THE HOUSE *of* LOVE

BOOK ONE

The Incorruptible Crowns Series

ABBY AKIN

CLAY BRIDGES
PRESS

The House of Love: Book 1 of The Incorruptible Crowns Series

Published by Clay Bridges Press in Houston, TX
www.ClayBridgesPress.com

ISBN: 978-1-68488-158-1
eISBN: 978-1-68488-159-8

Special Sales: Most Clay Bridges titles are available in special quantity discounts. Custom imprinting or excerpting can also be done to fit special needs. Contact Clay Bridges at Info@ClayBridgesPress.com

DEDICATION

James 1:12

"Blessed is the one who perseveres under trial because, having stood the test, that person will receive the crown of life that the Lord has promised to those who love him."

For the characters in my mind,
waiting to go on a journey for a crown.

CONTENTS

PART 3

N
W
E
S

PART 1

Chapter I

THE FALL OF THE HOUSE OF JOY

Every collapse happened the same way—the earth announced the death of a House.

A crack in the plaster started at the window. I watched as it spread upward, exposing the brick beneath. As the shaking grew more violent, I knew something had to be wrong. I quickly got to my feet to stand in the doorway of my studio apartment. Bracing myself, I willed the shaking to stop, only to realize I had no control over it. My apartment was not spacious enough to hold items large enough to protect me from falling debris. I did not have a bed frame or desk. My life's belongings were a standalone sink, a mattress, a shelf, and a dresser.

My life was in the hands of the doorway leading to the hallway.

With this earthquake, I knew The House of Joy had officially fallen.

This cemented the predictions of the end of times.

The House of Joy was the largest of the nine Houses in the kingdom. There was still one House immune to the darkness - the House I had come to call home.

The House of Love.

A shudder shot through the walls as if they were trembling in pain. Plaster began to break off the walls and fall to the ground when the cracks reached the ceiling. It coated my modest belongings below. The ceiling dusted my sheets with white powder and large tiles bounced on the mattress springs. The drawers of my dresser peeped open, getting a thin layer of white plaster themselves. In a moment's breath, a furious shake freed the wooden panel I used as a shelf from the wall. In turn, my books crashed to the floor. The shelf fell on the edge of my dresser and split in half, surrendering to the hard cherry wood. My leather-clad books scattered around the broken shelf.

I had neglected to open the books since buying them three months ago.

Now, they only opened for ruin.

They were purchased on the night of the Norda Festival when I stumbled into the Merchant Corridor after three pitchers full of hops. The festival was the celebration of the new House Pillar's coronation. House Pillars were the royal family of each House. The date of the coronation was marked by the twenty-third birthday of any living descendants of the Forgotten King. It is typically a joyous occasion that comes with dancing in the streets, proclaiming love for all, in addition to celebrating the new ruler.

In the Merchant Corridor, the books' colored leather bindings drew my attention. I finished my last drink and flipped through the pages. I discovered they were some kind of history book for the House of Love. Maps and timelines and family trees, all dating back to the age of the Forgotten King. I drunkenly convinced myself I needed them, paid handsomely, and smuggled them back to my apartment at the House of Love Estate.

I displayed them on my shelf as a reminder to open them in my free time. I did not get the chance. My work within the Estate didn't permit any time. Since then, they had collected dust. I was hoping to sell them to someone with enough time to revisit their stories.

Now, they rumbled in the chaos of the quake.

Within my lifetime, there have been three collapses, the years growing shorter and shorter between them. The last collapse was four years ago. I was nineteen and living in the House of Kindness when it fell. The Pillars in the remaining Houses decided it was best to close their borders indefinitely after the fall of the House of Kindness. To my benefit, they gave a three-day window for travelers who wanted a fresh start at a better life.

I left Kindness and journeyed through the snow-capped mountains of Joy. I was a day's journey away from The House of Love's border. The borders closed indefinitely only hours after I made it to the House of Love.

In my apartment, the jolts of the quake intensified. It was too dangerous to leave the safety of the door.

A vase atop my dresser, holding fresh willabees, fell to the ground. As if I saw it happen in slow motion, the flowers departed from the glass, the glass broke, and the water ballooned. A second later, the balloon of water rained on my festival books. I saw specks of yellow pollen from the willabees stick to the leather cover and the pages.

I rushed from the door jamb to dry the pages before they were destroyed. Snatching the only hand towel I owned, I attempted to dab the saturated leather covers and delicate pages. Stains formed on the towel, colors of blush and azure, from the dye on the leather. The quality of my towel did not allow for quick absorption, but rather assisted in the pollen's exfoliation of the brittle pages. The pages had begun to rip due to the friction from the towel. In my frustration,

I collected the red leather-bound book into the towel and threw it aside. The remaining two books were tossed in the sink to give the water a place to drain.

The floor was becoming increasingly unsteady. The shaking, coupled with the water, made it difficult for me to stand barefoot on the wooden floor. If my bed did not rest under the window, I would tuck myself under the covers and pray for the earthquake to stop. With the help of my enhanced adrenaline, I made my way closer to the door. Now, my only task was to avoid cutting myself on the scattered glass. When I stepped towards the door jamb, a large, uneven shake broke my balance. In a second's time, my body plummeted to the ground. I knocked my face on the edge of the splintered shelf on the way down. I could feel my neck hyperextending upon contact and my skull thud shortly after on the cherry wood.

My body rested limp on the dirty floor. The remaining water began to soak into my long, russet hair.

The shattered glass was beginning to pool in water and blood on the floor. It was all I could focus on as I lay motionless from the trauma. The shards scattered and bounced like grains of sand echoing the tremors of the quake. With each bounce, time seemed to stretch. The seconds lulled as if the world were slowing to a halt.

I could feel the veins in my head throbbing and a heartbeat thudded in my ears. One shard danced erratically across the floorboards, synchronizing its rhythm—not with the quake—but with my heartbeat. I couldn't help but *fixate*—watching it rise and fall. On a descent, it morphed from solid piece of glass into a droplet of water. My body exploded with too much pain to really care. I watched as the droplet of water splashed softly against the wood, insinuating the spectacle had been water this entire time. The sound of a crashing wave echoed in the chambers of my mind. I began to close my eyes and drift into unconsciousness before I was able to truly comprehend what I had seen.

Upon waking up, I heard more prominent droplets of water. They were falling and forming and growing a pool on my pillow. The color of the pillowcase only existing when I was the age of nine years old. A large droplet crashed into my temple, causing me to blink water into my eyes. I looked up to find a bubble—a leak from the storm raging outside—filling with rainwater. If it burst, my bed would be a soaked casualty.

An earthquake, an explosion beneath me, erupted in my childhood bedroom.

Lying as still as I could, hugging the blanket covering me, I rocked to the motion of the earth. I was frozen, unable to move from my mattress. My worst nightmare came true when the bubble above couldn't withstand the shaking. I was covered in cold, muddy rainwater. Screaming from surprise, I sat up, wiping the water away with any dry surface I could find. My eldest brother, Rafe, crashed through the door momentarily following the scream.

"Wren, get under the bed!" he commanded.

Confused and freezing, I crawled out from my wet bedding and under the metal frame holding my mattress. I was barely skinny enough to fit my body underneath the frame. The cool metal gave off no warmth, trapping my body in an endless tundra. I shivered while water dripped onto my face. My mattress was now soaked through. As I winced at the cold water and air and metal, the earth kept moving.

Items were thrown to the ground. The sounds alone felt like hell was being released, like roars and screams coming from the earth. The ceiling caved and more rain started to fall in my dark room. It filled the floor with a thin layer of water. Rafe was standing in the door frame to protect himself from the falling items and water. My body tightened; the warmth in my toes and hands was quickly disappearing.

A table beside my bed tipped over. The glass oil lantern shattered upon impact. My body instinctively winced, jolting my head on the metal above. I screamed in pain.

Rafe lunged into the room to help me get out from under the bed frame. Open and exposed, my brother couldn't find his footing to balance. In a single swing, the earth nudged, sending him to the ground. With sharp glass and random objects thrown on the ground, his skin was sheared open. He lay on his stomach as still as stone with water falling on his body from above.

I wouldn't dare leave the safety of the metal frame now. Cold and afraid and wet, I stayed under the bed and endured the earth's wrath, watching for any sign of life from my big brother.

From that moment on, I wished to never see a pool of water full of blood and glass ever again.

The memory shattered like glass as I was back on the floor in my apartment. The walls continued to shake in agony like they were sympathizing with my pain. The quaking continued as I looked to the doorway for safety. I hoisted myself off the ground and took cover. Glass stuck to my hands and hair. I could feel my arm bleeding from a puncture. I wiped away the excess glass on my pants and headed for the one place I knew that could protect me.

I stared into my destroyed apartment. The heaps of paper and leather in my sink were bleeding colors into one another. There was no chance at salvaging the pages for resale. The pieces of shelf couldn't be saved either. Their fate was set for the furnace later that night.

Slowly, the quivers subsided. Enough time had passed for me to feel comfortable reaching for my broom and dustpan tucked behind the open door. The straw bristles were against the floor, sweeping the shards into a dustpan. I looked over to the window, with the sun now shining through, and was reminded of the books. I left the dustpan to be dealt with later.

Tending to the books was my main priority now.

Quickly, I took the deeply soaked coverings and spread the pages that stuck together. I left two of the books fanned open around my apartment, giving the pages a chance to drip dry. I took the book from the towel and wrung the excess water into the sink. As I inspected the inside for any damages, the following words were highlighted in bleeding red.

I found myself walking the streets of Amoora as the sun began to set. What a glorious night to be in the capital of the House of Love. I bet there are celebrations happening all over the House, but none do it better like the people of Amoora. The singing and dancing had commenced in the square by the time I arrived. The Festival of Norda was in full swing! Our new Pillar's coronation ceremony had only finished an hour prior. Our people cannot wait. It feels like it was only yesterday that Permella was born. Now, on her twenty-third birthday, she takes the throne; blessed with gifts from her father, the King. It's turning out to be quite a family tradition. She will be a blessing to her family and her father's legacy. I'm glad to see she adopted the Pillar of Understanding. The strongest House remains in the hands of a worthy leader.

In another lifetime, I would dance, I would explore, I would love. I couldn't now or in the future. Not with this quake.

This was the third quake in my lifetime.

One more would be the end.

Every member of court had one—a small bell attached to the

Pillars' chambers. The bell above my door started to fill the room with repeating notes. It was the signal that I was needed elsewhere—and urgently. Jolted into a cleaning frenzy, I quickly tended to the water on the floor. Taking the damp towel, I soaked up any remaining water, the bulk of it being absorbed by the books.

Wringing out the remaining water, I cleaned the scrape on my arm from the glass. Tidying my clothes, I tried my best to breathe away the effects of the quake for a second. Its significance itched like a spider bite. It was disturbing to think another House had been destroyed by darkness. We haven't had a quake in four years.

There were no other obstacles.

The House of Love was the last safe haven.

The bell didn't hesitate for a second. In the midst of its ringing, I lifted the large wooden pieces that were once my shelf into the open doorway. I dusted off the faint white powder from my bedding to sit at the edge. Lacing my boots, I quickly checked the mirror above the sink to examine my wet hair. I don't worry about my appearance most days. With my fall and the ends of my hair damp, I wanted to double check everything was in order before heading to the throne room.

My reflection was blurry at first. Jarred from falling, my focus lagged. As I straightened my collar, my chin finally came into focus, then my lips. There was fresh blood in the corner of my mouth. With further inspection, I opened my mouth to see if anything was damaged. To my surprise, my front tooth was broken at an angle.

A chipped tooth.

During the earthquake with the shelf and the books and the memory, I hadn't noticed the break initially. My persisting headache didn't help either. The extra awareness of my mouth brought the pain to the forefront of my mind. My tongue passed over my teeth, feeling a substantial gap in the line. I wondered how I could have missed it. The sharpness of the break almost cut my tongue.

The temperament of the bell exploded for another round of fury. Louder and faster rings filled my room. I had to leave now. The Pillars called.

Inhaling a deep sigh, I headed for the door.

Chapter II

THE HOUSE OF LOVE

I closed the door to my apartment and proceeded through the intricate labyrinth of corridors to the throne room. It was nestled deep into the heart of the Estate.

My steps were hurried and frantic.

In the back of my mind, I couldn't help but think about the House of Joy. I had only visited once. Its snowcapped mountains and endless tundra took your breath away. It was hard to imagine a life in the everlasting cold; however, it wasn't *impossible*. It was sad to think it was all gone now.

The darkness has never been a secret. Growing up with brothers, they always liked to tease and scare whenever they could. I can vividly remember the tales they would share about the darkness.

It was a pure evil set to capture all of the souls in the kingdom. It awakened during the reign of the Forgotten King. A surge in darkness forced the King to scatter his nobility throughout the kingdom. He appointed nine noble families to govern each of the nine Houses. The separation of the kingdom was followed by the independence of each

House, making them a target. The darkness was a shadow of destruction and continues to be to this day. It attacked the weakest House first, the House of Self-Control.

The most sinful thoughts became actions. Neighbor against neighbor. Friend against friend. Days, even weeks, went by and the commonwealth of the House of Self-Control collapsed into the hands of the darkness. They were the first House to fall because of the people. To this day, no one has ventured into the House of Self-Control and returned alive.

That was only the *beginning* of the chaos.

Evil spirits bled into the surrounding seas seeking weak souls to capture in other Houses. The darkness grew stronger and harder to overcome. Tempted to fulfill their darkest desires, outweighing justice and righteousness and the virtues imprinted on their souls, the common folk began to destroy the very kingdom the Forgotten King built—House by House.

And now, only one House remains.

Throughout the centuries, safeguards were enacted to protect the remaining kingdom; however, the scales still favored the darkness. Selfishness ran rampant throughout the kingdom and no matter how hard the Pillars tried, there was no reversing any collapse. The remaining Pillars used policies to enforce the House virtues. In the House of Kindness, we were required by law to meet every wrongdoing with a kind word. The House of Love passed a motion stating there would be no tolerance for outspoken hatred.

I had turned the corner to enter the Grand Forum. My head became fuzzy as I emerged from the dormitory corridor. The Grand Forum was the centralized location for all House activity. It was a large circular room with various corridors jetting out in all directions. At the center, a tiered fountain splashed life and a cool mist into the air.

A flurry of activity had been ignited after the earthquake. Other department heads surfaced from their corresponding corridors to meet in the throne room.

The Estate not only housed the Pillars but their servants and appointed officials. Within each House, three Pillars were established as the leaders. During their coronation, they selected a trait that both revitalizes the House during their reign and remains true to the House's core value. Their primary duty was to uphold the written laws of the Forgotten King and provide an example of order for the common folk of the House. Departments such as agriculture, trade, and defense were split between the Pillars upon their coronation.

The Pillar's most trusted advisors were required to meet after the summons of the bell—everyone from the Head of Trades to the Royal Ambassador, the General of the Lovian Legion, and me, the Foreman of the Adora.

I observed many discussions about policies and discourse and the future of the House. My role as the Foreman of the Adora earned me a place in these discussions for the Adora was not only a magnificent clock towering in the courtyard of the Estate—it also served as the scale for the House of Love.

Each House's scale weighs its virtues against the darkness in its own way. Hourglasses and waterfalls have been used to represent some of the other Houses. The Adora's unique design measures the presence of darkness with time. Taking the shape of a giant clock, it symbolizes the ongoing love flowing throughout the House. Its ticks are steady and unyielding. By tracking the endless amounts of adoration, passion, desire, admiration, and warmth within the House of Love, it creates an impenetrable shield.

I followed the curved walls of the Grand Forum, looking upward to admire the mosaic dome colored with blood-stained glass. My hand traced the rounded, tiled wall to keep my balance while my attention was fixated on the glittering rubies above. They sparkled and hypnotized with the daylight beyond. I stepped into one of its crimson spotlights.

My head buzzed in response.

I merged with the crowd into the throne room like a fish swimming with the tide. Three long cherry wood tables lined the center of the room. My assigned seat, farthest from the entrance, beckoned me.

The three current Pillars of Love who embody their chosen virtues—Protection, Intimacy, and Devotion—had striking thrones atop a stage placed deepest in the ornate room. Stone steps separated us from them. Their thrones were aligned with each table to correlate to their respective departments and specifically crafted to represent their chosen virtues of Love. They were masterpieces of their own.

The most striking was the Pillar of Protection's throne. Sitting on the right, its design mirrored the House colors, displaying a crimson velvet upholstery on the backrest. An indentation was permanently engraved on the maroon seat by the long-reigning Pillar. Rubies embedded at the hilt of the chair rested above its ruler like a false crown. Stones of gilded scarlet rubellite studded the arms, alternating every other one with polished garnet. The reflections made the arms twinkle in the light and always caught my attention upon entering the room.

As I took my seat, the Pillars stood conversing behind their thrones. One of the men had his back turned, facing the blank wall behind the thrones. He was in a heated conversation with the woman facing us, looking out on her people periodically. Her brows furrowed and her nose was a deeper shade of blush than normal. A sign she had been crying recently.

The other Pillar, standing apart from the others, darted his eyes from one person to the other, mouthing - no, counting - the number in attendance. The counting stopped when he took notice of my entry. Once I took my seat, he discreetly approached his brother, interrupting their conversation with his presence. He leaned in to share a whispered message to both of them.

The ongoing conversations around the room began to hush as Adonis, the Pillar of Protection, broke the murmuring with an announcement. "Let's get started. We have much to discuss."

"All rise," said the Court Marshal.

Those of us seated joined those who were standing. Lifting our right hands, we repeated after the Court Marshal's directed words.

"I, as a chosen court official, solemnly swear to uphold the laws of the King," he declared.

Repeated in tune, I, along with the Pillars and the officials, spoke aloud in the hall.

"I know the dangers of this world but chose to remain righteous and holy. By the law of the land and the words of the King, we submit to act out of Love."

I glanced around the room to see the worried faces of my peers around me.

"For the Love of the House and with Love in our hearts," he finished.

"Aye," we spoke all together, thus concluding the introduction of the meeting.

"Thank you, Court Marshal," Adonis said. "Please be seated, everyone."

The Pillar of Protection was dressed in a tunic that matched his throne: a burgundy, loose-fitted garment, with a complementary belt. His pant legs were covered by the same-colored material as his shirt. Dark black facial hair speckled with aging gray hairs covered the area around his mouth. His brows matched his beard. Lines that crowded his eyes indicated his age and were not kind. Adonis, in his younger days, would have been a very handsome man; now grown and mature, his life fighting against darkness has taken its toll.

He continued, "For those of you who were unaware, that earthquake was the last line of hope for the House of Love."

The throne of Intimacy was located at the center of the stage, belonging to the Queen of the House of Love. Its ivory structure inlaid with gold features had a calming effect. It held significant weight next to Adonis's neighboring throne. White chocolate upholstery lined the body of the chair with smooth and pure fabric. It shifted to a lustrous honey in the right lighting. The arms and frame were plated with a similar resplendent gold cushion. Pearls were embedded into the highest point of the backing, crowning it as the *queen*.

My eyes fell to the woman sitting below the crown of pearls—our distraught Queen. Her eyes never locked with any of us sitting below her. They were too puffy and too watery, for if she blinked, tears would fall.

"Don't be so disheartening, Adonis." Jeston, the Pillar for Devotion, slighted his brother. He remained seated and refuted his brother's negativity. "Our policies prohibit any hatred, loathing, or animosity to surface within the House border. Not to mention our many lines of defense at the border have served us well for centuries. All the evils of the world can try to penetrate our forces; they wouldn't survive a second."

Jeston was seated farthest from Adonis. His chair was dull compared to his siblings. Its significance was harder to detect, unlike the others. Jeston's fixtures were still grander than the seat I rested in; however, the throne lacked color and was very boring. The natural wooden frame hinted at a light cherry color. The wood constructed the entire chair, the backing and all. The only upholstery was the burlap material

Jeston sat on. In the summer heat, I predicted it would be the itchiest seat in the throne room. There were no studs to raise interest in the arms of the chair, only the hand carved cherry wood. Following suit with the other thrones, it featured carnelian stones at the top.

I did not think highly of the throne or the Pillar. He was as shallow and dull as the rocks that crowned him.

With his coronation only a few months ago, Jeston was the newest addition to the Pillars.

The Pillars in all the Houses were subjected to centuries-old regulations, set by the Forgotten King, as they reigned. With their own set of rules, once the next generation of Pillars turned twenty-three years of age, they were required to ascend the throne. Jeston had recently replaced his aunt, who held the position of the Pillar of Affection. Now, as the Pillar of Devotion, his job was to see that the House of Love citizens were reminded to care for their loved ones with the utmost devotion.

My opinion aside, he brought youth and energy to the throne room but also a lack of sophistication to the Pillars.

"You can't be so sure," Adonis rebuked. "Where are we in terms of numbers, General?"

A man dressed in a dark maroon peacoat, adorned with patches and insignia, stood to answer his question. He removed his beret before speaking. "Five thousand young men are at the ready. Whenever given orders, they are capable of defending our borders. Our Aluna operators haven't seen any spike in activity beyond the border either." He stayed standing as he looked at each of the Pillars.

General Quillion headed the special operation teams in the last three collapses. With The House of Love being the largest target, he had perfected our ground defenses to keep the House safe. Without his leadership, the House of Love would cease to exist.

"General, do you foresee any threats to come our way with the downfall of The House of Joy?" The silent queen had finally spoken.

Her voice was soft. Queen Sylvanora was dressed in a powder-blue gown. Her corset contoured her torso, emphasizing her waistline - desired by many. Her skirt of pastel chiffon neatly covered her legs. Her hair was voluminous, with waves of vanilla and champagne falling past her shoulders. Delicate lavender pearls set in silver crowned her head, making her unmistakable as the Queen of Intimacy.

The queen's appearance correlated directly to the Pillar she controlled. Her skin complemented the warm cream upholstery she sat upon. Contrasting the soft tones, her lips were carmine rich. Her eyes shimmered silver, creating a hypnotic iris. They darted to the General for an immediate answer.

"No, my Queen. My Aluna men tell me that there is no sign of the darkness. We have time to prepare as it wreaks havoc within the House of Joy." General Quillion straightened when addressing the Queen. He was firm in his word but intimidated by her question.

"Is there an update with the Adora? Any malfunctions or recent concerns?" Adonis shifted his attention to me. "Wrenna?"

Meeting his gaze, I felt the muscles in my back tighten, forcing me to sit straighter. As if a pulley system was attached to my body, I rose to stand across from the General. I held my lips tightly, careful not to reveal my broken tooth in a room full of the most powerful people.

"I haven't noticed any irregularities. However, given these recent developments, I plan to run some tests after this meeting concludes." My lungs were completely depleted of air by the end. This was my first time speaking, let alone being addressed directly by a Pillar, during these meetings. Until now, I'd merely observed the others exchanging conversations on diplomatic matters.

I patted my sweating palms on my pant legs. Intending to go to the Adora before the quake happened, I was dressed to be smothered by grease and intertwined in the dirty gears. I wore black, loose-fitting pants that wouldn't show any accidental mishaps while working. My shirt of the same color gave me peace, knowing they wouldn't see the stains growing from under my arms.

As the General took his seat, my palms dampened more. I remained standing.

I would only sit when given a signal from the Pillars, but this created an awkward moment in the room.

Jeston, relaxed in his chair, broke the tension. "Excellent."

He propped his head with his hand against the chair's armrest, fingers splayed around his mouth. "Please keep us informed on any progress." He shifted subtly, hardly enough to disturb the room.

I nodded, refraining from showing my teeth under such scrutiny. He motioned for me to take a seat as Adonis resumed questioning the other leaders present.

A wave of relief surged through me, as I felt the collective attention of the advisors and officials wane. I let out a breath, releasing my nervous energy, refocusing on the Pillars.

Adonis persisted with his inquiries.

The Queen remained silent after addressing the General and Jeston, whose eyes were now locked on mine.

Adonis continued, unaware of his brother's intense focus on me.

Jeston's gaze traced me, from the wisps of my hair to the rings adorning my fingers. Intrusive, even from a distance. It felt almost taunting. His fixed stare ignited a fresh wave of heat through my body.

His stare felt inviting.

Adonis broke his trance by seeking his input.

I struggled to concentrate on his response, preoccupied with the blush creeping across my cheeks.

My presence went unnoticed throughout the rest of the meeting, as usual. Once we adjourned, I tried to slip away inconspicuously. Some of the elderly cabinet members obstructed my direct path to the Grand Forum.

"Wrenna?" His voice struck me like lightning, freezing my steps. Turning on my heel, I found the Pillar of Devotion motioning for me to meet him at the foot of his throne.

The rest of the members brushed my shoulders as I walked in the opposite direction. Jeston lingered near his throne, waiting for me to join him. Once arriving at the base of the steps, I squeaked out, "Yes?"

My response was barely more than a murmur, opening my mouth enough to let the slightest sound through. I was wary of what might follow my question.

"You shouldn't be so nervous in these meetings, even in those clockworker rags. You still have the ability to draw the eyes of everyone in the room."

His compliment sent a discomforting shiver down my spine. There are plenty of servants who would gawk over any acknowledgement from him, and some who would choose to return it. Contradictorily, I thought flirting with a Pillar, especially one from the most powerful House, had troublesome consequences. I wasn't going to fawn over him or his attempts at flattery. I wanted to be admired for my work, my talents - not my looks.

"Thank you," I said quietly.

Worried I sounded dismissive, I still attempted to conceal my chipped tooth.

"You don't have much to say today." He was eyeing my lips as he paused. "You seem rather distracted; is everything ok?" He spoke slowly.

Every word was like walking on hot embers, never ending and scorching my mind.

I nodded my head, hoping my expression signaled *please don't press further.*

He closed the space between us, leaning in to whisper into my ear, a stark contrast to the cryptic one he shared with his brother earlier. "If there's something you are hiding, Wrenna, I will find out."

I bit the inside of my cheek while glancing around the empty room, debating whether I should show him the effects of my clumsiness.

"Am I making you nervous?" He studied my movements as if he knew exactly what I was thinking.

I could feel the sharpness of the chip with my tongue. My already crooked smile elevated my embarrassment, especially in the company of a Pillar, no matter his age. However, I wouldn't want to disrespect a Pillar. Stepping back, I took a deep breath and revealed my fractured tooth—chipped and broken. His stare shifted to my mouth.

His eyes danced with amusement as he revealed his own smile. "When did this happen?"

Irritated by his amusement at my discomfort, I responded, "During the quake."

I paused to see if he wanted a further explanation. As I suspected, his eyebrows raised, inquiring for more information.

I continued, "The willabees you sent me fell during the quake and the vase shattered. There was glass everywhere. When I went to clean it up, I slipped. I didn't notice my tooth until I was summoned here." Although I was unashamed by my smile now that I didn't have to hide it anymore. I raced through the words, leaving me out of breath again. Silently, I wished the conversation would end.

Jeston drew near once again, reaching to tuck a stray hair behind my ear. He whispered into my ear, his breath warm and enticing, a similar feel to his stare from earlier. "I can fix it for you. All you have to do is ask."

Retreating from his warmth, I hesitated. I did not want to repay the debt if I agreed. I met his eyes instead of answering. Unwilling to give a verbal answer, my stare said enough. *Yes, please, but don't make me say it out loud.*

As if he could read my mind, he retreated slowly toward his throne. "It's a shame. Your smile was so charming." A part of me felt he was telling the truth. "You wouldn't even have to beg," he teased.

Fixing my tooth was as simple as blinking for him, yet he played with me like a mouse chasing the cat.

"I'm not begging," I said firmly and rolled my eyes.

Irritated at his games, I dismissed myself with a curtsy. If the exchange for the end of Jeston's games and flirting and flowers was to live with a broken smile, so be it.

Nearing the threshold of the door, I felt a pop in my mouth. My tongue passed over the missing gap to find my tooth had been restored. Blessed by the Pillar's powers, I feared what was to come from it. I faced him in the narrow room, surprise creased on my face.

"Why do you—?"

"You shouldn't have to hide your smile," he remarked. "I'd actually like to see it more."

A sigh escaped my mouth before I could stop it. Jeston's eyebrows rose for the second time, this time in response to my ungratefulness for his generous gift.

I offered my gratitude to save myself.

"Thank you." I said, hoping it was enough.

"I'd like to see it *soon*, without—" his eyes pointed to the throne room's walls.

"Why?" I repeated.

"A Pillar, such as I, does not need to explain his reasons." He went on to command, "Have dinner with me."

By all the Love, I'd rather be tortured by darkness.

As he waited for my response, I kept my body still. I'd gag at the thought of myself sitting at dinner across from him, but he had the power to break my neck if he lost his temper. I wasn't about to set him off.

I remained silent, drawing the conversation longer in search of finding a way out.

Impatient for a response, Jeston added, "As a return of favor, join me tomorrow night. After your time with the Adora. Just have dinner with me." He was eager to hear my obligatory response.

He fixed my tooth; I felt like dinner was the least I could do. I wouldn't even have to talk to him. I could sit and eat and leave.

Keeping my lips pressed tightly together, I grinned, reluctant to show him my smile.

"Excellent. I'll send a note with the details."

With that, I exited the throne room, heading for the Adora. Thanks to him, my workday would extend well past sundown; however, on the bright side, I didn't have to worry anymore about my tooth.

Chapter III

THE ADORA

The Adora was veiled by its own byzantine network of corridors within the Estate. Only the team and I knew how to find the entrance, an access we were granted by the Pillars themselves.

The enclosed tunnel, illuminated by crystal chandeliers with House gems, took many confusing turns. Multiple forks prevented servants and advisors from nearing the entrance. The wrong decision would take you back to the start and the other would continue your way to the magnificent clock. In my four years, I've only gotten lost twice—a current record among the Adora staff. Also in that time, I've never encountered an unwelcome guest.

The path was rather challenging to remember, but one I took every day.

As I neared the Adora chamber, the ticks of gears grew louder. Muffled by the busyness of the Estate, surprisingly no one has heard it before. The face of the clock rose high above the Estate grounds, inaccessible to everyone but a few select people. It was one of the more notable features when journeying to the Estate for the first time. As you enter the main gates, the Grand Forum dome catches your eye with its glittering rubies and next, the prominent clock tower.

Climbing the metal stairs, I stepped through an archway into the main compartment, passing the wooden birds that were fit to sing any moment now. I navigated through the different archways and steel passages with ease. Once the catwalk straightened, I veered to the left toward my office. I wouldn't call it much of an office. It was once a storage closet, constructed to hold the extra bell chimes and leftover paints. With my promotion, I invaded the space and added my own touch, officially deeming it my 'office.' It was a place to put our belongings while we worked and a place to hold meetings for my crew.

Five clockworkers were under my care: two gear train operators, a calibration expert, a weight engineer, and a safety inspector. They were the sole reason for the clock's proficiency. Our latest project included the yearly cleaning and lubrication.

Among our team were siblings, Piston and Pax, expert gear workers. Their recent project involved replacing an aging spindle tucked deep in the core of the clock. Had it not been replaced, the quake could have affected the rotations of the Adora. I quickly glanced at the bulk of the machine displayed just outside my office. Unfortunately, the catwalk remaining on the perimeter of the Adora gave little access to the innermost gears. The graphite gears clanked with one another repeatedly. I closed my eyes and counted the turns. Thankfully, it rotated without hesitation. I raised my voice to speak over the constant turning and tuning and humming of the Adora.

"Pax? Piston?" I yelled into the void of machinery. Even with the constant sounds, the Adora seemed eerily quiet.

Pax and Piston brought laughter to the machine with their sibling bickering. Piston provided the manpower to tighten screws, and

Pax was flexible enough to climb into small spaces. Coming from a multi-generational House of Love family, they were very close. The holidays were spent together, feasts and wine and games with people they enjoyed around them. It's ironic to see Piston and Pax nip at each other so often. If I hadn't accompanied them to their home for the holidays, I would never have known there was love in their hearts. I guess when you've known someone for so long, tension comes easy.

"Rev?" I yelled again, hoping someone would answer this time.

Reverie, my technician, couldn't have been more opposite. Quiet and calm, she was from the House of Faithfulness. She managed to escape the darkness and journey to the House of Love. Her stories start at the time of her arrival in the House of Love, for she doesn't speak much of the time she spent in her homeland. She doesn't offer much to conversations, but I knew she was the smartest person in the room. She was always coming to me with new ideas about how to improve the Adora. Her role as the calibration technician complements her personality. It is a very precise job, with large costs when it's not done correctly.

Reverie works closely with Runa, the engineer in charge of the pulley systems that hold the weights. The weights provides energy for the Adora. They are a vital piece to the success of the House, not only powering the Adora but most of the House. While being extremely heavy, they are also incredibly fragile. Each of the three weights could easily flatten the whole crew if dropped.

Bolt would never let that happen, though.

I tried calling out for both of them as well. There was still no answer.

Vaughn 'Bolt' Smotherton was without a doubt the worst name to be given at birth. The nickname Bolt was given to him by Runa when they first met. As our safety inspector, he is in charge of weekly training and strict protocols for the Adora. Bolt ensures every knob and screw is secure before he dismisses us. With the large gears constantly turning, they could easily crush an arm or leg if we were not careful.

I began to feel uneasy. I needed to start my tasks for the day, assessing the Adora for quake-induced damage. The machine seemed to keep tumbling uniformly, nothing to be worried about. I still wanted to run tests to confirm my intuition.

I took to a higher positioned catwalk situated adjacent to my office. With a bird's eye view, it revealed the lack of clockworkers in the Adora.

"Hello?" I shouted over the knocking of the gear trains, with my hands cupped around my mouth.

No answer.

Descending the platform, I heard footsteps on the metal slats near the entrance of the Adora.

A broad-shouldered man walked gingerly on the catwalk. It was a face I couldn't see clearly. My head was still hurting from my fall earlier. It could have been Piston, who had the same tall and muscular build as the man I saw from a distance. The closer I got, the longer it took for me to register who was standing there.

He had to duck to avoid hitting the archway where I had passed it with ease. His hair, the same color as mine, was a deep chestnut. At that moment, I knew something was wrong because it was a shade neither of my two male workers possessed. He wore a maroon outfit. A cotton t-shirt fitted tightly around his chest and arms, and his matching cargo pants had multiple pockets. His boots were the color of sand, an odd pairing to the deep red he wore everywhere else.

I shook my head to clear the fog.

My shoes screeched on the metal floor, giving away my position hidden by the sounds and in the shadow. All I could hear were the counts taunting me for how much time had passed. It was impossible to have strangers in the Adora. They needed special access granted by the Pillars, so this unfamiliar face was very dangerous.

"Can—Can I help you?" I forced the words out. I wished at that moment to have some form of protection at my side.

He stared at the grinding gears a second longer before looking in my direction.

"I'm looking for the foreman of this place," he said, only glancing in my direction for a tick and a tock. "Do you know where I could find him?"

His voice was calm and loud enough to hear over the knocking of the gears.

"You are not supposed to be here. How did you find this place?" I asked.

His feet turned toward me, the metal catwalk groaning under the weight of his lofty size.

"I'd beg to differ. I really need to speak with someone in charge. Can you tell me where I can find the foreman?"

He stood absolutely still, not offering his hand or glancing in my direction. He stared intently at the core of the Adora with no change in expression.

"Who do you think you are?" I prodded with a fiery tone.

"Tev," he said.

"Well, I am the Foreman of the Adora. Why are you here?" I pressed.

"I was sent to replace your crew." He spoke firmly.

This took the wind from my lungs. I said breathlessly, "My crew?"

"The Pillars of the House have deemed the Adora a classified job. With your former crew's lack of security clearance and I having a surplus, they sent me here with the news of the House of Joy. I was also told to speak to the Foreman to clear up any confusion on their behalf."

"But- but, they help me run this place!" I retorted. "How are *you* supposed to replace a five-person crew?"

"I was told the secrecy of the Adora needs . . . some fine tuning." He smiled out of his own amusement.

"Without my workers, the Adora will break down. Two people couldn't possibly manage the undertakings of the clock," I explained.

"There's no time to waste then. Where should I set my things?" He turned his body fully toward me, implying I would show him to my office.

"How do I know what you are saying is truthful?" I asked hurriedly.

"I know this might come as a shock to you, but I was sent orders. I intend to obey them." He shrugged as if I were to just accept it as a fact.

"Which Pillar sent you?"

"I'm not at liberty to say. All I know is that your crew was sent home for the day. They will receive a notice with orders to stay away. I was told this machine needs careful monitoring to ensure the safety of this House."

"But they are the reason it works!" I was close to shouting, as my temper was rising.

"Obviously, someone with *authority* does not agree," he shot back at me. He was unwavering in his placement on the catwalk, ready for me to show him the Adora's complexities and inner workings.

He was the messenger, and I got the message.

Biting my tongue to prevent any curse words from coming out, I said, "Right this way."

He observed every move I made in the Adora, meticulously transcribing every bolt and joint I worked on. The way he stood and watched drove a flare of irritation through my body.

He was sent to replace my crew, but didn't lend a hand in any way. Sweat formed on my temple. I hadn't been this hands-on with the Adora in months.

As the foreman of the Adora, my tasks were to oversee the hourly chimes, uniquely selected by every Pillar, one of their perks as Pillars. They determine the tune that rings on the hour. It is set on a daily rotation to ensure each Pillar hears their tune throughout the week. Everything from bells, to whistles, to the wooden figures that dance around the clock every hour—they decided it all.

Every part of me was twisting and turning to tune the dials to the right timing. He observed every part of the process, even when my shirt caught on a tick of metal. It pulled my cotton shirt up past my navel. He remained still, offering no assistance. His eyes remained glued to me. I shuddered at the thought of him watching me, vulnerable to his gaze.

These military brats who gain an ounce of authority from General Quillion think they are free to act however they choose. Their encounters with the darkness have led many of them to the wrong vices: wine, rum, herbs, you name it.

Drinking well into the nights, the inebriated soldiers would take hot irons and brand their horses. The animals were unable to move from their posts with their reins tied. The soldiers would stick them with a branding tool, casting permanent scars on the horse. The screams of the horse would wake neighborhoods in the dead of night, including mine. Laughter would soon follow from the soldiers. I wondered how the House has stayed out of darkness with those types of men defending our border.

The gears of the Adora clanked effortlessly after the maintenance routine. I spent the early hours of the morning applying grease to the center turnstiles to ensure they turned with time. With Tev's unannounced arrival, I was too preoccupied with his presence to thoroughly run my performance testing on the clock. That was tomorrow's problem now.

We headed back to my office. When I gathered my keys, he packed his belongings and left without saying a word. After locking my office full of chimes and whistles, I peered through the pockets of metal and iron. Tev was nowhere to be found.

Leaving through the archway, I stepped to the rhythm of the Adora until reaching my own door. The repetition of the gears rang in my head. As I drew closer to my apartment, my back stiffened. I was due for a good night's sleep. I opened the door of my apartment to find the dustpan of glass still on the floor, waiting to be thrown away.

Disregarding it for a moment, I went to the mirror to look at the work of Jeston's powers. To my surprise, not only did he fix my chipped tooth, but he also straightened my crooked smile. With a blink of an eye, he managed to fix something that would have normally taken years. Truly grateful for his work, I still wasn't fooled.

Jeston's advances had started during his first week as a Pillar.

In previous years, there wasn't a need for clockworkers to be present. We managed the gears and saw the Pillars whenever they wanted a different tune for the hour. With suspicions of the House of Joy growing in the darkness, the Pillars wanted consistent updates on the Adora.

For my first meeting, I arrived with a stack of notebooks to show the Pillars the Adora's performance tests. Power exports compared to its intake, potential areas of concern for maintenance, and its magic's strength—a test I designed myself. My over-preparedness sparked Jeston's interest. It's known that the Pillars' lives are cursed to embody their throne. Where they might lack one area of love, they are indefatigable in compassion or intimacy or devotion, or protection.

I was not a fool.

With Jeston, his devotion seems to border on lust. His advances continued and varied. Harmless flirtation progressed into him sending me flowers. I took it with a grain of sand. His devotion to the House compelled him to do it. I was a victim to his games. However, I was smart enough not to show my hand.

I'd rather suffer in a cell than be his mistress.

I'd rather live in darkness.

I left my apartment with the dustpan in hand. I wanted so badly to relax after a chaotic and long day; however, work still needed to be done. The dump chute was down the hall. Its cold metal handle indicated no one had been up for hours. It was early morning already. The halls were silent, peaceful, and quiet. I enjoyed these rare times of silence. I never experienced them during the day. The absence of noise was as pure as golden treasure. I basked in it. With a deep breath, I closed my eyes briefly and, on the exhale, I retreated home.

Slowing upon arrival, I saw the door to my apartment had been opened. I hadn't left it that way. Pushing it open a little more, I found the five unemployed clockworkers consuming every inch of my apartment.

"What's going on?" I inquired.

Reverie and Runa, the siblings, and Bolt shifted their attention toward the door. Pax and Piston sat on either end of my disheveled bed. The white powder from the plaster lingered on their dark clothing. Reverie and Runa leaned against the dresser. They paused in their inspection of the cracks to stare at me.

Brandishing an open envelope torn at the seam, holding it up to indicate it needed to be the topic of conversation, Bolt replied, "We need to talk."

I wasn't sure how to start the conversation. I needed time to process the day, with Jeston's invitation to dinner and Tev's sudden appearance at the Adora. My head spun for a second before I said anything.

"What's there to talk about?" I asked, trying to fake my surprise with them in my room. I wholly ignored the letter Bolt held in his hand.

"Did you know anything about this?" He raised his hand with the letter. "About our termination from the Adora?"

I stared down at my worn hands. They were stained from the grease I used earlier. They were a dead giveaway to where I had been for the day. "No." I bordered on lying at this point. Leaning against the door, I crossed my arms to hide my hands in the shadows of my dark clothes.

"The Pillars didn't tell you anything at the meeting today? After the quake?" Runa spoke, untangling her own arms to lay them at her side.

My mind shot to the meeting this afternoon. To Adonis asking me about the Adora. To Jeston's inquiry afterwards and fixing my tooth. I was suddenly more aware of opening my mouth. Surely, they would notice my smile had been straightened.

Preparing to talk with tighter lips than normal, I went over the words Reverie said again. Puzzled, I met her eyes. "How did you know about that?"

"It was more of a guess until now. Joy was the last House protected until today. I assumed the Pillars wanted to hold a meeting to discuss future strategies in the line of defenses, especially Adonis." Reverie tended to be one step ahead of everyone else. She could draw conclusions faster than the experts. From stories of her father, he was similar to her in that regard. They would write riddles for the other to solve.

"The meeting was about the city's defenses because of the quake. I'm not sure what's in those letters. It wasn't discussed this afternoon."

I spoke only the truth; hopefully my friends would see that. Even if the truth was stretched.

Piston stood from the bed. A groan of relief from the mattress springs escaped as he got up. Standing a foot taller than me, his head almost grazed the ceiling fan. He made the room feel even smaller with his presence. It was unbelievable how he managed to seem so small whilst sitting on the bed. He reached for his back pocket where his letter had been tucked for safekeeping. Without saying a word, he extended his arm and handed it over.

I unfolded it to read:

Dear Mr. Piston Passean,

We regret to inform you today that you are no longer needed, as your position with the Adora has been terminated. If you attempt to seek the Adora, the maze you have come to conquer will reset, thus concealing you in it forever.

Choose wisely.

Have a Lovely day,

House Pillars

I didn't know if I wanted to scream or throw up or sit down. The whirlwind of emotions I'd experienced today was enough for the day. I handed the letter back to Piston without saying a word. Tears started to form in the crease of my eyes. Before a tear fell, I pressed those emotions down far enough to where they wouldn't surface again.

"We all received a letter." Bolt spoke. "After the quake, we waited here for you. Rev concluded that you might be in a meeting with the Pillars. Hours went by. We worried that you had been hurt. Runa had a ceiling tile fall on her. She has a concussion because of it. If it weren't for Pax, we probably would have thought you were dead."

What was Pax doing this early in the morning to see me come home?

"You were spying?"

"We needed to talk." A hushed voice came from the back. Pax didn't meet my eyes. "We wanted to make sure you weren't hurt."

Irritation had rattled my bones. I took a deep sigh instead of yelling like I wanted to. I had enough of unwanted shadows for the day. Retreating from the doorframe, I confronted all of them. "It was a shock to me too why you all didn't show up. But work still had to be done."

In order to bring this conversation to an end, they needed something. They needed hope. Steadying my breath, I reassured them, "I will speak with the Pillars the next time I see them. I'm sorry; there's not much else I can do right now." I spoke sincerely and conveniently left out my dinner plans with Jeston. It was a detail I didn't want them to know about. It was a possible lapse in judgment agreeing to go to dinner with the Pillar. The fact would cause my crew—and my friends—to question other decisions I have made and will make. As their boss, I can't let that happen.

As for telling them about Tev, I didn't want them to think they were terminated because of their lack of production. They were replaced by someone who didn't know the first thing about mechanics and would never learn. They each brought unique qualities to the Adora, and I am—was—grateful for their contribution. Their job meant everything to them, the same for me. If they were permanently replaced, I did not want to be the one to tell them. As their friend, I couldn't do it.

The conversation died after I attempted to lighten the mood by asking about their day off. It wasn't received well. All but Bolt left shortly after. When the door shut, he let the silence linger before asking, "Are you hurt?"

"No." I was quick to respond.

"Are you lying?" He wouldn't release me from questions until I answered truthfully.

I conceded easily, pausing ever so slightly. "Yes."

"Where?" he insisted.

"I chipped a tooth—during the quake." I extended a pause, hoping he would speak before I finished my story. He didn't, so I continued, "Jeston fixed it after the meeting."

Bolt let his nostrils flare slightly, taking in heavier breaths. Jealousy overtook a small portion of his mouth. He spoke quietly to suppress his rising anger. "Why would you let him—"

I rolled my eyes. Before he finished his sentence, I interrupted, "I didn't. He offered, but I declined it. As I was walking away, he fixed it."

"At what cost?"

"Dinner," I snapped.

The anger now made his face beetroot red.

"Looks like he fixed more than a broken tooth." He glanced down at my open mouth. I guess I didn't hide it as well as I thought.

He went on, "You know he is dangerous, Wren. I don't want to see you dead because of him."

"You don't need to protect me anymore," I snapped in his direction.

Before I knew it, Bolt was standing inches away. I could feel his breath on my face and the steam from his ears. I looked from his eyes to his mouth and back to his eyes. He contemplated his next move, and I could see him meditating on which avenue to take.

"I want to protect you," he said softly, his jaw feathered for a moment after.

With him this close, it was difficult to remember our friendship. At this distance, it was a reminder of the times I had spent wishing I would bump into him at the Adora. A reminder of the comfort he provided with his strong arms. Of his warm company during the cold months. Of him cradling me in my bed to soothe my fright after hearing the horses' cries. Of us cuddling under the sheets during crashes of thunder and lightning. A reminder of his affectionate kisses in the quiet of night. Where I *was* protected by him.

"I don't need your protection." I said quietly. The words flowed like lava out of my mouth, destructive and hot.

Bolt peered down at his shoes. His shoulders sagged in defeat. When he inhaled, he lifted his head. He met my gaze for one last time with a line of water at the base of his hazel eyes.

He left without saying another word.

Chapter IV

BRAMWELL'S BOOKS

The next day, I was set on finding the truth.

Before I left for the day, I collected the damaged books from their various places around my room. The pages were wrinkled like raisins in the sun. The bleeding colors generated images artists only wished to master. However beautiful they were, I was disappointed in the fact they were now damaged. I should have known the shelf wasn't large enough to hold the weight of the books. The quake just solidified my foolishness.

Momentarily opening one of the books, I examined the pages inside. If I hadn't known the pages were originally white, I would have guessed the book was written on red paper. There was no trace of the white paper throughout the entire book. I noticed the first page sticking to the leather cover. A scarlet pigment splashed on the page as I peeled it away. The dedication was scribbled in black ink and difficult to read.

My Ella, my love for you stretches far wide. This book is written for you, my love.

Looking past it, the colors of red and plum were interrupted by a text written in white ink. The text was written in flowing letters, a stark contrast to the handwriting in black above. A delicate hand was the owner of this portion.

Oh, to the lost one, for night's bitter cold.
You who lie awake, look in the old-
Your power belongs to the mud and mire.
Love will be in ruins, if you so desire.
For there is a glory beyond the riches you seek.
Found not in a Heart full of pride, but one of the meek.
Seated on a throne by the one true artist,
I hold a gem you shall never harvest.

I closed the book in search of the author on the spine. There was no name. Flipping through the chapters, I found the same handwriting as the black ink dedication. On the last page, I saw the name of the person who I would only assume belonged to the handwriting.

Bramwell.

The name screamed at me like a kettle on a stove. These were Bramwell's journals? Notes and ideas and scribbles of his life, here in the Estate at the time of its founding. He was the royal tutor for the Pillars in the House of Love, the hand of the King. He trained the first Pillars in battle and speech and royalty. He built the kingdom for the Forgotten King. And this book belonged to him.

I set the book on top of my dresser along with the other books. Setting aside the singular name that burned in my mind, I headed for the door. Upon opening it, to my surprise, there was a box bearing a note with the House crest and a large silver bow. It remained undisturbed in the hall. The note read,

Dinner in my quarters at 6.
The dress will match your eyes.
All my Love,
Jeston

I should have known he was going to do something like this. He wasn't going to allow an opportunity like this to slip through the cracks. He upheld his part of the deal and now it was my turn.

I brought the decorated box into my apartment, unveiling the dress inside. Its muted cerulean color would indeed match my eyes. Reaching for the dress, I removed it from the box. Hanging it high above my dresser, I fanned the skirt open to loosen the wrinkles. I stepped back fully take it in. Its chiffon skirt was the type that would sway back and forth during a dance. Ruffles and little beads elevated the monochromatic fabric. It was a dress that little girls picture in their daydreams. Despite my awe for the dress, I reminded myself who sent it.

Bringing myself back from the clouds above, I returned to the reality that I would have dinner with Jeston tonight. Most importantly, I was nervous. I've been alone with Jeston before, but that was in the throne room where someone could walk in and see us talking. I didn't want to be trapped in his quarters where the only people to know that I was there were the servants. They wouldn't help me if I were to be in danger, especially not against a Pillar.

Taking another second to admire the dress, I couldn't help but smile ever so slightly as I left for the Adora. I was excited to put it on later that day.

At work, I didn't waste any time looking for variances within the Adora. Once again, the military man observed at a distance. Having a deep understanding of the tests because I created them, I combed through the sets of data I collected in my office. Each case was designed to measure different aspects of the clock. Undoubtedly, the Adora passed with flying colors.

Tev watched as I worked. He didn't say much. We had hardly spoken since yesterday's introduction.

"So, have you always lived in the House of Love?" I asked curiously still looking at my papers on my desk.

He did not respond.

"How old are you?" firing another question right away.

He continued to scribble on his own notepad.

"Have you gotten enough sleep? You seem awfully tired," I said.

I was only met with silence.

The knocking of the gears outside my office counted the time.

"Are you shy? Is that the real reason why you won't speak to me?" I asked again, trying to get a rise out of him.

He glanced up at me, but only for a moment

"Why are you always so serious?" I poked.

"Look Birdy," he said with a snarky attitude.

"It's Wren," I corrected.

"I am under orders to be here. I don't have to talk to you and you don't have to talk to me. Now, if you don't mind, continue with your work and I'll continue with mine." He tapped his fingers on his notepad waiting for a response.

"You don't do any work. You just watch me," I muttered under my breath. I didn't appreciate him calling me a bird either.

Through narrowing eyes, I prodded for another time, "Who sent you here?"

Letting out a sigh, he dropped his pen, "What do I have to do to get you to stop chirping?"

"Maybe answer some of my questions."

Thinking it over for a moment, Tev brought his pen to his lips. *Tap. Tap. Tap.* He smirked at me and said, "Three. I'll answer only three."

I held out my hand for him to shake. Firmly grabbing his hand, we shook. I thought hard about my first question. I knew he was sent here on orders. Orders from who? If he didn't know then it would be a waste of a question. He was sent here to ensure the secrecy of the Adora. Why was he chosen for this job?

I finally settled on, "What qualifies you to ensure the safety of the Adora?"

Pausing to think of each word carefully, he replied, "Before my time here, I was in the Queen's guard. My job was to transport packages for the Pillars."

His voice was deeper than I remembered from yesterday. The sounds of the Adora were muffled by the office walls. If it weren't for the barrier, I wouldn't be able to hear him speak.

"Next question," he urged.

What else did I want to know about him? What about his family? He couldn't have been much older than me.

"What did you do before you were in the Queen's guard?" I asked.

His expression hardly changed. He looked to the corner, where the ceiling and the wall met, then he said, "I belonged to team that specialized in missions outside the borders of this House."

"You mean to tell me you were an Aluna operator?" I asked. In all my meetings with the Pillars, the General never discussed the missions to the lost Houses.

"Is that your third question?" he said in response.

"No! Wait," I hesitated before saying anything else, thoroughly thinking through the next words that would come out of my mouth.

With more questions coming to mind, my last one better count.

Tev shifted in his seat, revealing the red ink scribbled on his paper. My mind thought back to the red pages of the book with scribblings of mysterious white ink. Maybe a shot in the dark, but I proceeded, "What do you know of the name Bramwell?"

His eyes grew big as if there *was* something he knew.

"Why do you wish to know about Bramwell?" He answered my question with one of his own.

I could see his mouth started to twitch, possibly thinking of a lie.

"What do you know about Bramwell?" I asked again.

"Bramwell was the House Tutor for the first Pillars. He established the armies and the rulers of the House."

"I could have told you that," I said, unsatisfied with his answer.

"Bramwell was an ambitious visionary," he explained in further detail. "He wanted to build a united kingdom. That vision failed the moment the King divided the kingdom into Houses. The nine Houses grew powerful distinct from one another. Bramwell saw destruction among them. He was accused of treason, hiding cryptic clues in his studies. He wanted to restore a fallen kingdom to what he once knew—strong and unyielding to anyone or anything. When the Houses learned of Bramwell's studies, they called for an execution. The King, believing Bramwell—his most trusted advisor—kept him safe in the House of Faithfulness. Corruption continued to grow in the separate Houses regardless of Bramwell. Some say the King forced the first collapse by protecting Bramwell."

"The House of Self-Control?" I asked.

"That was the first house to fall to the darkness but these are all myths, of course. No one in centuries has found texts to prove Bramwell's innocence."

I took a big gulp. I thought those books were just old history books. I bought them in the market during the celebration of Norda. The seller didn't mention any significance, especially the fact of them belonging to Bramwell. I needed to take a look at those books again. My body started nervously shaking, my legs twitching up and down, my hands moving like a spider's legs. My head filled with pressure.

"Are you all right?" Tev watched me carefully. Concern hinted in his voice.

"I feel fine." I lied. My body heated quickly. Under my arms began to sweat and my temple, even my feet. My stomach twisted into knots. I tried shifting in my chair to relieve the sudden pain.

"You don't have any color left in your face," Tev said, "Are you going to be sick? Maybe we should step outside."

His brow furrowed in worry.

Flashes of the pages cursed my mind. I could see the swirls of scarlet and folds of sapphire. Turning the pages in my mind, I read the name again, bright in contrast to the bleeding colors.

Bramwell.

Leaning into my uneasiness, "Now that you say something, I am feeling a little lightheaded. Maybe I should end the day early. I don't have any further testing to do today anyway."

It was an escape.

I stood quickly, eager to leave. Tev stood simultaneously. Black spots formed in my vision. I disappeared into the void of my mind. He braced my arm. Once the spots subsided, I recoiled at his touch. "What are you doing?"

"You looked like you were going to pass out."

Letting go, Tev kept his hand close to my arm. Warmth was radiating off of it. "I'll walk you home. Get your things."

"No," I protested. "You don't have to do that. I'm fine," I said.

My headache was fading slowly, but not fast enough.

"I'm walking you home." he commanded, as if it was an order I must obey.

I nodded.

Locking my office, Tev guided me through the corridors of the House of Love. We walked in silence. Passing the Grand Forum, I pointed in the direction of my apartment, and he followed my lead. His hands relaxed in his pockets a few steps behind mine, close enough to catch me if I stumbled. We arrived at my door and although anxious to sneak inside, I waited for him to say goodbye before unlocking the door.

He scanned my face before asking, "How are you feeling?"

"Better, thank you for walking me home." I forced my tone to be as courteous as possible.

Giving an assenting nod, he turned to leave, and I slid the key into the lock. The deadbolt cracked. After turning the knob, I leaned into my apartment, anticipating rereading the books to find out more information.

Without warning, an overwhelming sense of nausea flooded my stomach. I paused at the threshold, tightening my grip on the knob for extra stability. Within a heartbeat, Tev was standing behind me, his hand thoughtfully placed on my lower back and my arm gripping the door. Providing extra support, he eased the door open with a soft push and escorted me inside.

His hand led me to the bed.

I gradually sat down at the edge of my mattress. Doubled over in pain, I couldn't straighten myself. I placed my elbows on my knees, which held my head in place. The sink in the corner rushed with water.

Tev filled a glass and kneeled onto the floor to meet my face. Through the knuckles of my fingers, I could see his knees resting on the dusty floor. He handed me the water glass.

"Drink this. It will help."

I took it from his hands, my own shaking from the weight, I lifted it to my mouth and sipped. It gave some relief to the acid I could feel gurgling in my stomach. In the corner of my eye, I saw Tev's eyes glance around the room. Thankfully, the way the skirt of Jeston's dress hung on the nail; it concealed Bramwell's books underneath. Otherwise, they would be exposed to curious eyes. I finished drinking and held out the glass for Tev to take.

He placed it on the sink where he found it. I stood, fighting every urge to stay on the bed. I wanted his attention to be on me.

I stumbled my first steps on purpose, and he caught me from losing my balance.

"Thank you," I said.

"I don't think you need to be anywhere but in bed," he said.

While standing, the color of the leather caught my eye, peeking through the chiffon.

"I think you are right," I agreed, pretending to moan.

"Do you have plans for the evening?" He shuffled his feet alongside mine while he asked.

He eyed the dress hanging on the nail where my bookshelf once hung.

"Oh, that? That's nothing." I snorted.

After assisting me to the bed, he strode to the door. With his hand on the knob, he said, "Have a nice night."

Before I could say goodbye, he closed the door behind him.

Jumping out of bed to hear the fading footsteps down the hall, I locked the door. The tightness in my chest relaxed with relief. I headed to the wall where the dress was hung over the dresser. After another sigh of relief, I removed the dress from the nail and laid it neatly on my bed. Exposed on the flat of the dresser, the set of colored covers popped. I set the red book to the side with the intention of exploring the others.

One book had a cover of sapphire blues. The water droplets left distinct marks on the cover. These drops echoed within the pages, mirroring the cover's spots but in a duller shade of blue the farther I dove into the book. The first page similarly clung to the cover like a magnet. My body quivered with anticipation to see another dedication with similar black ink scribbled below.

To my Aruleah, my heart belonged to you—wholly until its last beat.

My eyes fixated on the name.

Aruleah.

I'd never heard a more beautiful name.

I remembered the other dedication addressed to an Ella. How many lovers did Bramwell have in his time in the House of Love? It wasn't uncommon for men to have more than one, but to write to both of them was odd. My mind began to spiral into the thought of a love triangle. Burning passion for Ella, but a tender love for Aruleah. I wondered who he chose in the end.

I couldn't imagine a love where your heart belonged solely to another. I knew it was possible; I just had never felt love that intense before. With Bolt, it was lust that fizzled quickly.

Below, there was another poem, written in the same flowing letters as the book in red.

I claim no interest in the words you say.
Our time of bliss has turned to gray.

Your power shall fall as the days turn to one,
The Pillars hold the weight—they do hum
a tune, you see, muffled by your cries.
Be wary, be warned: Love will be your demise.
The day is upon us, just you wait—
Enough with empty words—it is too late.

While I looked out the window, lost to my thoughts, the sun neared the clock tower of the Adora. The time read 5:30.

I had to get ready for dinner!

I was to be in Jeston's quarters in thirty minutes. An urgency surged. Abandoning the journals I had escaped into for far too long, I scrambled my way to the tiny mirror above my sink to assess the work that needed to be done.

Stripping my black, oily clothes, I carefully unzipped dress and slipped inside. With a tug on the corset to secure it in place, I fastened the zipper and buttons. It fit perfectly. It accentuated my waistline especially. The pinned skirt made flowing folds in the chiffon.

Ready to leave, I stopped myself before I got to the door. I was forgetting one key thing. Shoes. My Adora boots were stained with grease and polish. I only had another pair of white shoes for leisure.

A rattle at the door jolted my attention from questioning my footwear. I went to answer the door and to my surprise Pax opened my door before I had the chance.

Bursting her way into the room, she exclaimed, "Oh! I was walking by your door and these were outside. Did you forget about them? I was just going to just set them in here."

A pair of delicate shoes, ones with a tall heel and lacy straps, dangled loosely in her hands. Gems, clear as water, adorned the straps. Catching the light from the dying sun, they lit the room with a mirage of color.

"Those are beautiful," I said, in awe of them.

"Where are you going?" Pax had finally taken note of my dress.

"I have a dinner," I said, purposefully avoiding one major detail.

To no surprise, Pax pressed, "With who?"

"Never mind that; now, if you don't mind, I need those shoes," I said calmly.

As I reached to take them out of her hands, she snatched them farther away.

"Tell me who you are going to dinner with and I will hand them over," she negotiated.

I contemplated the events that would follow if I told Pax where I was going tonight. She had a reputation of sharing secrets with the crew. After I told Pax about my relationship with Bolt, Reverie asked me about it the following day.

"You can't tell a soul," I argued.

She beamed.

"Deal," she said with a smile.

Hoping she wouldn't hear the answer, I spoke softly "Jeston."

"You're joking," she said incredulously.

"Look, I don't have time to explain." I snatched the heels from her and put them on.

"I'm running late. I'll explain later," I told her.

I fussed with the strap for a second and secured the diamond shoes to my feet. Standing straight, I felt off balance. Walking was just as difficult, if not more. I considered my work boots for a moment. At least I would be able to walk. Out of the window, the sun was dying behind the tower. I didn't have time to change.

"I hope you know what you are doing," Pax said.

If only she knew, I had a plan.

Chapter V

DINNER WITH JESTON

Pax wished me good luck and left as I was collecting my things to leave. I checked the mirror one more time. My hair was where I wanted it to be, my lips the perfect rouge, and my teeth - thanks to Jeston - straight and whitened.

I opened the door to find a folded letter just outside the threshold. It stood lonesome in the hall. I picked it up with an idea about who it was from.

Change of plans:
Meet me in the Grand Forum.
I will escort you to dinner myself.

My window of time was narrowing. I was appreciative with the change of plans. I was worried about getting lost in the maze of corridors on the way to the Pillar's quarters. This ensured I knew where to go. Hurriedly, I tossed the note into the room, not needing to hold onto it any longer, and locked the door behind me. I cantered through the halls in the direction of the Grand Forum.

Entering the circular foyer, the candle lights made the space dance with shadows. Nighttime had come quickly. The room lacked the usual shine from the rubies above, creating an eerie vibe. My eyes fell to the center of the room where Jeston was standing. He wore a cloak which covered most of his body in a deep maroon, similar to the fabric on Adonis's throne.

"You look . . . enchanting," he said with a grin. That word stuck like a knife.

My heels echoed in the room as I stepped closer. I had to focus to control my breath, making it appear I sauntered into Forum instead of running.

"What happened to dinner?" I asked between breaths.

"Turns out my brother was hosting a family gathering this evening and I would like some privacy tonight," Jeston explained with a smirk. "I told him I had better things to attend anyway."

He finished with a wink.

Adonis, the Pillar of Protection, was a father to two children and a husband to Amelia. His children were toddlers by the time I arrived at the House of Love. They make seasonal appearances for holidays and festivals but otherwise their lives are kept hidden even to the Estate workers. I hardly see them or hear their names while in the Estate.

"So, what's the plan now?" I inquired, curious to see what plans Jeston had for the night.

"Well, being a Pillar of the House, I have some connections." He adjusted his cloak's collar. "Shall we?" He held out his hand for me to take.

"Why are you wearing a cloak?" I asked.

"I don't want to be recognized. I am a Pillar. I need the disguise." Forgetting to pull his hood up before, he did it now.

"Are we leaving the Estate?" I asked.

"A night on the town," Jeston said beaming.

"Will I need a cloak?"

"No. No one will recognize you. They don't know the clockworkers by name or face," he said nonchalantly.

Struck by his comment, I didn't know if I should be relieved or insulted.

He continued, "Besides, why would you want to hide that stunning dress? No cape or cloak would complement it anyway."

He held his hand out for me to take. In a swift moment, we were off down a corridor I had never been down before.

"When was the last time you visited the city?" he asked, creating a filler conversation.

I needed to play along. He needed to feel comfortable confiding in me with the truth. No sneering or wincing or rolling my eyes. I needed to act polite and kind and loving.

Taking an internal long sigh, I thought of the last time I visited the cobblestone streets. Forgetting the last time, I could only recall the last weeks. Machinery clinked in my head and the tracing of the carpet on my way to the Adora.

"It's been months," I said, settling.

I wiped the disappointment off my face before he could notice.

"What about you? When was the last time *you* visited the city?" I asked in response.

He took a sigh, indicating it had been longer than he liked. I wondered if he enjoyed life at the Estate. All the committees and meetings and politics must be boring, but he had quarters and amenities—servants even. All the women stewards doted on him. Even Runa and Pax would stop me to talk about the latest Jeston gossip. I was unfazed by it all. I saw the women he would stop in the Grand Forum after our meetings. Women, all the same size and shape, who were consistently petite and curvy.

A category I never quite fit into.

"It's been too long. This will probably be my last chance to leave the Estate with the news about Joy." Sneaking a look at his face, I saw he had the same expression that I was quick to erase. He let the emotions show as he continued to speak, "I enjoy the energy of the city, walking through the streets and listening to the music. I mostly keep to myself during my walks though. It gives me a chance to observe our people. Even if I don't talk to them, I see how they live. I see what I could do to make it better. My siblings don't necessarily agree with my adventures. They say it's too dangerous to be exposed like that as a Pillar. I don't really care much about their policies and rules. I wanted to go yesterday after the quake, but they stopped me before I could leave. I'm lucky to be leaving now."

"Here I thought this was a date," I joked, lightening the mood.

He smiled and explained, "Don't confuse my intentions, I'm thrilled to take you to dinner. However, I care for our people as well."

He had a point. After the last earthquake, the weak foundations of some buildings caused them to crumble. Upon my arrival at the House of Love, I was involved in the clean-up and recovery before landing my apprenticeship with the Adora. I helped search for missing people and cleared roads from debris to allow medical soldiers to easily get to people. The destroyed buildings were reconstructed with stronger materials; however, the buildings left unharmed from the last quake could be in danger from this one.

A deep breath to calm myself was restricted from the tightness of the corset. I could only reach half of a breath before thinking I would explode out of the dress.

Trying to lighten the mood further, I joked, "Well, you already managed to help one person." Making eye contact as we walked. I smiled at the Pillar. "Thanks to you, I don't have to fuss with dentistry."

He let out a soft chuckle.

I continued, "I am curious, however—why did you *straighten* my teeth? You could have easily left me with a chipped and crooked smile."

He grabbed my upper arm to slow our pace. Pausing in the corridor, his eyes flickered in the candlelight. "The times I would see you in the throne room, you would cover your mouth when you laughed, when yawning, even relaxed I noticed you still trying to hide it. After a few conversations of calling you up on the steps, you still wouldn't smile at me. I figured if I wanted to see your smile more, you needed a reason to not hide it. If you would like, I can change it back with the chipped tooth."

"No!" I reacted quickly to his offer.

He let out a roar of laughter. Echoes bounced off the walls, suspending in the air.

This would explain his long stares during the meetings. "What else have you observed?"

His eyes scanned the ceiling as he thought of something to say.

"You bite the inside of your cheek when you are nervous and twirl your hair when you daydream." He met my eyes once again.

The urge to start biting my cheek itched. I tried not to move to prove him wrong. A shiver went down my spine, causing me to shake. I didn't hide it well because Jeston offered his cape.

"You can wear it until we get to the city. These corridors get drafty at times. We don't have much farther to go." He placed the maroon cape around my shoulders. It lingered with his body's warmth. The tension in my shoulders relaxed with the heat.

"Thank you," I said quietly, pleased.

We walked in silence for a little longer, until the corridor walls turned stone cold. Shivering beneath the cape, we approached a door with large iron hinges and a lock. A key appeared in Jeston's hand, pulled from his pocket. He inserted the key into the lock, and, like the deadbolt of my apartment, it shifted to unlock the massive door.

"Right this way." He let me enter first, trailing close behind.

A dark tunnel ignited with torches. The light was contained within an alcove of the wall. Other flames ignited farther down the tunnel in tune with every second. It beckoned us to follow. Jeston's hand pressed into the small of my back, guiding me forward. He stood beside me, providing the comfort I needed to confidently walk.

"I'm going to have to ask for my cape," he said.

I obliged, shivering more.

Within minutes, the tunnel opened up and we found ourselves standing in the center of the city, Amoora.

Chapter VI

THE LICKITY SPLIT

I loved the city of Amoora.

There was charm in the colorful canopies that extended over the streets. There was endless delight in the pastries found at the bakeries that lined the streets. Narrow streets were crowded with tables overflowing from the cafes and restaurants. A mixture of bitter and sweet smells emanated from them at all hours.

We passed a couple dancing to the music flowing from the square.

Music in the city never ceased.

"Do you know how to dance?" I asked Jeston.

He sighed and stared at his feet as we continued to walk.

"I shouldn't make a fool out of myself this early into the night," he responded.

We found ourselves standing outside of what Jeston claimed to be *his* restaurant. The executive chef, a good friend of Jeston's, had prepared a table for the two of us separate from the main dining room. The table was set with dazzling details. Pristine linens, porcelain china, crystal glassware, not to mention the food was spectacular.

A three course meal.

Dinner with Jeston wasn't as bad as I was preparing myself for.

He was courteous.

And he was kind.

He pulled my chair when we arrived at the table. He gave me his dessert when he saw my eyes lingering on his plate. He laughed at my sarcastic jabs, and remained humble when I tried to pay him a compliment.

"You hold so many surprises," he said confidently.

"What do you mean by that?" I asked with a blushing smile.

"I had a feeling you were holding something back in our meetings. I couldn't place it. You were so—politically poised as the Foreman of the Adora. I'm glad I finally get to see this side of you. You're relaxed and yourself and fun to be around."

My cheeks only grew a deeper shade of red.

"Would you like to explore the city before heading back to the Estate?" I proposed.

His eyes lit with excitement, "Absolutely."

Jeston called the waiter over to the table. The man presented the check and a second bottle of wine with two glasses.

"I would assume the Pillars wouldn't need to pay for dinners like this," I whispered loud enough for only Jeston to hear.

He scribbled a signature and stood, holding the wine bottle and glasses between his fingers, "It makes me feel somewhat normal. Now, what spot did you have in mind?"

The quickest way was following the river that divided the city. There was a path near the water edge, bringing a cool breeze to the shore. Jeston held the wine bottle in one hand and the glasses in another. As we walked along the path, his attention was lost in the ripples of the water. The crescent moon provided little light tonight; however, the water seemed to soak up all of it.

Striding along the bank, he recounted a memory. "When the borders were open, The House of Joy—we called them Joymen—would journey through here. We could see their sails coming from the Estate. The passage through the city would cut their voyages in half to the eastern Houses. You wouldn't believe the size of their sails. My mother—" At the mention of his mother, his words trailed off.

Queen Aeliara, the Pillar of Trust, was the mother of the three Pillars. She passed away before my time in the House of Love. Queen Sylvanora had just been crowned as the Pillar of Intimacy before she fell ill. Poisoned by darkness, the former Queen suffered until her dying breath. There was no saving her from it, unfortunately. I didn't blame Jeston for not wanting to speak about his mother.

"I heard your mother was a Lovely woman. I never had the pleasure of meeting her, but I haven't met a single soul to tell me she didn't live devoted to her Pillar." I tried to pick his spirits up with a compliment.

"She was a Lovely woman. She taught me everything I know." He didn't explain further, thus signaling to me to stop pressing.

Luckily, we approached my favorite spot in all of Amoora. I jetted off the path, away from the water, with a grin.

Jeston stayed watching the ripples reflect the moonlight.

"Jeston?" I waved for him to follow and he did.

Steps led us away from the cool breeze of the water and we climbed to the level of the street. Cobblestones paved the narrow path until reaching a gate that allowed us to peer down on a garden surrounded by buildings on all sides. A gate prevented us from falling, but I knew the only way to access my favorite spot.

"This way." I directed Jeston, encouraging him to follow.

Similar to before, he caught my stride. I could hear the cling of the glasses in his hand as he chased me. The clang was overcome by music. The blessed sound of trumpets and bass were pounding, like my heart, as we neared the corner of the building. Turning the street corner, I was standing at the top of a staircase leading down to a basement cellar. Yellow and red lights illuminated the stairs while the music buzzed.

I paused a moment for Jeston to catch up before I descended.

"What is this place?" Jeston questioned, smiling from ear to ear. His chest didn't rise and his breathing was steady, unlike mine.

"Well, Mr. Pillar of Devotion, welcome to the Lickity Split." I said with a wink.

I sped down the flight of stairs, eager to introduce Jeston to the band that blessed our ears.

The tune was fast and changing rapidly. The movement of staccato beats filled the underground bar with listeners and dancers alike. The musicians were an all women band. The plain observer could see the music flooding their souls; the instrument was simply a tool or an extension of their bodies.

A dark-haired woman played the keys, highlighting the melody, without flaws. The trumpeter, her sister, blared in the background, taking over the melody only for a second. A toe-tapping beat whisked me away into the bar, leaving Jeston at the door. The large stringed instrument stood taller than the woman playing it in the corner of the stage. It obviously didn't intimidate her whatsoever. She plucked and pried the strings effortlessly, providing the steadiness of the tune. The final sister struck the snare drum to keep the beat rolling, moving, and flowing.

I was noticed by the trumpet player, who smiled through pursed lips and waved. I returned the gesture. Over my shoulder, I saw his majesty's dark figure creep through the shadows, trying his best to be unseen. Jeston kept to the outside walls in his cape, unsure about where he fit in a place like this.

Ridges, the bartender, sat behind the bar. A friend of Runa's at first, he poured our drinks the last time the crew of the Adora were out on the town. Running up, I gave him a big smile.

Leaning over the bar, I greeted him loud enough to cancel out the music for a split second. "Hey Ridges!"

"Hey doll! I haven't seen you in a while. You doin' all right?"

"I'm doin' all right," I repeated back to him. "I was actually wondering if I could get the key to the back? I brought a friend and I'd really like to show him the garden." We both peered over my shoulder to view Jeston in the shadows. He was watching everyone enjoying their time and trying hard to blend into the walls.

"Looks like quite the character." Ridges gave me a smirk.

"I won't be longer than a few minutes." Leaning in close, I held my dress tight to my chest to ensure I wouldn't give him a free show.

"Alright doll face." He reached down past the bottles of alcohol for a silver key. Holding it up for me to see, he said, "Take all the time you want."

"You sure?"

He nodded to the music, snapping his fingers as soon as the key left his hand. The lively beat was strong enough to feel the vibrations on the bar.

"You're the best, Ridges!" I committed to leaning over the side and gave him a kiss on the cheek. I could have sworn I saw him blush as I left for the back door.

Getting Jeston's attention was easy. Every other beat his eyes darted from the floor to the stage then to me. I motioned toward the back door. Within a key change, we were standing face to face at the back door. I swung it open. Holding the door ajar, Jeston let me walk under his arm into the hallway leading to the restrooms. Little did he know, around the corner was a locked door that led to the garden we saw on the street. Using the key Ridges gave me, I unlocked the door, with Jeston peering over his shoulder to ensure no one followed us. He snaked through and I turned the lock behind him, leaving the music behind and us alone.

The garden was a treasure in the middle of the city. I used to sneak away here when the mixture of alcohol and music made my head throb. This was my safe space, untouched by the bustling city outside. The residents of the buildings were the luckiest people to have this oasis outside their windows. A path overgrown with flowers and trees and bushes covered the entire garden leading up to the gate. I used to enjoy the days where I could lay on a bench and watch the birds above sing and soar.

"What do you think?" I asked Jeston. His eyes were exploring just as I had the first time.

"Pleasantly surprised." He kept his words short. "*Again.*"

I worried about bringing him here through the crowd of people. I knew this place was peaceful, we just had to walk through the bar first to enjoy it. Hoping to get his mind off the crowds, I asked, "Are we going to open the bottle or just have you hold it all night?" I looked at the glasses and bottle dangling from his hands.

His awe of the plants shifted to me. Raising both the glasses and the bottle, he said, "Let's drink."

He popped the bottle and poured the wine into one of the glasses. Handing it over to me, he poured himself a glass next. We sat in silence and embraced the beauty of the garden with the music playing in the background for a moment.

"I'm glad you brought me here." Raising a glass to his mouth, Jeston didn't veer from looking at the garden.

"I am too," I said genuinely. Despite how I felt about Jeston before, my biased opinions of him have changed due to this evening. He was pleasant to be around too, shockingly.

Nevertheless, the questions burned in my mind.

Now was as good a time as any to ask them.

Thinking of the best way to start, I settled for, "Would you like to play a game?" I turned my body toward his to fully face him on the bench.

"Depends, what's the game?" He played along, turning his body to face mine.

"A drinking game. I ask you a question, you take a drink for courage then answer honestly. I'll do the same after your turn. You have to answer truthfully though."

Intrigued, he agreed. "Who goes first?"

"You go first." I gave him the upper hand.

Taking his time to think about his first question, he asked, "What's the story with you and the bartender?"

Puzzled, I had to remind myself that he was a stealth observer. He watched me closely and often. Answering honestly, I said, "Nothing. Just a friend."

Laughing doubtfully, he said, "I don't believe that for a second. I saw the way you flirted with him at the bar. And the kiss on the cheek—it was natural, like you've done it before."

"I can't be kind?" I asked with a chuckle. Finding a button, I pushed further, "I'd say someone's jealous."

Raising his glass, Jeston took a sip, "If you say so."

Changing topics, he proposed, "Your turn."

I paused thinking of how to phrase the question I needed. "Did you have a hand in the decision to terminate the crew from the Adora?"

"No. I haven't heard any news regarding that." Jeston finished his glass and topped himself off with more wine.

"You must be joking."

"What happened?" The honest concern in his voice caused me to doubt my accusation.

"Yesterday, after you fixed my tooth, I arrived at the Adora, and no one was there. A man showed up and told me someone with 'authority' thought the secret of the Adora was in danger. He told me they were released from working on the Adora. My crew are not the type of people to share the whereabouts of the Adora. They know to keep it a secret."

"Did you know the name of the man?"

"Tev."

Pride hid in my chest as I presented two of my questions in one turn. Studying Jeston's face he kept staring into my eyes with concern. I doubted he would be able to tell me more about Tev. "He mentioned being a bodyguard of the Queen."

His eyebrows raised. I hid the anticipatory excitement from seeing a reaction.

"Do you know of him?" I asked.

"Yes, taller? And burly?"

I nodded my head in agreement.

"He was, as he says, a bodyguard for my sister. Tevarian Foxwood, Aluna operator. He recently left the guard for an opening at the Estate. I can't imagine you are implying my sister had anything to do with your friends' dismissal."

"But, what if—" I started to suggest, before being interrupted.

"Remember your place, Wrenna. My sister is still the queen of the people's hearts."

Remember my place?

I scoffed internally. I refrained from rolling my eyes. He meant my place as a clockworker. My place in *his* court. My place below him and his family.

Taking a sip and a long breath, I suggested moving into a different discussion.

Jeston quickly spit out another question as if processing aloud, "Why did you agree to come to dinner? Why did you even show up?"

I took a long sip from my glass, giving an extension to find the right words. "You fixed my tooth. It would have been a risky move if I denied a Pillar."

The honesty in my tone flowed like honey.

He didn't seem to like my candor.

The conversation was headed somewhere tricky to maneuver. I was beginning to see I poked at buttons I shouldn't have with Jeston. But there were so many things that distracted my attention from politeness—Bramwell being one of them.

"You did it because you were scared? Of *me*?" he questioned with a heartbreaking tone.

"It would be a lie if I said no."

Playing games was his forte; mine would be riddles.

He poured the last of the liquid courage in his glass and kept quiet. He started taking larger sips, and more often. By the time I could ask my last question, he would have an empty glass.

I went ahead and asked, "What do you know of the name Aruleah?"

Asking about Bramwell was too obvious. Maybe a name associated with him would jog his memory.

Jeston's eyes widened. A burp crept up but he coughed away the slight amount that escaped his mouth. Shock had tightened his body. He met my eyes, one last time. "I think it's time to go."

Shocked, I probed for a reason. "Why? What did I say?"

He stood with his empty glass and bottle in hand. "That's a name from the ancient world. We don't speak of that name. We need to get back to the Estate."

He started walking to the locked door.

I stood from the bench, anchoring us to the garden until he answered the question. "Why? What's going on? Who is she?"

He spun around quicker than lightning, standing a breath's length away from my face. He spoke softly, "That name is dangerous, Wrenna."

My full name stuck like a knife in my gut.

"People have died protecting the secret of that name."

It was just us in the garden. We shared a beautiful space, yet he needed to be this close to tell me that. I needed answers now. Firmly, I asked, "What secret?"

Jeston kept his lips tight; the sound of the wind could easily mask his voice if it picked up.

"She started as a House Ambassador for Love, a voice for the King to the other Houses. He trusted her. When visiting the House of Self-Control, she felt the draw of the darkness. After that encounter, she was convinced to give up everything, her status, her security, and her soul. She allowed it to claim this world. She was the reason the Houses have fallen. We don't speak of her name because the darkness seeks to find it. It strengthens at the mention of her name. Generations of Pillars fought hard to burn all the texts with her name inside for fear of it drawing it close."

His eyes full of fire, he took a gulp. "*Never* say that name again. If you need an order to obey it, I will give you one. Never say that name."

His voice was stern and commanding. "We need to leave, now. Before it finds us." He held out a hand for me to take.

I declined stubbornly.

"Wrenna, stop playing games." His voice weighed with impatience.

I huffed.

The irony in that sentence.

As Jeston body began to sink in defeat, an unworldly scream screeched from the street. Something was near the water. Carried by the wind, it echoed off the walls of the garden. From one end to the other, the screech haunted the flowers and trees. The baby buds shrank to flee from the noise.

Our eyes widened and we both silently agreed it was time to leave.

Jolted alive, we hurriedly made our way through the bar, up the stairs and back to the Estate.

Chapter VII

A DEATH CONFESSION

Vulnerable in the streets of Amoora, we quickly made our way back to the safety of the tunnels. Fearful of speaking after the garden, we hurried through the dim corridor without saying anything to one another. If he was right about the noise, the darkness could be listening for our voices. Through the door, he asked if I wanted his cape in the cold part of the Estate. I declined his offer.

I wished the night had ended differently. His authoritative tone in the garden reminded me of the hierarchy in the House. The freedom I had to venture off the Estate tonight was purely because of him.

Mulling over our conversation in the garden, I truly wondered how dangerous the name was to say. A part of me wanted to test it. To see what darkness would come when I would say her name. I watched my feet as I was walking, pondering questions like how could Bramwell love a woman so corrupt? To wholly give his heart to her, only to sell him out to the darkness. To love a monster?

Upon our entrance into the Grand Forum, the moment we exited the hall that led us to the city, the bricks and plaster began to seal the passageway. Quiet rumbles caught my attention, and I turned to see it close.

"What's happening?" I asked, not looking in Jeston's direction. My attention was solely on the bricks shifting.

"I don't want to take a chance if the darkness was looking for us. I commanded it to seal itself. I didn't want it to transform until we were safely back on the grounds of the Estate," he simply explained.

I gave him a look to explain further.

He did. "There are many passages in the Estate that open and close at the will of the Pillars. That's why the secret of the Adora has been well kept since its creation. The Pillars at the time created a web of corridors to open and close for the clockworkers only. The maze you feel walking to the Adora—the Estate shifts its halls to allow you to pass. It knows you can be trusted. The Estate is more alive than you think." By the time he was done talking, the plaster had been reshaped with no trace of an empty corridor just behind it.

I never thought that the Estate was a machine similar to the Adora. It explains how my friends could be lost in an endless maze if they pursued the Adora after their termination.

I turned my head to say goodnight. I was only going to give a bow, knowing my place, before he spoke my name.

"Wrenna, I—" He looked as if he regretted the ending to the night. As if he was going to apologize. But he didn't finish his sentence.

"Good night," I concluded, bowing my head and adding a curtsy at the end. I walked away before he could say anything else.

The closer I got to my apartment, the more my anger softened. I regretted saying the words with revulsion on my tongue. Unapologetically, I enjoyed the night despite the ending. I paused in the hallway outside my door, facing the direction of the Grand Forum. I thought of dinner with him, his conversation with the chef. Then walking down by the water, seeing the crescent moonlight bounce off the small waves. Then finishing the night at the Lickity Split and experiencing the liveliness with the music. I enjoyed watching him admire one of my favorite spots in the city, as well. It all replayed in my mind.

If only I hadn't spoiled it with my insatiable need for answers.

He would be long gone by now anyway. Back to his quarters, asleep in a comfortable bed. Where servants waited on him and he never worried about the warmth of the room or lighting it properly.

I turned toward my apartment, not wanting the night full of surprises to end. I unlocked the door, opening it to shadows and closing it on a daydream.

My bed was the only place I wanted to think about for the next several hours. The past two days had been eventful for my routine life. Before I would undress, I needed to light a candle for me to adequately see in the dark of night. My window, still open from earlier, provided the little light I needed to see my way to the matchbox and candles without stubbing a toe. Striking a match, I reached for the first candle.

Before the match touched the wick, a drop of wax burned my finger. My candle had been lit recently and burned halfway down.

"Ouch."

Shaking my finger from the pain, I was preparing to strike the match when my world went black—darker than before.

My neck was wrenched back. A cover had been placed over my head. I started to scream for help but before a sound was made, a large hand wrapped around my mouth, pinching my nose. It suppressed any sound loud enough for someone to hear. A big, muscular frame pulled me into their taut body and whispered hot breath into my ear, "If you make a sound, I will snap your neck—right here, right now. Choose wisely."

I didn't recognize the voice. It was husky and deep, as if he woke up recently from a deep slumber. Another voice over by the window whispered roughly, "Tie her hands."

The tone carried the authority of a Pillar guard.

I tried to fight their strength but before I knew it, they had my arms secured behind me. I thought my legs might be used as a weapon until they started pushing me around and disorienting me. The skirt of my dress tripped me and a rip in the chiffon sounded as I fell backwards to the ground. My headache and nausea made a resurgence with the violent shaking.

One of them grabbed under my arm to pull me off the ground. The other did the same. This one yanked me closer to him, almost claiming me as his own. One of them swung open the door, the knob smashing into the wall behind it. As they shoved me out of the room, I stumbled into the hall with a hand still attached to catch my fall.

It was well past the witching hour for anyone to hear the subtle shifts in the hall. If only Pax was still spying on me. I'm not sure how her small figure would match up to these men. Her brother would be a better option.

The muscular men closed the door and sped down the hallway. My feet couldn't keep up with their stride. The farther we walked, the more I thought about what was happening.

The books.

They are probably after the books.

I attempted to fight one more time, using my legs to kick off the ground. I could feel my skirt catch in the air and float down as I tried. Losing my shoes in the process, I heard one of the men say, "Quit it!" after a thudding sound.

The failed attempt left me drained of energy and them pissed off.

Hopefully, we were still in the Estate. I tried to look through the stitching of the linen to see exactly where we were. If the candle lights still lined the wall, we were in the safety of the Estate. Only blackness filled my field of vision. With the movement under the hood, my hair became a tangled mess, creating more darkness with the shield of cluttered strands. My mind started playing tricks on me too, as I rapidly blinked to make sure my eyes were indeed open.

Instead of dragging my feet in protest, I walked at a brisk pace. The tops of my feet had become raw from the carpeted hallway. The men were in a hurry to get somewhere. At this point, my only worry was what was going to happen when we arrived.

I heard the clack of their shoes hit a different ground; we made it to a different location. Echoes of their footsteps bounced off the high walls. At the same time, wooden doors opened to my right. There was only one set of doors that massive on the Estate. I knew where we were headed, based on the time it took, the clacking of their boots and the sound of the doors.

The men paused a few paces after turning a corner. Unlinking their arms with mine, they each set a hand on my shoulders. Taking one knee out from under me and forcing me down, I fell backward into something hard, catching my fall. My hands still tied behind me, I felt around to only confirm my suspicion.

At the same moment, the drape that had covered my head was taken off. My eyes needed a moment to adjust; however, I already knew where I was.

Before me, the three Pillars sat on their thrones.

As my eyes fully adjusted to the rapid change in light, I shot a wicked glare at Jeston. His cape was the only article missing from his evening attire as he sat on his throne. His downward gaze never intended to meet mine. With the lack of acknowledgement, I moved my stare across the stage. The queen was dressed in a silk pearl robe, and Adonis in a cotton robe bright as blood. All but Jeston grimaced at me.

Maintaining eye contact, I shifted my focus to my legs. They were exposed due to a rip in my dress. The color of my gown had been dirtied by the guard's forceful shoves onto the ground. My attempt to adjust my dress in the chair only made things worse. The slit of the dress opened more, further exposing my leg. With my hands tied, I couldn't move properly to fix it or my hair.

I fidgeted in my seat while Adonis addressed me. "Wrenna Reedwater. Do you have anything to confess?"

Adonis questioned me as if speaking in a courtroom, and I was his main suspect.

I peered over at Jeston; his eyes finally made their way to mine. He was as white as his sister's robe. The look on his face said, 'Deny, deny, deny.' So, I did what I was told.

"I assume you are going to tell me." Sass crept into my tone. If I wasn't careful, the fire burning inside would show soon too. "You realize a civil conversation could have worked instead of all the theatrics." I said, peering behind me at the massive guards.

"We have a witness claiming you are hiding valuable information from the Pillars of this House," Adonis said authoritatively.

I stole a quick glance in Jeston's direction for more clues. All I could understand was an air of shock. A part of me was furious at him for letting Pillar guards handle me like barbarians, but a part of me considered his involvement was limited, if at all.

I commented again, "Valuable information? Do you mean from the Adora?" I kept my answer ambiguous.

The Queen stood from her throne.

My heart skipped a beat.

Wasting no more time, she reached for something behind her.

When she faced me again, Bramwell's red-covered book landed at the base of the concrete steps, thrown by the queen with vile force. The red leather landed face-up. The pages were most likely crinkled now. Bitterly, she said, "Explain."

For the final time, I blinked in Jeston's direction. He was as stunned as I was that the book was in the room.

Lost for words, I mumbled under my breath.

Adonis, listening closely, took this as a confession and started calling for the guards. "Wrenna Reedwater, you are a traitor to this House and a traitor to your Pillars with the possession of this book. Your refusal to present this book to a Pillar at the time of discovery is treason!" The guards took hold of me again, standing me up. Tears welled at the base of my eyes. I fought against them; however, my strength was incomparable to theirs. Struggling under their grip, I began to scream, "Get off of me!"

Adonis finished with, "This is a call for an execution!"

"What!" I stopped fighting the guards to confirm what I had just heard, shrieking in desperation. "No!"

"Your execution will be scheduled for the morning. Get her out of my sight at once," Adonis said.

He stood from his throne.

Losing all composure, I let my tongue slip. "You bastard! All of you!"

If I had any chance of convincing them of my innocence, it was now lost with my words.

Jeston stood from his throne, racing down the steps to meet me below. I continued to struggle under the grip of the guards' hands. As he shooed them away, they dropped my body to land in front of the Pillar. A backhand struck my face with enough force behind it to send me to the ground. A scream escaped my mouth and Jeston stood over my paralyzed body.

He turned to face his siblings. "Obviously, this clockworker is deranged. Too many nights tending to the gears. Brother, may I suggest another option? She deserves to suffer in a perpetual hell. A ceaseless torment of agony and pain." A deep chuckle left him. "Death is too easy; let's make her suffer."

His brother, intrigued, let him continue.

"Give her to the darkness. Let her cross the border to be eaten alive by the spirits that haunt our other Houses," Jeston said sinisterly.

I could only see the back of his head between my tangled hair and temporarily losing sight on the side he hit me. My guess was a smirk never left his face as he was proposing the ideas to his siblings.

"Exile," the Queen said.

She gave a nod, agreeing I deserved a fate worse than death.

Adonis was the deciding factor. Reaching a quick decision, he said, "Exile it must be. Wrenna Reedwater, you, my little bird, are banished from the House of Love."

My whole world was gone. Falling into the gears of the Adora would have been easier. I was shattered into tiny pieces lying on the floor.

Before the guards could take me away, Jeston was quick to insert himself. "Brother, I'd be honored to see to her demise myself. My devotion to this House cannot be undermined by a mere clockworker like this."

Purely disposable—a clockworker like myself.

Adonis was quick to exit; a wave of a hand was enough to allow Jeston to take me to the darkness however he saw fit.

Yanking me to my feet, Jeston pushed me toward the Grand Forum. Holding my restricted hands, he steered me in the direction he wanted me to go. He knew any resistance on my part would cause my shoulder to dislocate, forcing me to comply. I succumbed to the embarrassment of being paraded out of the throne room past the guards and into the Grand Forum. His heels clacked on the polished floor, alerting the few department heads to withdraw into the shadows.

Following the curve of the room, we marched toward an empty wall beginning to deteriorate. Crumbling bricks and plaster shifted to form a passageway similar to the one he concealed only an hour before. Its deep void terrified me. There was just enough space for our bodies to pass through the threshold together. Before I knew it, we were encased by total obscurity within the Estate walls once again. This time, my life was completely stripped away from me and I was on my way to be exiled from the House of Love.

Chapter VIII

THE FLICKERS OF FIRE AND FLAME

"Get your hands off of me!" His grip tightened around my upper arm, dragging me farther into a newly opened tunnel. Stopping abruptly, he unclenched my arm.

Impenetrable darkness surrounded us. An escape was impossible.

He didn't hesitate to raise his voice to mask mine. "Are you out of your mind?" Echoes ricocheted off the stone walls.

We were in a tunnel.

"Two men kidnapped me in my own apartment! I was just sentenced to an execution! You're asking *me* if I'm out of *my* mind?"

Squaring his shoulders, he yelled, "Explain to me why my brother thinks you have any connection to that book!"

I stammered, not knowing how to respond.

"Well?" He was still yelling, waiting for an answer.

When nothing came out of my mouth, Jeston continued his thought. "The Pillars from all the Houses have searched for centuries for the books of Bramwell. They burned all but one. Wars were started over that book, dividing the kingdom further. Spite and jealousy had fed the darkness because of it." His chest rose and fell, taking heavy breaths.

All but one? He must not know about the others. I could use this to my advantage, to save myself from exile. "Why should I tell you anything? You are just going to deliver me to your brother again. You are the reason I am in this mess!"

"Control your tongue," he said menacingly. "My brother does not know anything about our evening in the city. I've barely had time to breathe since we returned. You think I had time to tell my brother what you told me in the garden? He will never know, and no one ever will."

Angry, I poked further. "You may be a Pillar, but you don't have the authority to speak to me like a peasant. I hold a seat in your court."

Raising his voice even louder, anger hit him too. "Are you unaware of my position? How daft are you?"

We both huffed at each other, willing to take shots at one another in the dark, not worried about the consequences. I bet if we could see one another, we wouldn't be this explosive. Sight grounded us.

Calming his voice, he said, "If you knew the history. That name—that book—you would have done the same. It's historically defiant."

I paused, taking an extended breath, before pleading, "Please enlighten me. I'm sorry for playing games earlier. Why is Bramwell's book so important to the Pillars?" I chose my words wisely to not give away my shot at freedom.

"I don't have much time. We need to start walking." His words were snippy.

I persisted, "I'm not moving until I get answers. Why did you sell me out to the darkness? Sentence me to exile? Execution would have been much easier for you to handle. Less pieces of the puzzle to mess with. Why bring me here?"

"This wasn't my fault. You needed to know that. My brother sent the guards. Sending them to do his dirty work, like always. I didn't know he sent them to hurt you."

The feeling of the rips in my dress hit my leg. I could feel the bruises starting.

The shock of it all was starting to fade away. Tears from the back of my eyes were surfacing. The thought of their hands covering my mouth, forcing me to comply with their strength. Shoving me around in my own home to take me away. I wondered how many bruises would appear over the course of the next couple of days from their force. I tried to settle my breathing, but the memory of their hands wouldn't leave. My fury settled in fear. If it weren't for Jeston, I would crumble into a mess on the floor.

Hearing my breathing intensify, he spoke gently. "There are ways to avoid the darkness, Wrenna. There are pockets of good that have survived each collapse. My siblings' paranoia is projected in court, growing substantially larger these last few weeks. The General himself said the border hasn't seen action yet. There's a chance you will live an amazing life outside of the House of Love. Would you rather be *dead* by morning?"

The word stuck out like a thorn in my side. My adrenaline was now completely gone; a wave of exhaustion crashed inside me. Tracing a silent path down my cheeks, my tears carried the weight of unspoken fear.

He continued with kind words, seeking to reassure me, "My siblings have convinced themselves the darkness is *clawing* at the border trying to find any weakness. Understandably, my brother's fear comes from wanting to protect his family. He has allowed himself to blend his duties as a Pillar and a husband and a father. He can't tell where one starts and the other ends. My sister feeds it with her own worries.

He doesn't have a moment to consider that the truth of the matter is, that's not the case."

I thought about the influence of the Pillars. They could feed us information biased with their own fears, and we would be none the wiser.

"My sister lets her worries take over her life. She sent Tev to the Adora to ensure she was up to date firsthand. It's a good thing that fear will not send our House into a collapse because we would have been ruined by now."

A surge of contentment flooded me instead. The knowledge of Tev, no matter how small it was, made it easier to process his sudden appearance. The hard fact to swallow was I'd never see the clock again, or my friends. Tears welled continuously and fell effortlessly. I didn't have to blink.

The black void allowed me to feel no shame in crying.

My life in the House of Love had been completely different this morning. My friends asked for help, and I failed. My job, one I was really good at, was no longer part of my life. The job made me happy. I got the chance to sit with powerful people, yet it held no weight in the court. To the Pillars, I would be only a disposable clockworker, no matter how surprising I could be.

With the thought of Jeston standing there, I needed one more apology for all to be forgiven.

Small fires sparked to life, lining the walls.

His eyes sunken from the long night and the angle of the flames, he whispered, "I'm sorry for hitting you. The devotion to my throne is stronger now with all but the House of Love fallen. Any form of disrespect calls for immediate action from me or my brother to defend it. I stood before he had the chance. I can't fight my instincts when it comes to those things. My body struck you and inside I was screaming the entire time." His voice broke a little at the end.

Recalling how many times Jeston vocalized how surprised he was tonight, I could say the same. He surpassed any previous expectation regarding him as a Pillar. Toward me and toward the House.

"I had no idea it controlled you like that." Forgiveness hinted in my tone.

He explained, "If I don't obey, there are consequences. Physical, mental, emotional, depending on how severe." He touched my arm softly with no intention of hurting me, yet I still jerked away. "That's *why* I would like to start moving. I need to escort you to the Barracks."

Seeing how I reacted to a brief touch, he hesitated with his next words. "I promise, you can trust me."

Testing the waters, I asked, "So, if I told you the truth about the book, would your devotion to the throne turn me in?"

His eyebrows raised. "It depends—does it put the throne at risk?"

Not knowing the full history behind the books made my answer harder to determine. I could only make a guess at this point.

"I'll assume, yes, based on how your brother was talking about it earlier," I said.

"To keep a secret like that from them, especially involving the safety of the House, would cause a lot of pain," Jeston acknowledged. He shook his head, trying to forget a memory of the pain he had felt before. Drawing a conclusion, he suggested, "Unless my devotion to something else was greater than my devotion to the throne."

"What could mean more to you than your throne?" I asked.

His eyes stared at mine for countless seconds, as if the Adora herself stopped working altogether.

"Friendship," he said.

"Friendship?" I repeated.

Jeston reached for my arm once again, nudging me in the direction we needed to walk. I obliged.

Heading to the Barracks, we wound through the endless passageways of the Estate. On our journey, Jeston began to clarify what he meant.

He began with, "Being the youngest in a royal family comes with its challenges. The people my age in the House are either confined to the fields, the barracks, or in the city. Other than the servants and some workers—like yourself—there aren't many people my age in the Estate. You know how my family feels about the city; they feel the same way about the fields. We shouldn't be associated with the working people, being Pillars. There needs to be a constant divide. I have always argued against that opinion, but I have given up in recent years.

"So, that left me to the soldiers. My family would send me to the barracks to train with the soldiers starting around the age of ten. I learned to fight, handle weaponry, and got to know the boys my age. Every year since, my mother would allow me to visit in the cold months 'to boost morale' as she put it. Every year following, I looked forward to when the trees lost their last leaves, knowing I would be with my brothers soon, not Adonis, but those boys I grew up around. With the Fall of the House of Kindness, they were deployed to the border on orders, and I was tucked away in the Estate since."

Making sure my math was right, I asked, "You haven't seen your friends in four years?"

He nodded his head. "Unfortunately, power comes at a price."

I would remember that.

He continued, "As for my brother, he had started his own family, spending time with them outside of the duties of being a Pillar. My sister, on the other hand, had her lovers to keep her company. Other than my family, I have never had a friend who I could trust in court."

Without the friendships I made while working on the Adora, I'd be lost. Those were some that I would treasure for the rest of my life. That was another thing to mourn as we walked farther and farther away from the Grand Forum. I wondered if they would return to work, now that I was gone. Or be notified about my leaving at all.

Without having much to input, I let Jeston go on. "I see the lust in the eyes of my servants. The idea of being with a Pillar. It's nice to be sought after but the separation of power is far. Then, the discussion of a clockworker sitting in on the meetings came around."

My ears perked up.

"I knew most of you were around my age. There was still a separation of power within the House; however, if approved, you would have a seat in court. I pushed hard for it when members were hesitant and almost convinced my siblings to reconsider."

I thought my preparedness was the reason I deserved a seat at the table; instead, it was because of a lonely Pillar. I am forever indebted to Jeston though. He elevated my position as foreman to sit in meetings. If it weren't for him, my whole crew would have been overlooked and disposed of long before the Fall of the House of Joy.

He carried on, "Seeing you at the first meeting felt like the first day of training again, exciting and new. I started to send you flowers to see if you were amused by the attention of a Pillar. Next, I flirted with you to see if you would flirt back. After nothing in return, I needed a way to show you my intentions were good. I realized my tests caused a repulsive effect, so I decided to twist your hand into saying yes to dinner. I just got lucky with your tooth."

"It was all a game, with the dress and shoes as well," I scoffed.

"No, the evening attire was because I wanted you to have something nice to wear. I noticed what you wore to committee meetings and figured you needed something nice. I wasn't about to have you taint my reputation with the servants based on your limited wardrobe. Do you understand how quickly that news would spread to my family? They would disapprove immediately, and you would lose your seat in court."

I started to feel the heat rising in my cheeks. I didn't know if I should be offended or not.

"My brother's sudden dinner plans gave me an excuse to leave to check on the people of the city, especially after what happened in Joy. I was planning on coming back here right after but then you suggested the music bar. I don't regret it either because to see the crowd dancing and people laughing gave me a sense of relief. Our people were not only alive, but almost unfazed by Joy's demise. The integrity of that city was still intact, which is all I really care about."

I wanted him to stop there. Knowing what came next, I didn't want to relive it.

"Then, we spoke in the garden and when I heard you say that vile name, my role as a Pillar shone through. I snapped. You wouldn't speak to me on the walk back to the Estate, even when I offered my cape. From the harshness in your words in the Grand Forum, I didn't want to give you more of a reason to be disgusted with me. I thought I had ruined the potential of ever changing your mind about me. Then, in the throne room—"

I studied how uncomfortable it made him to bring it up. He looked down at his feet. I could tell he was truly bothered by striking my cheek. As we walked, he fidgeted with his fingernails. Over the course of the conversation, he convincingly led me to believe him.

I responded, "You were going to say something in the Grand Forum before we parted but stopped yourself." I let him connect the dots of what I meant.

"I wanted to explain to you why I lost my temper. Fear was the main reason. My siblings' conversations regarding the darkness are a constant reminder that the House of Love is next. The name was a trigger enabling those fears into existence. The second reason was my devotion to keep the throne safe from danger. Wren, I mean it when I say evil will come with that name on your tongue."

The truth had finally come. Granted, there were still pieces missing; however, I didn't need much more convincing to believe what he was saying. I felt as though it was time I returned the favor by telling the truth.

Seeing light ahead, we neared the exit of the tunnel. Now was my chance to say something. Reaching for his arm, I tugged at his body. "There are other books."

Registering what I said, he rebutted, "That can't be. Any books by Bramwell have been burned—for centuries now."

"There are two more," I argued. "And one with *her* name on it."

His eyes went wide, similar to when he sat on his throne. Perplexed, we stared at each other in the flickers of fire and flame.

Chapter IX

THE BARRACKS

"How could there be more books?" Jeston asked.

"It's almost like there was a reason I was asking about the history of the books! I don't know. You're the one who knows the history." Irritability struck a chord in my tone. "I bought them in the market during Norda," I replied.

He blurted out questions, his thoughts scrambled together. "Well, what do they look like? Where are they? Are you sure they belong to Bramwell?"

I proceeded to tell him about the books. I described the quake and the water spilling on the books. The colorful ink bleeding onto their pages, revealing the white ink underneath Bramwell's dedications. I tried as best as I could to recount the words exactly.

Jeston stayed silent as I spilled every detail.

By the time I was finished, he didn't say anything. We reached the end of the tunnel. Still trying to process all the information about the books, we paused before going into the opening.

"I need to treat you like a prisoner," he explained. "There will be news from Adonis already. They will be expecting us. It will need to be a good act to get where we are going."

"Ok," I said cautiously.

Jeston kept with the same theatrics he used when we first slipped out of the Estate.

I was a prisoner.

I could sense my time in the House of Love was drawing to a close. Our arrival at the barracks was one step closer to exile.

Upon exiting we found ourselves soaking in the sunrise. Morning had come.

The tunnel emptied into the courtyard of the Barracks just beyond the Estate walls.

From dusk until dawn, the rollercoaster of emotions had left me exhausted. If I were to survive beyond the border, I needed rest.

Men dressed in uniforms patrolled the courtyard of porticos lining the camp with their long shadows trailing behind them. The sun left a golden tinge on their maroon uniforms, highlighting the fabric a bright reddish orange. Buttons hid beneath cloth on their chest and pockets lined their pants. It was a different uniform from what I remember the General wore. Instead of a beret, these men wore a more versatile hat, meant to hide their eyes from the sun's rays.

Their uniforms reflected the current Pillars. Similar in style to the thrones, the color of their camouflage was a shade of maroon to represent Adonis. To pay homage to the Queen, each button, hidden under a thin strip of fabric, was an iridescent pearl. The buttons peeked out, reflecting the sun as Jeston and I walked by. The tribute to Jeston's throne must have been the pattern of the uniforms. Lines striped vertically on each torso represented wood grain like the bark of a tree, patched together with leaf prints. The pants were a mixture of the same pattern, and a series of shapes randomized on the fabric.

You could tell which men were higher in rank because of their uniforms. With a peacoat material, their uniforms looked sharper than those of the lowly soldiers. Still in a maroon color, they also wore badges of honor. I assumed the higher the number of badges, the higher the rank.

All the men noticed us as we parted from the safety of the tunnel. First formation must have been soon because the numbers of men roaming the courtyard skyrocketed after the sun had fully risen over the horizon.

If the soldiers didn't salute, they bowed to Jeston as he marched through the center of the camp. I, still wearing my ripped and tattered dress, drew the eyes of most of the men from afar, like animals deprived of food. I was now their prey. Easy to stalk. Easy to secure. There was no doubt in my mind that these men were dangerous, maybe more dangerous than the Pillar guards. My battle with those sentinels lasted seconds; here, I wouldn't be able to blink before being taken to their bunks to be devoured. If it weren't for Jeston's protection, I would cease to exist.

Touring the main training area, we meandered toward the edge of the camp. A canvas tent with a soft door flapped with the slight breeze. Just inside was a short mudroom. Dusty red boots of all sizes were thrown everywhere, stacked on top of each other and beside one another. Behind another wall of canvas, six beds lined the perimeter of the room on each side. The sheets, printed with the same wooden fabric as the uniforms, gave the giant tent the feel of a mortuary. Twelve coffin beds lined the perimeter, waiting to be filled and planted into the soil soon. I took a big gulp.

Jeston let go of my hands as we took cover in the room. He veered to the left to the lockers lining the wall adjacent to the bunks. Opening the farthest one, he took out a maroon shirt, a pair of the pocket-lined pants, and a pair of socks.

Throwing them in my direction onto one of the beds, he said, "You can change into these. They were mine from years ago. I won't be able to wear them anymore." He searched in the mudroom for boots. He estimated my shoe size and threw a pair on the ground, almost hitting my toes.

"I'll step out and watch the door. Please hurry. It will be easier to hide a dress rather than someone in a dress." With that, he did as he said, and I was left with the canvas hitting the steel frames and company of the coffins.

Grabbing for the zipper of my dress, I slowly took it down, hesitant that someone was going to step through the canvas door. My body ached from the guards' use of force. As I slipped out of the dress, I searched for bruises. Three misshapen blots were starting to form, purpling my skin. I reached for the t-shirt quickly to cover up any skin before someone burst in.

A pack of footsteps shuffled on the ground outside.

I hastily assisted my legs into each pant leg, hoisting the belt up to my waist.

There was chatter just outside the door. Multiple voices cheered with excitement, growing louder with each passing second. Before I finished the last button of the pants, a group of soldiers flipped open the first layer of canvas.

I grabbed the dress and rolled it into a tight ball of chiffon and tucked it behind my back. I backed myself into the side of the tent nearest the lockers, trying to remember which one Jeston messed with. In a second, I opened the locker door, shoved the dress into the corner and shut it. Later I'd burn the dress, just for the memories it held.

Laughter roared in the tent. Some of the men jumped up and down, almost tackling Jeston at the center of the pack while others trailed behind, waiting for the storm of excitement to calm down.

Jeston had a huge grin on his face, with fire in his eyes. I hadn't seen him like this before.

These men had lit his soul with Love.

My feet resting in the cold dirt, I reached for the socks to put them on. Then the boots. By the time I was fully dressed, all the men dispersed to their distinct bunks, each carrying different conversations. I made eye contact with Jeston and he signaled for me to join him.

Stepping into the center of the tent, a fit man, similar build to Adonis, cut in my path and studied me. "Who might you be?"

Some of the men stopped their conversations to see me for the first time in their tent. My body tightened at the sight of him. "Um . . . "

I looked over his broad shoulder cascading in front of me, asking with my eyes for Jeston to save me.

He stepped in next to me, facing the large man, and explained, "There's a situation at the Estate I need to oversee. She's going to stay with you for a couple of days." Making the decision for them, he carried on, asking, "Did I make a bad decision by thinking you would help?"

My eyes widened. I was unaware of the plan; this was the first time I heard about it. The men, silent, didn't want to answer the question.

"What about Command?" A man sitting on his bunk, centered on the canvas wall, pulled a knife from its sheath to inspect it. He glared at me momentarily with it in his hands.

"I'll make sure they won't be an issue." Jeston raised his voice. "I'd hate to have to remind you who actually runs this place, Knifehook." He spat the threat, jokingly, toward his bunk.

As he backed off, another man from the other side of the room chimed in, "What are we supposed to do with her?" His voice was softer than the others, with a slight lisp. His bunk was two down from Knifehook's in the tent.

"She'll need food and water. Rotate taking extras at meals so you don't raise suspicion. Leave her to rest."

Stepping back, he projected his voice and resumed, "No one in Command must know she is here. I'll be sure they stay away, but protect her at all costs. If it's her life or yours, choose yours. She risked her life for all of you; it's time to return the favor. If she is found, we're all dead anyway." Jeston addressed the whole tent at once.

That incriminating word gashed in my brain, reminding me of the throne room, of Jeston's hit. It brought my attention to my tender cheekbone, swollen for sure.

A man sitting beside Knifehook joked, "This boy becomes a Pillar and assumes the world will bow at his feet." Laughter fell on the room. He continued with a wink, "Only joking; it's no problem, *boss*."

Facing me, once again, the burly man spoke. "We'd be honored." Speaking for the collective bunch, he bowed his head in *my* direction.

The farthest point from the door, there was an empty space wide enough for another person to stay. The patch of dirt would be my bed for the next few nights.

Whispering in my ear, Jeston said, "Watch the door for me."

I glanced in the direction of the flapping canvas door.

A thump behind me caused the dirt to plume. A cot had appeared thanks to Jeston. A wool blanket matched the wood grain of the uniforms, a complement to the devotion throne too. Resting for a moment by lying across the mattress, he basked in the comfort of the familiar bed. He sat up and tapped the space beside him for me to have a seat.

Sitting down, I could feel every muscle relax. I laid similar to how he did and immediately understood why he wasn't eager to move. The warmth of the blanket underneath to the firmness under my back made it a hard combination to budge from.

A man adjacent to our bunk asked in a hushed voice, "How is everything at the Estate since the quake?"

Another man next to him chimed in, "How's your sister?"

A few men joined in laughing, waiting for the answer.

"The consequences of the quake have my brother scared. He has bunkered us in. We can't leave our quarters most of the day. It's driving me nuts. His wife—"

"The hag?" said the man next to me.

"Yeah, she has been rearranging furniture in our living quarters to make room for her and her two little monsters." Rolling his eyes, Jeston carried on, "And my sister wouldn't be able to see you even if you stood on the steps next to her, Ronan."

Ronan gave a smirk, taking the jab like it had been a while since he and Jeston joked.

A trumpet sounded. The men all stood at once, running through the canvas door. I noticed Ronan was the shortest of the bunch as he exited the tent. I waited for a signal from Jeston to know what to do.

Once all the men were gone, he stood, advancing for the door before shifting his attention to me. "I better get back to the Estate."

"What's the plan? Why did you bring me here?" I was nervous to hear the answer.

"I can't trust the commanding officers. My brother heads this section of the House as their chief Commander. They could easily rat me out if they found you here."

I raised my eyebrows, tensing at the information.

He reassured me, "The men you just met are the Aluna operators. They report to the General himself and he remains in headquarters for the most part, as do his subordinate officers. The boys just got back from a mission and are required to get enough rest between each departure. You won't be found here."

I could feel myself sweating beneath the layer of cotton.

Noticing a shift in my mood, he restated, "You'll be safe here." He knelt down to meet my eyes, drilled to the dirt. "I promise."

My heart pounded. My brain tried to process which was the worst punishment: being left with twelve woman-hungry, dirty, mouth-breathing men or being exiled to the darkness. Through the thick fog of my mind, I asked, "Why are you going back to the Estate?"

Resuming his walk toward the door, pausing before exiting, he replied, "I'm going to look for the other books. Hopefully, the guards were stupid enough to only look for the one."

My finger brushed over the mushroom-topped wax burn. "My candles had been lit before I got home. We might be out of luck."

Proceeding to the open the flap, he pivoted to say, "Well, fortunately, luck seems to be on my side. After all, I managed to have you join me for dinner, didn't I?" He winked.

He dipped behind the first layer of canvas, "Get some rest. I'll be back before you know it."

He slipped away under the second layer, leaving me with the twelve coffin beds again. However, this time was different as I had one of my own to occupy.

Chapter X

THE THIRTEENTH SOLDIER

Jeston's voice rang in my head.

Never say that name again!

He raced in a corridor. Chasing after me in the Estate. A section I had yet to visit. Portraits painted on every wall. Some men, some women—all holding positions of power. Their gaze fixed on me as I ran, and he chased.

Stop playing games!

He was harsh.

And afraid.

Tripping on my own footing, my eyes were now fixed on the ceiling. I traced the gold-laced crown molding, searching for any irregularities to find if this was real. I looked for a darkness so unfathomable that my soul would burn at the sight of it.

That name is darkness!

I thought of the painted book.

To my Aruleah . . .

Her name sounded the way honeysuckle smelled or how I imagined the ocean felt on my feet: powerful and familiar. Part of me trusted her without knowing anything about her. I believed she was *good,* based purely on the sound of her name. I yearned for another chance to say it out loud, to enjoy the sweetness on my tongue.

The next scene had flashes of Adonis standing at his Pillar throne. His shoulders were wide enough to carve the canyons. His height was large enough to conquer the trees. The Queen shivered in his quake beside him. She threw the crimson book like a spear, piercing my heart in the process. Darkness bled from my wound, like it was my punishment for owning such a dangerous book.

Exile.

The echoes rang.

Exile.

It was etched on my soul.

The scene changed again like the curtain call of a play. I was back with Jeston. He was escorting me through the newly made corridor as we exited the Grand Forum.

The walls folded in. Emptiness followed.

But I knew he was still there.

I knew there was no escape.

Fires erupted in the tunnel before he said anything. Sunken eyes were my first sight. I knew it wasn't Jeston behind those eyes.

Only darkness resided in his eyes. There was no reflection. His carved sockets were completely absent. The whites of his eyes were gone, and I stared darkness in the face.

Taking complete control of the Pillar, it opened Jeston's mouth and velvety liquid fell. Dripping down his chin, it left streaks of black on his skin. The whites of his teeth were stained the same. A hand—its hand—cold as ice, wrapped around my throat and began to squeeze.

Droplets of sweat fell into my ear, jarring me awake. A concoction of salt and horror fell into my eyes, gluing them shut for a moment. I snatched the wool blanket, hoping to soak up any of the remaining liquid in my eyes.

Fully awake, I found the men were unfazed by my sudden awakening. I feared I looked, and smelled, as if I was one of them. I adjusted to lay on my side, to watch them covertly. My lingering exhaustion could have allowed me to fall back asleep after I scooted myself into a comfortable position. I was caught with my eyes open by one of the soldiers, which prevented me from falling back into a slumber.

To my right, I heard, “Boys, the girl’s awake. Behave yourselves.”

My head was still fuzzy. I focused on the person sitting next to me on his bunk. He was resting with one arm behind his head, leaning back on the taut canvas. He was the only one in the entire group with a beard. The gray hair on his head matched the hair on his chin, cheeks, and upper lip. He wore the same maroon uniform I did.

“Nightmares. They are common in this place,” he said.

My dream of the sunken eyes was easily accessible for a moment longer. However, the more I thought about it, the more I lost my grip on it.

My face felt hot. Under the layer of wool and cotton, my body was moist. Concealed under the blanket, a layer of protection. The heat was growing unbearable, but I didn’t dare leave the only safety I had left. Reclining against the canvas, my feet hung out from the cover for a bit of reprieve.

When I sat up, I felt a collective shift in the tent. The ones that were awake didn’t want anything to do with me.

The relaxed soldier beside me retreated from the canvas to the end of his bed. He whispered loud enough for me to hear, "You were talking in your sleep. They also aren't used to women in here. They'll get over it, it'll just take some time. You can call me Thad."

"Thad?" I asked while rearranging my body to better face his. My side now rested against the canvas with my legs curled up.

"Yes ma'am. Thadeous Ritter. Third generation Aluna operator for the House of Love," he stated while extending his hand with the expectation I return the favor.

The words Jeston told me before he left rang in my head: *You can trust them.* I wasn't stupid enough to blindly believe him, even if he saved my life from exile.

"You can call me Enna," I responded with a version of my name, one that hadn't seen the light in the House of Love; a nickname from my father. My voice was raspy, still warming up from my nap. I took his hand. The shake sent a signal of strength down my arm. I trembled behind mine.

Hopefully, he won't sense the lie.

A false name made it easier to believe I was safe. The Estate would be looking for Wrenna, the clockworker, but these men would know me as Enna, the refugee.

The man beside Thadeous introduced himself, even though I remembered his name from before. "Enna, I'm Ronan O'Shae, born of the Good." He had a thick accent I hadn't heard before. He held out a hand for me to shake as well. Pride echoed behind his handshake.

"You aren't from the House of Love?" I asked.

"Oh no. We come from all over, representing all of the Houses, fallen or redeemed," Ronan said. "Thad is one of the only ones from the House of Love. I'm from Goodness—the blessed meadows region—and proud of it too.

"This is River Lynxshade," Ronan introduced a dark-skinned man, resting on the bed beside his own, "from the House of Peace, and Maasten is from the House of Kindness."

My heart fluttered to the sound of the wetlands I grew up in.

The soldier Ronan called Maasten spoke up. "You must be special if Jeston brought you *here* of all places. Most people try to stay far away from the Barracks. He's never dumped someone off with us before. You must be in serious trouble if not even a Pillar can save you."

"Maasten is right," said Thadeous, "Jeston wouldn't come here, risking his life, if it weren't for something important. What happened, if you don't mind me asking?"

I didn't want to reveal my sentence to exile. I needed a lie. A believable lie. One that would make sense to them.

"I was wrongfully accused," I explained simply.

A man with thick auburn hair had stopped in on our conversation. Curious about the details, he asked, "Why did you arrive with Jeston holding you as he would any other prisoner?"

Freaked by the question, I said the first thing that popped into my head. "My alibi incriminated him as well. At his request the secret of our affair needed to remain, well, a secret. Adonis sentenced me and Jeston played his part as a jailer to keep the theatrics up."

"What did they suspect?" the redhead pressed further.

Anxiety building, I simply said, "Treason."

They all looked at each other silently.

I caught judgment in each of their eyes, so I clarified, "Adonis didn't host a trial for the truth. I'm sure he suspected we had been seeing each other, and it was the easiest way to get rid of me. To keep the Pillars strong, especially Jeston, with him only being coronated a few months ago."

Some nodded, believing the story. The redhead walked away before I could see his reaction.

One of the more attractive men came up to my bunk. He too had a husky build. Jet black hair twisted into dreadlocks that complemented his dark skin and amber eyes. He looked directly at me and spoke about something unrelated. "Next time you have a nightmare, can you speak quieter? Some of us were trying to sleep."

Embarrassed, but relieved about leaving the other conversation, I sincerely apologized, "I'm sorry, I didn't mean to disturb you all. What was I saying?"

"Yeah, let's hear it Dakari," Thadeous encouraged him.

Closing his eyes, the soldier cleared his throat then spoke with a lyrical hum to the following words:

Oh, to the lost one, for night's bitter cold
You who lie awake, look in the old—
Your power belongs to the mud and mire.
Love will be in ruins, if you so desire.
In shadows deep, where light once bled
Ocean eyes with ember's thread
To the place of decay, where water once flowed
A past left behind, where new seeds are sowed.
With eyes of blue, bound by plenty
Cursed with folly, lost and empty.
This one lost soul waits for the day,
Where a crown is restored, and gem to pay.

A roar of laughter erupted at our end of the bay. Dakari walked away with a smile and high fiving the other soldiers around.

Replaying in my mind, I recognized some of the words. They were from Bramwell's books. The sung phrases made it easier to remember.

The laughter settling, Thadeous changed the subject. "If you are hungry, Bokehart brought you food."

Waking from my spell, I shifted my focus to the food at the foot of my bed. There were napkins lying in the dust with slices of bread sitting atop.

"Oh. Which one is Bokehart?" I was curious to see who was kind enough to bring me food.

"Bokehart!" Thadeous screamed across the tent, drawing the attention of almost all the soldiers. Whoever Bokehart was didn't respond, so he yelled again. "Bokehart! Beau!"

Finally, a soldier sitting beside Beau elbowed him. He dropped the conversation to look over in our direction. He was the most beautiful man I'd ever laid eyes on. Sharp jawline with matching cheekbones with a high and tight haircut to elongate his neck. He smiled with straight teeth, pure and white, in our direction and gave a wave of his hand. I could see the definition of muscle lurking underneath his shirt from where I sat. I tried hard not to blush from him noticing me.

Bringing the slices up to my lap, I found they weren't spongy anymore. My stomach hungry for food, I tore apart the stale bread. I took a bite of it and my jaw popped from the pressure of biting down. Each bite was like chewing rocks. I risked chipping another tooth; luckily, I knew Jeston could fix it.

Thadeous looked over and said, "The food here sucks. We couldn't find anything better."

Grateful, I responded, "I'll take anything at this point. Thank you." Although my mouth was severely scratched from the hard bread, and my jaw hurt from chewing, my stomach was happy. The hunger subsided enough to last me until the night.

After the long nap, the taste of food, and getting increasingly more awake, a new issue had arisen. My bladder. With the urge rising, I quietly asked Thadeous, "Is there a toilet?"

Thadeous looked troubled, like he hadn't planned for this part. He projected his voice for everyone to hear, "Boys, we got a situation."

As I tried to hush him, he continued to say as everyone gathered around reluctantly. "She's got to take a leak. How are we going to get her to the stalls without being seen?" He looked to his brothers for answers.

The man, River Lynxshade, suggested, "She's dressed like one of us; just throw a hat on and she'll be good to go."

The crowd of men surrounding our edge of the bay turned back to what they were doing, after a solution was given. They were uninterested and not needed any longer.

Thadeous encouraged the answer. "Good thinking, Riv. You've always had a knack for sneaking around."

Maasten handed me a hat and Thadeous stood to escort me to the stalls across the camp.

The sun was beginning to set by the time I got my boots on and received a quick lesson on how to walk through the camp pretending to be one of the Aluna operators.

Close to two dozen buildings lined the camp. Each of them had a deck surrounding the body of the building. We called them wraparounds in the swamps of Kindness. There were guards stationed at all four corners on the porch. I wondered what needed such intense security to have so many guards surrounding the building at once. I took a mental note of where the bathrooms were located in case I needed to use them again and didn't have an escort. Hopefully, that would never happen.

I walked alongside Thadeous until he stopped just outside the door to the open stalls. There were no doors for privacy at this latrine.

A trough full of water sat near the door's entrance, alluding to be the place where I was to wash my hands or even bathe in the near future.

This would be my downfall.

My eyes widened; I refused to pass the threshold of the door.

Noticing my hesitation, Thadeous whispered, "Take the last stall. I'll stay at the door, so they know not to go all the way to the back."

Swallowing hard, I nodded and proceeded into the open-air stalls, trying hard to keep my eyes straight on the last stall.

Chapter XI

NEVER SAFE

With the sun growing closer to the horizon, the shadows grew by the minute.

Heading back to the tent, I could barely keep up with Thadeous. His stride was much longer than mine. I tried my best not to run beside him.

"Dinner will be called soon. I don't want any officers to spot you," he said cautiously. "Keep up. I'm trying to avoid you joining us in the mess hall."

We hit the first flap, then the second, retreating to the back of the bay where we were safe. We passed everyone lacing their boots for dinner. The moment I sat down on my bed, a familiar tune rang over the camp summoning them. I recognized the tune. I was the one to program it at the Adora. It was the tune for the Pillar of Protection. An image of the chimes striking on the hour flashed in my mind. I could hear the ghost of the gears notching from the body of the beast.

As I sat in a trance, Thadeous placed his hand on my shoulder.

"I'll try to sneak you some dessert this time." He winked before his swift exit with the others.

I watched the soldiers as their feet made imprints in the dirt floor of the tent, kicking up dust in the process. A long streak of light suspended in the air from an opening in the canvas door. The dust sparkled in the light, moving at random and eventually gliding down to its original spot. As the dust settled, my eyes grew tired again. The coffin bed called my name.

For fear of another nightmare, I fought the annoying urge to fall asleep. I could feel my body starting to tense at the thought. Taking deep breaths, I calmed my nerves. By the time the dust had fully reached the ground, the sun was no longer in the sky. The wool blanket now cradled my body, and my mind drifted into a dream.

I lay in the center of the forest floor staring at the sky of terracotta leaves. A slight breeze caused the trees to shed their leaves. Some shot straight down with brittle branches. Others floated, catching the last moments of freedom before resting on the ground forever. The sun was hidden behind clouds but illuminated an area in the sky with a soft light. A web of branches zigzagged in all directions above. The branches gave a home to a dozen apricot leaves while others were completely bare. The wind, continuing, rustled them again.

The crisp and brittle texture below me poked through my clothes and into my skin. Since I was still in my military attire, the fabric of my clothes was only a shade darker than the ground. It was almost a true camouflage with the leaf pattern stamped onto the fabric.

The wind brought cool air to my cheeks and arms. Its delicate touch sent a shiver through me and the leaves. Winter was ahead. The scent of damp soil and earth filled the hillside.

I felt a sense of peace wash over me. I had no desire to leave. I could have stayed hidden there forever. Hidden from the House of Love, from the Pillars, and from exile.

I stood, against my better judgment. With the weight of my body, the leaves underneath crunched. Dust and straggling leaves lingered on my clothes with a helpless, silent plea to take them away from this place. I reached down to brush them off. Before straightening up, I heard large footsteps thud through the forest floor. I set my eyes on the edges of the dying landscape, hunting for the cause of the sound.

The brittle leaves underfoot prohibited me from a stealthy escape. Someone, or something, could easily hear where I was going. Staying completely still, I listened. The rhythmic pattern continued. Twigs snapped and thuds continued. Whatever it was, it had come from behind me.

Turning on a dime, I found four muscular hooves scraping against the dry foliage. The once-tranquil forest had now morphed into an arena of cat and mouse. The body of the animal was a well-rounded, sporting massive antlers. They delicately and suspiciously balanced on the top of its head. A skull, similar to its kind, was tangled in its antlers. The remnants of a previous challenger knocked within the frame of its own antlers.

It stopped an uncomfortable distance away. Too close for comfort. It had spotted or—maybe—smelled me.

I froze. I knew *I* wasn't a threat, yet the animal stared at me like I was one.

A huff erupted from its chest. It was powerful enough to startle me. I took an unwanted step backwards. The leaves groaned as my weight shifted to a new set of crisp ones. Another deep breath escaped the animal. I could see it this time as the air bellowed out from its nostrils in a display of dominance. Another blast came. The animal's muscles were tensed. I could see them like they were perfectly carved out of stone.

He was the king of the forest.

I took another step, hopefully showing my submission.

Lowering its rack, the dead challenger rattling subsequently, the animal's powerful legs struck the ground, gearing to attack but not advancing. Another warning.

I began to retreat, excusing myself from the challenge arena and keeping my eyes secured to the beast.

Its hind legs were in a constant state of tension, ready to explode at any moment. There was no doubt it could sense my fear. Sending thunderous hooves to pound the earth, it stormed toward me. The skull attached to antlers rattled while both galloped in my direction.

As I sprinted away, my eyes were now glued to the ground, carefully spying my next step for a safe footing and an effective escape. I could hear his determined footsteps behind me, surprisingly agile for the size of his body. I weaved through trees in an attempt to confuse the animal, but still, it barreled onward, drawing closer.

Checking with a quick glance over my shoulder, I could see the rack and skull nearing. Distracted, I tripped on a hidden rock, which sent me stumbling into a pile of leaves. The thunder continued; this time I could feel its energy in the ground.

Twisting in the leaf pile, I braced for something to puncture me. I was met with the rack of the animal caging me to the ground. The ivory antlers constructed a perfect prison around my torso and head, only stabbing the ground. The attached skull was closest to my ear. I could smell the decay coming from it.

And yet, I was somehow unharmed.

Realizing my death hadn't come, the animal readied for another strike, lifting its submerged rack from the soil, spraying me with fresh dirt. I watched the eyes of my killer take a final and successful stab.

I woke up. My eyes opened this time to find a single lantern beaming in the mudroom. It provided only a little light in the bay. I couldn't see the bunks beside me, but I heard the snores of the men. For the second time at the Barracks, I woke with sweat on my temple and a dream fading fast.

The auburn leaves danced into nothing but a memory.

The beady eyes of the animal, however, remained for a longer time. Almost permanently engraved and never forgotten.

A penetrating stare twisted with a silent threat.

I rose from my moist bedding to wipe my temple with the wool blanket. I cleared my eyes to allow them to adjust to the new lighting. It was probably well past midnight at this point. Upon taking my hands away from my face, I saw something move in the dark.

Shadows were minimal in this lighting. Moreover, everything was in shadow. To see something move, it must have been darker than shadow. The presence of darkness.

The canvas to the mudroom flapped open, allowing more light into the bay. A man stood only inches from the edge of my bed. I jumped, trying hard not to wake the soldiers beside me.

How long had he been there?

My eyes dilated further so I could see more. The details of his face were hidden.

He only stood there. His head was angled, I assumed, to look at me. Placing his hands on the bed, he lowered himself to hover only a few inches above my face, "You shouldn't be here," he said.

His hair was highlighted with a tinge of orange by the lantern light.

The man who challenged my answers earlier.

I trembled.

Mustering all the courage I could, I whispered, "What are you talking—"

I was unable to finish my sentence. He placed his hand over my mouth to muffle any other words. This wasn't another dream. This was real. He pressed harder to hide the terror in my scream. His hands scratched my face with a frigid touch. I could see the definition of his face better from this angle. Parts of his eyes illuminated in the dim light. Like the icy hands that held my mouth, they were reflected in parts of his eyes. However, instead of them looking into mine, his gaze was on my ear. I took breaths through my nose, becoming increasingly short and scattered with the threat of my life hanging over my head. I let out another scream behind his hand, now trying to wake the soldiers closest. I prayed Thadeous was a light sleeper.

Help me, I thought.

My breath from my nose condensed on his fingers, he continued, "I don't care why you are here or who you know, I will kill you."

He began to push my head into the mattress, cutting off air to my nose. In a last attempt, I used whatever air I had reserved to scream as loud as I could. Staring off center, he pressed me farther into the bed, gripping my throat harder this time. He was going to kill me. Whatever vision I had of him, buried in the shadows of night, I started to lose sight of it.

I could hear the faint release of mattress springs to my right. Thadeous ripped the soldier away from me. I gasped for air. It was followed by exaggerated coughs. Even under the strength of Thadeous, the redheaded soldier lunged to attack again. I screamed, a powerful pitch, waking everyone in the bay.

One by one, matches burst to flame to light their individual bedside lanterns. In an impressively short amount of time, all the men of the bay were awake and witnessing my escape from the redheaded man's attack. I ran to the other edge of the tent to put some distance between him and me.

Struggling under their strength, he shouted, "Get away from me!"

Another soldier rushed over to him, leaving his bunk in the middle of the bay. "Hey, Holden! Wake up!"

I heaved, trying to find my breath again, feeling his hands still wrapped around my mouth.

Now under the full control of his brothers, he cursed, "Wither and die!" His gaze was set on the dirt at the center of the bay—not me.

"Holden!" Thadeous shouted, trying his best to shake the dual-colored eyed man awake from behind

The man standing before Holden sent a backhand into his cheek.

I jumped from the impact.

Holden stopped twitching. His gaze lifted to the man who delivered the hit. I couldn't see over him, but quiet cries escaped Holden. Thadeous let go of him and the man who struck him put his arms around him, hugging tightly.

I felt a tap on my arm. I jerked away, not wanting anyone to touch me. It was the soldier Dakari, the man who recited my riddle back to me. I couldn't trust anyone in this tent, not after what just happened. His hand still outstretched, his voice was comforting. "It's ok. It's over."

Still rejecting his touch and choking back tears, I asked, "What happened?"

I wanted to curl into a ball.

Dakari joked, "I told you, some of us talk in our sleep."

"That was—something else," I spat back. My voice broke as the tears began to fall.

"The mind can play cruel jokes sometimes." Dakari spoke in a hush. "We aren't sure what exactly happened to him, but it's been happening for a couple of months. He went on patrol to the border, a mission for the Pillars. He was separated from his squad. After an hour of searching, they finally found him wandering in the desert, miles away from where he was supposed to be. Thorns from a jumping cactus were all over his hands and face. When we got him back to camp, the medics took out the thorns, gave him a wellness check, and sent him on his way. They said he was fine. Ever since, he wakes up in the middle of the night and relives that day. We have found he isn't in control of his body when it happens."

Terrified, I posed the question under my breath, "What did he see out there?"

"We think he was touched by the darkness," he said plainly. "There's no proof of it. That's just what we think. We brought it up to Command and since the medics can't find anything wrong, they won't discharge him. Some considered him a lost cause. Others fought to send him back to his home in Patience with an exile charge. Jeston convinced the General to keep him with us. He is our brother. We couldn't just leave him out there like that. The agreement was we wake him during his spells, and he stays in the House of Love."

Dakari spoke as if Jeston's word was golden. As if he admired the decisions of the young Pillar. As if he was right in the decision to keep the suffering soldier here.

Jeston's voice rang in my head.

To keep a secret like that my devotion to something else must be greater than my devotion to the throne.

He said before how much these men meant to him. Keeping Holden here was proof. He wanted to make sure he was safe in their hands instead of throwing him across the border to fend for himself.

Thadeous came over to us. Dakari stayed by my side, but I saw Thadeous give him a signal to give us some privacy.

Making distinct eye contact with me, he suspended his hands in the air above my shoulders. "Are you ok?" He scanned my body, waiting for a response.

I remained still. With his pursuit of touch, I wanted to recoil, but he only hovered his hands for a second then dropped them, almost knowing I didn't want to be touched. I gave an honest answer. "I'm not sure."

Processing Dakari's story was difficult. If Holden was touched by the darkness, he was a danger to the other soldiers and to me and to the House.

Thadeous reasoned, "He has been doing better with his episodes, staying in a routine every day. With the news of you staying here, it must have triggered—"

His voice became faintly distorted. I could see his lips moving but there was no sound.

With intense focus I could hear him say, "—with the others, we are going to rotate on hour shifts to stay up and watch him. That way you are kept safe."

Astonishment flooded my face.

Thadeous saw it immediately and reassured me, "We want to protect you and keep you safe as much as we want to help Hold—"

A ringing in my ears cut off all external noise. My chest tightened with the knowledge that I had to share a space with someone who, whether they meant it or not, wanted me dead. If it weren't for Thad, I would be only a memory right now. A corpse. Fear began to uncontrollably beat in my veins.

What if it happened again?

I looked past Thad to the other men in the bay and wondered which of them was the next person to threaten my life. The dizziness I had begun to feel gradually progressed to the point where I lost my footing.

Thad recognized it and grabbed under my arm to support me, calling another over to help stabilize. They walked my limp body over the closest bed. My vision blurred, only seeing the silhouettes of the soldiers. Thad fanned me, trying to provide additional air.

All the while, my mind flashed with memories of tugs at my throat in the dark. The feeling of brutal shoves into the hallway of the Estate. Visions of Jeston in the throne room and him stinging my face. The tunnel, black and absent. The name of Aruleah paired with the deepest colored shadows danced in my mind. The garden came into focus; where I said her name last shined.

The trees and flowers were not glowing like when Jeston and I last visited them. They were burning, withering away from the heat of the ignited fire. The bench where we drank was now becoming a pile of ash and coal.

My place of peace, the one to rid me of chaos from my life, was . . . gone. The spot that provided comfort when home was too far away. Pieces of it, not fractured, not bruised, not able to be mended, but completely obliterated.

Flames began to roar like a lion. They echoed off the stone walls.

"Enna."

My world was crumbling before me, and I had no control over it. What had I done to deserve it? I know I have made some poor decisions in my life, but *this?*

"Enna!"

I gasped for air. A group of men surrounded me as I lay motionless in a coffin bed. Similar to Holden, I began to cry.

The tears that dripped into my hands were a cry from my spirit and my soul. I felt broken, unwanted—and somewhat *shameful.* The emotions flooded the room. My hands covered my eyes but also my mouth. They were a shield, protecting not only my vulnerability, but the soldiers that had to watch and listen to the brokenness. My head buzzed with pressure and my nose stuffed with snot.

Nowhere was safe.

My home.

My garden.

My dreams.

In this time, I cried for never returning to the Adora and for my family of friends I'd never see again. For the position I worked so hard to secure in the House of Love court. For the questions left unanswered as to why I was such a threat. I sobbed over the garden, simmering in flames. Never given the ability to know if that was the truth or just my imagination.

For the touch of barbarian guards that tossed me off to the side like I was nothing, proving my insecurities that I tried desperately to hide.

It was true; I was disposable.

That the core of who I am—honest and kind—would only hurt me in the end.

I let my guard down, unintentionally trusting Jeston, confirming my naivety that safety was abundant in the House of Love. Everyone was supposed to love everyone here. The value of my life was a game to everyone else. My worth was insignificant. My values meant nothing. My loyalty to the throne was instantly discredited when threatened by the possession of those damned books.

Keeping them cost me my life.

Books that held their own secrets against the throne.

A secret hiding darkness.

A secret hidden in darkness.

In need of fresh air, I opened my hands to find a handful of soldiers empathetic to my situation. Furrowed brows stared earnestly at my crippling body. As if these burly men wanted to take away the pain that I experienced in this moment. That they wanted to take my place instead. That they were able to carry this burden. A reminder that I don't have to endure it alone.

My sobs turned to deep breathing, slowing by the second. I sniffed, wishing their eyes were fixed elsewhere. I wiped away the hot tears from my cheeks.

Thad sat on the bed beside me. With sincerity in his voice, he asked, "Are you ok?"

The thought of an answer sent a flurry of new emotions racing through my mind.

'*No!*' I wanted to scream.

It took everything in me to not place my hands back on my face and cry. Unable to speak, I shook my head. I could feel my face tense again. My lip was beginning to tremble.

"Relax," he said in a hushed voice. He lightly pushed my shoulders back into the bed. "Sit back and rest. This bed is empty; you can stay here for the remainder of the night."

I allowed my back to relax on the bed, resting my head too.

The group of men dispersed to their own bunks. Thad was the only one who stayed with me.

Noticing him moving to the foot of my bed, I lifted my head to ask, "What are you doing?"

He found a resting spot on the ground with his back pressed against the frame. He responded, "I'm taking the first shift. I want to make sure you can rest easy."

His generosity had compounded since I arrived yesterday. He was a perfect Lovian citizen. Curious, with heavy eyes and a tired voice, I asked, "Why are you so nice to me?"

He grinned and explained, "We all have experienced nights where breaking down was our only option. If there was a need, any one of us would stay up and comfort the other. That's what families do. That's what love is—sacrifice. You, my dear, are no exception."

A dam of tears welled at the base of my sight.

Lanterns began to extinguish one by one, falling in the same time it took for them to ignite.

As his brothers were headed back to sleep, Thad whispered in the tiniest voice to not be overheard by the other eleven soldiers in the room. "You might feel weak in this moment, but this will only make you stronger."

I took a deep inhale.

"You are brave. You are strong. You do not need to worry," he said.

I let my breath go with an exhale, it was choppy at best. Quivers of sobs lingered on my lips. I pressed them together to subside the shaking.

Repeating himself, he said, "You are brave. You are strong. Do not worry."

Another inhale. My eyes closed and my mind chanted.

You are brave.

You are strong.

Do not worry.

Chapter XII

THE STRUGGLE AGAINST POWER

I opened my eyes to find two muffins, an apple, and a carton of juice on the bedside table. My head was full of pressure. I lifted it slightly to thank the soldier who brought the food. To my surprise, Thad was the only one in the tent. I raised my head above the wool blanket, letting some warmth escape. It must have caught his attention because he rushed over from his bed to help.

My head was a balloon about to burst; there was ringing in my ear due to the pressure behind my eyes. I pressed my back against the canvas wall to stabilize myself. Thad sat tentatively at the foot of the bed.

"Where is everyone?" I murmured. Sleep still hung in my body.

"They were sent to the border," he responded.

I gulped. The horrors of darkness haunted the edges of my mind.

"Why did you stay?" I asked, clearing my throat.

"You needed someone here to ensure you were safe. We never know who comes in the tent while we are away, so I stayed."

"I bet your Command wasn't too happy about that."

"No, probably not. But they can go to the General or even Adonis for all I care. Jeston said, 'If it's your life or hers, choose yours,'" he said plainly.

The memory was vivid in my mind. Such a direct order for protection of someone as insignificant as myself. A clockworker caught up in a 'wrong place, wrong time' situation.

I eyed the food, a subtle hint I wanted to eat. Thad reached for the muffins and the apple and set them next to my legs on the bed. My stomach growled at the sight. If it weren't for Thad sitting there, I would have devoured it all like an untamed animal. Instead, I waited for an appropriate time to take the apple into my hands and crunch on the skin.

Biting the crisp skin away, I sipped the extra juice dripping down the waxy peel. I wouldn't waste any drops of its sweet nectar. I finished the apple, the core still in my hand, and began to eye the muffins next.

Thad returned to his bunk, reminding me I wasn't in my assigned one. As a matter of fact, I wasn't sure whose bed I slept in for the night. I faintly remember Thad telling me about it, but nothing concrete came to mind.

Dismissing it altogether, I snatched the remaining food and my carton of juice. I swung my legs to the side of the bed and neatly tidied the blanket as a precautionary thank you.

"That's not necessary," Thad said.

"Oh," I said, taken aback. "Why?"

"That bed has been vacant for months." He spoke in the lowest voice, barely audible, and with bitterness.

"Whose is it?" I asked, wanting to know more.

"One of our brothers left for a position of higher standing. One at the Estate, actually." Thad nodded in my direction, drawing a connection.

"Oh."

It was all I could manage to say.

"Guarding the Queen of Hearts, can you believe it? He left the only family he had ever known because of that witch. I've heard stories from Jeston. He has told us about her many lovers—men *and* women. The parties she would throw for pleasure and the vilest and most immoral of acts. I guess she lives up to the role she has chosen for herself as the Pillar of Intimacy. And is it true she has a wizard flip over cards to tell her the fate of the House?"

"She does. I've seen him in meetings with them." I didn't feel like being dishonest about the information I've learned about the queen. I'd heard the stories too. Reverie and Pax weren't the only ones keeping up with the drama about the Pillars.

Placing the cool wool blanket on my lap, I pressed my back against the canvas wall, watching Thad mess with a knife. Without finding my eyes, Thad asked, "What happened to your stomach? Those bruises—" He trailed off, unable to say more.

"What do you mean?" I tried to act inconspicuously between bites. I touched the bruise he mentioned, and the pressure of my finger was enough to make me wince.

"The coloring is a few days old. Those happened before you got here."

I could only nod. I didn't want to recall the feeling of that sack around my head nor the feeling of men handling me without care for my life.

"You don't have to tell me what happened," Thad said kindly.

"I'm not weak, if that's what you are implying," I snapped.

"Not at all." His eyes had an inviting warmth to them.

The soreness around my neck was more prevalent now that we were talking about bruises. I craned my head, trying hard not to notice it anymore. Unfortunately, I would have a painful reminder of last night for a couple of days at least. I stood on a knife's edge of emotions. Tears swelled and pressed against the walls of my swollen eyes. I knew the dangers I was in but hearing it out loud brought the reality of the situation alive. The tension of holding back my emotion was sure to explode at any moment. The rhythm of Thad's voice kept me in check.

"I believe you are a good person. You got tied up in something out of your control and are suffering because of it."

"Suffering?" I asked incredulously.

"Absolutely. The darkness, no matter where you are or what House you reside in, is always crafting a plan. It wants us to suffer as much as possible. You may not feel attacked in that moment, but it is always working against you."

"But the House of Love has not fallen to the darkness." My statement was more of a question alluding to the truth.

"I believe Adonis is a snake, just like those outside of this House. He is obsessed with power. He will do anything to keep his throne. As is the queen. They are human. Humans are flawed."

"They are Pillars," I corrected him.

"That doesn't make them gods," he responded. "Don't be fooled, Enna; you can't walk around with blinders on anymore. Don't believe all the Pillars have told you about the Houses outside of these borders. There is darkness here too."

"But the light?"

"There is light and where there is light there is goodness, and kindness, and peace, and patience—" he paused. "Do you see my point?"

Again, I only nodded. An uncomfortable silence hung in the air.

"How do I fight the darkness?"

"Staying calm is important but it's virtually impossible when you haven't fought it before. Confidence and composure will come when you start living with the light. Panic or impatience can cloud your judgment. So, keep your composure. Breathing deep always helps me."

The bells chimed with the sound of the Pillar of Protection, a tune I wished to forget, sending a steady chill down my spine and flashes of the Adora to my mind. Night had already come. Caught up in our conversation, I was tired and hungry. Dirt stuck to my body from the sweat I produced while sleeping.

Thad suggested, "How about you clean off while everyone is in the mess hall? It will make you feel better. I'll bring some food back for you after I'm done there."

Without much protest, I said, "Deal."

Thad headed to the lockers. Jeston's was at the end and unlocked. He reached for another pair of clothes, tossing them to me with a small towel.

"Hurry, you won't have much time," he said.

I took his advice, quickly tucking my hair into my hat and following his footsteps out from the tent. Hungry soldiers flocked into the mess hall and Thad inserted himself in line.

Not far behind, I waited for the door to the mess hall to close and to make sure there were no straggling soldiers. The last ones to enter were the soldiers stationed on the porches. It wasn't until the door was completely shut that I stepped out into the unguarded open. Remembering the location of the stalls, I made my way to the end of camp. I saw the trough from my first visit and shivered at the thought of being found bathing in it. With minutes to spare, I checked the corners of the building in hopes of finding something better. I discovered vertical stalls with a spout in each. A nozzle adjusted the pressure of the water flowing from it.

Turning the knob, I undressed and stood under a rainfall of water. Catching my breath from the cold temperature, I washed the dust and dirt off my body. I was renewed. Along with the water, the disappointments of the events at the Estate went into the drain below. I cleaned the disturbing touches of the men, leaving only the bruises as a reminder.

The water fell and carried my emotion with it.

Tears were nonexistent under the water. I couldn't tell where one began and the other started. I thought there was no sense of being sad.

What would that accomplish?

It could get me caught in a time like this.

My hair held the most dirt. I looked down and the water had turned brown when I let my hair run under it. Once the water was clear, I turned the spout off. I wrung out my hair with a twist and placed my hat on my head to hide the length. Grabbing the towel to dry off, before I knew it, I was wearing the clean clothes and walking back to the tent.

I couldn't help but smile as I walked the path. My hair, soaking my hat, dripped down my back, leaving water marks on my clothes. The freshness from the water left me recharged and brand new. I looked forward to the food Thad would bring back from dinner.

As I reached for the first flap of the canvas, the lantern's light shone like a star. I set my dirty clothes next to the massive pile of dirty boots in the mudroom and entered through the second flap. To my surprise, there were three men at the center of the bay. One knelt while another stood behind him. A third man stood between them and me. The one with his back turned towards me had a tall and broad frame with shoulders masked by dark, flowing hair. Paralyzed with terror, I stood in the doorway of the tent, stiffening at the sight of Adonis.

Two guards swooped beside me, securing the entrance.

I was trapped inside.

The Pillar faced me, casting a shadow over a figure covered in dirt:

Thad bowed with his head hanging low. Seeing him defeated by Adonis tightened my stomach, like a wrench would a bolt. Thad was the epitome of skilled combat and an Aluna operator. His training should have guaranteed a victory against Adonis, even if he was a Pillar. Something told me there was foul play at hand.

I transferred my attention to Adonis. He greeted me. "Ah, my little bird. I was beginning to wonder where you had flown off to." His voice was crass and unforgiving.

Little bird?

I could have retched at the pet name.

"Adonis." I acknowledged his position by removing my hat, it dripped with water. I secured it tightly in my hands. My long, russet hair hit the back of my damp shirt.

"I guess my stupid little brother thought it was best to hide you here under the protection of his *pretend* brothers," he said, turning to Thad's body on the ground. "He obviously underestimated my authority." Tsking, he continued, "I guess he will never know the rush you get when you enforce the actual power of the Pillars."

His eyes glinted molten red, showing his true Pillar form.

I confronted Adonis with confidence I didn't know I had. "What did you do to him?"

"Nothing, yet," he stated crassly. "But he will lose his title and his power. And his throne will be burned. I might even convince my sister to send him across the border to join you. And for all this, I give my thanks to *you*."

"You're bluffing. You wouldn't do that to your own brother," I spat back.

"It is my job to protect this House. If my brother defies the rules of our ancestors for a friendship, then there will be consequences."

Friendship.

I had once scoffed at Jeston's idea of becoming friends and wanting a friendship within the court. Now I understand why. His brother was a monster, and his sister probably followed suit.

The rulers of the House of Love were hypocrites. Thad was right. Darkness can be anywhere. I only hoped Jeston managed to reach the books in time. That he was able locate and conceal them, ideally far from Adonis and Sylvanora.

Continuing my pursuit of answers, I asked, "How did you know I was here?"

"Some of my Command saw a few men from this platoon taking food from the mess hall. After this man," gesturing to Thadeous, "stayed behind from their mission, I thought there was enough cause for me to pop in and visit. And now I find you here, causing all kinds of trouble."

I examined Thad's body. His hands were tied behind his back, like mine in the throne room. A guard held him by his graying hair to look up at me. There were cuts bleeding from his face, under his eyes and on his lip. Blood dripped into his beard, leaving a scattered red stain. We connected eyes and he shot them to the door, signaling me—*warning me.*

The fight was two against four.

The odds were not in our favor.

I looked behind me subtly to glance at the men guarding the door. They stepped closer to me, closing the distance that separated us. With each of their steps, I took one myself, staying equidistant between them and Adonis. Glancing side to side, I searched the room for a weapon, a tool I could use to escape. I found nothing of use.

Adonis continued to rant, "I personally thought execution was the right call for your sentence. My brother's idea was surprisingly much better. I only wish I had seen to your exile myself."

Thad's eyes grew wider with the knowledge of my exile—a detail Jeston and I had purposefully left out. Thad struggled to free himself from the bonds on his wrists. He and I both knew they were here to throw me across the border. As he tried to stand, the guard behind him extracted a blade and placed it on Thad's throat.

Thad protested the threat. "Always sending your guards to do your dirty work, right, Adonis? Too scared to lose to a man who holds no title? What kind of Pillar would you be if you lost a fight? Why don't you fight me like a man? Jeston was right! You are no man! And he is right about her; she's innocent in all of this!" Thad spoke even when he didn't know the full truth. The guard struggled to keep him contained.

Adonis lifted his hand without saying a word, a silent signal to his guard to do what was previously discussed. The blade pressed further into the side of Thad's neck, drawing a little blood.

Placing his hands on his knees, Adonis lowered himself. Not by much, but enough for Thad to clearly see his face. In a prosecuting way, Adonis spoke, "You are just as guilty for keeping her hidden. I should have you exiled too."

"I was under orders from a Pillar." Thad gritted his teeth.

"I am your Pillar!" Adonis shouted. "And you will obey *my* orders. Not some child's."

Adonis straightened, only to be antagonized by me.

Heat rising in my cheeks, I provoked him further. "Aren't you supposed to be a Pillar in the House of *Love*?"

"I am the Pillar of Protection. You—you, you *clockworker*—you threatened the mere integrity of this House. My job is to protect the House from people like *you*."

I was a clockworker—a nobody who inconvenienced him. A servant he wanted dead. All for the possession of a book.

He took a step closer to me, dismissing the guards.

The closer he got the harder my heart started to beat. I told myself that I needed to stay calm if I was to get out of this alive. I took a turn down one of the aisles between two of the beds, making Adonis believe he was setting a trap by stepping in and closing off my only exit.

I asked the question, knowing he was going to draw out the answer. “And what’s so bad about people like me?”

Maintaining our strides toward a dead end, he snarled, “People like you cause problems, disrupt order, breed chaos. I can’t trust anyone, but myself, to rid people like you from this House.”

I backed into the canvas of the tent. With the cold from the night pressing into my body from the other side, I could feel the current of wind pushing me forward; egging me on with courage to attack. I took a breath and before Adonis could touch me, I sent my dripping hat across his face. His black hair coated his face in long, wet strands, blinding him for a moment, leaving him stunned and angry. I jumped on the mattress beside me to evade his trap. The guards at the door left their post to assist in my capture. The other guard holding Thad didn’t move. His objective must have been to detain the Aluna operator, but I knew if Thad was free, it meant death for everyone else.

Bouncing from coffin bed to coffin bed, I leaped off at Knifehook’s bed. Thudding to the ground, I searched for only an assumption. Sure enough, I guessed correctly. Knifehook stashed a dagger to the frame of his bed. Its blade was the shape of a talon, deadly and sharp. I took it in my hand before seeing a shuffle in the dust.

I began to crawl to confuse the two guards, careful not to cut myself with the curved blade. Clearing two beds, I rushed for the center of the bay behind the guard holding Thadeous. Unaware of the weapon in my hand, he watched his peers tripping over one another to reposition themselves into grabbing me.

The bruises on my stomach stung, reminding me of my desperation and helplessness. My ears burned recalling their hot breath. They were willing to take me from my own home in the middle of the night. They were willing to lay their hands on me, all to obey an order.

I grasped the weapon and sliced the calf muscle of the guard. Reaching for his bleeding shin, the guard released Thad. I cut him free and tossed him the knife. The Aluna operator plunged it into the heart of the guard in one fluid motion. Blood began to pool in his mouth as he collapsed on the dust-ridden ground.

Thad, now free from his captor, attacked Adonis by sending his head into the Pillar's, making hard contact. Adonis stumbled back a few feet, wincing and holding his forehead.

Shaking the strike from his own head, Thad instructed, "Run!"

The other men were making fast advancements on me. I tripped and sent my gut into the rails of Ronan's bed, knocking the wind out of my lungs.

Thad sent a flying kick at the first guard, leaving him incapable of attack. As he attempted to land another air-defying kick, the guard dodged it, so that it missed him by inches. Thad lost his balance, and the guard rushed him into the foot of the bed. Dust had sprayed into the air, leaving me blind to what was happening to Thad. I could hear his body hit the metal frame of the bed, and a shuffle of feet in the dirt. The other guard must have restrained him on the ground. His friend, now on his feet, was punting Thad's abdomen. Each kick massacred his stomach and rib cage as he took each blow with grunts.

The dust had settled enough for me to grab the lantern next to Ronan's bed, using it for protection. I stood and found Adonis uncomfortably close. I could see the spot on his forehead where Thad hit him. A glaze coated his eyes, driven by the power of Pillars, shining a deep red. He was full of anger.

One more step and he would be in striking distance.

For the second time, I swung at his face.

He caught my arm in the air and smiled. "Not this time."

He took my hand and forced it behind my body, testing the strength of the ligaments in my shoulder, similar to Jeston in the Grand Forum. This time, I yelled in pain. I submitted and pressed my face into the canvas wall. Full of fury, he expressed, "I can't wait to hear the terror in your screams when the darkness eats your soul."

With nothing more to lose, I cursed, "Go to hell."

He lifted my arm upward, forcing me to stand on my toes. I tried everything to subdue the pain.

Adonis walked me to the door, and I saw Thad lying motionless on his side a few feet away.

No.

"What would you like us to do with him?" One of the guards huffed as he recovered from the fight.

"I have something special planned for him," Adonis replied.

He laughed and kept steering me towards the door. I fought to release my hands from his grip. His grip was mightier than any human's strength, pressing my bones together as if they were meant to be fused.

This was the power of the Pillars.

We passed the guard Thad killed with the knife. Thad's body mirrored the dead one in the dirt. Every ounce of my existence wanted to scream for Thad. I knew hardly anything about him, yet he sacrificed himself to save my life, like Jeston ordered. He was someone who was kind and took care of me. He was one of my friends.

The lifeless guard had his eyes open, staring into an abyss of death. I left the tent, only to remember him as the man who smelled of blood.

By the time we reached the mudroom, a fierce worry overwhelmed me.

The darkness was calling, and I would greet it soon.

Chapter XIII

THE BORDER

Howls of wind swept my hair from my shoulders, blocking my view, as we exited the tent. Upon the release of dinner, Adonis and I surfed through a crowd of soldiers in the heart of camp. Lights shone on the frustration on my face and the outstanding power motivating him. Onlookers paused in their movements to allow us to pass with ease, some even tugging their friends' arms to make room for the Pillar.

No one was to stand in the way of Adonis the almighty.

Soldiers residing on each porch raised their arm in a tidal wave as we passed to salute their high Commander.

We turned down a paved alleyway between two buildings, with his guards following closely. After we reached the end, the path took a dive down a steep hill. He clenched my hands tighter, guaranteeing I would not slip away. Two tall lanterns provided enough light for me to see my next step but nothing further. Suspended in the air, the lanterns followed our steps as we dove down, down, down into the forbidden unknown. I could see a floating light in the distance with nothing surrounding it.

Standing alone, the light marked my greeting to exile.

The border gates.

As we approached, a metal gate towering dozens of feet into the air came into view. I was shocked to know the gates were within walking distance to camp. Although it easily reached above the size of the houses, I still hadn't seen it despite its massive size. I was so close to the border, so close to darkness.

A single lantern illuminated an intricate pattern of woven metal. Observing the exit, I could see the same metal gate reflecting behind it again and again and again. There must have been several gates protecting the border to the House of Love. In order to be completely exiled, I would need to pass through eight other gates.

The first metal door creaked open. Its ornate metal weaves gleamed in the lantern light, welcoming me into its wickedness. The door, while several feet wide, was only a few inches taller than Adonis. Its metallic groan echoed through the air, a testament to its weight and durability.

Letting go of my arms, Adonis shoved me into the first layer of gates. The door swung shut, locking itself. The geometric patterns began to weave into place. Like a prison cell, I had to wait for the next gate to open.

This was best time to say all that I wanted to without the hands of the guards or Adonis trying to silence me.

"You could have killed me and been done with all of this. It's pathetic, really, to know you'd rather be rid of me and yet lack the courage to kill me." I attempted to highlight his mistake with the intention to delay my inevitable exile.

I could see a mark on his forehead, a faint oblong spot sitting above his eyebrow and growing.

It would bruise nicely like mine in a couple of days.

Adonis stepped forward to meet me through the gate. He looked down with his sinister smile, eager to explain. "I would rather hear the echoes of your screams throughout the camp. For all the trouble you have put me through and for the danger you are to this House, I want you to suffer more than I want you to die."

He snickered. "My brother, wrong about every other decision, was right about this one. Death is too easy. With death, your existence is simply over the moment you take your last breath. Exile is a far better punishment.

"In the upcoming days and weeks and months, I will revel in wonder about your inevitable fate in the darkness. I will take joy in it. I will wonder about the sins of your life and how the darkness will make you relive them over and over and over again as it has done with so many before you. I will wonder what you said in your plea for mercy for it to stop, and after all of that, I will wonder how it devoured your soul. In all my days, I will enjoy the thought that you were eaten alive by the darkness."

His rhythmed speech edged with harshness. It cut like serrated daggers, leaving a permanent, well-constructed image of what was to come.

I breathed, "Such vile things coming from a Pillar of *Love*," bringing his position up again. "All of this, in exchange for a book," I added.

His expression changed in the dim light.

Determination.

Determination to prove he was right.

"That book, girl, will destroy all that we have built. It has the potential to unleash a cruel fate over all the Houses. Ancient secrets of this kingdom and this House will destroy life as we know it. Bramwell was executed for disobeying the word of his beloved King by hiding those secrets within his journals.

"All but one of those books had survived the test of time, until the last one showed up in our living quarters a couple nights ago, stained by Bramwell's wedding wine. We knew exactly who it belonged to and yet we found a note with your name written on it.

"Having that book in your possession risked the safety of this House, this kingdom, the safety of my family - my *children.* Therefore, I find nothing wrong with wanting you to suffer. After centuries, you are Bramwell's last loose end—besides my own blood betrayal. Soon it will not matter either way."

Jeston.

"What are you going to do to him?" I latched onto the gate. Power surged through it, rejecting my touch and shocking me. I retreated back, my hand aching from it.

Adonis reached for the gate himself. He did not seem to be affected by its power in the same way I was. There must be some sort of connection between him and the gates. "Unfortunately, the ancient laws forbid me to kill another Pillar without consequences of my own. However, Jeston still disobeyed them. He must be punished."

In my quest for truth, I managed to dethrone a Pillar. Jeston was only trying to help me. My wonderment and need to understand the secrets of the world, ones that have been kept hidden for a reason, had put too many lives in danger. I learned my lesson. I would rather be left in the dark, oblivious to what was happening, than know all the hidden secrets. I thought of the brawl that was to come when Adonis returned to the Estate looking to remove Jeston's throne. The thought of torture alone would make my heart ache.

The gate behind me opened, startling me out of my daydream.

I could set my own trap for him. For vengeance. For justice.

Complying, I walked through. The moment I passed the threshold, the door slammed shut. I pivoted on my heel and asked, "And what of Aruleah?"

His eyes widened just as Jeston's did in the garden. The color of his eyes was now visible in the light. They started glowing scarlet, a shade brighter than in the tent.

He growled, "How do you know that name?"

Finally.

The upper hand.

I wouldn't waste it.

I negotiated, "Free me and find out."

Knowing he was powerless against my knowledge of her, he demanded, "How do you know that name, bird?"

"I will tell you all you need to know, when you open the first two gates, and deny my exile."

Instead, the metal behind me squeaked with rusted hinges. The shadows of night masked my horror when I heard them swing. I wasn't done yet. I revealed my next weapon without advancing.

"And what about Aruleah's poems to Bramwell? What was she convincing him to give her?"

Red waves the same color as his eyes began to radiate from Adonis's body. The ribbons projected in every way off him, further signaling his anger. Heat was escaping his body; the metal before him turned red hot.

I attempted to persuade him to set me free instead. "I've proved to you I know more than you thought. Let me go and I will tell you everything."

Silence.

I had pressed to the point where yelling and cursing were insignificant. The braids of light expanded in size and blossomed to blue. Between the wires of the gates, I could see Adonis' guards taking several steps away from the gate. They fled into the shadows where I saw glimpses of their figures running. Faint dashes of their maroon uniform caught the light, indicating the danger to come.

The next several gates hummed with a buzz, set to erupt at any given time. Simultaneously, they opened, unlocking the deep void behind them. I half expected to be inhaled into it by an unexplainable force ready to devour my soul and sins, yet nothing happened.

My attention was on Adonis. He lowered his voice. It was barely audible. "I will force you out if I have to."

"What about Aruleah?" I poked again.

"My job as the Pillar of Protection is not to question but to protect. That name on your tongue is a threat to this House," he said in the same malicious tone.

"And if I stay?" I protested.

"Your death will come," he snarled.

I watched as the beams exuding from him turned white in seconds, almost invisible. Heat pressed against my cheeks. I realized that they weren't ribbons or braids or beams but *flames*. They grew hotter by the second, bending the metal of the first gate into liquid. It was the power of the Pillars in its raw form, ready to scorch the earth.

The heat increased, driving me toward the black that beckoned behind me.

"What is happening?" Sweat started to form at my temple.

"You ask too many questions." Adonis brightened with white flame, stinging my face.

I stumbled through the doorway of another gate. It closed as I winced from the pain of the heat on my eyes. Through another door and another. I watched as the Pillar of Protection liquified the first gate like lava.

The final gate came fast, with the heat intensifying.

My last chance at redemption.

"Adonis, I will tell you everything." My tone was close to begging.

He only stared and spoke sharply. "You have a choice. Stay, and your skin will eventually melt, exposing your bone, which will then dissolve into a puddle of flesh. Or leave and submit to the darkness. Choose."

Behold, the Pillar of Protection, burning as hot as the sun, giving me an option. Jeston's voice rang in my head.

There are pockets of light.

Find them.

Letting go of my life in the House of Love, I forced myself to make the decision with the hope of living long enough to find something good beyond the border. I took my last step from the House of Love. The door sealed shut. It wove extra pieces of metal into place to further secure the House. Any chance at saving myself was gone.

I could see the light from Adonis still through the holes of the gate. With me gone, he closed his eyes to bask in the power. His flame grew brighter and brighter. If I stayed to watch, the gates wouldn't protect me from the blast. He planned to push me farther into the abyss with an explosion.

Receding from the gate, I fell back into unknown territory. My foot sank, causing me to lose my balance. I rolled down a sloped hill, with rock and sand spewing in my eyes, mouth, and hair.

Slowing, I ended up on my back.

Through the strands of damp hair and grains of sand, I looked side to side, hoping to find something familiar. There were no impressions of trees in the shadows or large rocks to hide behind. The crescent moon had not risen yet, so I could only see the ambient glow from the camp and the Pillar set to detonate at any minute.

Before I could move, there was pressure against my body. Pressure that was sent to impact my heart, head, and legs. Drowning from the heavy air, my lungs couldn't inhale like they should have, taunting me with my imminent death. My bones vibrated and my teeth chattered from the explosion. A loud noise rang in my ears, as I was helpless against the wrath of Adonis.

I looked at the plateau for the gates. Their metal shined like molten lava for a few seconds, before cooling in the breeze. I wondered how many gates were still intact. They disappeared into the night sky shortly after.

Into blackness.

Into darkness.

The darkness of exile.

PART 2

Chapter XIV

THE HOUSE OF HOPE

Millions of stars witnessed my body lying still in the warm sand. The sky was expansive but still utterly distant. I could feel them, full of wonder, like a curious creature reaching for a new toy. Stretching across the entire sky and sparkling like diamonds, the stars sang to me like a familiar friend.

'Alone?'

It was like a voice was speaking into my ear. There was no breath, and I wasn't frightened.

I heard it again.

'Safe.'

From end to end, the sky was full of these speaking stars. Their air of mystery in the millions of constellations brought a surge of insignificance to the forefront of my mind. I had been taken from the safety of the House of Love. A place where love abounds, and its people care for you no matter the circumstances. Where no neighbor was a foe. But as I lay in exile, I was the contradiction. I was living proof that the concept wasn't true.

I was replaceable and expendable and valueless and unsafe and a foe in true form and . . .

I had to shake my thoughts away.

I willed my mind to focus on the sand I gripped, tethering me to the ground.

My time at the Adora never prepared me for this. I thought I was untouchable in the House of Love. But I secretly knew, it made me stronger than those out here. The House of Love gave me a purpose. It gave me something to love. The love of a job and the love for my friends.

Unfortunately, I wasn't lucky enough to be blessed by the House to fall in love with someone. I had Bolt when I was lonely. He was a love of some kind. I knew there was more out there. An unconditional love. One that never fades. One from a spouse. I didn't have the opportunity to find it. Now, I wondered if I ever would.

With my exile, I would come to miss the trance of romance blossoming around every corner and its cheerful people dancing in the streets. The excitement of the newest festival or parade to celebrate love for one another in all forms and even express one's own self-love.

Instead, I dreaded my new home, despising the fact that flowers were not guaranteed to bloom every year, and the sun brought sadness.

That's what came with darkness.

That was the cost of exile.

Another whisper rang against the walls of my skull.

'Protected.'

'You will not be alone for long.'

This was the first time I was alone since I was snatched from my apartment. Reminded of the jerks who took me, I knew my actions in the tent were out of revenge. Yet, they were blindly following orders. Orders to distribute protection. All from the hatred of a name written in a book. Those books, those riddles, that name. How could I forget them now?

Oh, to the lost one, for night's bitter cold.

I was a lost one now.

Lost to the darkness. I wasn't cold, but bitter with a cold heart. Hatred rippled in my veins. I knew this made me more vulnerable to the darkness. More than I ever wanted to admit. The darkness could easily swallow my soul—not just because of my exile, but because of the darkness in my own heart.

There had to be good in me still.

I am not all hatred.

I am only hurt.

There is a difference—I think.

I looked at the stars in the sky again. My back felt stiff and immovable. The crescent moon finally peeked over the horizon, shining dim light over the vacant land. I could see small bushes and jagged rocks placed here and there, covering the plains of my new home.

I was only familiar with three of the fallen Houses.

I knew the swamps of Kindness because that's where I grew up. I saw flashes of the willow trees with their branches hanging like curtains above a window. Summer nights were humid and stifling—falling asleep with sweat on my temple and waking up in a puddle of it. The fireflies would buzz around the swamps, lighting various coves just as the sun was about to disappear for the night.

But then I was reminded, I left that life behind.

Four years ago, I braved the tundra known as the House of Joy in search of a better life, a safer one. Its entire land is covered in ice with snow-capped mountains, misty fog, and glacial rivers. Only small villages have been able to survive the endless frigid winters.

I knew I didn't want to waste time in Joy. My goal was to make it to the House of Love.

My focus has always been on Love.

Never Kindness.

Not even Joy.

But Love.

I didn't even know the names of the other fallen Houses. Could this be the House of Hope? Or the House of Truth? Maybe Wisdom or Forgiveness or Humility? I wouldn't know. All I knew was instead of feeling absolutely destroyed sitting on the sand, I felt at peace.

Another wave of voices from the stars.

'*Chains broken.*'

I sneered at the thought.

'*Free.*'

They sang, again.

They were right.

I was not tied anymore.

I could wander.

I could explore.

I could learn.

There was hope.

It took all my energy to sit up. Using my sore arms, I hoisted my torso off the ground. My head buzzed with pain. I lifted my hair off the nape of my neck, now dried with clumps of sand, the weight pressing on me and worsening my headache. The ringing in my ears was less, but still an annoying high-pitched note that I assumed would never fully heal. It was a permanent reminder to never cross another Pillar.

The shirt I wore was damp from the compression of my body and the ground on my wet hair. There was a warm breeze. I took delight in the fact that I was not in the House of Joy. The one and only time traveling through was enough for me. I was thankful for the feeling in my fingers and toes, remembering the time I couldn't feel anything but the cold.

The warmth in this land was a comforting feeling. The blackness of the unknown, backlit by the moon, was, in contrast, terrifying. I thought of the mysteries that belong to this House. The breeze wrapped me in a warm hug. It was a reassurance I needed at that moment.

Beyond the cover of night, I heard something shift. Large footsteps crunched the sand and kicked pebbles underfoot. Thinking back to my dream with the wild animal, I stood quickly. I was dizzy for a moment as flurries of sand and stars swirled across my vision, then subsided. The sand swayed under my feet and made it difficult for me to remain steady. In the distance, I saw a shadow—a figure. I readied myself to face another animal, possibly one made of the darkness. Instead, I was met with a voice.

"Wrenna?" The shadow spoke.

It knew my name.

My first encounter with the darkness, I shouldn't be surprised that it knew my name.

"Wrenna Reedwater?" The voice grew louder, and the shadow grew along with it, forming itself into the shape of a man. It was a ghost already set to haunt me for the rest of my life. I closed my eyes, waiting for the impact of the darkness—to be touched by it like Holden Culpepper. I counted the slowing seconds for it to close its hands around my throat and cut off my airway. I knew it was going to devour my soul and make my body shriek like Adonis' prediction. I could feel my hands shaking and my body growing hotter.

As I prayed for a quick release, it said my name again. "Wrenna!"

I winced, my eyes tightly shut. It had to be in front of me by now. I felt a touch on my arm. I stepped backward upon opening my eyes,

I tripped over the ridge carved from my body. Two hands, strong and forceful, caught my body and steadied it like a plank of wood.

"Take me fast," I whispered to myself, submitting my soul to the darkness that captured me.

I could hear the breath of the darkness slow in succession, speaking for a final time. "Wrenna, relax. It's me, Tev."

Chapter XV

TEV FOXWOOD

"Tev?" My breath caught in my lungs like it was too good to be true.

The darkness had to be playing tricks on me, playing with my mind.

How could Tev be standing in front of me?

The shadows seemed to speak, not a man—and certainly not anyone I knew. A part of me was relieved to hear his voice, but another part of me wanted it to be someone else. Someone kind, like Thadeous.

I tried to remember the details of his face. Our limited time together had the lines blurred. All that came to mind was his height and tawny hair.

"Are you hurt?" He patted my arms to check for any broken bones.

I jerked away, not trusting the flesh standing before me. I had to admit—it was convincing. The voice was a match to my memory.

Disregarding his question, still needing more proof before letting my guard down, I asked, "What are you doing out here, Tev?"

"I was sent out here because Thadeous stayed back at camp and the unit needed a twelfth member. I volunteered. We've been monitoring the H.O.L.'s border for any activity."

"The H.O.L.?" I interrupted.

"The House of Love. The military uses all kinds of abbreviations."

"How did you find me?" I asked.

"The military is also known for their gadgets." He lifted my arm and consequently my hand touched his face. I tried tensing my muscles to resist him, but even with all my energy I couldn't stop him. I felt a device on his face, covering his eyes. "They are special goggles. They help during nightfall. You never know what kind of creatures can sneak up on you out here. It's best to wear them—you may not need them, but if you do, you'll be glad they're on."

"Tev?" I interrupted his train of thought to get back to my question.

"Oh, right. I saw you sit up. I was surveying the area and because of the explosion I wanted to make sure nothing bad left the House of Love."

"Do they happen often? The explosions?" I asked.

"We should probably get moving." Tev avoided answering my question. "We don't want to fall behind." Tev brushed his hand against my arm, leading me in the direction he wanted to travel. I took a cautious step farther into an unknown land where darkness dwelled. Everything in me thought of the gates to the House of Love.

Tev felt my hesitation. I could hear him take his goggles off.

He stepped closer to me, closer than I liked him being. I didn't give him the satisfaction of moving.

"Have you ever noticed that it's easier walking toward the dimmest of lights than walking into the brightest of shadows?" he whispered in my ear, hinting it was a secret I could never repeat.

I whispered back, "I'm not afraid of shadows."

I'm afraid of the unknown.

"How do you know what's out there won't kill us?" I asked.

I could feel the warmth radiating from his body. Over his shoulder, I could see a tumbleweed bouncing in the desert, each bounce counting the seconds Tev lingered close by.

"That's where faith comes in," he said with the softest of breaths.

"In what?"

"The pockets of light out here," he responded instinctively.

"How do you know they exist?" I asked.

"Because I came from one."

I stepped away from Tev to meet his eyes, blurred by the night. I could see a shine coming from them. Two beady reflections staring at me, one full of encouragement and the other full of hope.

"We better get going," Tev added. I could see his hand in the moonlight, outstretched for me to take.

With a deep breath, I looked behind me in the direction of the gate. There was nothing but a black void. Even with my own imagination, I couldn't pretend the gates were there. They had disappeared into the shadows and into the past.

Now, my focus turned to the man offering an answer.

Reluctantly, I took his hand.

Tev, in one move, put his goggles on and positioned himself behind me, placing his hands on my shoulders to guide me in the right direction. There were bushes and boulders to navigate as we walked in the night. Tev told me to take larger steps at times and to shuffle my feet in the dirt to help with finding my footing.

It probably wouldn't surprise him, given his position in the Queen's Guard, that I was exiled. I wondered, however, if the Pillars kept situations like mine a secret. It would be less gossip to control and chatter among the different corridors. As Foreman of the Adora, I doubt anyone in court would notice my disappearance. Only my coworkers would argue about a replacement.

Not to mention, the Pillars had another secret to hide: the Bramwell book.

I thought it best to simply ask Tev, "Do you know?" giving no other details into the meaning.

I could hear him behind me, taking a long sigh, then he answered, "I could take a guess as to why you are out here. I don't know the reason, but I know the Pillars and I know their tendencies."

Getting choked up hearing his answer, I breathed the truth. "He found me and threw me out."

Tears started to fall down my cheeks. Luckily with him behind me, he couldn't see them, although his grip tightened on my shoulders, probably from the muscles tensing underneath.

He attempted to rationalize my situation. "Adonis comes out to the border from time to time. Sometimes unplanned, sometimes to open the gates for the Aluna operators. You happened to be caught at the wrong time."

Adonis told me his commanders notified him about a soldier staying behind. He was probably checking on Thadeous and when he didn't see any true reason as to why he was still at the Barracks, he must have known something was up.

"I tried to convince him to reopen the gates. I thought I could persuade him to but—"

I couldn't finish my sentence.

"The gates tend to bring out the worst in Adonis. There were formed by previous Pillars. Each time a House fell, the Pillars combined their powers to create an intricate gate system for the ultimate protection against the darkness. Adonis recharges his powers through the gates. Backed by centuries of Pillars, full of emotions like worry and panic and despair, the emotions and power flow through him. It seems to be a delicate process because he can't always control it. His temper affects his level of control. If he is upset, he detonates."

"How does the border stay intact? It looked like it was about to fall apart," I said trying my best to keep up with the information Tev was telling me.

"He'll need to get Jeston and Sylva out to the border to rebuild it. They combine their power, like their ancestors, to reconstruct the different layers."

"How do you know so much about this? In my time here, I've never heard stories or rumors about any of this," I asked, glazing over the fact that Tev just called the Queen by a nickname.

I guessed we were in a field of dried flowers. I could hear them scratching on my pant legs. I had to remind myself to walk with caution. There were burrow holes belonging to small animals. I only knew this because my foot had dipped into two of them already. Tev gave no warning of the holes. His feet might have been big enough to walk right over them.

"It's a well-kept secret of the Pillars. When Jeston was a teenager, he came to the Barracks to train with us. He told us about the hidden passageways in the Estate and many more secrets. Ones to never repeat. I love him like a brother, but once he knows you can be trusted, he is an open book. No secret is left locked up."

Tev began to chuckle to himself. He must have recounted numerous stories in his head as we walked farther from the gates of the House of Love.

"Why did you tell me about the gates?" I wondered.

"The likelihood you will ever set foot in the H.O.L. again is pretty low."

His bluntness hit deeper than any bruise or scratch.

I stopped in the middle of the field and broke free of his hands.

Spinning to meet his face, I argued, "You don't know that. Jeston could save me from exile. You don't know him as the Pillar. He holds power; that means something."

"No one can escape exile," Tev retorted. "Once you pass the gates, they know never to allow you back."

He talked about the gates similar to the letter Piston got from the Pillars, suggesting the halls move and change and have a mind of their own. Hearing Tev's words so clearly, I could have wept. Tears resurfaced at the base of my eyes. To avoid Tev seeing me cry, I silently turned around and continued to shuffle my feet in the dry meadow.

Tev must have felt some kind of pity for me because he started to talk again.

"I've known Jeston for a long time. I was picked to be an Aluna operator around the same time Jeston began spending winters with the unit. The Pillars wanted a specialized a band of brothers, trained to run covert missions in the fallen House and stay one step ahead of the darkness. They wanted to stay one step ahead of the darkness. We trained together, ate together, and spent all of our time together. We became a family of sorts. After the Fall of the House of Kindness, the Pillars grew paranoid about the decline of the kingdom. They were worried our time here had become limited, like the end was near. Their response to the Fall was keeping us on a constant rotation. Ten days on and one day off. It's been like that for nearly five years. Luckily, things started to change when Jeston took the throne a few months ago. He has been giving us the option of pursuing other tasks, ones to free us from a life of fighting the darkness. I took the opportunity to protect the Queen when Jeston offered it to me."

Tev pushed harder on my right shoulder, guiding me in that direction. I couldn't hear the flowers against my legs anymore.

"I asked Jeston about you. He didn't give me any indication that you two knew each other or even grew up together," I countered, seeking answers of my own.

"If Adonis found out his brother was giving orders to military members, an organization that falls under the Pillar of Protection, he could possibly lose his throne. The Pillars have a strict rulebook on how to run the House, not to mention the egos of all of them. Jeston is willing to do anything for the people he cares about."

"I hope so," I mumbled, wondering to myself when Jeston would find the time to save me from this place. "If you are out here, how do you get back into the House?"

"The Pillars. Like I said, we have been pretty consistent with our ten days out here. When we need to return to camp, all the Pillars are needed to open the gates. They are the only ones to accept people into the H.O.L. One of their many measures for keeping the border secure."

My foot sank into another rabbit hole. I gasped because of the surprise. Exasperated, I said, "How much longer?"

"It's just around this bend," Tev said behind me, oblivious to mentioning anything about watching where I step.

Keeping with his stride, I could smell a faint smoke in the air. My eyes were left dry by my tears and the addition of smoke burned them. I winced, trying to keep my eyes focused on where I was going, but I had no luck. I reached for my eyes and subsequently stopped on the trail.

Tev left my side. "Wait right here."

I continued to rub my eyes, not giving him any verbal cue I heard his instructions.

"No!"

I heard Tev's voice bounce from boulder to cactus to the vast desert beyond. He was farther away than I expected. My body was tense hearing him shout.

"What happened?" I asked, still wincing at all the smoke.

I could hear his footsteps crunch on the sandy ground, closer and closer by the second.

"They're gone," he said plainly, trying to mask a sadness that I still could hear.

"I thought you said they would stay out here for days at a time? I thought you said they were your brothers? I thought you said they were—"

He cut me off. "I know what I said!"

I blinked away the smoke, still unable to see. I tried to shuffle my feet in the dirt to get closer to him. We were alone. He didn't want to say it out loud, but I knew it was the truth. Selfishly and full of fear, I instinctively needed to be close to Tev. I didn't know what was out here. Something foreign could try to attack both of us if we were not careful.

"Stop," he commanded.

By the tone of his voice, I did what I was told and stood helplessly in the desert, out of reach from Tev and closer to the darkness than I've ever stood before.

I could hear his footsteps pace toward me on the gravel. In a second's time, Tev touched my hand, and I just as fast took it away.

"They left a note," he said. "You should read it for yourself."

He took my hand again and this time I allowed it to happen. He placed his goggles in my hands and I lifted them to my eyes. I could see everything as if it was day. I could see the dusty, brown dirt beneath my feet as well as the sagebrush surrounding us. I looked up to meet Tev's face. He wore the same maroon uniform issued to everyone in the Barracks. The same one I wore myself. Behind him were the remains of the campsite. A fire pit built with various rocks and seating placed around it. The pit billowed with smoke, never ceasing in the slightest.

My eyes met Tev's once again when his hand, shaking and unsteady, gave me a note to read. Written on parchment, similar to Piston's in my apartment only days prior, a message read:

This should teach you not to take orders from a child.
Enjoy exile together.

With Love, beyond all borders,
The Pillar of Protection

I lowered the goggles from my eyes. There was a sense of privacy I felt I was invading while wearing them. An air of mystery hung for a second before I got the courage to say something.

"You weren't even there when I arrived at the Barracks. Jeston didn't give you orders to protect me like the others. Why would Adonis want to exile *you*?"

"He isn't talking about Jeston," Tev responded, his voice cold.

"I don't understand. If he isn't talking about Jeston then—"

Before I could finish my sentence, Tev told the truth I had been waiting to hear. "Sylva sent me to the Adora to spy on you, and I obeyed."

Chapter XVI

THE DESERT HOUSE

We collected ourselves enough wood to build another fire adjacent to the damp ground that was still smoking. With the help of the goggles, Tev found a dried cactus carcass that we could burn throughout the night. Luckily, Tev's pack was still secured in the last place he left it. It had a few jugs of water and meals to sustain him for the five days he anticipated being out here. Opening the dehydrated bag of rice and beans, he filled an empty container with water to rehydrate the food. We shared the meal by the fire in utter silence. Only until after we were done and I was about to fall asleep did he say something.

"I can't believe they left me," he said to the stars. He lay on his back, staring up at them.

Feeling an overwhelming sense of empathy, I tried to justify the unit's disappearance, "Maybe they left because something terrible happened. They wouldn't just leave you out here to die. Especially if they see you as a brother."

"I fear they don't," Tev said between the cracks and pops of the fire.

"They wouldn't do that." I retorted. "They don't seem like the type of people to—"

"Don't be fooled, Wrenna," he snapped. "We have protocols to follow. The unit is supposed to stay until everyone is accounted for. There is a reason they left me behind. They don't see me as one of them anymore."

"I just don't understand." I shook my head in defiance.

"I wanted to leave. I was given a choice, and I chose freedom over staying with them. We all agreed nothing would come between us. I went back on my word. That's why they left me out here. They turned their back on me just as I had done to them years ago."

I could hear the despair and defeat behind the anger in Tev's voice. I knew I couldn't take away any of the pain he was experiencing. I knew I didn't have much to offer him. So instead, I stood from across the fire and planted myself in the seat next to him. The heat radiating off of him was hotter than the coals that captivated our attention. It wasn't much. We were out here for no fault but our own. At the very least, and most importantly, we knew we were together.

"Are you worried about the darkness?" I asked.

"The darkness is—" he trailed off. I could tell he was working a puzzle in his mind, trying to find the right words to describe it.

I started to think the worst of the worst. I was beginning to fear what Adonis told me about the darkness. How it would seek out my soul and devour me from the inside out. I tried hard not to picture what it would look like or what it would feel like when the darkness took over. But, I was curious and that alone could lead me down a dark and dangerous path.

"I've spent the better half of my life journeying through the Lost Eight, and I haven't witnessed any kind of darkness that fits the description the Pillars claim." Tev finally found the right words.

Coincidentally, it was as if he could hear my thoughts. I sighed with relief upon hearing his explanation.

"The Lost Eight?" I inquired.

"That's what we call the fallen Houses instead of calling them each by name," he answered. "There are nine total Houses and eight of them have collapsed."

"Do you know them well?" I asked, "I've only been to a handful myself."

"Yeah, I've got a rough idea of each House. Though there are some I have never been to before. The Forgotten King's kingdom was quite spectacular," Tev explained.

"Which one are we in now?"

I anticipated hearing Tev say the House of Hope. I had a strong feeling that it was where we were currently sitting.

"We are in the House of Patience," Tev said. "The H.O.L. shares its southern border with the HoPat. There are other entrances to the H.O.L. but the gates at the Barracks lead to the HoPat."

"The HoPat.?" I restated.

"The military has abbreviations for everything. The H.O.G., the H.O.P.E., the Hok—they are an easier way to say the names instead of wasting time saying the House of Goodness, the House of Peace or the House of Kindness."

The mention of where I grew up made my ears perk. I sat a bit straighter when he said the words.

"You said you were from one of them—which one?"

"That was a long time ago," Tev dismissed the question.

My curiosity bubbled inside me. I wanted to press further and learn more about him but after the day he had, and the tiredness weighing my eyelids, I didn't bother.

After a few moments of the crackling of fire lulling me to sleep, a thought about the darkness crept back into my mind. Suddenly, I wasn't tired anymore.

"You say you haven't seen the darkness, but how do you explain the quakes after each collapse? Those can't be just a coincidence." I said. This time I was speaking to the stars as I lay on my back.

Tev responded over the bursts of the cactus skeleton burning. "There might be a correlation with them, but I know for a fact that it is not as bad as Adonis, or even Sylva, are letting on. I traveled with her to other forums and other Houses. I saw the other Pillars and their people flourishing in those Houses. At the Barracks, we suspected that they, the Pillars, had something to do with the House's demise. They were the ones blessed with power. That was before I caught a glimpse into their lives. Yes, they have power, but it's restricted with their own set of laws."

"You should have seen what Adonis was like at the gate. There was nothing restricting him," I countered.

"I sense there are secrets the Pillars keep between only themselves. Secrets they will do anything to keep well hidden. You said it yourself: You've never seen anything like it and you were with them often," Tev said.

I huffed at the fact that I didn't have anything to argue. Instead, I asked, "What does Jeston have to say about all this?" It was a test to see if Tev knew Jeston well too.

"Jeston doesn't know his brothers at the Barracks suspected anything. We decided to keep these theories from him. He is our friend and belongs to the brotherhood, but his title as a Pillar separated him from us. We were collected from our homes and built up. He merely tagged along."

As much as Jeston wanted a *true* friend in his life, he was always going to be differentiated. He would never truly be trusted due to his position. What he wanted most was impossible for him to gain. I never thought I would say this, but I felt sorry for him. All he wanted was a person to trust—a friend—and unfortunately, he was now stuck with his explosive brother.

Jeston saved me from a death sentence even when I was the meanest I could be to someone. He deserved better.

The fire stayed alive through the night, no thanks to my efforts. I had drifted to sleep with the thought of Jeston fresh in my mind. I could see his face in the tunnel he walked with me. His eyes were carved deeper and darker, like a walking nightmare. I woke with the dirt and sand coating my cheek, neck, hair, and hands. The feeling of it rubbing against me was absolutely unbearable, like it wanted to suffocate me slowly.

I gave up on sleep and told Tev I'd watch the fire while he slept. He added a few collected twigs before laying his head down on the ground for a little rest. I envied how easy it was for him to sleep. His guttural snores filled the campsite and distracted my mind for the time being.

After I poked the remaining embers for an hour, the sun began to light the sky. There was a sliver of hope with the light. In the back of my mind, I thought the sun would never rise in a land that was lost to the darkness. My worst fear was I would never see the sun again. Fortunately, I was wrong.

Open sky stretched for miles on end. It slowly turned from a velvety midnight to a globe of periwinkle. At the horizon, I could see the sun starting to peek its way through the ridges of mountains in the distance. It interrupted the slumber of the creatures nearby as it inched higher into the sky. Pastels of cherry blossom and peach sorbet painted the sky. As the sun rose past the horizon, a few clouds were highlighted with a brighter shade of peppermint pink and sunflower yellow.

The spectacle of such beauty left me awestruck and silent. An illusion of peace and hope lay before me. I had viewed the sunrise through a new lens—a lens of rebirth.

I was free.

I waited and watched as the desert floor blossomed with a stir of activity.

The rodents that peeked their heads from their burrows left a smile on my face while the lizards zipping effortlessly through the dirt left shivers. The birds chirped proudly with the rising sun. Most of the music came from inside the cacti. Nests, no doubt, were protected by the spires of the structure.

I watched as the sun's rays eventually reached Tev's body, warming his back. Little hairs of red highlighted his head, complementing his maroon uniform. The cotton t-shirt was stained with sweat in a line down his spine, reminding me of the sweat that accompanied my nightmares.

I followed a lizard dashing through the dirt. He would wait in the shadow of a bush then scurry away to the next. Leaving the safety of shelter, the lizard was snatched by the mouth of a snake. The joyous moment was fleeting when the beams of the sun hit my face.

This happened *every day.*

There was nothing special about this sunrise nor my presence here.

I was as lost as the land.

The beauty and peace slowly faded into fear and despair. The colors, faint and delicate, turned bold and bleeding. Hope must be hard to find in a land so vast, with creatures waiting to kill for their next meal.

Tev must have felt the shift in temperature because his eyes opened soon after the campsite was lit. He stretched his arms above his head and palmed his eyes, wiping the sleep from them. Tiredness weighing heavy in the dark circles around his eyes, he still managed to smile and greet me with a low good morning.

I returned, my voice withered down to a rasp, "Good morning."

I couldn't return it with much enthusiasm given the strain on my voice from the night before. My body started to feel the weight and toll from the past few days. Invisible chains were strung across my shoulders, never allowing for recovery or rest. I better get used to carrying them. I would need a miracle to feel them lifted.

"Did you get enough sleep?" I asked, wanting to distract myself from the evil thoughts happening inside my mind.

"It'll do for now," Tev responded, "We better get a move on before someone or something comes looking for us."

"Who would want to come out here?" I looked around in confusion at the desolate and barren land.

"Adonis will likely send a firing squad out here to ensure both of us are not a threat anymore," Tev said bluntly.

As if he called the rumbles forward, the sound of large hooves striking the ground grew and grew. A small object flew past my ear faster than a blink of an eye. I could hear the zoom and then impact with the ground.

"Get down!" Tev yanked my arm down, causing me to fall next to him on the sand.

"What was that?" I asked, my breath quickly increasing.

"We need to head for that mountain range. We will be safe up there. We are too exposed out here. On my lead, follow closely behind me." He was commanding me just as a soldier should.

"Tev—" I began to say.

"If you want to stay alive, you will do as I say," he said sternly.

I nodded and took his hand and we ran.

Zoom!

Whiz!

Crash!

Boom!

All in succession, bullets flew past us. I did not look behind me to see who was following us. I thought I heard the thuds dissipate as my legs grew more tired from running.

"Tev, I can't run much farther!" I yelled, still holding his hand and heading deeper into the desert.

He found a tall, thick cactus to hide behind. We crouched down to hide ourselves from whomever was chasing us.

I was panting, hoping air would fill my lungs as Tev scoped the area.

"We need to keep moving," he ordered.

"Who is chasing us?" I asked between staggered breaths.

"Bucknells," he responded.

"Who?"

"They are agents sent to fight. These are creatures with trees for antlers. A single step can puncture any bone, muscle, or body. Their spit travels faster than the eye can follow. They are ordered by the Alunas, who are following orders from a Pillar. These things are a form of defense for the House of Love within the Lost Lands," Tev spoke in a single breath. He met my eyes and said, "We need to go—now."

So, we scrambled through the desert, ducking behind tall cacti whenever I needed to catch my breath. Unforgiving, Tev yanked my arm more times than I cared for but slowly we inched closer to the mountain range and safety.

Chapter XVII

A DAY IN THE DESERT HOUSE

Before I knew it, we were climbing in elevation. I watched my feet sway back and forth send me into a trance for hours. The sun had fully risen almost directly above us by the time I was brought back to reality.

I was standing on a path of pebbles and dust. There were trees sprouting out of the ground beside the trail. I halted and spun on my heel. I found Tev a few paces behind me, watching my movements with high intensity. He came to a halt when he saw I was awake.

"What happened?" I asked, my voice was burnt out from fire duty the night before. "One moment we were running through the desert, hiding behind cacti, and the next we are in the trees, climbing."

"You caught a whiff of the dust from the Postuells," Tev said.

I raised my eyebrows, silently asking the question, giving my voice a reprieve.

"You underestimate the power of the Lost Lands," Tev scoffed. "The dust kicked into the air from the House of Patience can send people into a state of meditation. I've heard stories of people who intentionally seek the desert—for their own health. They would wake after a few hours and head home feeling much better than when they arrived."

"How does it work?"

"No one truly knows. These lands have an inherent air of mystery. Your guess is as good as mine."

"And if you were to guess?" I pressed.

Tev shrugged and stated, "I'd guess that if time is stripped away at the core, then whatever the task, whatever mountain you face, the more attainable it appears."

Scrunching my face, I was perplexed by the notion that these places were alive.

This House was captured by the darkness and yet, it still held power.

These weren't *wastelands* like I had previously thought.

"I picked these while you were walking," Tev handed me a sizeable fruit. Its magenta color and plump weight made my mouth water. There was a slit already cut in the skin for me to peel away the rind.

Tev motioned for us to keep walking on the path while I ate. He filled the space with a more thorough explanation of the Postuells.

"The first time walking the desert is the hardest to overcome. The desert is helpful in some regards. It calms people in times of distress. However, the darkness has a way of turning even the simplest of cures into a nightmare. Its main objective is to distract or confuse us from our true gifts. Over time—as you will come to learn—humans are *undoubtedly* weak. We concede to the darkness because it is easy."

"Is that what happened to me?" I asked.

"No, the darkness can't confuse you. You are protected," Tev stated so positively that there was no question. It was a fact.

And yet, I proceeded with, "Protected? But you just said humans are weak. How am I protected?"

"You didn't change course. Unfortunately, a person walking in the desert for the first time needs to wake themselves. There wasn't much I could do. You kept the course toward the mountains, so I predicted you'd wake up soon."

"You risked my life with a prediction?" I spat out.

"You woke up. I knew this to be true because you are protected," he said.

"You keep saying that. What do you mean? How can I be protected?"

Tev bit into another fruit from his pantleg and spoke as the juice was running down his mouth, "The darkness isn't just a being like you and me. There are spirits that constantly surround us. Ones that want to protect us and ones that want to harm us. Ones we can see and ones we cannot. That's the difference in Lost Lands from the House of Love. We can see either side—physical and spiritual—out here. They don't hide in the fallen Houses. And I saw you were protected."

"If that is the case, where is my protector?" I asked, wanting verification that what he was saying was true.

"You're walking in a line of fools. Even if I showed you proof, you would still think it wasn't real. Other people have sought the protectors and have been swindled into staying in the desert far longer than they hoped. Some never left and died here. Out of fear or convinced from the lies the darkness chooses, they stayed broken, and they stayed here."

I laughed, thinking Tev was being dramatic.

He snapped his fingers to shut me up, and it worked.

"This is your warning, Wren. The darkness is cunning. It can be blissfully numbing at times. It can deceive. Some have, and will, come to enjoy the company and ease of the darkness. Let that not be your case."

The warning shocked my system just as I bit into my own fruit. The juice of the fruit coated my throat with a sting, causing me to cough. Once my taste buds caught up, the fruit was deliciously tart. It made my eyes narrow and water along with my cough.

"Some soldiers take days to wake themselves," Tev scoffed.

Between slurps of juice and wiping my mouth, I said defiantly, "I wish I could have stayed there a little longer. I lost the sadness for a second."

Tev snapped again, "That's one way to welcome the darkness. It uses your past because it's watched you. It knows you're sad. It'll try anything to relieve you of sadness through lies. You need to let the past go to defend yourself out here."

Anger started to fester in my bones. "If only you knew what I went through. You'd want revenge too."

"Revenge is an excuse, Wrenna," Tev said bluntly.

He walked past me to continue the climb on the nearest trail.

I paused, shocked by his response. "An excuse?"

"The darkness wants you to think that to take control," he said with his back turned. "You might have been through hell, but that's in the past. You can't change it. It's done. What you can do is forgive. Through forgiveness, the darkness cannot hold you captive. It's sad to see you already have so much bitterness in your heart."

I straightened myself, uncomfortable at the proclamation he was making.

"Or," Tev continued his thought, "if you want, give into the darkness and see what happens. Continue down this road of revenge and see where it leads you. I bet the darkness would be very glad to have another soul."

I was left stunned, not knowing how to respond.

"Just know," Tev now turned toward me and looked me in the eye, "there are plenty of people who wish they could start over. They wish they could flee from the darkness or see it flee from their loved ones. You are lucky. You are a living testament to someone else's dream."

"I am not lucky," I argued the simplest debate. "I don't have a place to call home!"

Tev closed the gap between us. The soil under his foot crunched with every step closer to me.

"Answer me this: In the hours you have been here, how many times have you been surprised by the light still living in this land?"

I stood my ground and huffed through my nose.

"Admit it, you are surprised that it is not all bad out here. You were surprised that Adonis lied about the darkness. Your first encounter with a fallen House and the darkness didn't devour your soul. Instead, this land showed you mercy. Explain that."

I stayed silent for fear of telling Tev he was right.

"You are stronger than you think out here. Start believing it. Stop feeling sorry for yourself. Stop telling yourself you were cast out here to die. The mind is a wonderful thing. It's easily tricked if you tell it 'no' enough times."

I rolled my eyes and shoved Tev the best I could with my shoulder. I wanted this conversation to end.

"You are strong, and you are brave."

I could hear him behind me, repeating the words of Thadeous. Images from last night when we were ambushed in the Barracks came to mind. Then sometime after, the calming of Thad's voice.

You are brave.

You are strong.

Do not worry.

If I was brave, why did I have so much fear?

If I was strong, why did I feel so weak?

Stopping for a final time, I stepped aside and let Tev lead the way.

Approaching me, he said, "There is a canyon over that ridge with a river full of fish. Let's head there and get some real food and rest for the night."

I nodded, thankful we were done with the conversation, and we were on our way.

It took another hour for us to hike to the spot Tev mentioned. I needed to take small breaks while climbing to catch my breath. My body was not used to the exercise, and I hadn't eaten a proper meal in days. I focused my energy on the hope of having a fish to eat all for myself soon.

We had reached the bottom of the canyon when I realized the air had become sweeter and cooler. There were massive shadows that covered the walls of the canyon. Large, winged birds flew in circles above the canyon. The water from the river captivated my attention. It flowed with crashing rapids. The white water could have kept me dazed for much longer than the Postuells. I watched and listened to the water, counting the patterns of the waves. It reminded me of a time far into past—a single memory of childhood.

Tev asked me to collect river rock so we could build a fire. There were enough stones along the bank where I began to gather and build. Meanwhile, Tev searched for dry brush, twigs, and logs. He returned with a crumbly bush that didn't have the luxury of extending its roots to meet the river but provided plenty of material needed for a successful fire.

Once Tev ignited the brush, he assembled a fishing rod from his pack with thin wire and attached a metal hook to the end. A handy tool to pluck the fish out of the water. There was a pool of knee-deep water with soft pebbles underfoot that he waded in to cast his line.

I stayed on shore to watch. I was in charge of preventing the brush from escaping the stone pit and setting the rest of the desert ablaze.

Momentarily, I heard a large splash coming from the pool. I stood to find Tev, soaked head to toe wading out of the water. He held two fish on his line as he dripped his way to the campsite. He explained he was reaching for the fish and slipped on one of the rocks.

We both laughed at his misfortune of falling. Notably, and to my surprise, it was the first time I had laughed since being exiled.

Our bellies were full of fish in minutes. It was the first time my stomach ached being full of food in days.

I lay next to the fire, resting my back on the ground. My legs ached from the day's journey across the Postuell desert. I wiggled my body into the ground. My hair was coated in dirt again. I sat up, exhausted from the heaviness and the inconvenience my hair had become since leaving the House of Love. I tried spinning it into a bun. When it fell down, I let out a long sigh.

Tev could see my unease and suggested, "Would you want me to cut it for you?"

I nodded.

Tev patted the dust from his pants in addition to wiping his hand on his otherwise dirty pantlegs. He reached in his pack for a knife. The blade reflected in the gleam of the fire. He stood behind me and clumped my matted hair in his hands. His only instructions were, "Hold still."

I sat in silence as he sawed my hair to the length of my shoulders.

After my haircut, Tev snapped a branch from a near tree and used it to draw in the sand. I could hear the shift in the grains of sand as he etched away. I looked over to see what he was doing.

Pictures of the fish and the trees, leaves and even flowers were temporarily sketched into the sand before him. I found a comfortable position in the sand to watch him silently. I could feel my body growing heavier and heavier. I began to drift into the beginnings of slumber, then I heard the question.

"Which House are you from?" Tev said, only slightly louder than the pops of fire.

I opened my eyes and shifted my body to see him still etching away.

"Kindness," I responded.

"Why did you leave?" he followed up.

This was a story I had buried the day I arrived at the gate of the House of Love. I wasn't ready just yet to bring it up again.

"The collapse happened," I said and in quick succession changed the subject. "How were you immune to the Postuells?"

He chuckled to himself, probably recalling his first time in the desert.

"I have passed through the Lost Lands more times than I can count. The darkness knows I will stand firm against it no matter how hard it tries to break me down. I know the good that abounds even in the darkest of shadows." He looked around to the large canyon walls that hid the sunlight from us.

"How do you know so much about this place?"

"We picked up a thing or two during our missions out here." He spoke calmly.

"Missions for what?" I probed him again with another question, as if I was trying to squeeze every last bit of juice from a fruit.

"We were sent on mission to gather information about the people out here. There aren't many tribes left in this region. We would spy on them and report back to the General with what we saw. Mostly, people go about living their lives out here, but with Adonis' skepticism and Sylva's fear, we continued with missions. Their thinking was: the more you know about the enemy, the more you can protect yourself against it."

"How many of the Houses have you seen? All of them?" I asked.

"No, we were sent on missions to most of the southern and western Houses. They were the most accessible from the House of Love. I've also seen the isle of the House of Self-Control. But, not as an Aluna operator."

"Why?"

"That's where the darkness is said to have formed. The House has been in darkness the longest. When it collapsed, the House broke off into the seas and has been an island lost in a dense mist. Adonis forbade us to go south of the House of Patience. He didn't want us to bring anything back from the isle."

"And you've seen it?" I was sitting, waiting patiently for his response.

"I called it home," Tev said plainly.

A howl had erupted from beyond the ridge. Screams and screeches followed joyously behind it.

"Yotes," Tev said, "*Vicious* animals. Mostly hunt at night. One of us will have to keep watch while the other sleeps tonight. By the sound of it, they are close."

My eyes had widened at the chorus of yelps coming from the black of night. The sun had fully set by now and the yells of the animals were bone chilling. Tev was listening just as intently as I. The trees shifted and scratched with a sudden breeze, and I jumped in my seat. Sand blew up where I sat.

"If we continue in this direction, we should reach the House of Goodness in a few days. There is a town tucked in the meadows that is welcoming to travelers. We could find you a place to stay out there." His suggestion was met with kindness.

"I don't know much about the House of Goodness," I stated.

Tev closed his eyes. The stick in his hand began tracing the little details he could remember from the Meadows of Good.

"If you could picture," his hand scribbled along, "hills, rolling, for miles on end. At sunset, the grass turns the color of limes and sunlight dances through every woven fiber of grass. Lush trees full of intertwining branches and leaves that change colors when the skies turn cold. Willabees lining every bank, and brook, of water visible. There are variations of purples and pinks you could not image with your own mind. There are open skies with fluffy clouds in every direction and the berries are the fullest and plumpest in the entire kingdom."

"Sounds like heaven." I smiled cheerfully at Tev.

He had drawn his version of the House of Goodness into the sand. He quickly erased the markings and started a new drawing.

"The seas were my favorite. The land curved into a cove at the southern tip where the water would rise and fall. The cliffs held the sea spray, and you could feel it in your skin. Sticky at times but inherently comforting. Warm when the sun was out and cold when it was tucked away. The birds would squawk loudly, flying into the sea to find their next meal. Only on special days could you see multiple fully enclosed rainbows at the height of the day. In the sky and in the water. They would sparkle for a time then retreat like a bear for hibernation."

"That's quite the talent." I motioned to his drawn cliffs with water and birds.

"I started drawing when my unit needed a map of the Houses. I added landmarks and important details to remember for the next time we passed through here."

To my knowledge, a map of the Houses hasn't been seen since the Forgotten King's time. Bramwell's books held an original layout, but after the fall of each House, their borders changed. The only House with its original borders, set by the King, was my former home. The House of Love.

Tev tore open a pocket at his knee to reveal a creased tan paper. I quickly met him at his side to get a better look at the map. Scattered on the page were ink drawings and wandering lines establishing the kingdom. A vast layout with mountains and waters and names of towns I had never heard of before.

"I never finished it," he explained. "There are still Houses I haven't seen or towns I have yet to visit."

"Considering that the House of Joy has hundreds of tiny islands, most of which are covered in ice and fog, you'll probably never see it to the end," I said.

A silence hung in the air at the comment.

"And the people?" I inquired, breaking the awkwardness.

"They gave me hope," Tev said without thinking.

I simply smiled at him with tight lips, waiting to hear more.

"The folks there are shorter and squatter than us, but they knew how to cook. Their stews would be full of hearty potatoes and carrots with fresh cut lamb. That was my favorite."

The description of food made my stomach rumble. Tev heard it too, but he continued, "The men wore their beards long, some rattier than others. I never met a Goodien that was opposed to an arm wrestle. Most are strong. Stalky, but kind nonetheless."

There was that word again, taking me back to my childhood of boat races and frog catching.

"I grew up in the swamps of Kindness," I blurted out. Upon realizing what I had just said, I continued my thoughts, "My family wasn't the richest. The six of us lived in a shack on the bayou with holes in the roof and mold growing in the corners. I had three brothers. During the collapse of the House, my brother Rafe was injured trying to get me to safety. I couldn't face being the cause of such pain for him, so I left. I journeyed through the House of Joy, only stopping for food and occasionally sleep. I came to find there was little joy in the land and less in its people. My sights were on the House of Love anyway. I had heard of the infamous ships that harbored at the ports and the cafes with the sweetest of treats. There was prosperity that came from Love and I wanted a taste of it."

"Did you find it?" Tev asked.

I thought back over the first of my days in the House and ended with the last of my days. I had been betrayed and, as a result, it tainted my perception of the House. As much as it hurt to say, I answered with the truth. "I'm not sure if what I found was real."

Chapter XVIII

THE SKY GIANTS

"Wrenna? Wren, wake up."

Tev shook me awake. The first light of the sun had begun to spread across the sky when I opened my eyes to Tev standing above me, panting.

We stayed up long into the night sharing tales we had learned. We laughed so hard, my stomach ached as I sat up to meet his face.

"What's going on?" I asked through narrow eyes and a yawn.

"We need to move. Now."

His tone suggested danger was arriving soon if I didn't listen to him now. The sun had been taking its time rising over the canyon walls this morning. My tired body was zapped awake with adrenaline as Tev yanked my arm, and we started running into the canyon. I tripped over small rocks, ones Tev conveniently dodged.

"Tev, what's going on?" I asked again, hoping to hear a response.

"I spotted a giant in the sky. I can explain later, but we need to find a proper hiding place first," Tev shouted.

He held my hand tighter as we sped through the canyon. The walls of the canyon were sheer. Layers of rocks passed us as we zipped in and out of the bends. The years of erosion were written in the walls. There was no escape but through. Vulnerable to the skies above, we didn't have much cover.

We kept running even when my legs would give out from under me. I would stumble and he would catch me. We darted around the jetting branches of bushes growing in the cracks and splashed in the water if necessary.

Before I could process it, we stopped. I nearly crashed into Tev. Before I could collide with him, he caught me and covered my mouth. I stared fearfully into his eyes and breathed heavily through my nose.

"We need to keep quiet and find a place to hide. It's not far behind us. Do you understand?"

His stare froze my veins. I nodded and we took off faster and quieter than before.

We found boulders from a landslide tall enough to hide two grown adults. My skinny frame was easy to slide between the entrance. Tev had a harder time fitting through with his muscular build. After a minute of weaseling his way in, he made it and instructed me to hide deeper into the cave. Stubbing my toe and tripping, I fell to the ground with my hands extended to catch my fall. My knees also crashed into something sharp on the floor of the cave. It looked to be in the same size and shape of a feather but cut like a knife.

Tev took note of our surroundings outside the cave.

I stood and found blood stains starting to form on my palms and pantlegs.

In the smallest whisper, I said, "Tev."

His head whipped to meet mine and he pressed a finger to his lips to signal to keep quiet.

I did as I was told and waited.

Not long after, I felt a thud on the earth. It shook the rocks, but our covert structure remained steady. Thumps began to crash on the earth, growing louder and louder; one after the other. Whatever it was, it was big, and its sights were set on us. The pebbles trembled violently at my feet. The light from the entrance where Tev stood was covered by a large shadow. He abandoned his post to comfort me, moving us slightly deeper into the cave.

"Tev?" I squeaked, quieter than the first time.

Standing inches from me, he pressed his hand to my mouth to prevent any other sound from escaping. His other hand was placed firmly on the back of my head.

His body was tense.

Inches apart, I swear I could feel his heart beating at the same pace as mine. I peered at his darting eyes, landing on me for a second before refocusing on the entrance. Each time he looked at me, it was as if he was checking to see if I was still there. That my body didn't crumble to ash before him. That my eyes stayed the same teal color. That my skin didn't boil underneath his hand. That my mind didn't melt out of my ears. That I was still standing and in turn protecting *him*. And that the darkness didn't take me from him.

With each look, I counted the seconds that passed.

The strongest impact with the earth came and as a result, Tev and I were launched into the air. I instinctively shrieked at the shock of being thrown into the air. Tev's hands never deviated from their spots on my mouth and the back of my head. Luckily, the sound was muffled. I watched as Tev trembled too.

A loud roar echoed in the forest. A roar of defeat. Whatever was out there, it lost. Another set of thuds collided with the earth, becoming less and less by the second.

Tev's body began to relax. He removed his hands, and I was able to take my first deep breath.

"What was that?" I whispered, still afraid it might come back.

"A giant. They serve the darkness. Only a few of them exist that we know of, but their hearts are full of evil. They are sent by the darkness to destroy anything good. They have the ears of an owl but are blinder than a bat and dumber than rocks. It could hear us, but it couldn't see us and therefore couldn't find us. Its roar was a declaration of abandonment. A signal to its master that it surrenders the search."

"A servant of the darkness."

"A stupid one too."

"How did it know where we were?" I asked.

"My guess is the blorks. They saw us in the river and the darkness needed reinforcements to keep us from moving forward. 'For fear is the greatest weapon of the darkness,'" Tev said like he was quoting someone. "We must be headed in the right direction."

We wrestled with the boulder entrance one more time, leaving the safety of our shelter.

Tev pulled the map out from his pocket and began scanning the area for any notable landmark he could use. Unfortunately, the blueprint of the canyon was severely changed by the giant's steps. A completely new landscape was carved from the destruction. The massive walls of rock and stone had turned to sand and dust. The river water was now filled with mud and murk. Any greenery that remained was completely scorched by the touch of the giant.

It was complete devastation.

A welcome home present from the darkness.

We decided to move north, farther into the mountains.

After climbing the steep pass for most of the day, we found

ourselves in a healthy forest, one with lush trees with thick trunks and full branches. These trees I had recognized from my time in the House of Joy, except these lacked a coating of snow.

Resting for the night, we nestled in a true cave we found on the mountainside. Tev searched for animals while I collected firewood. He returned with nuts and berries and onions by the time I had the fire built.

"No meat for tonight?" I asked.

It was going to be a scarce dinner.

"Not many animals live this high," Tev explained. "There are mountain goats, but the chances of me taking one down and carrying it back to camp are next to impossible. I was thinking of eating one of the meals in my Aluna pack too."

We ate and watched as the sun began to set in the sky. Our alcove in the mountain peered over the tops of most trees. We were able to watch the sun kiss the horizon before it descended fully.

Finding a spot to rest against, I closed my eyes and turned my back to the warmth of the fire. I lay still, but the events of the day kept my mind awake. After an hour of fading in and out of sleep, my eyelids shot open to find the shadows of the fire dancing on the wall. My silhouette blocked a part of it, but I was able to see enough.

I watched as I relived the earlier hours in the light of the fire.

A giant crushing every rock underfoot.

Tev and I weaving in and out of the canyon to find shelter.

The darkness encompassing the very spot where we stood.

Tev's eyes watching to see if I was still there.

Before the ending, I had fallen asleep.

For I knew the outcome: We were going to be *protected.*

I opened my eyes to find the sun hadn't risen yet. My back, still facing the fire, was burning hot from the simmering embers. The mountain walls that protected us didn't flicker with light like they did when I fell asleep. I turned onto my back to find the fire had no life at all and my biggest fear had come true.

I was alone.

Chapter XIX

THE SAND PIRATES

Tev was not splayed out near the fire like I expected him to be.

Thankfully, the light from the moon had grown in strength since my first night in the Lost Lands. As I rose to my feet, pressure rushed to my head. I stood too fast and now I was incapacitated. I thought once the pounding subsided, I was all better. Then I saw a shadowed figure lurking by the edge of the landing and I started to doubt. Its shape was unfamiliar. Tev had broader shoulders than the one before me, shoulders of a soldier. This one had shoulders like a corn stalk.

Narrow, skinny, and wiry.

My bones locked, anticipating the creature's next step, thinking of every possible means to get out of the cave. For all I knew, it could think of me as a shadow. I became extra cautious, not wanting to announce my presence. If the thing happened to stumble upon this spot on the mountain for the same reason we did—a place of peace for the night—whenever I had a window of opportunity, I needed to take it. Before I could think of a plan, the figure spun, looking in my direction. Hopefully the lack of light and a plume of smoke turned me invisible to anyone looking in. I pressed my body against the back wall of the cave. The shadow shuffled cautiously inside.

This couldn't have been another dream.

It felt all too real.

My thoughts screamed loudly in my head as I tried to maintain my breathing.

Step after step, the creature got closer to me. I willed myself to blend in with the walls. My access out of the cave was limited thanks to the threat of the hot embers at the entrance. The creature bled into the smoke. Light-footed, I rounded the wall and found myself close enough to escape. My focus was on the moon waiting in the sky.

I glanced over my shoulder to check on the creature—only to find stained teeth smiling inches from my face. Two yellow glowing eyes hovered above the eerie smile, inches away from my face. I screamed. The menacing face before me was indication enough to know I was in imminent danger.

I had no regard for keeping my feet quiet anymore. Survival was my main priority. I leaped for the forest floor below without hesitation or regard for my physical well-being. I landed on the needle-clad forest floor. My hands caught the brunt of my fall, leaving cuts from various stabs and pricks from pinecones.

I quickly got to my feet to find myself standing alone.

My attention caught a blaze of fire reflecting off the trunks of the trees. The golden light led my eyes to a horror I believed to only live in dreams.

Living skeletons, not humans, but animals.

Just as the smoke in the cave was visible with the light from the moon, the breath coming from their noses shone too. Two massive sets of antlers swayed back and forth, counting the seconds, waiting for their master to return.

These weren't statues.

These weren't part of a dream.

These were monsters that could crush me with a single step. Reins were placed around their heads, only seen due to contrast on their porcelain bones. Behind them, attached to them, sat a carriage.

Multiple glass boxes were held together by welded metal. Torches placed uniformly on each side lit the surrounding area and the boxes themselves. Speckled throughout the clear glass, spots of colored stones glowed in the firelight and moonlight.

Beyond the stones, inside the box, was my missing friend.

Tev started pounding on the glass. His body fragmented in bits and pieces, distorted by the glass. He yelled, trying to rip apart the walls of the enclosure, but his cries for help were muffled. There was enough light for me to know what he was saying.

He wasn't asking for help.

He was telling me to run.

I was paralyzed. I didn't know where to run. I had lost all sense of direction, already forgetting the direction of our campsite.

He was the one with the map.

My guide.

I was lost without Tev.

I chose to run toward him. I could see Tev's reaction, a bellow from deep inside him.

No!

He screamed, waving his arms, deterring me from coming closer.

I ignored him. I kept my pace toward the carts. Before I could grasp what happened, I walked straight into a spider's web camouflaged by the dark of night. Stretched between two trees, the silk threads latched onto my face and body. I paused to strip the thin debris from myself when a sensation started to numb my lips.

Disregarding it, I walked closer to Tev, trapped in glass. A venom-like feeling was spreading to the rest of my body, now inhibiting my stride. I almost stumbled into the breathing skeletons, sending a shriek from the animals into the air.

Definitely not a dream.

I crouched down to make myself small and unnoticeable upon my arrival at the carriage.

Tev increased his banging on the glass. His figure had become so distorted I almost forgot completely who he was. He sent a warning with one final blow on the glass. The yellow-eyed man had returned to his cart. By this time, I was fully impaired. My ability to run or fight was thwarted by the web's effect. The man snatched my hands and clipped them together in chains.

My capture caused him to send out a billowing laugh. A laugh displaying his pride. He won his prize. A significant and substantial one. One Aluna soldier and an exiled clockworker.

I was placed in a cage adjacent to Tev, sharing a wall of glass and stone. Unable to stand any longer, I crouched in the corner closest to Tev. I knew he couldn't protect me from here, but a part of me felt comforted by his proximity.

Tev slid to his knees, meeting me opposite the glass, pounding his hands against the wall. I could tell he was dedicated to breaking it. A small spot of bright red had stained the wall. I lifted my hands, bound together by rough metal, to touch the blood.

We were trapped in massive cages controlled by a man of walking death and pulled by animals missing flesh and muscles.

Probably due to my encounter with the spider web and its venom, I didn't care about our future peril. My muscles were relaxed. For the first time since my date with Jeston, I felt at peace.

The corner, although cool to the touch, felt comfortable and cozy.

I could curl up into a crystal corner and dissolve into deep sleep, my mind slipping away, becoming one with the crystal that I'd touch.

On his last attempt at breaking the thick glass, Tev smashed his way through the partition. Chunks of colored jewels and glass flew into my cage. I didn't mind; the sleep I sought was more important.

Swirls of unconsciousness coaxed my mind into shutting off. My heart rate was slowing to a sweet pace. My face numb, along with my hands and legs, I waded into the seas of tranquility.

I could hear Tev's muffled voice, this time, blocked by the will to sleep. I cared so little to be bothered. I didn't move. My bones interlocked with relaxation, a force that would send me down a chute of calm.

Scooping the clear rocks away from my body, Tev collapsed to the ground. I could feel the pressure of his hands around my arms, but it was more of an inconvenience.

But it kept me awake.

Luckily, it was the thing to keep me alive.

Awareness sparked back to life in my body. The nerves in my hands fired sensory pulses to my brain, gripping the cotton shirt below. With my eyes closed, I didn't know if it was mine or Tev's shirt that was braced in my hand.

My thoughts told my mouth to open next. I yearned for air, taking a moment for it to happen. I commanded my eyes to do the same after. They widened as if they needed to take a deep breath themselves.

My eyes and mouth were under my control, but my voice and body were still numb. Forcing signals to move them, I focused on my littlest toe. After becoming a master of that I moved to the next. My line of sight was directed at Tev, witnessing firsthand the control I craved in my body. I made headway by lifting my head off his arm that cradled me. It felt like I had planted roots deep in the soil and the earth still held some below.

There was no pain in my body; my nerves were likely damaged from whatever poison coated the spider's web. As I sat up, my head was clearest it had ever been, like waking from an eternal sleep and being reborn.

The carriage took us down the mountain the same way we climbed that afternoon. Our cage was lit by the torches and nothing else. The feeling of sleepiness was still strong, but I fought it.

"A sand pirate," he replied.

What felt like minutes later, sun had fully risen, casting beams across the sand and sky. The cage became a hub of rainbows, refracting the prisms caused by light through the crystals. Reds and oranges, blues and greens all dazzled on my skin and Tev's as we sat together. As the colors painted our skin, they dyed the maroon clothing we wore as well, leaving an impression on the fabric with richer, more interesting colors. The spectacle left me stunned and speechless.

Tev seemed to be completely unfazed, so stubborn to the point he was letting his frustration take over his entire mind.

We neared a dark blob, distinctly shown against the brightness of the sand. Wherever we were headed, it was large. Coming to a stop, the crystal cage opened to a blinding light, much brighter than the rainbows that rained on the inside.

Guided out by a copycat of the man with yellow eyes, the blob came into focus.

A land-baron shipwreck.

My nose was instantly hit with the smell of rotting fish and decaying wood. I could only guess this was the home of the Sand Pirates.

Chapter XX

THE CAPTAIN

I was pulled from the cage by the man with yellow eyes. He tugged on my clothes, almost ripping them with his grotesquely long fingernails. I towered over his small figure so much I could see the top of his balding head. His wicked smile and foul odor made me wince as he dragged me close. The wind picked up outside of the diamond box, unfortunately in his favor. It carried the smell right in my direction, making my stomach weak. Coupled with the poison still in my body, it caused me to almost lose my balance. This made it easier for him to direct me onto the ship without a fight.

I thought it would be best to stay quiet. I'd be able to hold my breath for longer periods of time if I did. To no surprise, there was no sound of retaliation coming from behind me. Tev was still trapped in the cage.

Grabbing at my clothes, the man with yellow eyes started to drag me by my chained hands. I entered the decaying ship through a large opening on the side. The wood looked rotten, cracked and split in multiple places. It was set to crumble in the slightest breeze.

Floorboards, holes of decaying wood mixed with sharp splinters, provided a path for us to walk. Before I could really take note of the details below deck, I was commanded to ascend a narrow staircase. I ducked my head at the top. When I lifted my head, the bright sunlight cast a spotlight on me. It blinded me as I stepped onto the main deck. The man with the yellow eyes had landed a second before and yanked my hands forward. My feet stumbled after him in succession. I was too distracted to see if Tev made it on board. My eyes adjusted to the light and there were rows of men.

I walked into a market, and I was the main swine.

The chatter between the men on the main deck fell to whispers. I was too far from the staircase to hear Tev's feet shuffling on floorboards or his own set of clanking chains. There was no sign that he was still with me.

Multiple masts large enough to graze the clouds stood proud in a sea of yellow-eyed men. I quickly realized that the stench coming from my captor was a trend among the crew of the ship. I held my breath in long intervals to keep from emptying my stomach on the main deck. Booming ropes scooped down from above, the largest of them housed at the center. There were many men, dressed in leathers around their chests and legs.

Fashion I hadn't seen before, if I'd want to call it that.

I thought it odd, to say the least.

Some men wore face coverings, protecting their skin from the sun. It didn't help much because the skin around their eyes and cheeks was tinted black and brown from long sunny days. I attempted to remember the ones without head dressings. The chatter between them turned to whistles as I drew deeper into the crowd. I halted their daily duties for a moment as I was paraded through them.

There was one man with an exceptionally round face. He stood taller than the rest of the men. I made eye contact with his canary yellow ones. Watching my every move, he kept his focus on me when someone nudged him about an offer. Didn't bother to look down at his friends, who began whistling and hollering around him.

Another man began shaking his leg up and down. The motion caught my eye, as I thought it was an obscene gesture, but he had been tapping his wooden leg on the floorboard to make noise. He sat rounder and squatter than the others on a box. His hair was exceptionally white. Even at a quick glance, I could see white hair poking out of his ears.

There weren't any women aboard that I could see. If there were any, I doubted they would help me.

My captor tugged at my chained hands to keep me in step with him. The crew thought this an appropriate time to appraise the prize set for auction. They began to reach out and grab at my short hair. Dirt was caked under their fingernails, some disgustingly long enough to scratch my face as the man with yellow eyes guided me through. Up close, I could see the color of their skin wasn't inherently black; their blackened palms were from dirt and feces. I looked down to find sand-covered mud—or what looked to be mud—between the splintering surface of the deck. It began to coat my shoes.

The man with yellow eyes walked me like a pet to the center mast. Whistles and shouts settled to mumbles while the man leading me in shackles addressed them.

"Where the cap'n be? I have a prize for him."

A door on rusted hinges creaked open behind the crowd. One by one, dirty, dingy men parted the way. Another man with heavy boots slowly stepped in our direction. I could hear his heavy footsteps and spurs clattering before laying an eye on him. His presence caused a quiet stir among the crew.

"Ah, cap'n, I found something worth your time."

The captain dissected the sea of men, creating an open circle around me and my captor. He wore a strange hat; its brim shaded his face so I couldn't see any details.

His body, a sculpture of muscle, looked to be stronger than Tev. Maybe even Thadeous. His hair, bleached by days in the sun, snaked out from the hat to provide coverage on his neck. He wore a leather vest like the crew, except his was clean; dirt seemed to evade him altogether. The vest exposed his sun-kissed and tan arms. His hand was resting through a belt loop. The belt with a large brass emblem was the focal point of his attire. Lastly, his weapon was secured in the holster at his hip, a symbol to his crew of dominance and utter importance.

I looked out of the corner of my eye to see the crew's reaction to their captain. They appeared frozen in time, awestruck by the captain's appearance on their deck. Mouths gaped open as he stood before them; they were surprised he emerged from his quarters in the first place.

The man holding my restraints explained the situation, "I stumbled upon her holed up in a cavern, side by side with a Lover boy. She's even dressed like 'em too, probably a spy for the court." His tone was persuasive, trying to swindle the captain into a good deal.

The captain, still watching our feet, was unimpressed by the man with the yellow eyes. I didn't know if I should be frightened or relieved.

Men surrounding us started to whisper. I overheard numbers throughout the crowd and caught other men counting with their fingers, as if they had the option at an auction if the captain didn't approve. The taller man with the round head continued to stare while the others around him negotiated deals.

"Cap'n, I assure you—" the man with yellow eyes began to speak before being cut off by the captain.

With a raise of his hand, the captain reached in his pocket in search of something.

A sack clanked on the floorboard, landing at the foot of the yellow-eyed man, thrown by the captain himself. My captor fell to his knees to count the blessed money. Fawning over the smell of metal in the bag, he rose to his feet to thank the captain with a bow. The man with yellow eyes shoved me toward the captain before retreating back into the crowd.

The captain's back was already turned, leaving the scene. The spurs clinked as they made their way back to the captain's quarters, a definite signal of disinterest in his latest purchase.

Stunned by the indifference, I stood still in the crowd. I didn't know if I was supposed to follow him or not.

Before long, I had a swarm of dirty men grabbing at my hair again. I didn't have a choice now. I followed the captain so I wouldn't be devoured by the crowd. I caught a glimpse of the captain whispering something into the ear of one of the crewmembers beside the door from which he had emerged. Another short and stocky fellow raised his voice to repeat the captain's words, "The cap'n wants her in his chamber, lads."

A collective *hurrah* erupted on the main deck. The men were congratulating the captain and joined in merriment by high-fiving the others around.

I was shoved in the direction of my new master by fingernails that scratched my back through my clothes. I obliged, considering the alternative that would be forced upon me if I didn't.

The chambers smelled of musk and cigars, a combination of someone who hasn't bathed and smoke from cloves. Fortunately, the smell emanating from the yellow-eyed man was worse in comparison.

Upon looking around, I saw the battered exterior was not mirrored in the captain's chamber. His quarters were well kept and seemed relatively new. The wood flooring wasn't chipped or rotten as I had seen on the main deck. Panels constructing the walls were uniformly cut and stained a dark tawny color, providing a sophisticated look to the captain's quarters.

A large wooden desk matching the walls was placed at the back of the cabin. On the top was a map with interesting looking instruments I had never seen before. One was metal and pointy. Another was round, creating two bubbles side by side. One of the instruments looked like a scope, perhaps something to use when peering at great distances. Maybe to see the stars better, or even the horizon at sunrise or sunset. I wondered how long it'd been since the ship felt the ocean's spray or the last time the crew felt the sensation of water. Based on their appearance, my guess was decades.

The captain didn't pay me much attention. I figured he was eager to see me undress based on the fact he paid the yellow-eyed man the equivalent of my yearly salary in coins. Instead, he opened a wardrobe built into the wall. He plucked a piece of clothing from it and without a word, placed it on a nearby chair. He walked over to his desk and took a ring full of keys from the drawer. The chains around my hands rattled as I watched the captain stride closer to me, stalking me as if he was the predator and I was the prey.

This was the first time I was able to see his face from under his hat. Immediately, I noticed his eyes. Never before had I seen eyes like that—a piercing blue, muddled with a layer of brown. Both eyes contained this mutation. Half brown, half blue. He looked younger than I expected. His body was that of a father, but his face hadn't matured from youth. Strong jawline and cheekbones with a prominent nose and ruby lips. He was handsome, but strange.

My heart raced, even though I anticipated his next move. As I suspected, he unlocked the cuffs, releasing my hands from the chains for good. He tossed the keys back on the table. The noise caused me to jump. Before I knew it, the captain escaped to his canopy bed tucked in the corner and shifted his hat to cover his eyes for a midday nap.

I made myself as unnoticeable as possible. I stood confused for a moment before hearing the sound of snores echoing in the room. Taking that as a sign of privacy, I strode over to the dress he picked for me. The dress was a dusty mustard yellow. It wouldn't be something I would pick for myself, but I was happy to put it on. Looking around, but not touching anything, I was scared to wake the sleeping pirate. I stripped off the maroon uniform to gladly replace it with a fresh set of clothes.

As the golden fabric grazed my head, a shower of cleanliness came with it. I could feel my tangled hair freed from any knots, as well as my fingernails polished to match the dress. Its loose fit was hemmed to the correct measurements seconds after I straightened up. A perfect fit. I was left gaping at what had just happened, startled by another snore from the captain. I folded my uniform neatly, setting it behind the partition and out of the way, hoping I would forget about it soon enough.

There were chests scattered about the floor, overflowing with crystals colored similarly to the giant box that brought me here. Amongst the crystals were gems of different shapes and sizes and colors. Emeralds with wild greens, sapphires like the sky and sea, and rubies matching the color of blood. I was reminded of the dome in Grand Forum in the Estate. When the sun would hit it just right, the floor of the foyer would dance with color, coming alive for only a moment.

Passing the captain's bed, I was sure to watch my movements with my new dress. I made my way to the rear of the cabin in order to get a better look at the map sitting on the desk. In contrast to Tev's map, there was a more detailed version of the House of Patience sitting before me.

I peered down, taking in as much information as I possibly could. The map showed an outline of the House of Patience, the same diagram Bramwell depicted in his books. The hourglass shape was easy to spot on any map. Lying flat on its side, it was meant to express the limitless patience that coursed through the House. Clearly labeled near the center of the House was the only thing I knew about the HoPat, simply by my experience when first entering the House.

The Postuells were written over a bit of land stretching farther than I originally anticipated throughout the House. There were other names I could decipher after walking miles within the House. Names like Glassblade Range and the Endless River. I could only assume those were the areas where Tev and I journeyed through before getting caught by the yellow-eyed man.

The closer I looked at the map, the more I found. There was a marking with different colored ink in middle of the area called The Dunes of Decay. A chicken scratch of a boat and single flag had marked the location of the ship where I currently resided.

It was labeled as The Sandshadow.

There were other names on the eastern side of the House that I didn't recognize, like Mirage Heights and Scorchfang Range and Glactus Garden. However, something else caught my eye with a closer inspection. There were two maps on the desk, one stacked on top of the other. As I lifted the map of the HoPat to get a better angle, a voice from under the hat spoke simultaneously. "Don't touch that."

I gasped and stepped away from the table, releasing the parchment paper. Rounding the corner, I anticipated seeing the captain's face for the second time. The captain still lay with his head tilted back under the cover of his brimmed hat.

Braving to speak a word, I said, "Thank you for the dress."

Without hesitation, he responded, "I didn't tell you to speak."

I was baffled but snapped back without hesitation, "You can't speak to me like that."

"Yes, I can," he said confidently, "I own you."

I scoffed, wishing I had the wit to think of something snarky to say back, but nothing came to mind. It was only a reminder that I wasn't in control.

Nevertheless, I combated his wishes. I pursued a conversation. "Where did my friend go?"

As fast as lightning, the captain sat up, removing his hat from his face. He had youthful skin with slicked back hair highlighted with natural streaks. For a second, I was completely distracted by his lips and strong jaw. He had dark lashes that contrasted against the most unique eyes I had ever seen. His left was a soft blue, the color of ice, spotted with dots of mud brown and the other was bisected brown and blue. Beau Bokehart had competition for the most beautiful man alive after this man showed his face. I never would have guessed a captain of dingy and disgusting pirates to be young and, dare I say it, attractive.

Just as I was judging his features, he looked at every inch of my appearance in the dress he picked. Reclining his head back without the cover of his hat, he said, "What do I have to do to shut that pretty little mouth of yours?"

I willed myself to refrain from blushing, to stay focused on the task at hand. I reminded myself this man paid for me to be a servant. "I need you to tell me where my friend is."

He responded, now his eyes closed, attempting to relax, "Probably dead or soon to be dead if I had to guess."

I couldn't let Tev die without me trying to save him. "Take me to him. Now!"

"You're not in any position to be making demands," he retorted unenthusiastically.

"What do you want from me? Why did you pay that man money for me if you aren't going to even look at me?"

"I have my reasons, darlin'."

"Care to share?"

"No," he said matter-of-factly.

Retaliating, I ran to the closest chest of jewels, dumping its contents out on the floor.

There was no reaction from the captain.

I went to the next chest and emptied it the same.

Again, no reaction.

I did not stop until every chest of gold and gems and crystals was completely emptied onto the floor.

The captain did not move. I swore I could have heard the faintest snoring under the hat instead.

Rage began to heat my cheeks. With no other option, I ran toward the bed. Crossing the threshold of the nook where the bed resided, I heard a cling and clunk over my shoulder. Before taking another step, I glanced behind me to find the disaster I created completely wiped away.

Every gem and jewel found its home inside the chests again, this time neater than before my outburst. All of them were sealed with a clasp matching the metal of the captain's buckle. The floor was swept spotless; not even the dust from outside the quarters could be seen.

My attention and curiosity landed on the captain. "Who are you?"

Ignoring the question, he snarked, "Honestly, what does a man have to do to get some sleep around here?"

"Answer the question and I'll let you have your peace," I negotiated. Hopefully, he would take the bait.

"Riperous, Pillar of Persistence for the House of Patience."

My eyes widened.

Just my luck, another Pillar.

"Now," he continued, "shut that mouth of yours, before I do—and trust me, you do not want that."

Abiding by our agreement, I did as I was told.

Chapter XXI

THE INITIATION

The day continued with little conversation between me and the captain. I curled into a ball on one of the plush chairs in the cabin. Reluctant to close my eyes in the presence of a Pillar, I couldn't help but nod my head and drift into a place where I felt safe.

I dreamed of being back at the Adora with her gears and clanks and rhythm. The beats pounded my heart like it did the giant clock. I could feel the vibrations even in my dreams, my veins pumping blood to my hands and feet, synchronizing to the beat of her. My friends were scattered in the gears, fine-tuning and testing various things.

I was home and for a second, I forgot the tragedy that was my life. The horror I had found in exile and the darkness that seemed to be getting closer. I planted my feet on the metal walkway and refused to move for anything or anyone.

A large bang caused my eyes to open, and my body jerked. I was back in the presence of the Pillar. A dirty, scrawny man came into focus as my slumber receded. He handed a note on a folded piece of paper to the captain. The captain opened it to find a message.

A smile grew on his face. He threw the paper in the air and gripped the little man tightly around the shoulders. It wasn't a malicious grab, but a joyous one. As the paper floated down, I caught a glimpse of the words: It is time.

"Come," the captain said to me. "We have a party to attend."

His smile was villainous, like he wickedly enjoyed the anticipation of what was to come.

Not moving at his desired pace, he took my hand, and I jumped from my seat. His hand was cold. Chilling but strong and powerful—nothing would come to compare.

The starved man opened the door for the Pillar and together we made our way out to the main deck. Towed past the stairs I had ascended earlier that day, we made our way to the back of the ship. We passed the main mast and several disgusting crew members. The closer I looked, the more I understood. Their skin was in a state of decay. It was peeling, shriveling, and dead on the surface of their bodies, and yet it seemed to faze no one. I wanted to crawl out of my own skin just at the sight of them.

A part of me wanted to cry for them. They were the darkness that Adonis warned me about. Their eyes warned me that evil lingered here.

And the daggers of ice holding my hand were confirmation.

The captain swung open a door leading to what I assumed was another cabin but at the front of the ship. I was wrong. The door exposed mustard-colored velvet curtains. He threw them aside and stepped forward with his arms outstretched. He boomed with a belly laugh simultaneously.

A performance—for whom I was not yet certain.

My intrigue soon turned to horror when thunder sounded beyond the Pillar. A roar like that of a crowd.

I carefully followed his path. Through the curtains, I stood on a balcony to accompany the show-king. There were two throne-like chairs waiting for us; however, the Pillar was too preoccupied to even notice them. He kept on with his waving and gesturing for more noise, more applause, more glory.

A spotlight beamed on the two of us. I was blinded but the Pillar instinctively grabbed my hand and threw it in the air to complement his own. Another wave of roars came over us. As my eyes adjusted, I could see an arena before me, one I would think was impossible to be contained in a ship this size. It defied the laws of science and logic, but I bore witness to it.

Beyond the balcony, rows upon rows of seats were filled by the decaying crew. Most of them were shouting and encouraging the spectacle of the Pillar, their attention never drifting from the showman. Mesmerized, they egged on the Pillar more by the second.

I took notice of the arena floor. Live animals, a herd of cattle, minding their own business and chewing on hay.

The crowd quieted when two gates at either end of the arena opened.

The Pillar shoved me into my seat, and I landed with a thump, knocking the wind out of me and disorienting me again. I could hear the Pillar yell. Something was emerging from the gates. Another rush of roars came from the crowd; this time, the sound stung my head. I peered over the balcony's edge for a better look only to find a man riding a rust-colored stallion. Broad shoulders. Tawny hair. It was a man that I had come to appreciate in my time in the desert House.

It was *Tev*.

My eyes grew wide as he carefully marched into the arena. The gates began to close behind him, and the Pillar finally spoke.

"Gentlemen," he addressed the crew with another round of open arms. "We come today to witness the passage of eternity onto another. With our pride, we gleefully accept this young man into the brotherhood of the fallen. May the decay in your soul translate to that of your flesh."

Another cheer.

"Ride your steed into death, my friend!" The Pillar now spoke to Tev.

The crowd began to chant, urging Tev to usher the horse closer to the other gate. I needed to stand to see the other end of the arena. I saw a yellow-eyed man sitting atop a skeleton creature, the same one that brought us to the ship. I realized the man was the taller man, the one with the rounder face that couldn't take his attention away from me when I first arrived. Now, his attention was on Tev, beckoning him toward a supposed living death.

The Pillar sat, exhausted by his part in this performance but watching eagerly to see the ritual begin.

"I always love welcoming our newest arrivals with the thoroughwights," the Pillar mumbled under his breath, loud enough for me to hear.

A tinge of fear sparked in my chest. I hoped I wouldn't face the same fate as Tev. I started to record Tev's every move, learning how to counteract the initiation in case I was thrown down there too.

Tev's horse reared on his hind legs and began to neigh. The neighboring animals scattered to avoid being crushed by the horse's legs. The stallion knew what kind of danger it was headed into, and it wanted no part in it. I couldn't help but watch the other creature, learning how it moved and thought.

The thoroughwight crept closer to the full-blooded stallion.

Slow.

Patient.

Like it already knew the horse would die.

Waiting for the attack to come, Tev seemed to calm the horse enough to look up toward me and the captain on the balcony.

"I'm not doing this, Riperous." Tev used the Pillar's name. "You cannot force me into darkness when I have the light."

Sitting back in his chair still, the Pillar muttered under his breath, "Watch me."

Another sinister smile sketched across his face. He waited a second longer before instructing the thoroughwight and its rider, "Take him!"

The skeleton horse darted across the arena faster than any living animal I've seen. Tev must have expected this because he moved with great agility through the other livestock on the dusty field floor. Breaking left and right around the herd to escape the grip of the thoroughwight, his hands reached around his back for something. In a second, he was looping rope in the air, trying to aim for a different creature.

He courageously dodged the man on the skeleton, but not for long.

Tev launched his rope for a head, and it landed. He tied a knot on the saddle, and the momentum carried the horse into a compromising position. The animal Tev's rope hooked onto was stronger and behind him and his horse. Tev's horse instinctively heeled the ground, trying its best to stop without getting hurt, but the force was too much. Both its front legs snapped at the knee, and a horrible cry came from the horse. It bowed as if it was saying one last prayer and Tev was launched into a sea of hides. The rider on the thoroughwight came as fast as light and cut the rope connecting the two animals. In one swoop, he managed to cut the rope and turn around, pulling a pistol from his holster at his chest. He shot the stallion behind the eye and its body went limp thereafter.

"Oh! No way!" the captain yelled in amazement. He began clapping at the performance by the rider.

As for Tev, he managed to escape the thoroughwight, but not its rider. The large man found him hiding amongst the herd and brought him into the spotlight. Facing the balcony where the Pillar and I sat, he projected, "Cap'n, what fate do ye see for this swine?"

Tev was being held by the collar of his shirt. I almost wanted to yell at him to try to run, but his body looked weak. He looked damaged and broken and crushed. And where was he to hide?

The Pillar stood to address the rider.

"Bravo, bravo." He clapped slowly, not for the rider, but for Tev. "Attempting to escape a cursed life."

The crowd started to boo, spitting and cursing in between.

"I've made up my mind," the Pillar stated.

He held up his hand to quiet the crew.

"You, soldier," the Pillar said, "You shall not be honored with a curse."

He smiled sinisterly.

"But with *life*."

For the first time this evening, I made a point to look directly at the Pillar. I couldn't move from my seat, but I wished I had the power to burn my stare into his brain.

"The life I bless you with will be a life in which you wish for a cursed one," the Pillar breathed. He said it in such a casual way that I thought we were back in his cabin talking over tea, but instead it was amplified for all to hear.

"Take him out of my sight," he concluded.

Just as instructed, the rider walked Tev through the same gate he entered.

"You're a monster," I whispered, still staring at the back of the Pillar's head.

Spinning on his heel, he lowered himself to meet me face to face. He placed one hand on the arm of the chair and the other under my chin. He whispered, "You'd be lucky if you were *only* dealing with a monster."

Chapter XXII

PILLAR OF PERSISTENCE

After the performance in the arena, the Pillar brought me back to his quarters for dinner. At the chime of a grandfather clock, hidden in the corner, members of the crew waltzed into the cabin to set the table with food. Lavish and luxurious heaps of fruits and meat and bread were brought in for the captain to have his pick.

I sat in another plush chair waiting for the Pillar's instructions. I hadn't eaten a proper meal since the fish a few nights ago. I itched at the chance to snag a bite of something, but if I had learned anything about Pillars, I learned that *everything comes at a price*.

If not my life, then my existence in the House itself.

The sun was beginning to set in the desert sky. The sunflower yellow glass constructed the windowpane. It brought warmth to the space, not only in color but also temperature. The temperature grew warmer in the room as the sun filled it, causing my body to become sticky and sweaty. The heat must have gotten to the Pillar too. I saw him take a handkerchief to his temple, patting sweat while sitting at his desk.

He joined me in the common area. His stride was set for the table of food, before stopping at the sight of me, shocked by my presence. I sat patiently, waiting to be instructed.

"You are still here?"

Using his terms, I couldn't hold my sass when I said, "You own me."

"Well, don't just sit there, join me for dinner," he commanded.

Practically jumping out of my seat, I followed him to the table full of food. From what I saw the men bring in from outside, I wanted to try the meat first. Its smell had livened the room with smoky and savory goodness, leaving me salivating in my seat. While the captain chose the place setting closest to us, I was left with the one up against the wall. There was not much room between the wall and the table for me to comfortably sit, but with a meal like this one, I wasn't about to complain.

Knowing my manners, I waited for the Pillar to take his first bite before I even reached for food for my own plate.

The meat was delicious. Its exterior was covered in a sauce, a sweet one with a touch of spice. It left my fingers sticky. I licked it off, loving the leftovers on my skin. The captain took note of it and asked, "When was the last time you ate something?"

The hours had blended together at this point. I responded with a curt shrug.

In response, the captain stood from the table. He opened a cabinet tucked away from plain view. His grin proclaimed he was the only one to know about this secret hideout. He removed a bottle from the cabinet with one hand, then grabbed two glasses with the other. Placing them on the table, he poured me a drink.

"When's the last time you had something to drink?" he asked.

I shrugged again, unwilling to give a true answer. I could smell the tang coming off of the bottle. *Rum.* The truth was, in the garden with Jeston, we split the bottle of wine. But out here, there was more danger in taking a sip. I didn't want to give the darkness even more reason to pay my soul a visit.

He offered the poured glass to me. I shook my head, rejecting his offer.

"I would advise you to think about this decision." The tone of a Pillar. One that dared me to cross him and think of the consequences if I chose poorly.

"I don't want to drink it," I said with a stern voice.

"That's too bad, sweetheart. You don't have a choice," he commented.

He lifted the bottle to fill the second glass. A double pour to the one he handed me. He patiently waited for me to take it. I guess I was up against a master of patience. I only had stubbornness on my side.

Picking up on my silence, he offered, "How about I make you a deal?"

I raised my eyebrows to show my intrigue.

"If you have a drink with me, I will see if your friend survived his visit to the low deck."

This could be my way out. I also wanted to make sure Tev was safe.

Testing the waters, I wanted to see how much I could get out of this deal and see how weak this Pillar was in comparison to the ones I'd dealt with before. "I'll have a drink with you if you take me to see him."

He raised his glass, adding a condition to my terms. "We drink the bottle first then."

I took hold of my drink and struck the edge of his. Downing the contents in one sip, I hoped I wouldn't regret my decision.

The captain refilled my glass. The sting and burn down my throat made me cough. After a couple more I was numb to the pain, which disappeared altogether after my third or fourth or fifth drink.

My worries about the days of darkness faded fast, glass after glass. The alcohol's effect created a lack of feeling and a lack of awareness. I was pursuing a new form of freedom. I was able to let my guard down with no care in the world, for the first time in ages.

My head swirled. The candle lights hanging from the walls flashed past as we danced to the music of the grandfather clock. The food was a blur too; I stuffed my face with more than enough. I hardly remember the taste, only the feeling of my mouth being full at all times. I couldn't decipher whether it was because of the food or because of the booze.

While he was filling our glasses with the last drops of the bottle, I tiptoed to the map of Patience at the captain's desk. An upholstered chair with a high backing was plated in gold.

A Pillar's true throne.

I had seen three just like it a few days ago in the House of Love.

I fell backwards into it as the Pillar handed me my last drink. We laughed in unison before the swig of rum hit the back of my throat. This time, no burn. I kicked my feet, throwing them over the arm of the chair. He didn't approve, signaling me to stand and move out of the way. I did as I was told, only to stumble, almost tipping over the clock that annoyingly chimed.

The Pillar crashed down with heavy, dead weight. He reached for my hips, pulling me toward him. I didn't care enough to fight him on it. After all, he was the most attractive man I'd ever seen. I sat in his lap as he combed through my hair, pushing it out of my face.

"You are more lively than any of the other women," he stated.

Something in the back of my mind didn't appreciate the backhanded compliment, yet I continued allowing him to touch me.

This was the closest I'd been to seeing his face. Where in daylight, he was youthful and muscular, in this lighting, he had developed wrinkles. Crow's feet around his bicolored eyes and lines around his mouth aged him unkindly. His other hand, resting on my thigh, was inching higher and higher by the second. A part of me cringed at the feeling of his touch, but another part of me wanted to give in.

I saw an easy escape when I noticed our empty glasses sitting at the edge of the desk. Standing from his lap, I went in search of another bottle of alcohol in his cabinet. He watched me stumble through the cabin full of jewels to the secret storage spot. More rum. I returned, bottle in hand, to find the captain passed out in the chair. His deep breaths were choppy due to the concavity of his body.

Circling the table, I counted his breaths before lifting the map drawn out in front of him. Even with the vast amount of alcohol in my system, I could see why the map was hidden from prying eyes.

Picking the first layer off the table, I saw another map, this one in the shape of a shepherd's hook. Its southern border was marked by three concentric circles depicting the coves and curves of the House of Goodness. I saw Tev draw a similar shape in the gravel only a few nights ago.

However, on this map, in blue ink there was a drawing of a crown etched at the center of the circles. The sight of the crown sparked a memory.

An Aluna operator reciting an old fable—a tale about a lost soul looking for a crown and gems. I lifted my eyes wearily to the cases of hand-crafted stones around the cabin.

Was this man the lost soul?

Underneath the shepherd's hook was another parchment. I lifted the second layer to find a completed map of the entire kingdom. I set the bottle on the table to study it. I interpreted as best I could with blurring vision.

With my back turned to the captain, his breaths became softer, quieter. I couldn't see his eyes, but I heard his voice. "I told you not to touch that."

Releasing the parchments, I retreated from the table and, better yet, from the Pillar.

The table, now separating our bodies, was the only thing maintaining space between us. The captain stood, crashing his thigh into the side of the table. All at once the illusion collapsed—he grew a gut and his once flowing hair thinned into a few strands holding on for dear life. A foul odor leaked from his body. The remnants of his soul, I'm sure.

I stumbled back, not from the rum, but from the surprise of his sudden change in appearance. This wasn't the same man who combed through my hair minutes ago; that man was young, almost trustworthy. This man was an elder. A man of severe decay. A dead man walking.

He noticed my repugnance. "What? You don't like the look of me?"

His voice was different too.

Deeper.

More *threatening*.

I kept my head from moving, but my eyes must have given me away. I didn't want to be near this man any longer. A darkness I had never known haunted this man.

As I stepped backwards toward the door, the Pillar forced the desk out of the way. The full bottle of rum fell to the ground, spilling the contents.

He shouted, "Where do you think you are going?"

I backed into the door. Reaching for the knob instinctively, I darted out of the room at a slight turn. Hopefully that would stop him long enough for me to think of a plan.

The deck was nearly empty. A few strangers patrolled lazily, drifting like wandering tumbleweeds across the desert floor.

I had no time to waste. Running for the staircase, I climbed down to land my feet on a rotten board. Grabbing hold of the railing, I yanked my leg free and consciously chose my next steps. I could hear above me the captain's footsteps. They were heavy and loud and haphazard. He was drunk and lost.

As was I.

Finding Tev was my main goal. He would protect me. He would save me. I rushed past bunks of sleeping pirates. They swayed in hammocks peacefully, unaware of the beast I had awoken above. There was no sign of the Aluna operator. Another hole, a ladder, led me deeper into the ship. Taking a risk, I chose to climb down in hopes of finding rescue.

I lost my footing on the last rung of the ladder. Crashing to the base floor, my hands took most of my fall. It was colder than the one above, retaining the cool ocean temperatures from its time at sea. Cold enough to feel a distinction, but not cold enough to see my breath. I held my arms close to my chest and walked gingerly through the ship, wary of my steps and the sounds I made. I prayed the Pillar's intoxication prohibited him from thinking of looking elsewhere on his ship.

Past another ladder I saw jail cells. A whistle from the darkness stiffened my joints. The man to my right sat in a cell. He was missing his right arm. A torch lit his cell. With his left hand, he grabbed the metal, showing part of a knuckle missing from the hand as well. He stood to inspect me like I was his next victim.

"Wren?" Just beyond the man with missing limbs, I heard the sweet familiar voice.

"Tev?" I whispered.

"Wren, I'm back here!" Excitement filled my alcohol clotted veins. "Look for the key. The jailer put it on a hook out there."

I followed the instructions to the best of my impaired ability. Another whistle pulled my attention back to the jailed man. He was pointing to a hook, too high for him to reach, but just outside his cell. Snaking it off the hook, I nodded a reluctant thanks to him.

Stumbling toward Tev's cell, I turned the key with the help of Tev's hands through the grates of the jail. He almost tackled me with a hug upon exiting, followed by cupping my face and checking for any injuries or cuts or bruises.

Seeing me lose my balance not once but twice, Tev was led to question, "Are you drunk?"

"Yes. I need your help," I slurred.

Taking my impairment into account, I could sense Tev was planning an escape. I staggered into his chest. He caught me and I said, "This one isn't like the others."

Distancing my body from his, he assessed my state. "Can you run?"

I didn't want to lie. It was hard for me to stand, but I made it down to the jails without being seen or heard. "I'm good," I said, trying to convince myself and Tev.

He winced at the smell of my breath. "Don't worry, we will get you out of here. Get you some . . . water."

"Tev, there is another problem."

Heavy steps pounded above. Time was ticking down before the Pillar found me.

"What?" He waited to hear what obstacle stood between him and his freedom from this hell.

"The captain—"

At that moment, the bald-headed, elder man collided with the bottom level of the ship. I shrieked, sobering up right then and there. Tev spun me behind him.

"What are you doing with my servant?" the Pillar yelled.

"We are leaving, Riperous," Tev said.

"I'd like to see you try," argued the Pillar, castling up to Tev.

The soldier stood his ground. I'd seen it before—soldier versus Pillar—and knew how it ended. I wasn't going to allow the same result to come out of this encounter.

I whispered to Tev, speaking close to his back, "Play along. Be fast when you get a free shot."

Tev's hand gave a thumbs-up, signaling to me he was on board with whatever plan I had conjured up.

I stepped out from behind him, addressing the Pillar. "Where am I? Oh, sugarplums, where did you take me? This isn't the bow like you promised."

The Pillar, perplexed by my comment, didn't know what to say next. Faking an appalled look toward Tev, I pranced over into the arms of the monster. At the feeling of my body pressed against his, the man held me tighter. His eyes never veered from Tev, however.

Detecting his awareness, I set another trap. "You saved me." Giggling with folly, I offered a reward. "Kiss me."

I could feel Tev's body stiffening at my command.

The disgusting creature planted one on my lips.

I tried my best not to wince at his putrid breath. Our lips only touched for a second longer before Tev was cutting off the circulation to the Pillar's head. His barbaric eyes rolled back and his body dropped to the floor. Tev guided his body down to the ground until he knew he wouldn't wake up anytime soon.

Knowing we were in the clear, I retched. From the rum and overstuffing my stomach with food to interlocking lips with a vile animal, I couldn't help it. Tev patted my back and pulled the loose strands of hair from my face. Once I was done, I wiped any remaining vomit or snot from my face.

"Feel better?" he asked.

I only gave a nod.

Chapter XXIII

ESCAPING THE SHADOW OF SAND

"We've been walking for days! There's nothing out here!" My voice was hoarse from dehydration. It was barely audible with the distance between Tev and myself. I would be surprised if he heard me.

"It's not much longer, Wren," he shouted over his shoulder. "We just need to pass that hill."

He pointed to the next mountain of sliding sand.

I fell to my knees at the thought of it. The sand had drained me. It was two days since we fled from the Sandshadow.

Just one more hill.

We are almost there.

That had been Tev's mantra since we left. Sinking deeper into the uneven sand, I fell, catching myself with a soft landing on sand. It crept into the cuts of my dried skin and lips, ripping them further apart. Glancing over his shoulder, Tev found me with my face to the ground. I had no desire to move. I didn't care if the heat from below would blister my skin. I was done.

I envied Tev's stamina. He was noticeably tired but still had the will to keep going, blindly trusting the next hill was sure to be the meadows of the House of Goodness.

Trudging through the sand, he sank next to me on his knees. His shadow shielded me from the hot sun. "Wrenna, please don't give up. We are almost there." He tried to encourage me, but I was hopeless.

Seeing him out of the corner of my eye, unable to lift my head, I spoke to the blur in front of me.

"We are never going to find it, Tev. We left the ship two days ago. We haven't eaten. We've barely slept. We are going to die out here."

"There's always hope," he argued. "We will find a way out. The darkness wants us to die out here to stop the pursuit of the crown. We can't let that happen."

Tev helped me to my feet by grabbing my upper arm and hoisting me up. My feet could barely withstand the weight of my body. Subsequently, with each step, pain seared through my aching bones. Tev held my arm to stabilize me, carrying not only half of my weight but his whole weight as well.

How was he so resilient?

How did he still have hope?

I could see his hope after the sun went down. He made sure we at least made it through the night. He protected me at all costs.

The scorching sand in the daylight turned into a cool desert at night. The chill made us sleep close to one another. I almost buried myself in the sand to keep warm until Tev decided to embrace me. Where I was shivering, he was stable. His warmth allowed me to relax through the night and his presence gave me a peace that I was going to live.

We wouldn't have survived the night if we were apart. I'd like to think I contributed to his survival as well. A purpose to stay alive and not give in to the vast, endless desert. I was glad to have his touch throughout the night too. Something to hold onto if and when my nightmares started. Something to ground me to hope, knowing he had some to spare.

With the combination of the whistles of wind on the sand and the howls of coyotes, my sleep was choppy. Both Tev and I tossed in the sand. Last night, I woke to find myself in a position nestled in his armpit with his face inches away from mine. I watched as his brow scrunched and furrowed as his mind dreamed of haunting horrors. Ones that made his body twitch, even in my presence and limited warmth.

The day and night blended together, but I could see the toll of those nightmares once the sun rose each day. But he still continued to have hope. He told me, "After years of training, the tests and trials we went through as brothers, there was a point where our bodies automatically knew what to do."

In times such as these—in times of distress—they know what to do. They would fight, and they would proceed, knowing the finish line would come.

Weakness had filled my life for so long. Weak with my discernment of my putting trust in the wrong people. Weak with no vision of a victorious future. Weak by allowing the world to navigate my thoughts and actions rather than by my own will. Weak physically, allowing people to force me into positions I did not want.

I don't want to be weak anymore.

I needed to force the darkness out like Tev had done. The light provided strength for him to live in the arena. I needed the light's strength now.

I could see the victory I had with light on my side. I knew I had to seek the light because the darkness would always seek me. My mission now was to find the crown the Pillar wanted. With the strength from the light, I could use the crown as leverage to establish a foothold of power. If I had power over a Pillar, my opportunities would be limitless.

If Tev could do it, so could I.

If Tev had hope, I could have hope too.

And if Tev had vision of victory, so could I.

At the base of the hill, we both looked up to the top. Looking at each other, without saying a word, we found our footing in the sand. Though it crumbled under our weight, we still managed to ascend. Tev let go of my arm to fight his own battle of sand falling out from under our feet. I fell to my hands and knees and began to crawl, lifting one leg at a time until I reached the top of the hill. My breath became deeper, wheezing in hot air. Sweat began to form on my temples.

Tev slipped a few times, sending him back to the starting line. He eventually stole my technique to manage the sand. I watched below as he fought to climb. His hands searched for a grip under the layers. Clenching something, he pulled himself higher.

He made it to the top and immediately planted his back into the sand. I lay next to him, tired and drained. Our breaths synced for a second, until his eventually slowed where mine kept its steady pace.

He lifted his head, smacking me with a loose hand to look in the same direction.

"I told you," he said snarky and out of breath, "just beyond the hill."

I peered to my left as sand found a new crevice and seeped into my ear. I winced at the uncomfortable feeling.

I found the grainy terrain, the one I'd come to hate these past couple of days, fading into a lush meadow of grass sprinkled with the colors of a rainbow. Sprouts, soaking in any ray of sunshine, stuck out between the pebbles and sand. Velvet greenery, a sight sweeter than candy, fell back into smooth rolling meadows, and flowers pranced on the edges of tomorrow.

"Took long enough." I confirmed it wasn't a mirage.

"I might have misjudged it a little," he countered, accepting his miscalculations.

I smirked. "A little?"

Before he had the chance to playfully smack me or tell me off, I tucked my arms to fly down the hill as fast as possible. Delusional and dizzy, I tumbled like a weed. The ground finally leveled out, causing me to come to a stop.

Tev wasn't far behind, following my lead again.

We both laughed before he helped me to my feet. I dusted off the sand that stuck to every inch of me. I wished this was the last time I would ever have to dust off sand. I wished never to feel it again. Its touch on my dry skin left cuts like glass. I wanted no more than to drown in a pool of water and to never have cracks on my face, hands, and feet again.

I didn't have to worry for much longer.

Crossing the border, where the desert met the green meadow, we took our first steps into the House of Goodness.

Or so I thought.

PART 3

Chapter XXIV

THE GOOD MEADOWS

I half expected to feel more sand under my feet, as if the House of Goodness was a hallucination all along.

Instead, we found a bubbling stream weaving through the grass. As we got closer there was an unspoken, mutual decision we would plant our feet, knees, hands, and faces into the wet mud. It covered our sores with silky, cool silt.

Where the river in the HoPat was lined with steep cliffs and mountain faces jetting high above, this stream grew flowers about its edges. Wild willabees sat happily by the water. Their delicate lavender petals and centers filled with pollen could be seen from far away in contrast to the grass.

Filthy and muddy, I sat on the bank to be cleansed of any lingering scorching sand. It was only a distant memory now. Soaking in the sun, recharged by the stream, we let our clothes dry. I struck up a conversation to pass the time.

"Do you know anything about the captain of that ship?" I thought back to Tev's forearm wrapped around the Pillar's throat and the thud echoing after the fight was won.

Tev had covered his eyes with his wet shirt. Not moving a muscle, he answered, "I know his name is Riperous. I know he runs the trading. He sends bounties out into the House to stalk and kidnap anyone they see; hence why we didn't see any tribes while we were in the HoPat. They were in hiding because of him."

"Why would the captain have bounty hunters?"

"Money. Power. Boredom even. The business itself is very lucrative." He shrugged and continued his thought, "I know he would either pay a decent price or trade them for another. The captain's men get paid a steep sum when they pick up someone interesting. I bet our uniforms gave away our value and importance."

I thought back to the man with the yellow eyes. He mentioned our House of Love uniforms, mine and Tev's, surely upping the interest of the captain, and it worked. I can still remember the thud those coins made when the captain purchased me. I wondered how valuable I must have been considering he hardly looked at me, paying the price he did.

He went on without waiting for me to ask. "The captain was by far the wealthiest man in the House, even after its collapse. He could burn money, and it wouldn't matter."

I remember the glittering jewels I threw about the cabin. The many chests full of gold and gems just sitting there. Sitting amongst the gems, it never occurred to me to wonder how he acquired so many of them. My fit of temporary rage blinded me from the truth.

Mumbling under my breath, I said, "Even the corrupt Pillars still have it easy."

Finishing with the section of boulders, Tev glanced back at me with a furrowed brow. "What do you mean?"

"The Pillars—they've never had a hard day in their lives." I said it with sarcasm but truly meant it. Even Jeston had everything handed to him on a silver platter.

"Why does it matter?" Tev sounded confused.

I thought it was easy to understand. Bewildered at the question, I stared at Tev, trying to find a way for him to understand.

He elaborated before I drew my conclusion. "Why do the Pillars have anything to do with it?"

He doesn't know.

He didn't know that man was one of the Pillars for the House of Patience. If I thought about it too hard, I wouldn't believe it myself.

I broke the news. "He is a Pillar, the Pillar of Persistence. For the House of Patience."

It was interesting; usually Tev was the one explaining things to me about the workings of Lost Lands and the creatures we encountered here. I liked being on the other side of it. Knowing more than him, especially about a place with so many deceptions.

Tev cocked his head to the side with an expression of realization. He pieced something together.

A secret of the Pillars.

Satisfied, he let out a little laugh. "The Fall of the House of Patience was set off by a Pillar abandoning his throne. Since then, only two Pillars rule in the Patian court. The Fall of the House of Patience was almost five centuries ago. The others in court tried to amend the House, sticking to traditions and coronations, churning out new Pillars when the candidacy ended. The cursed one became legend, lost to time. I didn't fully understand because if what you say is true, he still holds the third Pillar position."

I let my mouth drop open.

Tev went on to explain. "In the Pillars' by-laws set by the Forgotten King, it explicitly states that there must be three Pillars per House. It makes sense too, if you think about it—a house cannot stand with two pillars; it needs a third. I heard rumors from the tribes that he left to serve the darkness. The remaining two Pillars cursed their fallen brother because of his abandonment of the throne, ultimately causing the Fall of the HoPat."

I peered at Tev with bright eyes. "The captain's chair."

"What about it?"

"It was similar to the thrones of the House of Love Pillars. The two Pillars, resentful, probably sent him the throne along with the curse. A curse of immortality, perhaps? That's why he was looking for the crown."

Tev paused. "A crown? He is looking for a crown?"

"I saw a map on his desk. From my brief glance, there was a picture of the crown circled three times."

"Where?"

"The southern border of the House of Goodness where the shepherd's hook curves."

"The captain is looking for a curse-breaker. Trading people. Trading information." Tev finished my thought.

We strolled well into the House, conjuring up conspiracies about the crown and the darkness. We settled on a plan to search for the crown ourselves in the House of Goodness. I didn't know Tev's motive for finding it, but selfishly, I thought of it as a prize. A way of reconciliation with the Pillars. An offering for my freedom or even a reinstatement as Foreman of the Adora.

Passing a grove and surveying the area, Tev said, "We'll rest here for the night."

We were about two hours away from sunset. A little early to declare this as our campsite, but he was the expert in this area, not me.

"I'll see what animals I can find, if you want to start building a fire."

He pulled his fire starter from his back pocket, trusting I wouldn't lose it.

I spent the next hour collecting enough wood to burn through the night. My time outside the gates of the House of Love has taught me how much to collect for a comfortable night. My fingers turned to ice with the moisture in the air and from most of the wood, a contrast to the desert sun and dryness I had become accustomed to. Building a pit of river rocks to conceal the fire, I waited for Tev to round the bend with hunted animals in hand.

The light was almost gone before he returned with a black and white animal hanging by its tail. Its distinct sharp claws and stripe down the center of its back didn't help me identify it. As Tev got closer to the fire, I saw blood dripping from his face.

I jumped to attention, giving assistance where he needed it. He brushed me off to the side, grabbing for his striker from the fire starter set.

"What happened?" I asked.

"I had to wrestle this bastard from his hole. He caught me off guard and clawed me. I broke its neck in retaliation."

I ripped the worn hem of the dress Riperous gave me. A few paces away, I soaked it in the stream, wringing it out on my walk back to the fire. Kneeling next to Tev, I pressed the cloth against his cheek where the scratches bled. He winced but I kept the pressure on it.

As I pulled back, his hand held mine to remain on his face. His green eyes contrasted against the bright red blood.

My mind jumped to the beautiful man who offered me a drink. The same one who convinced me to finish a bottle of rum. The man I'd drop every conviction for if he had said the right words. With his thick blond hair, muscular build and air of mystery in his dichromatic eyes, I became almost desperate for his attention. Then I thought of the man I'd let touch my thigh, a different man, an older one. A cursed man.

I shivered at the thought.

Tev caught sight of it and asked, "Are you ok?"

I swallowed my memories and responded with a forced smile, "Yes. I'm fine."

"What is it?" he pressed.

"It's nothing," shaking away the conversation, I continued to smile to give him relief.

I let go of the cloth against his cheek, giving him full authority over it. " . . . Wren." He breathed my name.

Feeling inclined to share what happened or else it would eat away at me, I blurted, "I wish I never let him near me, much less touch me."

Tev's stare told me to explain.

"He cut me a deal. If I wanted to see you, I would have to drink with him. Glass after glass. I got drunk and fell into his lap, literally. He slid his hand up my leg. I jumped off before anything . . . progressed."

"Did you want anything to progress?" Tev responded, sitting still in the glow of the fire.

"Not after he turned into a monster. I escaped with enough time to find you down there. Thank Love from above." I raised a hand like I used to do in the House of Love when we would use that phrase.

He forced another comment through tight lips. "It sounds to me like you were open to the idea of falling into his bed."

I paused, long enough to show my true feelings about what happened that night. "I'm glad to know what you truly think about me, Tev."

Pursing his lips and nodding his head, his stare fell onto the flames of the fire.

"Are you *upset*?" I inquired.

He remained silent and still.

Taking another stab, I said, "Stop ignoring me. You didn't do anything when they took me from the cage."

He didn't take too kindly to that comment. "You don't know the truth about the cage, Wren. So, before you go making assumptions, how about you get your facts straight?"

"What happened, then?"

He huffed. "The cage was made from crystals found in the House of Patience, therefore the essence of patience was infused into every fiber of that prison. Whatever you saw or felt, it wasn't real. It was a mirage."

"What are you talking about? You broke through the wall. You held me. You sat next to me in the rubble."

"Wrenna, that never happened," he said calmly.

All this time, I had believed he cared. Come to find out—it was my own mind playing tricks on me., twisted by the darkness into lustful illusions.

"What did you see?" I requested.

He paused, unsure if he wanted to share. "The darkness played with my mind too. I was a ball of anxiety before they tossed you into the cell next to me, enduring the feeling of tiny ants all over my body. The darkness brought my worst fears to life while I was in the cage. I fought with smoke, repeatedly hitting the wall that separated us. By the time we arrived at the ship, I was exhausted from fighting with air."

I thought of him twitching in his sleep, probably the same terrors from the darkness.

"In your nightmares," I asked, "what does the darkness show you?"

Diverting the conversation completely, he asked, "How would you like your badger cooked?"

Sighing, I was done with his diversions. The day I died would be the day he'd finally be vulnerable with me—and it'd be too late. I walked the tightrope, getting bits and pieces from him. I'd fallen without a net into the pit of impatience.

I was through having to manage his emotions and mine. It was a hazy, foggy, obscure line, a game I had no interest in anymore.

I left the crackling fire for the ripples of the stream nearby.

After an hour, the water made me unbearably cold. Shivering my way back to the fire, I found a pile of bones stored to the side, suggesting Tev already ate. He gestured for me to take as much as I wanted.

I started with the meat from a leg.

Not wanting to speak after dinner, I laid my head down on a soft patch of grass.

"Before you fall asleep . . . " Tev's sentence trailed off.

I shifted, letting him know I could hear him.

"Wrenna, you should know . . . "

My face caught the light of the fire. I could see him trying to find the next words but something was stopping him. His tired eyes and low-hung shoulders were enough indication that he didn't have much energy. Especially one for a long conversation.

"I'm sorry that Thadeous and I couldn't protect you from the horrors of the world. When you told me about the captain and his advances, a part of me wanted to rip his throat out because he exposed you to a portion of the darkness no one should see. It's a darkness that could easily suffocate you if you aren't well equipped."

I sat up. My short hair collected a blade of loose grass on the way up.

"Tev, it was bound to happen. We aren't in the safety of the House of Love. We are surrounded by darkness. Don't beat yourself up."

"Wren, I tried my best."

"I know, Tev. I'm not blaming you," I reassured him. "Let's get some rest before another big day of travel."

"Will you be warm enough?" he asked.

"I'll be fine for tonight."

"Just let me know if I need to add more logs onto the fire during the night."

I smiled with small lips. He wouldn't meet my eyes. He only nodded his head before lying down with his back facing me.

I laid my head down for the second time, listening to the crackle of the fire behind me. Little did I want to admit, the fire hadn't kept me warm. I would surely freeze in the night thanks to the dewy grass.

He's an idiot.

He was driving me mad. The way he proceeded without any rhyme or reason. One hour we would be walking toward the sun, and the next, away from it. He had no clue where we should be headed. I was on the verge of speaking my mind.

I didn't feel like talking—what would be the use?

So, I sat in my thoughts and stirred.

A cloud enveloped my mind. I couldn't think anything positive, no matter how hard I tried to refocus, and it lingered for a long time. With each step I took, I wondered what would clear my mind from the irritability festering inside. A reprieve never came. As I watched the back of Tev's head, I was reminded how alone I was.

Tev had a home he could escape to.

Tev had a family out here to take him in.

I had nothing.

No one.

I had myself.

But that wasn't enough.

I had been exiled.

I had been discarded.

I had been forgotten.

Why should someone care for me?

What did I have to offer them?

I had no money.

No title.

I had a pretty smile.

What else was I good for?

Every so often Tev would turn his head to look back at me as if he could hear my thoughts and agree with what I was saying silently. Coincidentally, I would make eye contact with him every time he turned, affirming he was the topic of thought.

We continued through the lush grass, stopping to eat here and there, nibbling on bushes of berries as they came along. Only a few words were exchanged in these moments. There was nothing to be discussed.

As we walked, grass brushed my legs. I was reminded of the ticks that haunted my nightmares back home in Kindness. How I dreaded the days I had to walk through the tall thicket. It stalked me more than I in it. I hoped to never endure the torture of those humid nights, lying awake and praying for peace to come.

I hated stepping out of our family's house, automatically drenched in sweat. My body was coated in moisture, unable to move without sweat trickling down my arms and legs.

The birds' tunes carried far in those mornings. The dogs panted endlessly, with their hot breath filling the room with a despicable odor. Their noses were freshly dusted from their newest hole dug behind the house. My father watched them from the comfort of his chair on the porch, calling them off whenever they got too rowdy. I would watch from the window. They would play and never tire, jumping into holes and creating new ones.

They loved those summer nights.

The most notable childhood memory remained in summer. The lightning bugs dancing at dusk. A pink hue in the sky, the grass: a blue color from the elongated shadows and a lime from the descending sunlight that peaked through the trees. A sprinkle of lights would flood the yard from the bugs. From the house to the pond, many lightning bugs would appear every two seconds. When the sun was up, I dreaded the day; however, those endings made it all worth it as we watched a melody of lights bounce around in the yard—the only memory I miss about home.

The grass grew wilder the farther we walked. A stream up ahead gave us an excuse to pause for a few minutes. Tev excused himself and I remained by the water, watching the ripples cascade over the pebbles below as I stayed occupied in my mind.

I heard Tev say something over my shoulder; I turned in annoyance. To my surprise, he wasn't talking to me.

Chapter XXV

THE RAGSDALES

Leaving the water behind, I found Tev in a conversation with two girls about the same age as us. They were both striking. The one with fiery red hair stood taller than the other. As they smiled at Tev, their teeth were brilliantly white. Bouncy curls lay in the taller one's hair while the other had sandy blonde braids alongside her ears, keeping the hair out of her face.

I straightened my posture as I approached them.

"Oh, and this is Wrenna." He introduced me when I got within earshot of them.

"Hello." The shorter of the two spoke, giving me the same smile she did Tev.

"Wrenna, these girls say they felt a calling to this brook. They want to help any way they can." Tev turned to me with gleaming eyes, excitement hinted in his tone. After the days we'd had, this was supposed to be good news. Something inside me didn't like the idea of trusting people we just met.

"Could I speak to you over here?" I grabbed Tev's upper arm. His muscle contracted, leaving hard muscle underneath my hand.

He moved easily though, following my guidance away from the girls.

When we were out of earshot and the hum of the water muted our conversation, I asked him, "How can we be sure we can trust these girls? For all we know they could be working for the darkness."

"Unlikely. Look at them. They are harmless," Tev retorted.

I glanced over my shoulder to peer at them standing there for a split second before returning to our conversation.

"Tev, I'm not sure—"

"We'll be fine, Wren. We've been in more trouble before and escaped." He was trying hard to convince me.

"At the first sign of trouble, we are leaving."

"Deal," Tev agreed eagerly.

Joining the girls again, he spoke cheerfully to them. "Which way?" I could feel his smile growing bigger by the second.

"We live just beyond those trees. You must have walked right past the entrance," the fiery one explained.

"It's not very noticeable. Our father doesn't want strangers coming up to the house," added the other.

There's a whole family living within the Lost Lands?

How could that be?

"Excellent!" Tev said enthusiastically.

We followed the lead of the girls as we headed to their family home.

"I'm Ria, by the way," the fiery girl said. "This is my sister Nora."

The shorter sister gave a bit of a wave as Ria said her name. At a closer look, they had some similarities about them I hadn't noticed at first. While different in size and hair color, they had a similar walk and meekness to them. As I fell back to watch them side by side, their feet mirrored each other perfectly—never losing their rhythm. Waltzing down the road, they turned at a bush one could have mistaken for any other. Tev glanced around, noticing something I didn't, when we diverted from the path. With the sisters leading, we darted into thick bushes as tall as I stood. Before long, the bushes became fewer and fewer before we walked into a clearing of golden wheat and mountains hiding in the background.

I knew we had finally made it to their home when I saw the overhead gate to the property. In misshapen cast iron letters, the sign read:

RAGSDALE RANCH

Ria and Nora Ragsdale turned to wave us through. Tev and I were caught gaping at the sign and ranch house that was built just beyond it. The house was modest and unassuming at first glance. As we got closer, there were little details within the stone foundation and the wooden beams that covered the front door. Leaves were carved into the wood, forming an arch above the entrance. It was breathtaking work, but could only be seen at close proximity to the house. The door was also made of wood, with a large handle to push and pull it open. Nora opened the door, with Ria following her gesture inside. Nora held the door open for Tev and me too.

Ria skipped away to another part of the house before I could ask where she was going.

Nora explained, "She's going to get some new clothes for you."

Shocked by the news, I said, "That's not necessary."

Tev intervened by saying, "What she means to say is, 'that's very kind,'" giving me a glare afterwards.

Looking around the home, we entered a sitting room with colorful paintings on the walls. I stepped closer to admire the work. Nora saw my interest and explained, "Our mother is an artist, a really good one too. She did all these here."

The paintings were close to masterpieces. The one I fixated on was a lighthouse on a hill. Flowers covered the stretch of land before meeting the lighthouse. Waves crashed on the rocks, imitating the ocean as I once knew it. Wild and unpredictable. The sky was full of clouds, highlighted with a pink hue to represent the sunset. Waking from my trance, I could hear Ria coming from down the hall. I looked in anticipation for the new clothes in her hand when I realized that the girl who emerged wasn't Ria at all.

"Everyone, this is our little sister, Ellie," Nora said.

The similarities between Ria and Ellie were harder to distinguish. Their hair was a giveaway, however. Ellie's hair was bright and sunkissed, similar to the Pillar's on that nasty ship.

"Hi, nice to meet you both," Ellie said, not giving much emotion with the greeting.

Not only did her hair resemble Riperous, but her eyes were piercing blue with brown puddles, a trait I was starting to think was native to the area.

Tev gave a half smile.

I managed to squeak out the quietest 'hi' myself.

Ria now met us with hands full of new clothes. "This way, you two." She directed us into the hall Ellie emerged from. Tev gave a hand for me to go first and I obliged. Ria stopped after the second door to turn and face us. She handed me a pile of clothes, relieving her arms. "There's a washing room and a bed for both of you. I already told our parents we will be expecting company for dinner. Wash up, get some rest, and we will come get you when dinner is ready."

She handed Tev clothes too and shuffled us into the room.

"Towels are at the foot of the bed. Try not to get water everywhere. Our mother is pretty particular about the wood," Ria explained for a final time before shutting us in the room with one another.

Left stunned, Tev took to a bed and fell lazily onto it. He hugged his clothes, gifted to him by Ria, which were now lying on his chest.

"I don't know what you were so worried about," he said smugly.

"We still don't know who these girls are. How do we know we can trust them?" I asked.

"I think we will just have to see." Tev closed his eyes on the bed. For a few minutes he didn't move. Snores erupted after a while longer.

While he was asleep, I looked around the room. Two beds with a nightstand separating them sat opposite a large wooden dresser. It all fit very comfortably in the room. Two doors flanked the dresser—one leading to the washroom and the other a closet. Inside the washroom, there was a black bathtub that stood proudly in contrast with the white tile on the walls. Still holding the clothes in my arms, I spun around to find Tev with his mouth gaping open. The Aluna operator had fallen asleep.

He wouldn't mind if I delighted in a bath.

I grabbed a towel and shut the door to the bathroom.

Steam came from the faucet as it spurted water into the tub. I undressed, leaving my muddy dress folded as neatly as I could on the floor, making sure not to dirty the white counters with it. The bath was about halfway to full. I made my way to the sink and mirror. I studied my reflection while the tub filled. Dark markings of mud and dirt coated my face. My eyes were sunken from the lack of food. I had acquired a tan comparable to the captain's. It emphasized my cheekbones and highlighted my forehead with redness. Most notable, however, was my hair. It was jagged and uneven across the bottom where Tev cut it with a knife. I had such pretty hair when living in the House of Love.

As I entered the tub, a layer of dirt drifted from my body and hovered at the top of the water. I let the steam relax my muscles and calm my mind. I dipped my hair into the water, untangling the wisps coated in mud. After a few minutes, the water began to turn a swampy color, reflecting the amount of dirt I carried in my hair and nails and who knew where else.

Resting my head against the ledge, I closed my eyes. The warmth of the water felt like a warm hug, carefully and strategically comforting my body where it needed it most. I kept my mind busy by thinking of the places I'd seen since leaving the House of Love. My mind slipped into a memory of the desert ecosystem, the canyon and the river, the Sandshadow and the sand dunes. I could picture the captain's cabin and the deck below very clearly in my mind. I retraced my steps, walking up to the Pillar's throne and looking at the map of the House of Patience. The many names of places I hadn't visited nor wanted to visit.

Before I knew it, my body had lost its grip on the tub and slid into the water. My head fully submerged, I was released from my trance of memory lane. I resurfaced, coughing and wiping water from my eyes and regaining my sight at the same time, the door flew open. Tev was standing in the doorway with a concerned look on his face. Suddenly, the water turned an icy cold. I shuddered upon his arrival.

"Oh, sorry. I didn't—" He didn't finish his sentence. He turned away but remained in the doorway. He asked, "Are you ok?"

"Yes, I just slipped—that's all." I assured him. I had instinctively curled my body into a ball under the water, silently wishing he would leave and close the door.

As if he heard my thoughts, he began to back out of the room before I stopped him. "I'm almost done."

Without looking back into the room, he muttered, "Take your time. Dinner won't be ready for another hour. Nora stopped by to give us the message." He closed the door behind him without another word.

I uncoiled my body from the tightly wound ball. The water returned to its comforting warmth once again and I was left to relax.

There was a knock on the door in which Tev answered. Ellie stopped by the room to let us know dinner was ready.

After I dried off and changed, Tev didn't take much time at all in the bathroom. He was more excited about the bed and sleeping. Nevertheless, we were both refreshed and ready to eat.

We followed Ellie through the hall outside to a patio where a large wooden table sat at the center. Above it, lights hung in a unique pattern, one I suspected their mother had designed. The table was set with eight plates and bowls of food almost spilling out from them. Tev hanging back, I took the lead walking up to the table. Ria and Nora were already sitting, passing food from one end of the table to the other. They were accompanied by an older couple—mother and father, no doubt—and another young man like Tev.

"Our guests have arrived," Ellie said with a smile.

The father looked in our direction and stood from his seat at the head of the table.

"Brilliant! Come and join us!" He motioned for us to take our seats across from one another. I looked at Tev and he gave me a smile of comfort. I did as I was told. My seat was next to Ria, with their father beside me.

"Thank you for dinner, sir." Tev said humbly to the old man.

"Oh, posh, call me Finneous." The man tapped Tev's shoulder, welcoming him to dinner. He gave a wink to me. His eyes reflected his daughter's eyes, a striking blue with brown woven throughout. Motioning across the table from him, he continued, "And my wife, Adaline. We welcome you to our home! Now, let's say the blessing. Elena, would you do the honors?"

Finneous stretched his hands out to imply Tev and I take them in ours. Simultaneously, we obliged.

Ellie, sitting beside her mother, said, "We bless this food we are about to eat. We are thankful for the day behind us and the night ahead. By all that is *good* and *patient.*"

"Let's eat!" said Finneous shortly after.

Our silverware clanked with the plates as Tev and I devoured our food. Everything was prepared to perfection, better than the meals I had on the Sandshadow. There was a juicy meat, potatoes, crunchy greens, and warm bread. There was more than enough food for everyone to have a second helping. The sisters didn't partake in that option but the man sitting with them did.

"My cousins fail to introduce me, I'm Evanridge but you can call me Evan." Similar to Finneous, he stood to shake Tev's hand and then mine. He was quiet for most of dinner, eating his food and listening to the shrieks coming from the girls about this and that. It was hard enough for me to follow with the volume at which they spoke.

While the girls were cheering on their mother about something, Finneous in a quieter voice spoke to Tev and me. "What brings you to the ranch?" he asked inquisitively.

"Do you know of the Sandshadow?" Tev asked.

Finneous sat back in his chair with a concerned look. "I do." Not alluding to know more information than that.

"We were captured and taken there. We had escaped a few days ago before meeting your daughters earlier today," Tev explained.

The way Tev worded it was perfect; we were the victims in this story. We were the ones who needed help.

Waiting for Finneous to respond, Tev gave me a wink just as Finneous did at the start of dinner.

"I see. That ship has been a curse to our home for as long as I can remember," Finneous said.

Curiously, I questioned, "How long have you been in the House of Goodness?"

His head turned toward me. He smiled and patted my hand on the table, "My dear, this ranch is in Patian land. It has been in my family since the time of the Forgotten King. We wouldn't ever leave. This is our home. My wife and I reconstructed this house with our own hands after my mother passed on. I intend to be buried in my family's crypt, just like my father and his father before him and so on and so on."

"I thought we crossed the border into the House of Goodness. We followed the paths of willabees and creeks. We were in the meadows of Goodness."

Finneous laughed with his belly. "My dear, you are mistaken. Just because you see grass doesn't necessarily mean you are in the meadows of the House of Goodness. There are pockets of green within the House of Patience too."

I looked at Tev in bewilderment. It couldn't be. His map showed that we were going in the direction of the House of Goodness. That's where the crown was and that's where we needed to go.

Tev met my eyes and in a hushed voice said, "We must have taken a wrong turn in the dunes. We were both very tired and the sun was unforgiving."

I kept quiet for the rest of the night. The surprise of the night sent me into my own thoughts. I wanted nothing more than to rush out of dinner and back into the bathtub, but my feet stayed glued to the floor as we finished dinner. Tev was trying to tell me something with his eyes as we concluded the evening with the family. Finneous had instructed the girls to give us a tour of the property tomorrow after a good night's rest.

After a proper good night, Tev and I were off to bed.

I didn't say a word to him the rest of the night. I silently tucked myself in bed into warm coverings already placed on our beds. Without another thought, I was asleep.

Chapter XXVI

RAGSDALE RANCH

The crunch of leaves was unmistakable. I stood, this time faster than before. I scoured between the trees to find the beast, and better yet, a hiding place. I knew the beast was close. Thuds hit the ground as I shuffled my feet through the piles of fallen leaves. My breath quickened with every second that passed. My legs were sturdy underneath me, ready to sprint if I needed to. I found a hiding place under the root of a nearby tree. I tucked my gangly body into the crevice and waited. I felt animal's pounding steps in my bones. It was hunting and it was angry.

I slowed my breathing to hide myself further amongst the rotting leaves. A slight nip in the air caused my nose to run. I could hear the breath of the animal now; it couldn't have been far. It stalked the ground, waiting for the slightest movement. Snot reached my mouth and seeped into it. Moving the back of my hand to wipe it away, I gave away my position.

The creature whipped around a tree and found my hiding spot. I came face to face with it again. It attacked by thrashing its antlers at me, trying to free me from the spot. Immobilized, I stayed where I was with the knowledge that I would soon wake up. I would be free of this creature, if only I could force myself to wake up.

Without warning, a blast shot through the animal. Blood splattered on the dried leaves. A thunderous sound echoed throughout the forest. The beast's eyes, glossy and bulging, peered at me with the most agonized expression. It didn't want this outcome, but someone else decided its fate for it.

The animal's impact with the ground caused me to open my own eyes and conclude the nightmare.

The curtains were closed in our room. A ring formed around the windows, highlighting the curtains in various places where the sun peeked through. The bedding was warm, but the air around us was chilly and uninviting. I was glad to be protected under the blankets. Pulling it up to my nose, I watched the dust spiral and dance in the small beams that showed through. I could hear Tev making sounds indicating he was still asleep. I didn't bother to look in his direction or wake him just to have his company. The quiet moments were few and far between. There was a type of unexplainable peace in this house.

Not the first time I've felt this sensation before in the HoPat.

My mind jetted back to the night of my exile and the sands I gripped, holding my place in the world, not letting go until I knew everything was going to be fine.

Then Tev came and saved me. But for a second before, there was peace and weight lifted from my chest. Patience interceding and reveling in the outcome of my exile. Nevertheless, I was glad that Tev was my outcome and not the darkness.

Tev's breathing shifted, indicating that I was not the only one awake. Staying under the covers, I turned to face the other bed in the room. Tev was wiping his eyes and yawning simultaneously. I smiled plainly, soaking in the last moments of quiet.

"How'd you sleep, Wren?" he asked in a deep voice, one I've become accustomed to since meeting him. His voice in the mornings lingers in sleep itself, taking an hour to fully shake away the deep voice.

"I can't complain. How about you?" I asked in return.

"I slept great!" he exclaimed. "We are very lucky to have met those girls when we did."

"Tev, we are still in the House of Patience. We need to get back out there. We need to get to the crown."

"What do you think is going to happen if we stay here longer? No one knows about the crown. No one except you and me." He sounded sleepy still.

"And Riperous," I reminded him. "I'd feel better if we kept moving."

"We hadn't eaten in days, Wren. We were going to die out there if it weren't for those girls. If they hadn't brought us here, we would have been done. I only slept for a few hours in the night to be sure you were protected. That was the first night's sleep I didn't wake up worried about you or myself since—" he took a long pause to think, "the H.O.L. So, for my own sake, I'm staying right here for as long as we are welcome."

"I don't like it." I was starting to feel irritated by what Tev was saying.

"I don't care," Tev mumbled.

With perfect timing, there was a knock at the door. I sat up in bed, bringing the warmth of the covers along with me. Tev stayed in the same position and yelled, "Come on in."

The door swung open, with Ria and Nora entering with fresh clothes in their hands.

Nora started with a cheerful smile, "Father wants us to show you around the ranch this morning." There was a type of gleefulness in her tone, waiting for us to get out of bed. Her hair was done in a tight ponytail, keeping the hair away from her face. The jacket she wore bubbled off of her but looked fairly warm. There was a little pink in her cheeks and nose too, complementing the cool air in the bedroom.

"Not before breakfast," Ria countered her sister. Very exact and proper, she set the clothes on the dresser opposite us. "We brought you new clothes, perfect for a tour about the property. It's going to be a bit chilly, but mother is an excellent tailor. She hemmed some of Father's old clothes for both of you after you went to bed last night."

At first, blinded by the little light in the room, my eyes were suddenly averse to the sudden brightness when Nora ripped open the curtains. The sun was already high in the sky. Tev readjusted in his bed to hide from the light like a vampire. The girls gave a giggle and left the room, eager and excited to show us around their home.

The ranch was built on a hillside. There were three pastures for the cattle and one for the horses. There appeared to be other animals I didn't recognize as we walked the property. I kept quiet for most of the day. Tev, however, was curious about everything.

"What are those?" he asked, pointing to two large animals at the top of the hill. They had Two tusk-like bones extended from their cheekbones, meeting in front of their faces and flattening into shovel-like plates.

"Oh! Those are dustbacks. They are very friendly," Nora said happily. "Would you like to pet them? They really like people."

When we got closer to them their faces looked flattened as well.

It looked like they smashed their faces into the ground to cover as much of it as possible. Their brown eyes glared at Tev and me when we walked up to meet them.

"Why do they look like that?" Tev asked.

"They help break up the tough ground for planting season."

"They have shovels for faces," Tev commented.

"Exactly!" Nora said.

I wondered how—in the name of Love—something like this had been roaming around. They must have certain qualities horses and cattle don't.

"They like the dirt. They roll around in it all the time." Ria patted the back of the larger one and dust flew from her hand when she made contact. A groan came from the beast as she began to scratch its underside. "They are really harmless. Big teddy bears if you ask me. Give him a pet. He won't kick."

I stuck out my hand. The skin of the dustback was dry, imitating the ground with its sandy and grippy qualities. It left my hand dry as a result. I wiped the remaining dust on my pantleg and backed away, giving the creature a smile when I did.

"Hey! Finneous needs some help up in the barn. He's not in the best of moods, so I would hurry and get up there." Evan was mounted on a horse's back, shouting from the gate we all had entered for the dustbacks.

Ria gave a thumbs-up to her cousin and he kicked his horse to trot along in the direction of the barn.

"Where's the barn?" I asked Ria.

"It's just over the hill. We better go now," she replied.

The four of us walked along a dirt path—one the dustbacks wouldn't mind rolling in—while heading to the barn. Its bright red color stood out against the canary yellow dirt and the pastures full of green. It had a large white door, propped open by a rusted machine, one I didn't recognize.

As the four of us walked inside the barn, we found Finneous in the midst of several large birds. I'd seen these birds before. They were perched above the cavern where Tev and I went swimming a week prior. These were blorks. I shuffled my feet in the dust, delaying my entrance into the barn. There were five birds in total. Three were staring down at us from the rafters of the barn while two of them were fluttering around Finneous.

"Wow! I've never been this close to blorks before," Tev exclaimed. He wasn't frightened, unlike me.

"Good morning," said Finneous. "I hope I am not interrupting your tour. I needed the girls to help me with feeding this morning."

My expression must have given away my unease. I stood at the door while everyone else rushed inside. Little did I know Evan came in after me. I jumped in my spot by his hushed voice.

"They are extremely misunderstood creatures, given their size and their talons," he said.

My eyes shot to the one perched on Finneous's thigh. The curve of the talons hooked slightly into his pant leg but didn't puncture it. From where I stood, I could see Tev grab a slab of meat from a bucket beside the girls. Finneous, holding the bird to brace it and himself, gave Tev a signal to throw it. Tev threw the piece of meat into the air and the blork snatched it out of the air with ease, swallowing the chunk in one gulp. Tev turned to the sisters with a grin as wide as the bird's wings before glancing to me and waving me over.

I smiled reluctantly and whispered to Evan, "Why are they here?"

"We use them for protection," Evan said.

I watched the blork swallow the meat whole.

"Protection from what?" I asked.

"They scare off any unwelcome guests wandering in the deserts. They are the reason our ranch hasn't been consumed in darkness for generations. People don't like the looks of them. When they see them, they run, thinking they are beacons for the darkness. In actuality, they are protectors for the ranch."

"We saw some in the canyon. Perched up high."

"These birds will wander, just like cattle grazing," Evan explained.

"Do they ever attack?" I asked quickly, barely listening to him but keeping a watchful eye on the giant birds.

"Sometimes," Evan said. "They have a temper just like all of us. Just don't pluck a feather or put your hand near their beaks when they are feeding." He held up his hand to show me a missing knuckle from one of his fingers. "I was eighteen. I thought I could feed them myself. They took it right off as soon as they saw the meat. I'm glad that's all they took. Finneous stitched it up. It's a cool story getting bitten by a blork."

If they could take a knuckle, they could slash a throat.

I stopped shuffling my feet in the dirt. I didn't want to take another step into the barn. This distance was enough to satisfy me. In the background, I could hear Tev laughing with Ria and Nora while throwing another piece of meat into the air for the blorks to grab.

Evan noticed my hesitation and asked, "Do you want to get closer?"

"No, not really," I said, simultaneously shaking my head at him.

How could they let something so dangerous around them?

And continue to use them as protectors after Evan got hurt?

I don't understand.

I don't think I will ever understand.

I looked up to the ceiling of the barn to take note of the others. They had their heads cocked to one side, interested in the food down below. I saw the curiosity running through them.

Their heads tilted in perfect unison, watching the movement below.

Watching the meat.

Watching the *people.*

"Evan?" I said in a quiet voice. "Are they going to attack?"

Looking up, Evan saw what I was looking at. The birds were getting ready for a dismount from the beam supporting them. He yelled over to his family and Tev, "Incoming!"

Ria and Nora grabbed Tev's shoulders to give room for the remaining blorks to land. The wingspan of the birds was greater than I expected. Still standing in the doorway of the barn, I could feel the wind from the birds, pushing dust into the air and softly landing around Finneous. My fixation was on the descending birds, as the birds who were fed took flight. I missed the brief exchange when dust flew into my eye. Before I knew it, Tev and Nora and Ria were inching closer to feed the next set of blorks.

Evan, standing between me and the blorks, turned to me and asked, "Would you like to see more of the property while they finish up? They can meet us in the back pasture."

I nodded my head and followed him outside into the warm sunshine. His horse was eating a pocket of grass beside the barn.

"Do you know how to ride?" he asked.

"No," I responded, still shaking off my unease from the giant birds. "Can we walk?"

Evan gave a half smile and spun around with his hands in his pockets. "No problem. She seems to be enjoying herself anyway." He pointed over his shoulder to the horse plucking grass wherever she could find it.

We walked to the same path we came from the dustbacks, but instead of heading toward the house, we went in the opposite direction. The barn was built at the base of a small hill. Once we reached the top, we could see the rest of the property. Two large herds of cattle were grazing in different pastures. There was a tree along the path and Evan took a seat with his back to the trunk.

Patting the dirt, he motioned for me to take a seat next to him. I did and when I finally settled in my spot, I could see for the first time the magnitude of the property. The pastures were mostly dirt with little greens popping up, far away from the cattle. There were purple mountains in the far distance, similar to my first day in the House of Patience. Fence lines cut the property, separating the pastures and boxing in the cattle. I traced the fence to a grouping of trees. There was a stone shed as well. Behind it, rows of crops, enough to feed the family and a small village if they wanted to. Last night's dinner and the abundance made more sense after seeing the rows of vegetation.

Everything here was thriving.

In a world that was dying.

"This is it," Evan said as he took a deep breath in and closed his eyes.

"It's incredible." It was all I could really say.

"It's been in my family since the Forgotten King. Most of my relatives are buried down there." He pointed to the shed in the trees. "Granddad and Maw. My parents and my sister."

I looked at him with concerned eyes.

He continued, "My dad was Finneous's brother. My parents were stung by a time scorpion and instead of slowing their age, it sped up their time. They died a few years ago. My sister, on the other hand, got captured by a pirate."

The word itself made me squirm in my seat. A flashing image of a man with small strands of hair jetting from his head popped into my mind.

"Those men have always been on the hunt for beautiful young women," Evan continued. "She was in the wrong place at the wrong time. One of them took her and left her to die in the heat. She died of heat stroke just outside the property line."

A shiver went down my spine. I thought back to the captain's hand as it inched higher and higher on my thigh. I shook the memory from my mind and focused on the cattle out in the pasture.

He continued, "I was the one who found her. Finneous doesn't like it when we leave the property, but I felt a calling. I barely recognized her when I found her. Her face was burned and scabbed over. I brought her body back to be buried next to my parents."

"Sounds like you've had a lot of loss," I said, not knowing what else to say.

"Yes. There are still blessings to be thankful for though. Uncle Finn and Aunt Ad took me and my sister in after our parents died. They have been like a second family. I help out around the ranch, fix things when they break down, and take care of the cattle. I don't know how else I could repay them."

"Would you ever want to leave? Be on your own?"

"Oh man, outside of the property there isn't much left. Our home was destroyed in a fire not too long after my parents died. There's just too much darkness for my liking. I'm pretty content here," Evan commented.

The breeze brushed my hair across my face. The tall stalks of wheat effortlessly flowed like the mane of a horse. I inhaled, smelling the dirt, the cows, and the dust.

I simply responded, "I can see why."

Chapter XXVII

TEV'S WISHES

"Wren, we wouldn't survive out there. Not yet," he said after our second day at the ranch.

Since arriving at the ranch, I argued daily with Tev about resuming our search for the crown. He combated me every time with a different excuse.

"Can we talk about this some other time? I just need to crash," he said after helping Finneous mend a blork's foot. It got caught in the fencing while chasing a rabbit. He walked past me in the hall to the bedroom and I didn't see him for the rest of the night.

"I'm about to fall asleep. Let's talk about it in the morning." He yawned as he spoke. The words were muffled as he smooshed his head deeper into his pillow and covered his head with the blanket.

Tev avoided my eyes when we would talk.

It wasn't the answer that bothered me.

It was how quickly he found something else to do.

One morning, I shuffled my blankets off, loud enough to wake him, but quiet enough to not make it obvious. Walking into the bathroom, I started a bath. I hoped the running water from the tub and the movement inside the adjacent room would prolong his drift into sleep. I peeked my head into the bedroom before the tub was full, letting in a little light to see his face. He was turned on his side, so I couldn't see his face. Judging by the sound, I knew he was asleep. He was still and snoring, by no means fazed by anything I had done.

I shut the door with a fury and the crash from the door made the mirror rattle on the wall. I instantly regretted it. I didn't want my anger to destroy this place. I was grateful for this little room and the peace it brought at the end of the day.

I undressed and slid into my resting position in the bath. Steam was rising from the water. All my frustrations with Tev were being lifted away. First, my anxiety with the delay in my search for the crown was melting away. Secondly, my bruises and sores were being treated by the warm water.

Finneous had put us to work around the ranch. In the mornings, I helped either Ria or Nora brush the dustbacks and Tev helped with feeding the cattle. We all broke for lunch and joined Adaline and Ellie at the house. It was becoming quite the routine. During lunch, the boys would discuss the day's ranch details and the girls would giggle about something funny only to them. I kept quiet watching the two groups develop bonds I didn't envy. Bonds would make it harder to leave.

After lunch, there were different chores around the property every day. Tev would often escape with Finneous and Evan on horses to the pastures. They would come back for dinner, covered in manure or mud—the smell alone made me think it was one over the other, but I wasn't too sure.

I was lucky. I stayed close to the sisters and their mother after lunch ended. We fetched vegetables from the garden, prepared the food for dinner, and swept the dust from the house. There was a constant thin layer of dust on the floor, no matter the time of day. My least favorite, however, was helping Ellie collect the laundry, simply because of the boys. Their clothes smelled ten times worse than the girls,' always coated with a silky texture I couldn't place—and didn't want to.

Ellie was the sister I found myself in conversation with the most. She was shy and soft-spoken, only talking to her mother for direction in her chores and helping me do them correctly. When the group was all together, unless she was spoken to directly, she would blend in amongst the louder talkers, like Ria and her father.

Ellie was the youngest of the sisters. Two years separated each of them and yet, I found the youngest was the most mature. I did not know if it was because of her timidity, but she had an elegance to her that the others did not. Her hair was brilliantly blonde, similar to that of Riperous. Wisps were kept under control by braids tracing her ears and falling behind her shoulders.—like mine working at the Adora. When we cleaned, the pair of braids would fall forward and she would whip them back faster than they fell. Her eyes matched her father's. They were a piercing blue, like snow in the shadows muddled with brown holes. They complemented her straight smile well too.

My bath water was getting colder, but I didn't want to leave my sanctuary just yet. I pulled the stopper, holding the water from the drain to let the cold flood through. The level went down a bit and I resealed it. Turning on the hot water back on, wanting the steam to rise from the water, just how I liked it.

I would stay in the bath for as long as I could, until the water grew cold.

Feeling guilty for using up so much water, I drained the tub fully and covered myself in a warm towel. Not too long after, I was tucked in bed, ready for a fast sleep to take over.

The next day was similar to the previous. Tev was awake and out the door before I opened my eyes. At lunch, he questioned Finneous on blork lore while they ate and soon after he finished, he mounted a horse and trotted to the nearest pasture. At dinner, he recalled seeing an abscess on one of the mama cows and wanted to check it out before the day got away from him.

I finally cornered him while clearing away the silverware from dinner to ask, "Is now a good time, Tev?"

He jumped at the question, surprised I said something to begin with. He was interrupted before he could answer when Finneous brought out an instrument and started playing a melody, plucking the strings. Tev followed his lead and started singing a tune in coordination.

Out of frustration, I dropped the utensils on the table, creating a loud clang. Loud enough to disrupt the concert beginning on the patio, yet no one noticed. I slipped inside the house, silencing the music behind me and returned to our bedroom—my safe haven. I drew a bath, washed, and put myself to bed before Tev made it back to the room.

He was kind enough to change his whistling in the hall to soft humming once he entered the room. I pressed a pillow over my head to help drown out the noise and slowly fell asleep with a pillow cupping my ears.

The next morning, Tev stirred in bed for a few minutes before ripping the covers off and trotting to the bathroom to change. Adaline had been so generous in lending us clothes to wear while at the ranch. Two pairs of old shirts and pants were given to both Tev and me, one for wearing and one for washing. I typically wore my clean clothes for the next day to bed. While Tev was washing up, I lay in bed wishing to sleep more. Wishing I didn't have somewhere to be. Wishing I could stay in the comfort of the covers for the whole day. Then the thought occurred to me—*why couldn't I?*

There was work to be done, but they didn't need me.

The ranch would run just fine without me for a day.

Tev made his way out of the bathroom. He noticed my lack of movement for the morning and asked, "Are you all right, Wren?"

"I'm not feeling the best this morning. I think I am going to stay in bed." I said plainly.

I could see Tev shift away from me as if he didn't want to catch anything I had acquired. Still, he kindly asked, "Do you need anything? Are you hungry? I could grab something from breakfast for you and bring it back."

I spun around, turning my back on Tev and further entwining myself in the blanket. Pressing my head against my pillow, I closed my eyes once again. I softly responded, "No thanks."

Tev's feet shuffled on the wood floors as he walked over to the curtains, drew them closed, and walked out for the day, leaving me with nothing but solitude, silence, and slumber.

Throughout the day, there were knocks on the door by Ellie and Adaline, asking if I needed anything. A few times I ignored them, pretending to be asleep. Around midday, I got out of bed to acknowledge a knock.

Ellie stood with a tray of fruit and bread and a glass of water. "Mom says if you are feeling sick, you need to eat. Your body won't heal all on its own if you don't take care of it." She handed over the tray without my permission.

My eyes hadn't fully adjusted to the light spilling in from the hallway. She was a blur, but I agreed to take the food.

"Thank you," I said before closing the door and setting the tray on the dresser. I went back to my bed without consuming anything.

Grabbing the blanket, I whipped it over my head and pretended to fall back asleep.

Later that day, I heard the door open again. This time, footsteps entered the room. It was Tev. I looked at the window with its closed drapes and there wasn't a ring of sunlight around it anymore. The day must have turned to night. I slept the entire day away. Waking, not only from Tev's movement, but by his smell, I could hear the water starting for a bath in the background. By the smell of him, he needed it. I turned over and watched through the crack, the only entertainment I had for the day. He must have assumed I was unaware he came in because he undressed with the door slightly ajar.

His frame caught my eye at first, not for the bare skin, but the red lashes he examined in the mirror. There were three, diagonally drawn down the middle of his back, burning hot with crimson blood streaking in some areas. The water running in the background created a steam room. He quit his examination due to the foggy mirror and proceeded into the bath. The moment the water reached his back he paused. I could only see his hand gripping the side of the bath, turning his knuckles white. He was in a lot of pain. He slipped into the tub, out of sight.

I turned over again, giving him some privacy. I was starting to get warm under the blanket. The steam from the bath crept into the bedroom. I stuck my leg out to cool a part of my body but otherwise stayed under the blanket, almost as a prisoner would a cell. The blanket was my prison now; however, I didn't want to move from it. Not much of a prison if I chose to stay here, tucked away in this house, secluded from people I didn't want to talk to, hiding from the sunlight. But it's how I wanted it to be. The alternative was too taxing: to put on a façade that everything was fine all the time. It wasn't.

I was sad.

I was mad.

My life was uprooted, and I had no control over it.

No input to where I wanted to stay.

My life was handed over to the darkness without my input.

It was my life that was destroyed by someone else's hand.

And the outcome?

I was exiled and now, an outcast.

Water sloshed around in the bath, signaling Tev was done. He opened the door, to my surprise, with a towel around his waist in search of something. Whatever it was, he found it and made his way back to the bathroom. I lay still. I didn't want to have a conversation with him. In the dark, he couldn't see if my eyes were open or closed. We both assumed they were closed.

Momentarily, he reentered, this time fully clothed. He walked cautiously. His steps were slower this time and purposeful. A warmth covered me. I thought for a second the blanket fell on my leg again, but I was wrong. Tev stood hovering over my bed. Sensing his presence, I adjusted to lie on my back. He sat on my bed, where my legs weren't occupying space.

"How are you feeling?" he asked in a hushed voice, almost afraid.

"Better, still not great," I replied weakly. "What happened to your back?" I asked to change the subject.

"I was helping Finneous feed the blorks because Ria and Nora were feeding the dustbacks. Someone needed to help because you were in bed. One of them got agitated while feeding and I was too close. It scratched me before I could get away."

A twinge of guilt festered in my stomach.

"Do you want to join us for dinner?" His voice was stronger than the time before.

"I already ate," I lied. The idea of food was fine, but the idea of being around a lot of people right now was worse.

I like the bed.

I want to stay here.

Tev glanced over his shoulder at the dresser where the fruit and the slices of bread remained untouched. He looked back at me; I could barely see his face in the dim light. "Wren, it's not good for you to be away and alone. Please come to dinner."

I reassured him, "I'm fine, Tev. I'm not super hungry."

His hand stretched out to mine on the blanket. His face moved closer to mine to see it in detail. His eyebrows were furrowed, and he looked sad. One of the corners of his mouth was pinched into the cheek. Gentler than before, he whispered, "I'm worried about you."

I wished in that moment I felt relieved that I finally had someone in my life to care about me deeply enough to worry about me, a feeling I have longed for since leaving my home in Kindness. A feeling I searched for in overnight lovers in the House of Love. Instead, I was overwhelmed with anger. It felt like Tev was hinting that something was wrong with me—something I needed to fix.

I kept quiet after he said that, with confusing thoughts running through my mind.

He was worried about me, but he kept brushing me off about the search for the crown.

How important am I for him to treat me like that?

Whenever I brought up the search, there was something else more important than what I thought. How infuriated it made me whenever he would find a way out of a conversation. As I sat there in silence, the anger rose and rose until, like a kettle on a stove, I needed to scream.

Because of Tev's proximity to me, I contained a portion of my anger. Through gritted teeth, I said, "That's not your job."

"Wren—"

He tried to mutter something, but I cut him off.

"No. You don't get to blow me off for days and then come in here and tell me that you are worried about me. How does that make sense to you?"

I paused long enough for him to respond, but before he did, I continued my thought.

"I haven't had a conversation with you since we arrived. You have been too caught up in the ranch life to give me the courtesy of a conversation about the crown. I want to plan. I want to leave and find it. I believe it is out there."

My thoughts were screaming in my head. The ones that lulled me to sleep while I lay in bed today. Random ones coming to the forefront. I didn't know which ones to say and which ones to hold onto. The thoughts started to roll off my tongue out of order, not making any sense to Tev or to myself.

"You leave in the morning, and I don't see you until lunch. It makes sense why we don't talk then. You seem to talk just fine to Finneous or Ria or even Evan, who hardly talks to anyone at all. But whenever I come around, there's this wall that goes up. You don't look at me. If we didn't share this room, I doubt you would be near me.

"Tev, we were exiled together. We were captured and escaped together. We protected each other. We laughed and shared stories.

I don't understand what happened here that made you turn on me. What did I say or what did I do to make you think I was your enemy—that I was part of the *darkness*?"

My voice broke on the last word.

It was how I truly felt.

It was how Tev made me feel by his actions.

He was now standing with his arms across his chest, waiting his turn to say something. After a long pause, we both acknowledged it was his turn to speak.

"Let me be very clear: you do not have the darkness." He spoke gruffly.

I only nodded, encouraging him to continue.

"I've realized something out here and it might be the reason why I've kept my distance from you. The longer you remain bound, restricted, tethered, the more foreign freedom feels. We are free out here, Wren. We could do absolutely *anything*. We can laugh. We can sing and dance. We can cry. Look at the Ragsdales. Their family has been here for years, and they are protected. I know you want to have a conversation about finding the crown. But I've come to love it here. Leaving this ranch scares me. For the first time in my life, I have found liberty in a place where time seems to stand still. Where I can be anything I want to be. The military told me I had to be lethal and scary, so I was. I had eleven Aluna brothers tell me to act big and bad, so I did. I had Pillars give me orders and direct my life, so I obeyed. I don't have to live that way anymore. But you— you want to form a plan to charge back into that life, leaving this feeling behind, leaving this *freedom,* and I don't want to do it."

He uncrossed his arms to relax at his side. The truth was out now. He didn't have to hide it anymore.

He continued, "I care about you, Wren. I want to see you safe and happy, but you have been so focused on what you don't have instead of focusing on what you do have. You have been blessed more out here in the desert than you have ever been in the H.O.L."

My face must have said something because he went on to say, "Don't disagree with me. I see it in your eyes—in the way you talk about the Pillars. The meetings you had with them where you were finally given an opportunity to be in the room with them, but you and I both know they didn't care what you had to say. They made you feel small and insignificant. But what I don't understand is why you want to go back. You are dwelling on the fact that your life was taken away. You can't see the blessings in front of you."

I remained quiet. I couldn't look at him any longer, whether because of anger or shame, I had yet to figure it out.

"All day today, Ellie has been asking me if you are all right," Tev said.

This information got me to look in his direction. Tears started to pool at the base of my eyes. The light from the bathroom was seeping into the room. Hopefully, Tev wouldn't see my tears fall.

He spoke softly. "I have never heard her talk before, but I was approached three times by her today, asking about you. There must have been something you said or did to make an impact on her. And Evan noticed you were missing too. He asked me around lunchtime where you were hiding, and we laughed about you missing out on the chores today." His voice mirrored the laughs shared between the two as he recalled the memory.

"These people here care about you, Wren. They want to see you happy just as much as I want that."

I finally got the courage to say something. "Tev, we have a mission to get this crown."

"It's *your* mission, Wren. Ever since the border, you have been looking for something to give you purpose like the Adora did. You've found it in this search for answers with these riddles and the books. Have you stopped to think that maybe the crown doesn't exist? That this feeling you seek, redemption or reconciliation or revenge, will never happen? Or do you believe that if you obtain this crown that you will have a foothold against Adonis? That you can leverage your way back into the House of Love you love so dearly? *Why do you want the crown so badly?*" Tev's anger started to rise in his questions, rattling them off as I did with my thoughts.

"You don't understand, Tev." It was all I could say.

"Then tell me!" He became animated when he said this. "Tell me why you feel such a strong pull toward the crown?"

I couldn't answer the question. He was right. Ever since my exile, I'd had questions, and now I thought the crown would possess all the answers.

Tev sat down on the bed again, his voice returning to gentle. "Look, if you still want to search for the crown, go ahead. I don't know what you will find when you do, or how much better it will be. If you leave, you are going to have to search for it on your own, though. I'm not letting go of something that I have been searching for much longer than you've known about this crown."

Shocked by what I had just heard, I was overwhelmed with thoughts again. This time, I was disappointed in myself.

Tev was right.

I needed to give up my search for the crown.

But a quiet voice inside me said, *don't give up.*

Chapter XXVIII

ARULEAH'S GRAVE

Tev and I were on better speaking terms in the following days. I did not give up my idea of leaving Ragsdale Ranch, but I quit bothering Tev about it. I didn't want to stir up friction between us again. I knew where he stood.

Over the next couple of days, his demeanor toward me changed. In the mornings, he would wake me up gently before getting ready himself. We would walk to breakfast together then take to our separate duties on the ranch. He was much kinder in passing too. Something as simple as a smile or we'd stop to have a quick conversation here and there. Whenever the time came for us to do different tasks, he would squeeze my hand in thanks for understanding why he wanted to stay.

In truth, I didn't understand. His desire to stay went against all that I wished.

My quest to find the crown had turned to mere thoughts. My call to action was subdued to please Tev. I hadn't spoken to anyone else about it. I was tempted one afternoon to talk to Ellie about it but couldn't muster enough courage to say anything.

Where do I start with something like this?

There was too much to say in a quick passing. I thought of dropping hints, to see if she knew anything about the name Bramwell or Aruleah or the Pillars or even a crown, but I didn't want to scare her off.

Our friendship grew after that day I rested in bed. In the afternoons when we were sent for chores, we would joke with one another about the smell coming from the clothes. I made faces of disgust at her, and it would make her giggle. We bonded over lighthearted laughs like that. For the first time, I thought it was nice to have a friend other than Tev.

The mornings became colder as the weeks went on. We moved our breakfasts into the kitchen. Since the kitchen couldn't hold us all, breakfasts became a time to eat and then get to work, instead of chatting. Ria and Nora would be in argument over the latest book Nora was reading. I would often shoot Ellie a glare of annoyance when their voices got to an intolerable level. Ellie typically ate in the corner while her mother braided her hair. Evan and Tev wouldn't talk partially due to the fact that they were shoveling food into their mouths, hardly breathing between bites. Finneous would be enjoying a hot tea quietly while simultaneously reading a large, creased paper, one of the many items the blorks would drop at the doorstep for the family. His nose drifted to the middle section where the weather report was written. I could see his eyes scanning side to side with the latest updates.

"Snow drifts are coming from the north," he read aloud from the paper between the shuffles of feet to and from the kitchen.

In big letters on the front read: THE GUILDHOUSE. Finneous described it to me as a way of knowing what was going on between the fallen houses without having to venture far into the House itself. The paper was written in the House of Patience as it was centralized for all the others, easier to distribute.

"There were other people who chose to stay after the borders closed.

Besides, there are other ways into Houses if it was necessary. But we were still all given the choice. It's been centuries since the Fall of the House of Patience, and my family has done fine."

"And multiplied!" said Nora from the kitchen between bites of her breakfast.

Her sisters laughed at the comment.

"We've made it work; I can't see why people in the other House couldn't either," he explained.

I thought of my family in the House of Kindness. This was a common occurrence while being amongst the Ragsdale family. I thought of my mom and dad sitting at their dinner table chatting about the latest recipes or my dad's issues with the pests outside. My brothers would be zooming from one end of the house to the other playing soldiers. It wasn't all peaceful or kind. There would be times when we didn't see eye to eye. When the Fall of the House of Kindness happened, they chose to stay, whereas my fear drove me away. The threat of the darkness lurking around every corner overcame me at times even before the Fall. With a weighted heart, I left, thinking it was the best thing for me. I wanted security and safety, and the House of Love was where I could find it.

Ironically, now there was nothing I wanted more than to risk my safety in search of the crown. The prospect of answers was stored wherever the crown was hidden. I just needed to find it.

Before we left for our morning duties, Adaline stopped Tev and me to give us an extra layer of clothing: a scarf and coat for me and a knitted cap and gloves for Tev. We thanked her and met up with the others shortly after.

I was very thankful for the coat. The temperature had dropped significantly overnight. As Ria and I fed the dustbacks, we had to cut our brushings short due to the cold winds picking up speed.

"The extra dust will keep them warm. We only needed to brush out the knots so they wouldn't tangle further," she said with chattering teeth.

I could tell she wanted to be inside.

We made our way back to the house and to my surprise, Tev and Finneous were already inside and building a large fire to warm the entire house.

Tev turned to me to explain, "We fed the cattle but with the winds picking up, we needed to get the horses inside. The animals should be fine for now. If it gets any colder, we might have to move them, so they don't freeze."

I gave a look of shock, questioning the very proposal that the desert House would get cold enough to freeze cattle.

Finneous caught my bewilderment. He filled the fireplace with chopped wood as he said, "It's unusual weather for this part of the House. The rapid change is the most harmful. There must be a big storm in Joy for it to reach us all the way down here."

I found Ellie sitting alone comfortably in a wide armchair with enough room for me to sit beside her. Her mother was in the kitchen preparing something warm for all of us while Ria went to her room to change into thicker clothes. Nora, wrapped in a knit blanket on the other side of the room, was reading a book. Her book gleamed with the title in big red lettering: *The Prism Guide: Unlocking the Secrets to Gems and Glass.* Just like her father, she kept her nose buried deep in the book.

Glancing around the room, I noticed a person missing. I whispered to Ellie, "Where's Evan?"

Keeping her eyes on the makings of the fire, she whispered back, "He didn't come back with the others. He is probably down at the family crypt. It's always hard for him to be around my family on the anniversaries."

I looked at her for more information, but the fire began to bloom and smoke. She gave a laugh as her father started to cough and comically wave around as if he made the mistake on purpose.

The time to ask her questions had passed, so instead, I slipped my coat on again and walked back out into the bitterness. Only to leave the cheers just as the fire sparked to life.

I could feel the ground stiffening under my feet with cold. The wind twisted my hair and whipped it across my eyes and ears uncontrollably. Cold crept through my clothes. I crossed my arms to maintain some of the heat from the fire inside. Passing the blork's barn, I began to climb the small hill beside it. I walked along the path by the tree Evan took me to on my first day at the ranch. Looking back, I could see puffs of smoke coming from the chimney while wild dust blew at the base of the house. I kept walking toward the pastures, finally arriving at the family crypt. White gravestones were bursting out of the ground between fallen canary leaves and dried grass.

Evan was sitting on the ground, staring at two headstones. He stood when I was in earshot of him, giving a half smile as a kind acknowledgement.

"I thought you might be here," I said over the howls of winds and the shaking of leaves in the trees.

"It's their anniversary today. Three years it's been," he muttered between sniffs. He had been crying.

I didn't know what to say. I walked over to him and put an arm around him, for comfort and, selfishly, for warmth.

"The scorpion took them in the night while they were sleeping. Those pests are all over the place around here. The blorks typically hunt them, but one must have gotten through. My parents were the best. Supportive in every way. If I had my mind set on something, they were the first to encourage me to pursue it with a full heart and at full steam.

"My dad was Finneous's brother. He was quieter though, not as loud as Finneous likes to get. And my mom—" his voice broke. "She was beautiful. She was from the House of Joy, of course. That's where she met my dad. They were always laughing together. She would brighten any room whenever she walked into it, as if the light followed her around. You remind me of her, actually. Pretty and *kind*."

Looking at the headstones, I saw two names joined together on one and a single name etched on the other. Their names read:

Donoralius Ragsdale
Born: Patian
489 – 3 – 15
Died: Patian
540 – 12 – 17

Glorina Ragsdale
Born: Joyous
491 – 6 – 27
Died: Patian
540 – 12 – 17

Evanlina Ragsdale
Born: Patian
521 – 9 – 16
Died: Patian
542 – 5 – 18

Before I could say anything else, Evan said, "My mom and dad weren't very creative with our names."

We both laughed.

"I'm sorry you didn't have more time with them," I finally said after the laughter died. "Losing family is hard."

I tried to comfort him the best I could, but I left my family. It was different. I didn't know the feeling of losing them completely. I had always hoped there would be a day I would see them again back in Kindness. I never entertained the thought that they might be dead.

I started to shiver. Evan could feel it through my quivering arms around him.

"You should head inside. It's starting to get cold out here," he said.

"What about you? Aren't you coming too?" I asked.

"I would like to stay out here a little longer, but I don't want you to freeze."

"I don't want to leave you alone." My teeth began to chatter like Ria's earlier.

"At least go inside the crypt. It'll block the wind and be a little warmer. I won't be much longer," he said with a pat on my shoulder, sending me into the stone building that was the family crypt.

There was a statue standing near the back. It was carved out of the same white stone as the large rectangular ones outside. The walls had names etched into them, generations of Ragsdales. There were no lights, except the one coming from the doorway. Time wasn't a friend to the names etched in stone. It was difficult to see some of them.

Bestor Ragsdale and Juniper Ragsdale. Cardace and Unity Ragsdale. Trennon Ragsdale. Periwink and Simion. Walter and Meriweather.

I looked behind my shoulder to Evan. His entire family was here. People he never even knew and maybe some he did.

The stone woman stood proud and stoic. There was no emotion on her face. Spider webs covering her face indicated she hadn't been paid a visit in a long time. The plaque at her feet was nearly hidden under cobwebs. I wiped away the dust with my sleeve. The name carved into the stone made my stomach drop.

Aruleah Ragsdale
Born: Lovian
16 – 4 – 17
Died: Saved
61 – 4 – 17

I shrieked at the name.

Aruleah?

Aruleah from Bramwell's books?

Aruleah, the writer?

The poet of riddles?

Was this really her?

She was a Ragsdale?

"Wren, are you ok?" Evan came inside. He must have heard me.

I could only muster pointing to Aruleah with wide eyes.

"Oh, her? Yeah, she was the matriarch of the whole family. Twenty generations of family names are in here. All because of her. She was born in the House of Love and escaped here. Weird lady from the stories my mom told me. One of her favorite sayings is carved on the statue."

I frowned, unable to see any writing on the white stone. "Where?" I asked.

He reached up and brushed away the cobwebs. Something caught the light above her head.

A crown.

I didn't notice she was wearing a crown beneath the cobwebs. Evan continued to swipe away the debris to reveal a stone crown sitting on Aruleah's stone head.

He read aloud, "*Follow the light and it will follow you. Give the light and you will be given too*. Have you heard the nursey rhyme about Aruleah?"

I shook my head in silent response.

"My mom would sing it to me when I was little and restless."

Evan began to sing.

In shadows deep, where light once bled
Ocean eyes with ember's thread
To the place of decay, where water once flowed
A past left behind, where new seeds are sowed.
With eyes of blue, bound by plenty
Cursed with folly, lost and empty.
Forsake the vices, passed down by many
Break free from chains, twisted and heavy.
Give up the past, the hunger, the flame,
Restore the gems and the claim.
Seek the light where darkness sways,
For the path ahead, as long as your days.

The tune was very familiar. Evan sang it the same as Dakari, the soldier I met in the Barracks. I looked at Evan with confusion but excitement.

Soon after, I rushed us out of the crypt, buzzing the entire walk to the house. I couldn't wait to tell Tev everything.

"Wren, you told me you were done with searching for the crown," Tev whined as we both got ready for bed.

I thought it was probably best that I didn't share the information about Aruleah with the family. I kept trying to get Tev alone, but none of my hints landed with him. After the fifth attempt I cornered him.

"Tev, do you understand what this means?" I said excitedly. "Ocean's eyes with ember's thread. Do you know anyone with blue and brown eyes? A place of decay. We need to go back to the Sandshadow."

"Are you crazy?" Tev said sternly. "We can't go back there. We almost died Wren. You almost -" He didn't finish his sentence.

"I know what it sounds like, but I really think the answer is on the Sandshadow."

"How do you plan to find it again? We wandered in those sands for three days without food and water."

"The snow coming in will show us our tracks and how to get back. We won't get lost this time. I have a good feeling about it."

"Why do you want to do this?"

"It just feels like *this* is something I need to do."

"You aren't afraid?" he asked timidly.

"I'm terrified, but I've let fear direct my life long enough," I told him.

"You can't just leave. Finneous will try to stop you. They will notice if you are gone." Tev was trying everything to keep me from going.

"We can leave together, during the night." I suggested.

"Wren, I've told you; I want to stay here."

"If all goes to plan, we will be able to come back." My eagerness was fading. His negativity was discouraging me from trying to convince him further.

"What exactly is your plan? Walk onto the Sandshadow and talk to Riperous? Convince him to walk a straight path into the light? Convince him to turn against all his selfish ways to reclaim the throne as a Pillar?"

"Yes," I said plainly.

"For Love and Patience, you can't be serious. You'll be killed! It's a suicide mission!" Tev's voice was tinged with anger now.

"I've waited long enough—"

"Maybe you should wait longer," Tev interrupted.

I continued my thought as if I didn't hear him at all, "Other people have told me what is best for me. I'm not going to let that happen again. I'm going—if you come or not."

The room became very quiet. With the abrupt ending to the conversation, I turned over in my bed to face the wall instead of Tev.

Aren't you afraid?

I didn't linger on his question long. Instead, I told myself:

I'm going, whether you come or not.

I fell asleep shortly after, not saying another word to Tev.

The next morning was colder than the day before. Snow whirled in spirals with thick flakes falling from the sky. I joined Nora to brush the dustbacks. We cut our morning short due to the weather again. Tev and Evan passed us on the way to the house, before I stopped Nora.

"I think I'm going to stay out here longer. I have never experienced snow before," I lied, using any excuse I could think of to get a closer look at that statue.

She didn't give me much of a fight before following Tev and Evan inside. I turned toward the family crypt. The ominous clouds were growing darker by the hour. The hill was slippery with fresh snow beginning to stick to the ground.

I made my way inside the family memorial and the statue of Aruleah was the same as I had left her yesterday. Without hesitation, I approached her to take a better look at the crown myself. With Evan, I didn't want to make a scene, but today, I could stare and search and wander the entire crypt without the judgement of another person, or so I thought.

I could hear footsteps crunching on the fallen snow just outside the crypt. My stomach tightened. No one else knew where I was. The steps grew louder. A boot clacked with the stone. I spun around. Finneous stepped inside.

"Hello, Wrenna. I thought I might find you in here," he said.

"Good morning, sir," I responded, confused.

"Oh please. Call me Finneous," he chuckled and proceeded to step closer to the statue of Aruleah. "Evan told me about yesterday and your fascination with my ancestor. Do you know of her?" he asked.

I didn't want to lie to him; he had done so much for Tev and me already.

"I know her name, but that's all I know," I said the truth.

"She was a wise woman," he started to explain, "She escaped the House of Love. Not many knew the reason why. Aruleah was a keeper of journals. I stumbled upon them when my mother passed, and I inherited the property. This woman here escaped the House of Love because of a man. A man who desired her so much, he was willing to do anything he could to have her love. He advanced but she refused. She did not feel the same way. She wanted to choose her love, not have love forced upon her. She found he was tricking her to benefit himself, so she fled to the House of Patience, where, after a couple of years, she met Riperous, the Pillar of Persistence."

My eyes widened at the sound of *his* name.

"So, you've heard of my other ancestor?"

"I've met him."

Finneous gave a tight-lipped smile and continued, "Riperous and Aruleah were unstoppable. Riperous, being a Pillar, and Aruleah, being an informant for the House, there was nothing they couldn't do. They eventually married and had a family, taking on the Ragsdale name. In those times, the entire House was land for the Pillars. Together, they were responsible for establishing the eastern border and trade between the Houses through this area. Aruleah settled here at the ranch while Riperous visited but remained predominantly and permanently at the Patian capital, Mirage Heights.

"She grew bitter her husband wasn't around to spend time with his family, and the guilt ate at him. In time with tearful suggestions, he left his responsibilities as a Pillar to come here and be with his family. Little did he know that would cause the first collapse of a House by the actions of a Pillar. By the laws of the King, a House cannot stand on two Pillars alone. Three must accompany the throne at all times. Riperous knew this but defied the King's laws to better his family and himself. He left the guilt of one and inherited another. On the journey to the ranch, his ship was lost in the Endless River. Casted with a curse in the Sands of Decay, he would remain there for the rest of his life. In order to save her husband, Aruleah wrote to the man in the House of Love."

"Bramwell," I whispered.

"Exactly," Finneous said with a wink.

Bramwell's books.

Aruleah's riddles.

She wanted to save her husband.

"I believe you have seen these notes yourself," Finneous deduced.

I continued to stare at him. I wanted to lie and say I had no idea what he was talking about; however, my desire for answers drove me to speak the truth.

"I didn't know what they were at first. I was in the market during one of the festivals in the House of Love—"

"The Festival of Norda," Finneous interrupted.

Shocked, I retorted, "Yes, how did you know?"

"I was the one who sold them to you that night," he said.

A flashback of that night ran through my head. There were fireworks and cheers and music moving throughout the street. Pax, Piston, and I went for drinks at the Lickity Split before heading into the markets. The merchant's face who sold the books to me was fuzzy. I couldn't remember it being Finneous or not.

"How did you enter the House of Love without the Pillars?" I asked, recalling a conversation with Tev the first night of exile.

"There are many entrances into the House of Love, unknown by any Pillar, my dear," Finneous said as a matter of fact. "I wondered, after selling the books to you, if I would see you here at some point. I wondered if you would make it to Patience." He stated, "When the girls told me they brought home guests, I had hoped it was you. The name Aruleah has a knack for attracting those who know it to this place. I knew there were secret codes embedded in those books; I just needed some help finding them."

"The dye from the leather got wet and soaked the pages. There were riddles hidden in white ink on the first page of those journals." I spoke fast, as if there wasn't enough time to say it all.

"Of course! Bramwell loved his wine," Finneous exclaimed. "What did they say?"

I spent some time explaining to Finneous about Aruleah's riddles in the books and the possibility of a blue- and brown-eyed soul being saved. I finished with the mention of the crown.

In response, Finneous explained, "Riperous has been trapped in the Sands of Decay for a long time. He hardly knows who he is anymore. He knows he is looking for a young, beautiful woman. The very reason Evanridge's sister was taken. She bore the trait only a few of us Ragsdales carry now."

"Blue and brown eyes," I answered.

"Yes," said Finneous. "It was a trait of Aruleah *and* Riperous, one they both shared. Looking into Evanlina's eyes must have sparked a memory in Riperous. When she told him the truth, that the person he was looking for had been gone for centuries, he hurt her in ways no one should. She escaped, the same as you, but battered and beaten. It took everything in Evanridge to stay here and not seek revenge. I told him, the day will come for Riperous to redeem himself. And as for Aruleah, she left us with this."

Finneous pointed to the statue bearing the crown.

"She loved riddles, the meanings behind which have been lost through the generations from father to son. Only a few of them remain now, including the one on that crown. 'Follow the light and it will follow you. Give the light and you will be given too.'"

"Why did you sell me those books at the festival?" I asked, changing topics to seek more answers.

Finneous looked at me and took my hand. "I saw your kindness. To your friends and the other merchants in the market, but I also saw someone who was lost."

I cocked my head to the side, needing more information.

"I held onto those journals since my father gave them to me, with the intention of figuring out what messages they held and, more importantly, excited about the adventure they would set me on. I brought them with me to the House of Love on a whim. I decided to give them to you, thinking it was time to let someone else have a chance at an adventure. When I passed them off to you I knew, in that moment, I would see you again."

He patted my hand and then dropped it to my side. Tears were starting to form in my eyes.

"I'm not naïve to the fact that you want to leave the ranch. My advice to you: Give it three days. Let the storm settle. Patience has a funny way of showing us more than we hoped for in the waiting period."

With that being said, he exited the crypt, leaving me with only the statue of Aruleah to keep me company.

Chapter XXIX

THREE DAYS' TIME

Shortly after Finneous left, I made my way back to the house. The weather had gotten worse. The winds were picking up and the snow was turning to rain.

By the time I entered the house, my clothes were soaked, and my hair was dripping. As I stood shivering in the doorway, Tev rushed to me with a blanket. He draped it over me and whispered in my ear, "I'm glad you decided to stay, especially with this weather."

I gave a half smile to him. I didn't want to be back in the house. With a single look, we agreed that this was where I needed to be for the night. With the conversation in the crypt still echoing in my mind, I whispered back, "Can I talk to you?"

Our eyes connected like magnets. For a second, he looked worried about what I might say. He took my hand in his. I followed his lead to our room for a private conversation.

I proceeded to tell him all that Finneous had told me about Aruleah and Riperous. By the time I was done speaking, my voice had become hoarse.

"You didn't recognize Finneous when we first arrived?" he asked.

"No. That night of the festival was such a haze. There were drinks and crowds and music and—" My voice trailed off with shame attached. My reckless days in the H.O.L. were behind me but the memories lingered still.

"What are you going to do now?" Tev asked.

"Finneous didn't deny there was a crown, but I doubt he knows where it is. He just said give it three days. What could possibly happen in three days?" I asked, not looking for an answer but thinking out loud.

"A lot could happen in three days," Tev said confidently. Holding out his hand for me to take, he said, "Let's get back to the group. Nothing spectacular is going to happen in here tonight."

He looked around the room like the walls were closing in on him. For once, I agreed and followed him to where the rest of the family was in the house.

When we emerged from the hallway, Evan saw us first.

"Feel better?" he asked.

"Glad you could join us," Ria said with a smile.

I sat down next to Ellie in the armchair. We faced the now raging fire. The flames caught my attention before Ellie whispered to me, "I was getting worried. You have been missing out on the game. Nora's won the last three times and Mom once before her."

The family was huddled around the small table at the center of the room. They were staring at a wooden maze with glass figurines perched on the perimeter of the board.

"What's the game?" I asked Ellie.

Just then, there was an abrupt cheer from Finneous and Ria. Nora looked upset, like they ruined a plan, advancing in the game in their favor instead of hers.

"Colorspire. We play it only on special occasions, like stormy days," Ellie said.

She took her piece and slid it on the board. It looked like an owl with sharp feathers pointing out of its tail. One I had recognized. One that cut my leg in a cave.

"That's my piece. It's a sunspiked owl. They are silent creatures. They hunt during the day instead of night. They have these razor-sharp feathers to protect them," she said with an excited smile.

"Those things are sharp," I commented, drawing from experience.

"Exactly! Their tails reflect the light best," Ellie said in response.

Confused and distracted by all the noise, I decided to sit back and watch. I peered over at Tev, who looked equally confused at the game.

After her turn, Ellie explained the objective of the game. "The pieces are made from the glass in the Glactus Garden. Each piece reflects light differently. When two pieces create a specific color, your character moves toward or away from the center, depending on the color. The resulting blinks determine how far you advance or retreat." She moved her piece toward the one that looked like a turtle. The turtle's shell emitted a yellow light. Ellie, disappointed by this, moved three spaces back.

"The goal is to be the first one to the center of the board," she said as she sat back in the chair with her arms crossed.

Next was Evan's turn. His figure looked like a rabbit with large horns growing at its ears. He moved it in the direction of the turtle and the light between them turned purple. He let out a laugh and moved his piece forward until the light faded.

The turns continued around the table, some with cheers and others with groans. Ria had a blue light with her glass lizard, sending her forward one space. Adaline's coyote caused a green light, letting her pass an entire row.

Then it was Nora's turn.

Ellie whispered to me, "Nora is the best at the game."

Nora's piece was in the shape of a dustback, and she moved it toward the center of the maze. She arranged the piece to face a certain direction and the glass dustback began to display all the colors of the rainbow, a signal she had won the game based on the moans coming from everyone else. As the colors danced around the room, Nora smiled. She was proud to win another game.

The family had dispersed from the table shortly after. Some were grabbing a snack from the kitchen while Ellie and Evan stayed by the fire.

"I don't know how she does it," said Ellie, discouraged, her arms still crossed.

"She cheats," Evan admitted.

"Really?" I asked Evan sincerely.

"No," Evan said chuckling to himself. "She's really smart when it comes to the way the light bends in her favor. It's just not fair."

"She studies it," Ellie added.

I remembered the book that hooked Nora's attention yesterday afternoon. Looking for the red lettering around the room, I found it resting on a lower shelf next to the chair Nora sat in yesterday. I picked it up.

The title of it read: *The Prism Guide: Unlocking the Secrets to Gems and Glass*

I opened the first few pages to find the table of contents. There were seven chapters:

Chapter 1: Reflective Properties of Different Glass
Chapter 2: Positioning of Prisms
Chapter 3: The Art of Light Dancing

Chapter 4: Maze Beams
Chapter 5: Mining Reflective Gems
Chapter 6: Rainbiotics: The Power of the Rainbow in Gems.
Chapter 7: Pillar Gems

The farther I read, the more confused I was about the contents of the book. There were scribbles inside the book as well. Written in ink, next to the last chapter labeled *Pillar Gems,* was 'untrue' in curly handwriting. I could feel my palms starting to sweat with anticipation as I flipped to the seventh chapter.

I started to race through the words, just as Nora did yesterday.

The Pillar Gems are unique stones selected by the Pillars during their coronation. Mined from individual Houses, the choosing of the gemstone inducts the Pillars into their House. After they were chosen, the stones were embedded into the Pillar's throne. This not only amplifies the Pillar's inherent attributes but stores the powers of the Pillar. The stones can only be removed once the Pillar has completed their term as Pillar. If the stones or gems are ever removed from their throne, the stone would retain the powers of the Pillar not the Pillar himself or herself. The stones could be transferred into any item to imbue it with the Pillar's power. For example, if the stones were set into a desk, the desk would inherit the powers of the Pillar.

This rule applies not only to inanimate objects but to wearable items. For instance, if a person wears a piece of jewelry, such as a head piece, watch, or ring, the wearer will inherit the Pillar's abilities.

If the Pillar abandons their throne with the stones attached, their House will fall into darkness, just as it happened in the House of Patience. The Pillar of Persistence, home to the House of Patience, caused the Fall by leaving his duties as the Pillar to pursue a woman of lower nobility. He still suffers the consequences by remaining trapped by time in the Sands of Decay forever.

There was a scribble in the margin with a drawn arrow to the underlined words 'woman of lower nobility' reading: *this is false.*

It is unknown how to restore a Pillar after he or she abandons their responsibilities as Pillar and their stones.

My eyes searched the room but the person I was looking for was already focused on me. He knew I found something. I smiled at him. He gave me a wink. I could feel heat rushing into my cheeks. Tev motioned his head to the bedroom, where we could talk in private. I shook my head and closed the book. I walked back to my seat next to Ellie, feeling the eyes of puzzled Tev from across the room. He wanted to know just as much as I wanted to tell him. Now was not a good time. Nora and Ria and their parents were returning to the room for another round.

Tev crept beside me to say loud enough for the others to hear, "Can I talk to you for a second?"

I gave him another smile and said, "Can it wait? I really don't want to mess up my first turn."

Cheers from the family sounded in the room and we started another round.

Adaline gave me my own character, a horned hog. Periodically, I would catch Tev looking at me with anticipation of the game ending. He was eager to listen to what I had figured out.

The wood for the fire was running low, so the family decided to turn in for the night. The girls shuffled to their room together. Evan left in the midst of a long yawn. Adaline left to clean the kitchen before heading to bed. With the embers on the fire, Tev and I sat together under a blanket in the chair. Finneous, insisting we stay where we were, began cleaning up the game.

"Finneous?" I asked innocently.

He looked in my direction. "Yes, my dear?"

"What is the Glactus Garden?"

One of the pieces reflected the red light coming from the fireplace.

"It's the House Garden in Mirage Heights, the capitol. It was founded at the same time as the House. The cacti, only found in that area of the House, have a coating of glass on them. It's partly due to the sand and wind and heat. The glass is spectacularly reflective and harvested to create piece like this one." He held up his own, one shaped like a blork. Its wings were outstretched, taking up a lot of space.

"Do you all have different pieces?" Tev asked.

"Oh yes, Adaline and I took our girls to the garden for their fifth birthday, just as my parents and hers did at that age. It's a House tradition to pick your piece."

Finneous held up his glass blork, admiring the way the light sparkled in it. "I have always loved the wings of mine."

He placed it in a special case to protect them all and sealed it shut. He set it aside and stood, heading for his bedroom.

"Could you be sure the fire has died before you leave?" he asked.

"Of course," I said.

"Goodnight," Tev added.

Then we were left, just the pair of us.

Tev's attention was now on me. I looked up to see his face and noticed his cheek was bunched into his shoulder in order to meet my eyes.

"What did you find in that book?" he asked.

"A clue. I thought you didn't want to talk about it," I concluded.

"I think my approach to discussing the crown has been a bit harsh. You obviously need someone to talk to about it and I want to be that person. I don't want to argue about it. I want to help, Wren."

His arm stiffened when he said that.

The warmth coming from the fading embers and Tev were lulling me to sleep, but I stayed awake long enough to tell him what I found. It had been a day full of answers leading me in the right direction. A night full of fun in a land where good was supposed to be lost.

This concluded the first day.

The next morning, Tev and I were woken up by the smell of food coming from the kitchen. We stayed on the couch talking for the rest of the night. Evan emerged from the hallway, stopping in the doorway at the sight of me and Tev. Saying a quick good morning, he walked through the room to the kitchen to help Adaline with breakfast. Wiping the sleep from our eyes, we headed for our room to change into different clothes for the day.

"What's the plan now?" Tev asked.

I was in the bathroom, freshening up, when I responded, "Maybe we should ask the family. Finneous seemed to know a lot about Riperous. Maybe he passed stories down to Ria, Nora, and Ellie. Like his dad did to him."

"Do you think it's best to include them in this?" he asked tentatively.

"It's their family after all. Their history. Why shouldn't I?"

The question seemed to kill the conversation as we finished getting ready.

We joined the group near the end of breakfast. The chatter melted into a hush as we entered. We were late. Tev and I took a seat, placing food on our plates in the awkward silence. Hurrying through our meal, we left with the rest for the pastures to complete the delayed morning chores.

By lunchtime, the sun had begun to shine again. The few days it was hidden away behind dark clouds made me miss it. With the sun came some normalcy. The dustbacks were happy to have their coats brushed again too. The temperature was beginning to rise too, making it bearable to be outside again.

Ellie and I were tasked with sweeping and cleaning the house following lunch. Without thinking I let out a question directed at Ellie, "Can I ask you something?"

Her stare in my direction read as if curiosity was sitting behind her eyes. "Sure. What is it?"

I stuttered my next words, not knowing how to fully explain what I want to ask. "I'm—I'm looking for a crown. I've been looking for one ever since Tev and I left the Sandshadow. Do you know anything about where I could find it?"

The curiosity abandoned her. She shook her head and continued to sweep.

"Ellie, please, if you do know something, would you please share it with me?"

She gave a sigh before saying, "I'm not sure. My dad told us stories when we were little, but I was too young to remember all the details. They are just stories anyways."

I let out a disgruntled sigh.

"Nora would know," Ellie added. "She is the historian of the family, always putting her nose into those books."

"I knew I should have asked her," I muttered to myself.

Ellie didn't take too kindly to what I said. To be compared to her sister in that way. To be seen as less than. Leaving her broom behind, she walked into the kitchen without another word to me for the rest of the afternoon.

My obsession with the crown flowed into the evening. Tev, Evan, and Finneous were done tending to the animals for the day.

"The cattle were really rowdy today. Eager to walk around and explore after days being huddled together to stay warm," Tev told me.

He walked gingerly. A full day of riding after taking a few days off was a hard adjustment.

Later that night, the family found themselves in the living room once again. I decided this was the best time to ask Nora about the crown.

I had made my way over to where she sat in her chair. She was reading again, this time a different book. The title was *The Fall of Houses*. She kept it close to her face, not able to see me approach her.

"What's that book about?" I asked an obvious question.

"The history of each Houses' fall into darkness," she said plainly.

"They keep records of that?" I asked.

"Oh yes. Illsi Tollar is a brilliant historian. She's written several books about the Houses and their downfalls." Nora had lowered her book.

"Is there any mention about a crown?" I asked in a hush.

"A crown?" she said loudly, grabbing the attention of the rest of her family.

Their attention now on us, I decided to address them directly. "I'm looking for a crown. Your ancestor, Aruleah, wrote letters to a man named Bramwell. These letters were hidden in journals, and I happened upon these journals toward the end of my time in the H.O.L." I glanced at Finneous when I mentioned the books he had sold me—the ones containing Aruleah's letters.

Continuing without interruptions, I said, "They were written in riddles. Aruleah was asking for help to find a crown to restore a House Pillar. This Pillar was her husband, Riperous, who is currently sitting on the Sandshadow, the same ship Tev and I escaped."

Nora's eyebrows rose at the mention of his name. She had obviously retained the knowledge from the last chapter of her book.

"He has been trapped in time, the effects of aging coming and going, but something keeps him suspended in time. He has been collecting gems too."

Nora twitched at the mention of the gems.

I addressed her directly. "Yesterday, I found in your book the chapter about Pillar Gems. They are chosen on the day of the coronation and hold the power of the Pillars. I've seen with my own eyes the true powers of the Pillars. I know what their stones look like too."

Nora gulped, stunned by what I was saying. The rest of her family was hanging onto every word I said.

"These gems on the Sandshadow—they are only the first step to restoring Riperous as the Pillar of Persistence, aren't they?" I asked Nora.

She was silent like the rest of her family.

"Aruleah mentioned a crown, an incorruptible one. One that could save Riperous. Do you know anything about it?"

Nora's eyes shot to her father and mother across the room, then to her older sister, Ria.

"Have you visited the family crypt?" Ria finally spoke.

I looked again at Finneous, as he was my witness to my answer. "Yes, I have. I saw the statue of Aruleah."

"Did you see the crown?" Ria asked.

"I showed her," Evan said, not meeting my eyes, but Ria's.

"Yes, he did," I agreed.

"What's your point, Ria?" Tev scoffed, impatient with her vague questions.

She glared at him, not liking his tone. "The crown on the statue has been there since I was born. When my sisters and I were little, we used to play in that stone room. One day, we got in trouble because a piece of her flowers broke off from us climbing on it. We found the stone that makes the statue is very brittle, unlike any of the gravestones set outside."

The fire began to pop and crack, breaking the silence that hovered in the room between the sentences and thoughts.

Eager to see it for myself, I said, "Well, let's go now."

Finneous stood and said, "It can wait until morning. I think that's enough for tonight. Time for bed. All of you."

He eyed me in particular. Everyone stood. I moved toward the door, defying the directions of Finneous. He grabbed my arm to stop me.

"Finneous, let me go," I said sternly.

I tried to shove his hand off, but it was no use. His grip tightened. Tev stood as a protector but didn't advance in respect to Finneous.

"I know your thoughts. I know what's going through your head. I know you want to go see it now. Trust me and wait," he said softly.

I yanked my arm from his grip and marched to the room. Tev followed shortly after me.

I had already escaped to the bath before he entered the room. I didn't say another word for the night.

This concluded the second day.

The next morning, I woke before the sun. I was eager to see the statue of Aruleah again. After I accidentally woke Tev, he stopped me before I could make it out of the door. My skin vibrated as I stood near the exit.

"Remember, Wren, the Ragsdales are letting us stay here. You ought to be kind to them. They are not asking us for anything in return. Keep that in mind when you leave for the day," he said.

Half listening, I nodded slightly, inching toward the door.

"Wren?"

"Tev, let me go," I said impatiently, gripping the doorknob. My knuckles were turning white from tension.

"Hold on. I want to say one other thing."

My body was facing the door, ready to leave. Out of respect, I turned toward Tev, signaling I was willing to listen.

"Whatever you find out there," he paused, drawing out our time together, "please say goodbye first."

There was a sadness that crept into the room. The end was drawing near, and questions were to be answered soon. With his decision to stay at the ranch, our time together was limited and coming to an end.

I nodded politely and raced out the door.

I didn't truly know where I would end up.

I hope not back at the ranch.

I hope I will have an adventure—like Finneous suggested.

The sun beamed through the windows of the house, casting a golden light on the chairs in the living room. Reaching the door that led to the pastures, I was stopped by a hand on my shoulder. Spinning on my heel, I was face to face with the head of the house, Finneous.

"Good morning," he said.

"Good morning," I repeated quickly.

"I would like your assistance with the blorks this morning."

My shoulders sagged with disappointment. Finneous raised his eyebrows at the sight of it. Remembering Tev's comment about us staying here, I straightened up and produced a tight smile. As he led the way outside, we walked to the barn to feed the blorks their breakfast.

"I appreciate your help this morning, Wren. I wanted to give the others a break before you left," Finneous said as he was putting away the bloodstained bucket.

We worked until mid-morning with the blorks. They seemed to sense my hesitation upon entering the barn, making them reluctant to descend from the perch on the barn's rafters. Finneous had me on bucket duty, tossing the raw meat into the air for the giant birds to catch. It took a few tries before I threw it high enough for them to snatch it out of the air. We had cleaned up everything, and I was just about to leave for the crypt when Ria came into the barn.

"There you are," she said to me. "I need your help with the dustbacks this morning. Nora's been vomiting since we woke up. Must have caught a stomach bug." She shoved a brush into my hand and grabbed the other with her own. She pulled me in the direction of the dustbacks' pasture, whether I wanted to go or not.

When we walked up to the dustbacks, there was a thick coat of mud on their front tusks and mud caked into their tangled hair.

"They were rolling in the mud yesterday. We need to brush it out before the hair mats," Ria said, grabbing a water bucket whilst walking into the pasture. "This will be for their tusks. They're filthy."

I looked in the direction of the crypt, thinking to myself, *it will have to wait.*

We worked on the dustbacks for what felt like hours. It was well after midday when I decided to covertly drop the brush and bucket off at the fence. Before I got too far, Ria yelled, "Food is ready. You should eat something. I could hear your stomach making noises."

I reached for my stomach, which felt hollow. I had skipped breakfast and lunch; I needed food. The sun hadn't begun to set yet. If I ate quickly, I would still be able to visit the crypt with enough light.

Against my wishes, I made my way into the house to join the others for food. Nora was sitting at the table looking green over a bowl of steaming stew. There were other bowls placed around the table for the rest of us. The boys, not far behind me and Ria, took their boots off when they entered the house. They, too, had a day full of mud.

"It's disgusting out there," Evan said. "You can't tell which is which."

"Evan got his foot stuck in a pile of it." Tev laughed at me.

I forced a little smile, making it appear I was paying attention. Images of the statue were shooting through my mind. My foot twitched under the table as I hurried through my stew. It burned the roof of my mouth, but I would have done anything to rush through supper. To make matters worse, the meat was very tough and it took a long time to chew. One thing after the other started to annoy me. The laughs between Evan and Tev. Nora slurping her stew weakly. Adaline shuffling her feet from the table to kitchen clearing the finished bowls, including mine. Just then, another hand was placed on my shoulder.

Without thinking, I shouted, "What now?"

I turned to see whose hand was touching me. It was Ellie. She was holding two brooms. Tears started to form in her eyes because of my outburst. The brooms fell, clattering on the floor. Everyone's attention was on us. She stood there not wanting their attention, only mine.

Finneous had just opened the door when Ellie ran right past him, racing to the pastures.

"She's been looking forward to it all day. Wouldn't stop talking about cleaning with you all morning. I think she senses you are going to leave soon," Adaline said regretfully.

I was instantly flooded with guilt. My cheeks heated red and my palms were sweaty. I picked up the brooms and chased after her.

"Ellie!" I called after her.

I found her at the top of the hill, sitting under the tree where I once sat with Evan.

"Ellie, I'm sorry," I said breathlessly.

"I don't want to hear what you have to say," she spat back.

"Ellie, please—"

"No! You know what your problem is, Wren? Whether you want to admit it or not, the darkness has gotten hold of you."

I looked at her as if she was knocking the wind right out of my lungs.

Her chest was rising and falling fast, as if calling me out was difficult for her to get off her chest.

She went on, uncontested, "I feel like it has had hold of you for a long time. Before your time in Patience."

I remained quiet, not by choice, but by shame.

Ellie huffed, "Huh, imagine, *Patience.* Something brought you here, Wren. Not this quest for the crown. Not whatever happened in the House of Love. You are here for a reason. This quest for the crown has blinded you. You are so desperate to find it that you have become selfish and irritable. There's something bigger right in front of you."

She wiped her nose but let the tears fall.

"Do you know why there aren't a lot of people who live in the House of Patience? Do you know why we are one of the only families in this area for centuries?"

She didn't give me time to answer.

"The House of Patience is one of the hardest Houses to live in, not only for the virtues it upholds, but the darkness that lurks in the shadows is the strongest here. Impatience can drive people mad. They become unwilling to wait for a solution and unwilling to hear the side of their opponent. Their time is more valuable than that of their counterpart. People who are not inherently patient in life—well, they suffer in this House.

"My aunt was one of them. She was a great woman. She loved her family, or so my mom and dad told me. She was so blessed to minister the light, but in her selfishness, in her being, she thought she needed more. This drove her to the darkness and ultimately to her death. The time scorpion wasn't by surprise; it was out of desperation. In the black clouds of darkness, you cannot think straight. She thought her time was coming to an end and she wanted to hit the pause button. Evan's dad tried to save her but was stung in the process. Instead of delaying time like she hoped, the scorpion's sting cursed them both right then."

I looked anywhere but at Ellie as she told the story. "And Evan—he still doesn't know the real story. He thinks it was all an accident. Not by my parent's fault, but by his own stubbornness to hear the truth. Then his sister—"

Ellie took another deep breath.

"Evanlina left the ranch in search of her purpose. She struggled like her mother. The darkness saw her as a target and lured her away from the light. She wanted something more and set out to find it. She met her match on the Sandshadow, barely escaping, only to die in the sands a few days later."

"How do you know all of this?" I asked Ellie.

"My parents don't want to hide the truth. They don't lack the integrity that most people struggle with nowadays. As horrible as it may be, they shine a light on the darkness for us to be aware of how to handle it in the future."

I had never thought of it like that before.

The darkness should not remain in the shadow.

What good would it do to bring it out into the light?

"My family's roots are planted deep in the soil of Patience," Ellie continued. "We have seen the effects of the darkness. We know it haunts in the shadows. It lingers in the arguments. It is quiet and tricky and when the time is right, it is a creature of destruction, taking all that is good."

My mouth was dry. I didn't have anything to contribute to the conversation.

Ellie continued, "Lina was my best friend. I begged her to stay. I told her it was a mistake, but she insisted on going. I didn't speak for weeks after Evan brought her home. And now, I see how the darkness is using this crown against you. It wants to drive you mad, just like the rest of them."

I opened my mouth to protest, but before I could say a word, Ellie interrupted.

"It's like an itch you can't stop scratching—each clue drives you further. At first, it just irritates you, but then it starts to hurt. Still, you push on, desperate to uncover the mystery, ignoring the consequences, it scabs but you pick it."

I could feel a hot spot on my neck forming an itch as Ellie spoke. I wouldn't dare reach to touch it.

"Sooner or later, you've reached the bone, but it's too late. An infection has grown and then you are *dead.*"

The last word hung in the air, a reminder of my fate to come if I continued down the path of the crown. The sun had fully disappeared behind the mountains. The light was fading from the sky. My time was up, and I had no desire to see the statue anymore.

This concluded the third day.

Chapter XXX

A HIDDEN SURPRISE

"Do you want to go inside with me?" I asked Ellie with an outstretched hand.

"What about the crypt?" she asked.

"It's getting too dark out here; we wouldn't be able to see anything."

Just then, out of the corner of my eye I saw something small on the ground move. Climbing from a hole dug in the ground was a small creature—its shell glowing faintly red.

Ellie knelt beside it, smiling. "The thornmounts are waking up," she said.

"What are they?"

One walked right past my foot as I recoiled.

"They are desert tortoises. Haven't you seen them before?"

"Only once. The night after Tev and I left the Sandshadow. We thought they were the pirates searching for us. So, we decided to run from them," I said.

"They surface in the desert when the sun goes down. Their shells glow a fiery red to attract bugs and insects to feed on. They are used to lead the lost in the desert. They are harmless. When they are all together, they look like *stars*," Ellie said mystically.

"How many are there?"

"Dozens. They are just waking up now that the sun has gone down."

A few more of them were emerging from the ground, gathering around Ellie. I could see her clearly in a casting of red light. She stood and dusted off her pant leg.

"If we start walking to the crypt, they will follow," Ellie suggested.

My heart gave a bit of flutter at her mention of the crypt. As much as I wanted to go, I also wanted to be respectful of what Ellie said before the thornmounts rose.

"We don't have to go tonight," I said.

"I'm still mad at you, however," she paused for a moment, "I'm curious to see what is in the crypt myself. Don't think because I've agreed to accompany you means I forgive you—yet."

"I wouldn't dare," I said with a smile.

And after that, we followed the red lit path the thornmounts provided to the crypt.

Arriving at the crypt, we both carried a thornmount into the crypt and set them on a ledge opposite one another. Ellie left for a brief moment to pick some vegetables to keep them satisfied and still. When she returned, other thornmounts followed her into the crypt, blasting the stone walls with red light.

I began scouring the statue, in search of anything out of the ordinary. The stone that Aruleah's figure was carved from dusted my fingers, leaving them chalky and dry. Ellie joined me in the hunt. She lifted a thornmount to the statue, giving us a better chance at finding something. I attempted to remove the crown from Aruleah's stone head, but it did not budge. I took hold of my own thornmount for better lighting.

We searched for the better part of an hour and found nothing. The statue stood clueless. Anger started to boil inside me. The blank expression on Aruleah's face made me want to hit it repeatedly.

Placing my thornmount back on the ground, I huffed, "You were right. Clue after clue and it led to nothing."

Sitting beside my thornmount, I picked up a nearby rock the size of my palm with plans to chuck it at the statue. Passing it between my hands, I thought of the wasted time. The journey through Patience Tev and I endured. The tease of redemption with the crown. The little hints of there being something worthwhile at the end of the day but still coming up short in the end. My palms began to sweat holding the rock. It was growing hotter and hotter the longer I sat and stirred in my anger.

Standing to my feet, I threw the rock as hard as I could at the center of the statue.

The collision cracked the statue, creating a sound neither of us expected. I instantly looked at Ellie. She was thinking the same thing I was. We approached the statue one more time and to our surprise, there was a hollowed hole in Aruleah's stone chest. I pressed my fingers to worsen the hole and found that Aruleah's statue wasn't made of stone at all. It was plaster.

Gripping the layer of plaster, I pulled back with all my might to open the cavity wider. A chunk of white remained in my hands as I stumbled back, almost stepping on my thornmount in the process. Ellie let out a laugh.

"We found it!" she yelled.

"Not yet," I said.

Both of us began to remove large pieces from the statue. White powder was coating the air as we destroyed the statue. Creating a large enough opening, I stuck my arm in as far as I could reach. There was nothing but the outline of the statue.

"It's empty," I told Ellie.

She directed me to pull my arm out and proceeded to hold a thornmount to the gaping hole of Aruleah's chest and stomach. The light wasn't strong enough for us to see the entire length of the statue.

"This is ridiculous. Hold this," Ellie said, passing the thornmount to me. "Watch out."

I stepped back, still holding the thornmount, as I witnessed Ellie crawl behind the statue. Pressed between the stone wall of the crypt and the statue, she started to rock the statue back and forth. Leveraging her back against the wall, she pushed with all her strength to move Aruleah forward. I stepped hastily backward, tripping over a thornmount. I began brushing the by-standing thornmounts out of the way while on my hands and knees. I could see the statue starting to give way and with one final push from Ellie, it began to fall. Kicking the last thornmount to the side, I slid on the stone floor to avoid being crushed by the statue. It collapsed on the ground, breaking the white plaster into little pieces.

As we coughed from the plume of powder, the dust finally settled enough for Ellie and me to see each other. Ellie stood at the same time I did. The room was lit by the dulled light from the thornmounts, giving a pinkish hue to the stone room. We swatted the dust from our eyes and approached the statue that used to be Aruleah. As we surveyed the wreckage, pieces of thick white plaster filled the entirety of the floor. At the base of the statue, there was a limp piece, coated in the same white dust as everything else.

"What's that?" I pointed, signaling to Ellie there was something we needed to investigate.

She picked it up and dusted it off.

"It's a piece of parchment," she identified. "There's something written on it."

She began to blow on the paper, revealing the ink well enough for me to see something was written there.

"What does it say?" I asked.

She had begun to read it silently, but paused to look up at me. The glint in her eye made my heart race. There was something significant on this paper, I thought to myself.

She cleared her throat before she read:

Dear Reader,

By now, you will have destroyed the statue of my mother. This letter is written to the descendant distant enough to not know my mother, but who fears the name's reputation. The secret my brothers and sisters chose to hide within this statue was only to spite one person in particular, our father.

Allow me to explain.

Our mother, Aruleah Permella Ragsdale, was a kind, loving mother. I, Persimeous Ragsdale, am one of her five children. Riperous Ragsdale, the Pillar of Persistence for the House of Patience, was our father. Being the youngest, I remember the least about my father. My siblings retained fond memories of my parents in their childhood.

I wasn't so lucky.

Growing up in Mirage Heights, we were royalty and brought up as such. My mother, having escaped the Estate of the House of Love, wanted her children to grow up outside of the responsibilities of the

Pillars and the greed that comes with power. She decided to leave with her children for another home within the House of Patience. Pleading with my father to join us, my mother convinced him to leave his position as the Pillar of Persistence. Abandoning his throne, he caused the Fall of the House of Patience, allowing darkness to roam freely within its borders. An earthquake shook the kingdom. The effects caused the water from the Sea of Tranquility to recede and form the Endless River, thus trapping my father in the Sands of Decay.

My mother was desperate to save our father. She wanted us to have a loving home with kindness and goodness and most importantly, patience, not death and destruction. With the news of the Fall, a book arrived from the House of Love. I was there when my mother received the first one. She read the first page and threw it across the room. Later, she wrote back, hoping to never hear from the person who sent it again.

Dozens of books were flown in later that week, coincidentally gifting us with a flock of blorks for protection. These couriers were immune to the darkness, fooling the darkness by looking like a creature made from itself. They warded off any darkness wanting to capture my mother and my siblings. We came to tend to the birds, giving them food and shelter, and they stayed.

As time went on, the darkness learned other ways to infiltrate our home. It's a predator and it's crafty. It'll strike whenever it is given the chance. My mother knew it was only a matter of time. She attempted to write to our father, pleading for help. With many letters sent, a reply never came. My mother was left disappointed, heartbroken, betrayed, rejected, and lost—it was the final straw the darkness needed. It seized my mother, welcoming her with outstretched hands. It hugged her like an old friend and she basked in it. Her loving heart grew colder and colder as the seasons passed.

I felt anger toward my father for turning my mother into a creature of darkness. The light was completely drained from her life. She refused food and water and sleep. My once beautiful mother was now a shell of a human. Even her skeleton began to peek through her skin.

I took it upon myself to write the only person who had looked out for us since the Fall of Patience, the man in the House of Love. I begged for a remedy to restore the light to her life—something immune to the darkness, just as he sent the blorks.

A reply came from this man, unlike my father. A crown was mentioned, one that could restore life, one of light itself. This man did not say where it was kept but believed in the power of the crown. Hopeful, I showed my mother the letter, thinking we could find the crown to bring light back to her life. It lifted her spirits slightly, and she started her search for the crown. During this time, my desire to restore my mother's light backfired. She went from a cold and distant woman to an obsessive one over the crown. I wanted nothing more than to feel the love of my mother my siblings once felt, but the darkness knew it could still have a hold on her. In her manic episodes, she wrote riddles to remind herself of her findings. She was gifted with words. Should anyone else come to read the riddles, it would only confuse them, another ploy I believe the darkness brewed.

The years went by and there was still no crown. I grew bitter toward the man in the House of Love for giving my mother false hope. She was persistent until her last days, a trait my father imparted to her,

I'm sure. Growing older and older, she knew her time was coming to an end. The riddles she wrote were given to the child who was faithful to her in the days of darkness. She knew, even in her haze, she failed at this task. She passed away without ever finding the crown.

My siblings and I grew up and had families of our own. Some left the House altogether in search of Goodness and Kindness and Peace. One of my sisters returned to Mirage Heights to present herself as the rightful heir to the Pillar throne. Continuing the line of secession, she maintained the other thrones with her bloodline. Resentful that her family couldn't fully reign in the House because of our father's absence, she sent him his throne as a constant reminder of his irreparable action.

I remained at the ranch and had a family of my own. One day, a package arrived tied to a blork. The box contained the seal of the King. I opened it to find a gleaming gold crown with a note that said: For the one who was faithful.

Etched inside the crown's interior were the words Crown of Life.

Still very angry at my father, I kept it and did not use it. I alone built a family crypt to store the crown, hidden as a monument in honor of my mother. I manipulated it to look like stone, so the crown would be placed inconspicuously on her head, paying homage to the quest she never finished.

As the keeper of riddles, I chose to scatter them amongst my siblings and myself. Some chose to pass them down as stories to their children. Others chose to discard them altogether. I chose to hide the riddle containing the instructions on how to use the crown with the crown itself, only to be found long after I am gone.

Understand, this crown has powers neither I nor my mother could fully comprehend. My guess is the only person to know the truth about the crown is the King who bestowed it.

Use it however you see fit.

Go with Patience,
Persimeous Ragsdale

On the ground was another piece of paper, folded and covered in dust. Ellie unfolded it to find the riddle and read it aloud.

My dearest—the love of my life,
This long suffering will not end in strife.
The time apart we have endured
Was not a waste but should be revered.
The choices you've made—ones I encouraged—
Led our lives into pieces, some that are damaged.
You must know: The darkness has not won.
There is life beyond—light from the sun.
My heart aches with regret—please come to forgive,
For this life of light is pure, one you can live.
The message of a life restored, tied to a book,
Gave me hope and joy, for I did look.
Seek the crown and you shall find
A world of light in your heart and mind.
For my love abounds far and wide
But guilt and shame have blinded my eyes.
I wish I was the one to set you free.
Only the blood of love on bended knee.
I searched high and low for the crown;
The sands of Patience were only found.

The power of forgiveness is the key to heal
A broken heart—one of zeal.
Unsuccessful, I must be
If writing this letter is my legacy.
I know your burdens are heavy in the dark.
They can be lifted, like a song from a lark.
Bring them to the light and you will see
The burdens can't hold you for eternity.

Ellie looked in my direction. She had tears forming in her eyes, the same as I. The passage was heartbreaking. Aruleah wished she was the one to save her husband from the decisions both of them made, not to mention her children's desire to spite their father. The feeling of pity for that hideous man on the Sandshadow started to fester in my stomach. He wanted to be with the love of his life. He wanted to leave the position of power. And now he was trapped in darkness.

Wiping the fallen tears away from her cheeks, Ellie said softly, "We need to show him this. We need to take the crown to Riperous."

Chapter XXXI

RETURN TO THE SANDSHADOW

"Are you crazy?" I asked Ellie, my voice sounding harsher than I intended, almost like Tev's. "He will kill us if we step on that ship, Ellie."

"No, I am not. He needs to know about Aruleah," she responded.

"What makes you think he will listen to what we have to say?" I asked.

She gave a sigh. In my mind, I took a step backwards. I was the one convincing her we shouldn't go when all this time that is exactly what I wanted.

We found the crown.

The search was over.

There was a part of me that felt the quest was incomplete.

As if she read my thoughts, she argued, "What are we going to do with this crown if it's meant to save someone from the darkness—keep it for ourselves?"

"It could protect us. We could live without fear of the darkness," I said convincingly.

"It's meant to restore the light," she snipped back.

The papers from Persimeous and Aruleah were dangling at her side. The crown lay on the ground between us. I peered down at it. The moment I looked down, Ellie had already stepped forward and grabbed it out of my reach.

I told her, "You can't go. Think of Lina. What did you tell her when she left?"

"I told her that it wasn't the right time. That she should wait a little longer to be certain. I am certain about this."

"I can't let you go alone."

"So it looks like you will be coming with me," she added.

"I guess so," I said.

By the light of the thornmounts, we walked back to the house. We had devised a plan to go back to the house for supplies. Ellie stashed the crown for safekeeping in a hole belonging to one of the thornmounts, so we could grab it in a few hours when we left the ranch while everyone was still asleep. We both agreed not to mention the crown or the statue to the family when we made it to the house.

"They won't like the idea of us going to the Sandshadow," Ellie said. "They won't want to come with us either. I'll pack a bag for the trip with some food. I know the sands well enough to make it there before the sun goes down tomorrow evening."

I nodded in agreement and opened the door to the house.

"Look who I found," I said to the group inside.

The family was gathered around the fireplace: Nora in her usual chair reading, Adaline and Finneous cuddled together enjoying the fire. The others seemed to be in an intense match of Colorspire, not daring to look up when Ellie and I walked into the room.

"We were starting to get worried. I was about to send Evan out for you," Adaline said to both of us. "What—in the name of patience—did you do to your clothes?"

In the light, it was easier to see the coating of white dust on our pant legs, the remnants of the fallen statue in the crypt and evidence that something suspicious happened while we were away. We both began to wipe the dust.

"We hashed it out the Ragsdale way—arguing until someone gives in," Ellie said before I could think of an excuse.

"Who won?" Evan chimed in with a laugh.

"Who do you think?" Ellie smiled back with a wink.

Confused, I saw Evan give Ellie a pat on the back before she sat down next to him in the chair. The fire filled the room with a strong heat. Beginning to sweat, I could feel the dust sticking to my skin underneath my clothes.

"I think I am going to wash up," I excused myself and headed to the bath.

Footsteps behind me indicated Tev was following me. Per our agreement to tell no one, against my better judgment, that included Tev. I entered the bathroom before he made it to the room. Closing the door to the steam-filled room, I evaded his curiosity in a narrow escape. Over the rushing of water from the tub, I could hear his heavy footsteps on the other side of the door. The squeaks of springs in the mattress soon followed.

Escaping into the water, after taking a deep breath, I let out a little chuckle.

Finneous was right.

Give it three days.

His voice echoed in my head.

We found the crown. There was a purpose for all of it. There was a reason I was forced from my home. From the earthquake to my sentencing, I thought of my home in the House of Love. I missed my friends and my job at the Adora. I thought of Jeston and Thadeous and Adonis. I thought about how lucky I was to find Tev shortly after landing in the House of Patience. I could feel the meditation from the Postuells and the hollowness of my stomach still. The sting of the sun came to my mind next, before Ria and Nora found us, then our time here at the ranch and meeting Ellie and Evan. There had been many blessings to come out of those dreaded books of Bramwell, ones I could have never imagined.

The steam began to lessen. I quickly scrubbed the dust from my fingernails and rinsed my hair. Wrapping the wet hair in a towel, I changed into clean clothes and exited the bathroom. Tev was lying on the bed, drifting off into sleep. His chin was tucked deep into his chest and his arms crossed over his stomach.

This was the last time we would see one another before I left for the Sandshadow with Ellie. I remembered what he told me this morning before I rushed out of the room.

Say goodbye before you go.

If he knew about our plan and Ellie accompanying me to the Sandshadow, he would surely tell Finneous. A part of me wished he wanted to join us, but I didn't dwell on that thought. Tev drew his line in the sand. He was staying. And I was leaving. I couldn't help but think about how I would miss him.

Quiet enough so I wouldn't wake him, I draped the blanket at the foot of the bed over him. I gave a peck on his forehead and whispered in his ear, "Goodbye, Tev," before slipping under the covers of my bed and falling asleep.

The night went fast. Eager for the morning, I turned over in my bed six or seven times before abandoning my bed altogether. Assessing my few belongings, I stuck them in the pockets of my clothes. I left Tev snoring loudly in his bed, a once annoying sound that would soon turn into a fond memory.

I met Ellie in the kitchen to snag last-minute snacks before leaving.

"All set?" she whispered with bread spewing from her mouth.

I nodded to keep quiet, as she packed the last items into a bag. Pointing in the direction of the door, we shuffled our feet, being sure not to bump anything that would make noise. Reaching the door, I undid the latch and swiftly darted through, with Ellie close behind me.

The moon was out, casting a pale light over the pastures. Grabbing baby thornmounts for additional light, we headed for the hole where Ellie stored the crown and the letters.

"Got it," she said as she reached down. Storing them in her bag, she secured the strap over her head and around her chest.

"Are you ready?" she asked.

"Are you sure you want to do this?" I asked her in return.

"Absolutely," she said.

With her answer, I asked, "Which way should we go?"

"This way will be the fastest." She pointed in the direction of the crypt. "There's a shortcut, so we don't risk running into anyone by the house."

She darted past me, and, in turn, I followed her to the edge of the ranch and into the desert of Patience—one I was already too familiar with.

Facing our destination, we watched the sun greet us for a new day. Starting as a dark navy, silent and deadly sky, it soon became full of hope. Clouds constructed a masterpiece with the colors of soft pink and yellow. Before long, the colors turned vibrant and spectacular. The majestic display slowly faded while we walked; however, the entertainment of watching it made the otherwise boring walk exciting. Ellie thought the same as I, pointing at different times to the configuration of the clouds. Our conversations quieted when the sun fully rose for the day.

We stopped midday for a snack and to rest our tired legs. Walking in the sand was no easy feat. There were plenty of times my ankles gave way to the mound underneath, almost spraining them altogether. Ellie took her shoes off at one point to let out the sand that had built up in the soles. She rubbed the sides of her foot, relieving the aches starting to form. Upon putting her shoes back on, she pulled a compass from the bag that hung at her side.

Looking at it then looking off to the distance, she said, "We are headed in the right direction. My guess is we will get there right when the sun goes down."

"We better keep moving then. We don't want to be out here at night."

The sounds of the coyote howls and the chill of the desert night came to the forefront of my mind, as well as the discomfort Tev and I experienced trying to sleep in the sand.

Finishing our food, we started our walk again.

The day crept along at a pace I wasn't expecting. Another hour passed in what felt like a flash. The anticipation of arriving at the Sandshadow and delivering the crown to Riperous was immense. I began to bite my sandy nails, a nervous habit I hadn't engaged in for years. I could feel the anxiousness radiating off of Ellie too. The device she held had a switch. She flipped it back and forth, counting our steps the closer we got to the massive ship.

Cascading a large dune, we could see the ship and its immense shadow in the distance. There was a reason the ship's name was

Sandshadow. When Tev and I escaped it a couple of months ago, we ran, never looking back. Because our arrival had been hindered by the glass box, I never understood how massive the ship truly was. From where we stood, it looked small, like a toy boat in a bath. I knew once we walked closer, it would tower over us, dwarfing our figures approaching.

"Let's follow the ridgeline and enter in the shadow," Ellie said. "We will stand out too much if we approach it in the sun."

Doubtful anyone was expecting two girls to sneak *on* the ship, I agreed and followed her lead along the ridgeline of the dune.

The sun began its descent in the sky, elongating the enormous shadow. This made it easier for Ellie and me to slip into it at a safe enough distance. We wanted to make it onto the ship before we ran out of light. I made the decision to set off in a run once we made it halfway through the shadow. We were exposed out in the desert; the closer we were to the ship, the harder we were to be detected. The light reflected in the captain's canary windows beamed onto the sand. Golden light danced beside us as we ran closer to the ship.

A large hole gaped in the ship's frame, but my sights were set farther down. I wanted to be out of sight and catch my breath before we dared to enter the Sandshadow. The closer Ellie and I got, the more we could hear the ominous creaks coming from the barge, mirroring the time the ship was once at sea. Sand filling our shoes and sweat forming on my brow, we finally made it to the ship. I took deep breaths to slow my heart rate and clear my thoughts.

Ellie, reaching my side, did the same.

Between breaths, she whispered, "You—could—have—told me—you—were—going to take off like that."

Sticking a finger to her ribs, she winced at a pain in her side. She bent over with her hands on her knees to relieve some of the pressure.

"We made it—though," I huffed back at her.

With her hands still on her knees, she shook her head in disapproval. I dismissed it and focused my attention on the open door of the Sandshadow. A few dozen feet away, there was no movement coming from it. Another creak came from the wooden frame. Ellie sprang upward at the sound.

"What's that?" she asked.

"The ship. It still remembers life in the water," I said, recounting the words of Riperous from my last visit.

We were losing light quicker than normal in the shadows. I dropped to my knees to sketch out a layout of the ship. The ship loomed over us, silent but alive with memory. For a moment, I wondered if coming back here was the worst mistake I had ever made.

I showed Ellie my plan for getting to the captain's quarters.

"It's a bit confusing once you are in there," I prompted her. "If we get split up, deliver the crown to the captain, no matter what."

For a second, Ellie had a horror-struck expression. The idea of us being alone on the barge hadn't entered her mind until now.

"I will try my best to stay by your side," I assured her.

"Maybe you should take the crown yourself," she suggested, lifting the bag from her side.

I raised a hand to ease her. "We will be fine. We just need to get to Riperous before someone else finds us."

She nodded with a shaky grin and we trotted our way to the door of the Sandshadow.

The smell of rotten fish and salt graced my nose once I set foot on the wooden planks of the ship.

My stomach twisted.

I never thought I would step foot on this ship again.

The lower deck hadn't changed since my last visit. The wood was still splitting in some areas and the dim lanterns lit the corroded corridor. At the end of the hall, I saw the staircase that led me to the top deck. Ellie, right on my heels, followed my lead as we crept our way deeper into the ship. Maniacal laughs erupted from beyond the wooden walls. Ellie and I stopped our advance to listen to their proximity. Peering around my shoulder, I could see petrified emotion on Ellie's face. I grabbed her hand to climb the staircase and give her some sense of relief that she was not alone.

I could feel her hand tighten in mine as we helped each other ascend the steps. Our feet were light enough to miss a few creaks. Our breath remained steady as our bodies were rising closer to the main deck. Our grip was loosened due to the sweat forming on both of our hands. There were no sounds coming from above. The laughter below us boomed once again. Most of the crewmen must be in the lower decks for their dinner. Keeping stride, with our hands together, we made it to the top deck. It was barren. There was no soul in sight. I found a barrel to hide us behind. Dropping Ellie's hand, I fell behind it. Ellie did the same. Slow, drawn-out breaths—I was able to breathe through my nose after a few minutes.

I pointed in the direction of the captain's quarters and Ellie gave a thumbs-up. Glancing around the barrel, there were still no sign of men. I chose to stand with the goal of reaching the captain's quarters. Checking to see if Ellie was behind me, I hit something hard with my first step.

Something warm.

Something breathing.

A decaying man was standing as tall as the mast itself between me and the door to the captain's quarters. I recognized him from my first day at the Sandshadow. This was the man who stood in the back, staring at me, like a prize he wanted to win himself. The same man who chased Tev around the arena with the thoroughwight.

I stumbled backward but before I could say anything or get out of his reach, his arms wrapped around mine, securing my own in place. He had pulled a knife from a hidden sheath and pointed it in the direction of Ellie.

"Don't say a word," he croaked.

I shuddered. My back to Ellie, I was wrapped in the man's decaying body. He threw me back behind the barrel, letting me go at once. Crouching down beside me and Ellie, his eyes matching that of my captors a couple weeks ago, he asked in a low voice, "What are you thinking coming back here?"

The closer I looked at the man, the more familiar the face became. Underneath the layers of dead, sun-kissed skin and without the beard I knew him to have, the man smiled at me. Once I pieced it together, I wrapped my arms around Thadeous and held them there to embraced an old friend.

"What—How?" I stuttered the only words I could manage as I pulled away.

"Adonis sent me here. He thought this would be a punishment well-suited for the crimes I committed against the H.O.L. throne." He motioned to the rags that somehow stayed on his body and the boils on his hands. "I wanted to tell you the moment I saw you, but since I was new to the ship, the crew wouldn't let me near you. I tried to tell Tev at the initiation, but Riperous kept me under a trance. What in Love's name are you two doing here?" He looked at Ellie, who was awestruck.

I turned for her bag, still attached to her.

"We found something." The gold of the crown hinted in the now-dim light. "We need to get this to the captain."

Thad looked puzzled by the notion. I explained the story of the books and the crown to him in a brief summary. The bewilderment was fading into a plan behind his eyes. Once I was finished, he glared at me with the same thrill I knew at the Barracks.

"Do you trust me?" he asked with his grotesque hand outstretched.

I looked at Ellie.

Her wide eyes peered back at me.

She gulped then nodded.

My hand met his and we took off for the captain's quarters.

Chapter XXXII

CROWN OF LIFE

"Give me your hands," Thad said hurriedly.

Ellie and I did as we were told. We stopped at one of the masts at the center of the ship. Before we were spotted, Thad tied ropes around our wrists to make it look like we had been captured.

"This will discourage anyone from asking questions if they see us. I have a key to the door. Let me do the talking first, then you can say what you need to," he explained.

I could sense Ellie didn't like the idea of an additional layer of helplessness to our plan, but I shrugged it off. It was the best option we had. After Thadeous tightened the knots, we made our way toward the cabin in the back of the ship. As we walked beside him, he pulled a brass key from a hidden pocket. He twisted the key in the lock and the bolt cracked. He lifted the metal handle, and we entered the captain's quarters behind Thadeous. Seconds later, the large wooden door shut behind us, locking us in the room.

Heavy steps echoed as the captain strode to see who dared to enter his chamber without an invitation. This version of Riperous was young, with his blond hair peeking out of a large black hat with a wide brim. He was dressed in the same leather and boots as when I first met him.

"Good evening captain," Thad said strongly.

"What is the meaning of this?" Riperous asked.

"I found these two roaming the desert. Wanted to get a closer look at the ship. Trying to sneak food and water, no doubt. I brought them straight to you after picking them up. You might want to have your fun with them before the rest of the crew."

A fire boiled inside of me. It must have been written across my face. Thad noticed he struck a chord of irritation. As he motioned for us to come closer, he gave me an apologetic look. I stepped in front of Ellie, volunteering myself. Before Thad had the chance to reach for my hands, I spit in his face. Playing the part well, I also wanted him to know what was off-limits. A snarled glare came from Thad with his back turned to Riperous. He wiped the spit away and shoved me toward the captain.

I stumbled toward the Pillar, who caught me in his arms.

"This one is feisty," Riperous said amusedly. He forced my chin up to get a better look at my face.

"Bite me," I breathed through gritted teeth.

Thadeous had untied Ellie's hands as Riperous examined me. I was able to see his cursed eyes, passed down through the years. While Ellie only had one dichromatic eye, Riperous had both. The top halves were the color of rust and the bottom halves like a cloudless sky. A shiver went down my spine at the sight.

He discarded me to have a look at Ellie after Thadeous removed the ropes. I spun to find her shaking where she stood. Her sight was fixed on the polished boots of her ancestor which were drawing closer to her. Grabbing her the same way he had me, he lifted her face. Upon seeing the same as his reflection, he immediately stumbled away from her.

Almost tripping over the chest full of multicolored gems, he hissed, "What is the meaning of this?"

His question was directed at Thadeous, who was taken aback by the venomous reaction. I could see his plan was beginning to fail. Thadeous hadn't expected this kind of reaction from the captain. Riperous wasn't supposed to know who we were. We were lost girls in need of food. Thad glanced at me for help.

Now was a better time than ever to explain why we were on the Sandshadow.

"She's a Ragsdale," I said confidently.

Riperous shot a glare at me as I said the name. Another hiss, like that of a snake, emitted from him.

"We brought you something," Ellie muttered.

With both men shooting glances between Ellie and myself, Ellie decided to reach for her bag.

"How dare you bring these girls here!" His anger was directed toward Thadeous now. "Take them away at once!"

"No," Thad said plainly.

"I order you to take them away," Riperous commanded.

Thadeous, without saying another word, moved to the doorway and stood with his arms crossed, forcing Riperous to listen to us.

Figuring his fate was near an end, Riperous made his way to the back of the chamber. He sat in his Pillar throne behind his desk, muttering something to himself. Ellie met me at my side and we both advanced to the distraught Pillar.

"Those eyes—" he whispered to himself. "Those eyes haunt me."

"They are the eyes of your wife," I said softly to him. "Aruleah."

The name jolted him like a lightning bolt sparked in his chair.

"How do you know that name?" he asked.

"We found something that belonged to her," Ellie said. She held the handwritten poem Aruleah left for him, pulled from her bag.

Extending an arm, Riperous cried out, unwilling to take it. He began to shake in his seat as if we triggered a volcano erupting. Whimpering like a bleeding dog at the sight of the parchment, he convulsed before Ellie walked over to his side of the desk.

Behind me, I heard Thadeous take a step closer to us in case we needed a trained hand at a moment's notice. With Riperous hunched over, his head hanging in his hands, Ellie lowered herself onto the wooden floor for the Pillar to hear the poem. She read the poem with the sweetest tone. Sobs were expelled from Riperous after the first line. Louder ones left him halfway through. He hid his face for the entire duration of the poem. Tears and snot began to drip from his hands. At the conclusion, he managed to take in a much-needed breath but continued to hide his face.

The cries faded in and out in the passing minutes. It was the only sound in the room. When Ellie was done reading, she placed the poem at her side. Her body was hidden by the massive desk. I could see her face staring up at Riperous. She put her hand out, holding it in the air. Thadeous and I could see what she was thinking. We both took a step closer in anticipation of the Pillar's wrath directed toward her. She touched his back to comfort the cries.

Wrath, however, did not come. Riperous parted from his hands to look at Ellie sitting next to him. His face had changed from the young man we once met to an old one I had met before. This was the true form of the Pillar: old and wrinkled. Seeing Ellie stay at his side unafraid, he calmed down, taking longer, slower breaths. The moment he and Ellie shared was similar to a father and child, understanding one another on a level deeper than anything else. I could only imagine what he was thinking when he looked into the eyes passed down through the generations that followed him.

"You look just like my Leah," Riperous said to Ellie calmly. His voice was raspy and weak, a combination caused by the cries and the aging. He began to wipe away the snot on a part of his clothes, cleaning himself up a bit.

Ellie gave him only a smile in return.

"She was my entire world. Our family—" He broke off, unable to finish the thought. He continued after a breath of air, "It was all taken away by a decision neither one of us could take back."

Tears began forming at the edges of Ellie's eyes, and she let them fall.

"We believe there is a way," I said from across the room.

Ellie hesitated, reaching slowly into her bag. She then pulled out the glittering gold crown.

"Where did you find it?" he asked Ellie, not taking his eyes off of it.

"It has been with Aruleah ever since she died," Ellie told him, conveniently leaving out the part about his son wanting to hide it from him.

"I can't believe she found it," the Pillar whispered.

"We aren't sure how it works," I added.

Riperous, remaining motionless, took in the awe of the crown. I could hear another step from Thadeous behind me.

Breaking the trance, Riperous looked again at Ellie.

"Will you help me?" he asked.

The words hung in the air.

The Pillar of Patience—the king of the Sandshadow—was asking us for help.

Hesitating again, Ellie nodded in agreement.

"The same eyes you have, given to you by myself and my wife long ago, have been cursed all my life," Riperous said.

Pressing hard on the arms of the throne, the elder Riperous stood with shaky legs. Ellie stood with him to avoid being trampled by the Pillar. He walked over to the jewels in the chests that were scattered throughout the room.

"You see, I am colorblind. I cannot tell the difference between any of these gems," Riperous said. "I have been looking for my Pillar Gem for centuries, hoping one day I would be able to use its power again. Mine was a small canary diamond. I was fond of it and sad to leave it behind. I noticed it was extracted from my throne when my daughter sent it to me." He pointed to the back of his throne, where a small divot was carved out for a single stone.

"I've sent men out into the House in search of any gemstones they could find. Through the years, their searches have become destructive, looting innocent people and taking women from their homes, an affair I regret to have a hand in."

We were all listening to him intently.

"I need your help now to look through these gems. Help me find my canary."

Ellie was the first to dump the contents of a chest onto the wooden floor. Thadeous stood guard at the door. I followed suit once Ellie tipped the second chest. We scanned the gems, some larger than my fingernails, all different colors—from dark navy stones to the lightest pinks. They glinted in the light of lanterns.

As if the sun itself was shining on the ground, I found a little yellow gem between two emeralds.

"Ouch!" Ellie said from the other side of the room.

"What happened?" I asked her.

"I cut myself. This one is very sharp," she responded.

Blood was starting to trickle down her pointer finger. Hot, red blood coated the stone too, larger than a pebble. Ellie held it in her palm, careful not to cut herself again. She handed it over to Riperous, who had been hovering over us. Transferring it from her hand to his, he smiled, kindly, though disappointment showed in his eyes.

"It's smaller than I remember—chipped," he said softly.

He walked back to his throne.

"They must have cracked it to dig it out of the throne," I suggested.

"I believe you are correct," the old man said back.

He slumped in a nearby chair. Ellie brought the crown closer to him.

"It wouldn't hurt to try," she said in a hushed voice.

"No, my dear." Riperous patted her hand holding the crown, a signal to give up. He stared at the broken gem, lost in thought.

"May I?" Ellie asked for the stone back.

Reluctantly, he gave it back, careful not to cut either one of them. In one hand, she held the shimmering gold crown and in the other, the canary diamond belonging to one of the most powerful Pillars in the House of Patience. Teetering the small gem on the central crest of the crown, she fixed her grip to place it in the divot as best she could. Configuring a bit, she eventually got the stone to fit. With excitement in her expression, she looked at the old Pillar.

"Would you like to try it on?" Ellie asked.

Stunned, Riperous said nothing. Tears beginning to fill his eyes again, he bowed, giving Ellie a chance to place it on top of his head.

The crown stayed fixed on his head, but a liquid light washed over the body of the Pillar. It was a molded and moving cloak of light emanating from the crown. The translucent golden veil revealed scales around Riperous's eyes. One by one they fell off, crashing to the ground. A set of chains shackled around Riperous's wrists became visible under the cloak too. As if the light was the key that unlocked the chains, they too were released and joined the scales on the ground. Riperous's posture straightened under the cloak. Looking beyond Ellie, Thadeous, and me, he smiled like he was being greeted by an old friend.

"After all this time . . . " he whispered.

This was the light Jeston mentioned.

This was the light Riperous had missed for so long.

Centuries of obeying the darkness, completely shattered by the crown of life.

His life in darkness had ended.

His haze of confusion and anger and burden had been lifted.

This was his second chance.

The old man who welcomed the light moments ago transfigured again. His blond hair was restored to a healthy, silky length. The dark leathers he wore were torn away and replaced with a pressed, mustard outfit comparable to the outfit Adonis typically wore. The wrinkles and harsh lines on his face were erased. His teeth were straightened and white and smiling back at us. He appeared to be the same age as Finneous.

This version of Riperous was the kindest I'd seen.

From behind me, Thad gave a bellowing laugh as he looked down to find the boils on his hands were healed and his skin was returning to normal. His beard was back, with a little grey peeking through.

Ellie, eyes sparkling with tears, let them fall as she stood to hug her ancestor. Their embrace was a familial hug, one with understanding and forgiveness and patience, one a grandfather would give to his grandchild.

For the first time in centuries, the Sandshadow had a captain again.

The House of Patience had a Pillar again.

There wasn't much time to celebrate before we heard a roaring noise. Riperous let go of Ellie and ran to the window behind his throne. In the back of the cabin, the window was only large enough for him to see through. He scanned the Sands of Decay for the unexplained noise. Turning to us, he ran past us, yelling, "Hold onto something!"

I narrowed my eyes to see through the dark peephole. Something large and white was headed in the direction of the Sandshadow. The roar was growing louder and louder by the second.

Riperous ripped open the door, yelling at his crewman, "Steady yourselves! You there," he shouted at two crewmen, who were astonished by their appearance. They came to attention with the call. "Tell them to shut the door!"

The men raced down to the lower decks, yelling the captain's orders.

A few seconds later, the noise from beyond the Sandshadow crashed into the massive ship. I was jolted toward the door. Luckily, I landed halfway on Thadeous, who broke most of my fall. Ellie landed at my feet. Another crash sent me flying into a bookshelf beside me. I could hear Ellie screaming when she was thrown into the air to land on the steps of the cabin leading to Riperous's bed. Books began to fall on my body. I expelled a groan but before I could feel the stings, another pull drew me to the glass cabinet on the other side of the room. This time I let out a scream when some glass bottles crashed beside me, their contents dampening my hair and the floorboards. I looked around through the strands of hair and broken glass to find Ellie hunched over a chair, unconscious. Jewels were twinkling in the braids of her hair. A lesser but still powerful crash moved the ship. Ellie fell to the ground with a thump, and I rolled over into glass. Another crash came, this one less than the last. The movements settled into sways.

Finally able to feel the impacts of being thrown around the room, I had no desire to move from my spot on the ground. My head buzzed and my bones ached.

With glass crushing underfoot, Thadeous assisted me to my feet. Swinging my arm around his shoulders for extra stability, he walked me over to Riperous's bed and gently placed my limp body onto the sheets.

My focus was unable to hold on to the world. Swirls of nothingness floated in my vision. I closed my eyes to dispel them. It was impossible to deny the slumber. Drifting further and further, I didn't care what was happening around me. All I knew was that it was safe to fall asleep.

Chapter XXXIII

RETURN TO THE HOUSE OF LOVE

I woke to find myself wrapped in warm white sheets with yellow light beaming down from the wall of windows. The salt of the sea had tickled my nose in the first few moments as slumber and dreams drifted away. Or maybe I was still dreaming. The smell of sea spray couldn't exist in the desert. The House of Patience, the crown, the Pillar—it couldn't have all been real.

Lifting my head, I found Ellie sleeping next to me. She rested peacefully and unharmed. Her braids had become messy. Loose strands attached themselves to the pillowcase. Careful not to wake her, I eased my way out of bed. Anticipating bruises from the crashes of fallen books and cuts from the broken bottles, I found there were none.

The smell of food drew my attention. A platter of pastries and sausages was set out on a table placed on the other side of the cabin. Walking down the steps, I was greeted with a deep voice, coming from behind the desk, backlit by a wall of blinding light. The golden bricks of glass that constructed the wall behind him matched his robes as well as the crown and throne and even his Pillar Gem.

"Good morning," Riperous said with his deep voice.

"Good morning," I repeated back.

He remained behind the desk as I reached for a scone. He was scribbling on a parchment with a long feather quill. It almost tickled his nose as he etched it on the paper. I rested comfortably in one of the chairs, remaining silent but aware of the Pillar. Shockingly, the Crown of Life sat, not on Riperous's head, but on the desk beside the parchment.

"I would like to have a word with you," he said, not looking up from his work.

Although his physique was more like a Pillar, his shoulders were slumped and tired, like he had been up all night. A tiny messenger bird with white spots had flown in from the opening in the bricks. Tearing a slip of his parchment, he tied it to the foot of the bird.

"I remember you from your time here a few months ago," he said, completing his last knot on the bird. It zoomed off after he gave it a whistle.

Shooting my eyes in his direction, I remained silent in my chair.

He stood to join me, sitting in the chair adjacent to mine.

"In the haze of the darkness, I wasn't sure where I had seen you. Now, I can remember everything."

I swallowed my scone. It was very dry all of a sudden.

Grabbing my hand, the same way he did Ellie's the night before, he said, "I can say now, it was never my intention to show you the worst of the darkness. Your first visit on the Sandshadow was full of darkness. In the haze, I said and did things I thought were right in the moment and after some time in reflection, I have learned that they were not."

I opened my mouth to protest, but he spoke first.

"No matter how old or how powerful or how determined you are to find yourself in this world, you will make mistakes. There are times when you will be scared, and you end up hurting those around you because that's the easiest thing to do. There are times when the darkness will be a friend to you. A good friend too. I must be the one to tell you, whatever it says, it is all lies. The promises of riches are not worth chasing. Your selfish desires do not supersede the needs of others. When you put people above yourself, you will be rewarded. I know this to be true because it is what you did for me. I hope with time you will come to forgive me."

"I haven't thought much about it, honestly," I said hastily, hoping to be done with conversation soon.

"I don't want you to be quick with it either. Forgiveness is a tricky thing. My wife said it best: 'The power of forgiveness will come to heal even a shattered, broken heart'."

"Is that what you did? Forgive her when you heard the poem?" I asked.

"I had forgiven my wife many years ago. I knew she didn't want to hurt our family by encouraging me to leave my Pillarship. When I was cursed here, I was full of shame and guilt and all I wanted was to feel numb. She would write and I couldn't bring myself to respond—a regret I have had to bear since her death."

"If you were the reason for the fall of the House of Patience, why do the Pillars in the House of Love think Aruleah was to blame?" I asked.

"Over the centuries, I have seen the Pillars come to love the power they have been given. Just as I did. For them, it is much easier to blame someone else for the collapse of what was once good and true rather than take responsibility for their own actions. My wife visited the House of Self-Control—yes. She unknowingly found much more than she bargained for there, but ultimately, it was my decision to leave. My decision alone that caused the fall."

"Did you ever blame her for it?" I asked inquisitively.

"My dear, healing comes not only with the forgiveness of others but forgiving yourself," he said.

"Is that why the crown worked for you?"

"Not the only reason, I presume."

"What do you mean?"

He stood, tracing his steps from behind the desk. He returned with Aruleah's poem.

"The blood of love on bended knee—I believe that to be your friend over there. The girl with whom I share my eyes."

"She doesn't love you—"

"No, but she grew in love with her mother and father and came here because of the love of my wife. Therefore, she is the embodiment of love and love shines in light."

I looked at him like he was speaking in code.

"Ellie has always lived in Patience. I believe love exists in other places, but patience is the grounding virtue in these lands for its people, not love," I said firmly.

"Love can break any barrier, Wrenna. It can multiply when it is nurtured. Abounding love is one of the strongest forces. Don't forget that."

I nodded, not quite understanding why he was having this conversation with me.

"Before we head down another winding path, there is something I want to give you," Riperous said.

He reached for a small wooden box on the table with the pastries. His long arms could reach the entire distance without having to stand. When he handed it to me, I opened the lid to find a ring with a single stone. Uniquely shaped, the stone's asymmetrical setting was oddly appealing. The stone was the same color as the one placed in the crown the previous night, the counterpart to the one Ellie found last night.

"It's a piece of my Pillar Gem," Riperous explained. "When you two were sleeping, I had your friend help me clean up the jewels and he found it in the pile. I spent the night making two rings. A memento of your time on the Sandshadow, however brief it was."

"Why do you want to give it to me?" I asked.

"Well, I didn't need my gem to remain intact for the crown to work. There was enough light inside of me. The crown just amplified it."

I gave a kind smile.

"There's also another reason." He trailed off this time. "I wanted to thank you. I can only imagine how you felt when you stepped foot in here again, terrified, slightly worried. But you did it anyway. You thought I was a soul that needed to be saved. For that, I am grateful."

"Thank you, Riperous," I said, pausing at his name.

He gave a wince.

Letting out a chuckle, he said, "I've always hated how villainous my name sounded. My wife would call me Ripp, as can you."

A tug at the corner of my mouth along with a nod signaled I agreed to his subtle suggestion.

"I have a ring for her as well." His eyes turned to Ellie, still sleeping. "I was hoping to explain with both of you, but maybe it's best you know first."

"I'm not following." I shook my head, confused.

"You are now in possession of a Pillar Gem. These aren't just any gems. They have powers of their own," he said.

"I know," I said, recalling Nora's book. "They hold your power as the Pillar."

"Not necessarily," he corrected. "They hold the spirit of House. Our House, the House of Patience, is calm, time-altering, and now, in the light. This spirit is drawn to the light, especially hearts who have the light. My dear, you now have the ability to visit anyone who holds the light in their heart."

My eyes grew big at the news.

"I—" I stuttered, looking down at the ring I hadn't placed on my finger yet.

"How do you think we Pillars visited one another in the Houses?" he asked with a sincere smile.

"I—I don't know," I said, dumbfounded, still shocked at the initial news.

"The light is a follower. Some might be able to push it away, but it will always come when it is wanted. If someone has the light, you can speak to them as if you are standing right next to them. All it takes is one person to have the light for you to be there."

Placing the ring on my finger, I could feel the heaviness of the stone and the coolness of the metal. It fit nicely around my knuckle as I secured it on my hand.

"How does it work?" I asked excitedly.

"Run your finger over the stone and think of someone you want to visit."

I ran my finger over the stone, thinking of the one person I wanted to see most.

In the blink of an eye, I was no longer on the Sandshadow but being whisked away to the place I had seen in my mind.

Opening my eyes, I realized the power of the gem had worked. I was standing comfortably and unharmed in the place I imagined only seconds ago.

The Grand Forum of the Estate was shining like rubies more than ever. The last time I was here, I was exiled with the notion I posed a major threat to the Pillars in the House of Love. As I got my bearings about me, there were many people leaving the forum in brisk steps.

A meeting had just ended.

"Excuse me?" I asked, stopping the General in his recognizable maroon peacoat.

He rudely carried on without even a glance in my direction.

"Excuse me, I'm sorry to bother—" I tried stopping the woman in charge of stewards for the Estate, but all I was awarded was another dismissal.

From inside the chamber, I could hear Adonis speaking to someone. My heart quickened, ready to see the man who destroyed my life. I was ready to show him how well I was doing in exile. I was ready to tell him how I restored a Pillar. Eager to see him scurry away in fear, I waltzed into the throne room.

The soles of my shoes squeaked on the polished floor. The long cherrywood tables lined the room leading to the stone steps where, the last time I was in this room, Jeston struck me. I shuddered at the thought but continued holding my head high. At the other end of the room, two Pillars were speaking to two of their advisors. One I recognized as the mage, and the other's face was hidden.

Surprised they hadn't seen me yet, I let out a cough in my hand. The sound echoed in the room, yet they did not veer from their conversations. None of them reacted as if I had spoken. I inched closer; they were bound to see me now. I was about to speak, but just then, the tiny, white-spotted bird fluttered past me. Landing softly on the arm of the Pillar throne, the bird looked at Adonis. The Pillar reached for the bird's leg and removed a small strip of parchment.

Reading it aloud, he said, "The House of Patience has been restored. I, Riperous the Pillar of Persistence, request an audience at Mirage Heights this evening."

"That must have been the meaning of the dancing light last night," Sylvanora stated immediately.

Adonis, disregarding her comment, addressed the man standing in front of him. "If it weren't for you, Bolt, I would be surprised by this. We would be scrambling to protect our House from those idiots who claim the light."

Getting a better look, I could see the man standing between me and Adonis was indeed Bolt—my safety inspector. His shaggy hair was cut tight to his head. He wore glasses and a maroon coat, making him look taller and more mature.

"It was an honor to serve the House of Love," Bolt responded.

"The moment you told me of Bramwell's books in the possession of that songless sparrow, I knew you would be loyal to the throne," Adonis praised him.

At the mention of what I could only guess was me, I marched up the steps. Waiting to be questioned, I stood in direct sight of Adonis. To my surprise, he could not see me. None of them could see me. I went to grab the cards from the table, but I couldn't grip them. They fell through my hand as if I was a ghost to them.

If I could only speak to the people who had light in their hearts, then they must not have the light.

How could that be?

I was in the last remaining House.

The House of Love hadn't collapsed.

There hadn't been earthquakes since my exile.

"What do the cards say of our fate?" Sylvanora asked the mage.

His round belly filling the space around him, the mage pulled large cards from his pockets and started to flip them one by one onto the table.

"They are difficult to read, but there is an uproar in your future. A person from your past will come to disturb your peace and blood will betray blood. With the House of Patience restored, the House of Love is in danger," the mage said to both of the Pillars.

Sylvanora looked from her advisor to her brother with a frightened expression.

Adonis had turned the color of his throne underneath his dark hair and beard.

Through gritted teeth, he said, "If you will excuse me, I need an audience with our brother."

Peering past Sylvanora, I noticed the spot where Jeston's bare throne sat before. It was empty. Not even a trace of burlap on the stone. Fumbling for the stone on my ring, I felt the coolness pass through me while thinking of Jeston. By closing my eyes, I was gone from the throne room and whisked away to another part of the Estate.

Upon opening my eyes, I landed in an unfamiliar room.

The dark stone with jagged edges flexed on the walls. Swords of all shapes and sizes hung proudly next to a large metal shield. Small windows let in light from the outside high above where any head could see out. A mattress placed in a majestic wooden frame and complementary dressers and desk were scattered throughout the room. The same steps seen in the throne room separated the bed from the rest of the room. Comfy chairs and a table accented with books and a board game rested at the base of the steps. It was cold in the room. Torches, pairs of them, lined the room, but didn't add heat. An unlit fireplace had a mantel with wooden knights jousting at one another then resetting after one of them had won.

Before I had the chance to look around, the solid wooden door swung open, and a person was thrown beside me. It was Jeston. But not the Jeston who led me to the Barracks and certainly not the Jeston I shared a dinner with. This Jeston had dark bruises on his cheeks and a split lip. Catching his footing, he turned to whoever was at the door and spat. The door had closed before the spit took its desired effect, with laughter fading from the other side.

"Jeston?" I asked, hoping he would respond to me.

Not a hint of notice crossed his face. I peered down at Riperous's ring, wondering how it worked.

Striding to the mantel, Jeston examined his cuts in the mirror. Following him, I gasped. There were clippings attached to the mirror. A sapphire paper that matched a melting pot parchment. On both, a dedication written in black ink and a riddle written in white. He managed to find the books before Adonis did after taking me to the Barracks.

Jeston was now an arm's distance away. Reaching out, I tried to pat him on the back. I didn't want to scare him, but I desperately wanted to talk to him. I couldn't touch him, just as I couldn't touch the cards on the table. Something held me back. He glanced over his shoulder, in my direction, then revisited the mirror once he found nothing over his shoulder.

I watched his eyes in the reflection; he was reading the poems Aruleah wrote to Bramwell. Tears began to well at the base of his eyes. As he read them a third time through, the tears were beginning to fall onto his cheeks. Picking up a ceramic figurine, he threw it across the room. It crashed at the base of the steps. He snatched the riddles from the mirror and gripped them tightly in his hand. Hanging his head low, he went to retrieve the pieces he had just smashed. Biting his lip to keep it from trembling, he let out a scream while reaching for the first piece.

I couldn't help but jump from the noise.

There was nothing I could do to help him. All I wanted to do was let him know that I was here.

I made my way to the stone steps, and I sat beside him. Still unable to touch him, it was my way of comforting him, even if he didn't know I was there.

Folding my hands, I was met with the feeling of the new ring that adorned my finger. I studied the yellow hues that reflected the dim light. I wished that Jeston could see me.

"I'm here," I whispered. "I'm here Jeston. You aren't alone."

Closing my eyes, I continued to chant over and over again, "You are not alone. I'm here."

His cries began to quiet . . . as if something had reached him.

"I'm here." I repeated.

Silent tears began to fall on my cheeks. I could feel their sting on my skin.

"The light—come to the light, Jeston. Let the light in your heart," I pleaded to Jeston.

I began to rock back and forth on the steps, willing with all my might, using the spirit in the ring as Riperous said.

"I'm here, Jeston," I said, continuing my whispered prayer.

"Wren?" said a familiar voice, one broken, beaten, and bruised.

Chapter XXXIV

JESTON'S RIDDLES

"What—in Love's name?" Jeston asked.

"You can see me?" I asked, ignoring him.

"How did you get in here?"

"You can actually see me?" I asked again enthusiastically.

"Yes!" he shouted.

"Jeston, we don't have much time. Adonis is on the way."

"Move!" Adonis shouted from behind the bedroom door.

"Take these and hide." Jeston waved the riddles in front of my nose.

Snatching them from him, I jumped to my feet and sprang behind the door just in time for it to open, with Adonis standing in the doorway. Jeston had remained where he was, sitting at the base of the stone steps.

"Come to help clean my room?" Jeston jabbed at Adonis with pieces of shattered ceramics in his hand.

"Who were you just speaking to?" Adonis asked.

Dropping the ceramic shards, Jeston stood. He dusted the smaller pieces on his pantleg. He answered, convincingly, "I've learned to keep myself company these past few weeks. That includes talking to myself."

Ignoring him, Adonis thrust Riperous's invitation into Jeston's hand. "What is the meaning of this?"

Jeston read it silently before answering, "I don't know anything about this, Ad."

"You helped that little girl escape. I don't think it to be a coincidence that a few months later, a House has been resurrected."

"Leave her out of this," snarled Jeston.

Abandoning the archway, Adonis stepped into the room. Adonis moved closer to Jeston with every word.

"That little girl will be our demise," Adonis warned.

"Our demise? Or yours?" Jeston asked.

Pausing in his malevolent stride, Adonis answered, "That girl made you think it was a good idea to turn against your family and your throne. She has power neither one of us can grasp."

I thought back to our walk in the tunnels on the way to the Barracks, when Jeston said *my devotion to friendship would have to be stronger than my devotion to the throne.*

Caught in my own thoughts, I missed a whispered exchange between the brothers. Fists clenched, Adonis hit Jeston, knocking him in the jaw. Wrenching back his own fist in retaliation, Jeston set his sights on his brother, but Adonis was too quick. He tackled Jeston to the ground. Holding Jeston pinned beneath him, Adonis began to repeatedly hit his younger brother. Jeston put up his hands to block any punches coming to his head, leaving his torso vulnerable. Adonis saw the opportunity and took it. Thuds of the blows and Jeston's groans made me step out from behind the door.

"Stop it!" I yelled, trying to reach for Adonis, but something was holding me back.

My eyes connected with Jeston, and he let out a disapproving, "No!"

Adonis finished with a hard blow to the stomach, causing Jeston to cough up blood. He said, "Still won't cave, brother? You are lucky Pillar Laws prohibit me from killing you, or you would be dead by now. You should have seen me after I found out you hid that pet with those friends of yours."

"They are more about brotherhood than you ever did," Jeston spat.

Adonis stood over Jeston's trembling body. He was significantly taller than me and Jeston. His dark hair and beard made menacing shadows from the torches. Being invisible to Adonis, I stood beside him, staring at him with anger pulsing beneath. When Jeston was finally able to sit up, he saw me standing behind his brother and shot me a warning look. Adonis picked up on the subtle change.

Turning to see the thing his brother had looked at, Adonis, with a dark laugh, suggested, "Is she here? In this room?"

Racing behind the door to throw it open, he found nothing. Unsatisfied, he began to tear open the curtains behind the bed and turned over the chairs by the fireplace. He was determined to destroy the entire room in search of me while, unbeknownst to him, I was standing right in front of him.

Jeston became less worried about my safety when he realized Adonis couldn't see me. "I'm going to have to clean all this later, Adonis," Jeston said, playing the part of an unamused brother.

Winded, Adonis crouched over his brother in dominance. "You are hiding something in here. I will find it." His tone was determined, no matter the cost. He stood and glanced at the open books, "I see you have been studying." His attention was now on the open books on the table.

"I have nothing else to do in here," Jeston said nonchalantly.

Adonis, unconvinced, said, "Well, then I'll let my guards know that tests are on the table with punishments for every wrong answer."

"Adonis, this is silly," Jeston said. "I won't tell them anything. I don't *know* anything!"

"You tell lies, brother," Adonis retorted impatiently.

"Torture will not get me to speak; you might as well kill me," Jeston suggested with a serious tone. A part of me worried he wanted it to happen.

"I wish I could, brother," Adonis finally spoke. "If I fatally hurt another Pillar, my line of succession will cease with me, for murderers cannot rule the House of Love. My sons will rule this House when they are ready. I will build them up in power and might and strength with proud hearts, all the virtues of a strong Lovian leader!"

"You will fall to the darkness," Jeston spat.

"The darkness is a lie! A made-up story to instill fear into our people, making them turn to their Pillars for guidance and direction. It created the necessary separation to make us gods!"

"We are not gods," Jeston said plainly. "We are people born into the right family. At least I'm smart enough to believe there is evil in this world. How do you explain the curses? The collapses of each House? The road you are heading down will send this House into a collapse of its own. Do you want poverty and disease and destruction upon our people?"

"Don't lecture me about a collapse. I know it all too well. The House of Joy was easy to bring down. I planted the mere idea that happiness comes from wealth or wine or women. You don't know how many fools fell for it, including their Pillars. When they were disappointed, depressed, and sorrowful, the sadness followed soon after. The joy they once felt had abandoned them and the House. No matter how hard they tried, they could not seem to get it back. Thus, the Fall of the House of Joy and the eternal rule of the House of Love."

"Until last night when the House of Patience was reclaimed to the light with Riperous returning to power," Jeston mentioned, intentionally trying to provoke his brother again. "*You* are the traitor, Adonis."

"And yet, I am the one who rules," Adonis sneered.

"The light will always win."

"Not if I have anything to say about it," Adonis said darkly, turning his back on Jeston and heading for the door.

Jeston stared at his brother in disbelief, still huddled on the ground.

Spinning in the doorway, Adonis scoured every inch of the room. Speaking to the air, he said, "And you, my little birdy, be careful where you land. You don't want to be eaten by a sly fox, now do you?"

Jeston turned his attention to me, standing beside his bed. Thankfully, Adonis didn't catch the glance as he left, slamming the door shut and locking it behind him.

I knelt down beside Jeston on the floor, as he didn't look like he was ready to get up.

"What are we going to do?" I asked him.

What happened next, I was not ready for it. The way he looked at me was frightening and sad, like he was losing something he had just found. There were no tears. There were no words said. We just stared at each other with an understanding that I needed to go. A part of me wanted to reach out and comfort him. Another part of me was reminded of my place in this House: a low positioned, overlooked clockworker.

"Jeston, I—"

"It's too dangerous for you here. You need to go."

"What about you? I'm not going to just leave you here," I stated argumentatively.

"Adonis can't truly hurt me," Jeston argued back. "Pillar Laws bind both of us. They don't protect you, though. You must leave."

I remembered the riddles in my hand. "Here." I handed them back, prolonging my time with Jeston.

"Keep them. I could say them backwards if I wanted to. This . . . should be the last time we see one another." Jeston said softly, his voice cracking ever so slightly.

His eyes held both sorrow and determination.

I knew he meant it—for my safety as much as for his own.

I felt my chest tighten, as if the words had pulled a piece of my heart away.

"It's too dangerous for you to be popping in and out of here," Jeston explained. "What if one of the guards sees you? I think it's best we say goodbye now. Go—figure out the riddles. Leave me to handle Adonis. I know you are safe when you are not here. The more time you spend here, the more I worry. I can feel it."

"What if I figure out the riddles? Wouldn't you want to know about it? An update of sorts?" I asked inquisitively.

"I'll know. Pillars talk. Even my own brother let me know about Riperous's request. You don't have to worry about me, Wrenna."

From outside the door, we could hear the clang of metal hitting on metal. Feet shuffled closer and a rattle at the door's lock startled both of us.

"Go," Jeston commanded, "now."

I didn't want to. I wanted to stay. I didn't want to see him hurt again.

"Wren!" he said in a loud whisper.

Before the door swung open and before the guards had the chance to see me, I was whisked away with the coolness of my ring under my fingers.

"I wasn't expecting you back here so soon." A familiar deep voice spoke behind me.

Without facing him, I responded, "I couldn't think of another person with the light in time."

"I thought you were with your friend and the man with the beard."

"I visited the House of Love. I saw Adonis," I sniffled. "He was upset with your request."

There wasn't a retort. Riperous only listened to what I said.

With uncertainty, I turned around to face him. "Is the darkness real?" I had finally vocalized the question that burned in my mind since the moment Adonis said it in the room.

He stood from behind his desk. I met his inviting, bicolored eyes. "My dear, there is good in this world but there is also a force acting against it. If you want to call it the darkness, or evil or bad deeds or a void, that is up to you. There are many forms it holds and many names it possesses. Do not be fooled by it, for it is crafty. It can play tricks on even the wisest of men. I am proof."

Unsatisfied with the answer, I moved to a more pressing matter. "I was given these." I held up Aruleah's handwritten riddles.

Riperous's eyes widened at the sight of more of his wife's writing. Years of longing could be seen in the ocean of his eyes as they welled with warm memories.

"Can you help me?" I asked plainly.

"You have been chosen for a path that follows these riddles. I admire your tenacious spirit for wanting to find the truth. Contrary to your path, I have been chosen for a different one. I would love to remember my wife and the legacy she left; however, I have other responsibilities in this House. I've neglected them for far too long. I need to return to the Heights and start the rebuild of this House."

I must have given a disappointed look because he continued, "I have full confidence that you will figure it out. Look what you have done so far. You have persevered through many trials already. Take pleasure in knowing that you are strong. Consider it a pure joy to have endured so many trials, propelling you further into confidence you will overcome this one."

I nodded, not fully understanding what he said and still disappointed he was unwilling to help.

"I want to give you something that might help," Riperous said, reaching for a rolled parchment lying on his desk.

Handing it to me, he explained its contents, "This is the completed map of the Forgotten King's kingdom. I want you to have it. I don't have any use for it now."

I was awestruck.

I didn't know what to think. I held the map in one hand, feeling the weight of responsibility that came with it.

"There's only one map—" I started to say.

"And I trust you to keep it safe," he concluded, "Now, I believe your friends are worried about you."

I thought of the ranch. I thought of seeing Tev again. I imagined the reunion of Tev and Thad. Two brothers, not by blood but by Love, reunited in a land restored. I expected singing and dancing and good chaos to welcome me when I arrived at the ranch.

As I stared into his chest, Riperous lifted my chin so I would meet his eyes for one last time.

"Go be with your friends," he said.

For a final time, I felt the coolness of the ring and was whisked away, thinking of the home I had found in the House of Patience and the one person I knew to have the light inside of them.

"Wren!" Tev shouted my name when he saw me standing in the doorway to the Ragsdale house.

I dropped the map at the doorstep and ran to Tev. I wrapped my arms around his neck. He lifted my feet off the ground, spinning me in the air as we embraced, one arm wrapped tightly around me to keep me from falling. I could feel another hand reach for the back of my head to press me tighter to his body. Steadily, he let me down, but we kept our closeness for a second longer, long enough for me to say, "I'm sorry I didn't say goodbye."

Whispering in my ear, he said, "I'm glad you are safe now."

We parted. The moment after I was rushed with another hug, this one from Thad. He picked me up similarly to Tev but not as meaningful or as intimate. I noticed the family admiring Ellie's new ring and asking questions about what happened while we were away. Having only been a day or two, there were still many details we wanted to share. I let Ellie take the lead in telling the story since she was almost done with it by the time I arrived.

"Then this big crash sent us flying in the room." Ellie mimicked the rock of the boat in the water.

I watched Tev smile at Thad in disbelief, my stare lingering a little longer on Tev while he wasn't looking.

"And then he gave me the ring," Ellie said, showing off the canary stone in the ring on her finger.

After Ellie finished telling the story of what happened, Ria and Nora began their investigative questioning. Finneous had added logs to the fire. Adaline set out snacks for the rest of the family to nibble on, which Evan and Thad took no time to devour. Ellie energetically took the spotlight as her sisters' interest peaked. Their attention meant more to her than the quest itself.

With the riddles tucked into my pocket and the map still lying by the doorway, I didn't want to discuss them just yet. Instead, I wanted to enjoy the night, the celebration of restoring the House of Patience and returning to the ranch in one piece.

There would come a time when I would talk about my brief appearance in the House of Love with Tev, and we would set off on another adventure. But for right now, I enjoyed the family by the fire.

For I had finally found my house of love.

ABOUT THE AUTHOR

The desert runs deep for this Valley girl.
Mountains surrounding her home were her gem and pearl.
To Flagstaff she danced on the volleyball court.
Studying Mathematics and art along with the sport.
Then the Missouri Valley called her by name.
She left, for the seasons were starting to change.

Felt called by God to write such a story,
To share his Word and all of His glory.
A twist on the old, with the same theme.
After years of prayer, there came a dream.
Ideas of crowns, the journey to seek.
Not only for the called, but also for the bleak.

For Abby loves more than the stories she writes.
She loves painting and putting and puppies that bite.
Her favorite verse in Romans speaks to share.
"Be joyful in hope, patient in affliction, and faithful in prayer."
The Light sends a message for all to look,
For not by works but by faith, she wrote this book.

www.ingramcontent.com/pod-product-compliance
Lightning Source LLC
LaVergne TN
LVHW010559100826
845148LV00014B/2775
9781684881581